*Tethered Spirits*

# Tethered Spirits

## Wiaqtaqne'wasultijik na Kjijaqmijinaq

Corinne Hoebers

First published in 2025 by

Halifax, NS, Canada
www.ocpublishing.ca

OC Publishing is based in Kjipuktuk, Mi'kma'ki, the traditional territory
of the Mi'kmaq.

Edited by Marianne Ward
Cover artwork by Matthew Connolly, Speaking Wolf of the Qalipu Band
in Corner Brook, NL, Aboriginal veteran
Cover and interior book design by David W. Edelstein

ISBN 978-1-989833-56-8 (Paperback edition)
ISBN 978-1-989833-57-5 (eBook edition)

*Dedicated to Mi'kmaw Saqmawiey (Eldering) Daniel N. Paul, CM, ONS (December 5, 1938–June 27, 2023). My sincere gratitude for your time and patience during the writing of this book. Your insight and advice were invaluable to me.*

*In memory of the 215 Indigenous children found buried in unmarked graves on the grounds of the former Kamloops Indian Residential School in 2021 and the subsequent graves found since across Canada, and of all the remaining children not yet discovered. May your spirits soar with the eagles and collectively lift the survivors above their pain.*

*You cannot separate the People from the land,*
*it is who we are.*

> – shalan joudry of L'sitkuk Bear River First
> Nation, Mi'kmaw mother, poet, and storyteller,
> "Connecting to Wapane'kati," an address to the
> Mersey Tobeatic Research Institute's old-growth
> forest conservation meeting, October 21, 2016

*Creator, we ask for respect, so that we will know*
*that everyone comes from one place, from you.*

> – Helen Sylliboy, "Mi'kmaw Prayer
> of the Seven Sacred Teachings"

# Chapter One



*Bear Cub.* Like a duck to water, he naturally slipped into his new name. *Christian* sounded foreign to him now. He looked skyward to where Eagle Feather was pointing, and they watched the eagle slowly drift above the forest canopy before landing at the topmost part of a spruce tree. As his large, graceful wings collapsed around his body, he cocked his white head and looked down upon them. Then, this lofty creature, Kitpu, the messenger of prayers to the Spirit World, who soars closest to Kisu'lkw, the breath of creation, effortlessly lifted upward in flight. Bear Cub grinned at his brother as they too moved on.

Bear Cub now lived a life very different from the one to which he was born. He understood that in this circle of life, no living being had dominion over the other. The People addressed flora and fauna as people—non-human people. They asked flora for permission before harvesting and demonstrated their gratitude by minimizing harm. An Elder had taught Bear Cub about the practice of Netukulimk—take only what you need. If over-harvested, the plants and animals would leave. The Mi'kmaq survived by watching and listening to the world around them.

When he was seventeen years old, he had paddled from Dartmouth in search of his brother Jakob when their mother lay dying. Eagle Feather found Bear Cub alone and near death. Living with the Mi'kmaq, Bear Cub had easily adjusted to their beliefs; but a battle raged within him on whether or not to return to his birth family. Could he, after all this time?

Then there was Papa. Bear Cub pushed him to a dark corner of his mind and inhaled deeply to suppress the image of his biological father. The musty scent of decay in the forest breathed renewed creation. With each step, his feet sank deep into the living moss. Bear Cub relaxed. As in the old times, the rich undergrowth of the forest sustained the Mi'kmaq. Rain droplets dotted the toes of moccasin flowers—their roots a medicine used to treat headaches and fevers. Bunchberries, their tiny white flowers sprinkled amid the ferns, were medicine for the stomach.

Once again, Papa entered his thoughts unannounced. Bear Cub's body tightened. His father had forced him to become an apprentice to his uncle, to learn the weaving business. But Bear Cub could never trade the farmland soil he loved to sift through his fingers for the coarse wool and rigid pedals of the loom. His uncle taught him with the sting of his belt. As the memory festered, Bear Cub's temples throbbed. Papa had ignored his needs. Did he *want* to return?

Eagle Feather waved his hand at his brother. Bear Cub had not noticed they had arrived at the second weir below the river's tide head. Slipping the heavy basket of mackerel and eels from his sweaty back, Bear Cub plunged into the cold water. His exhausting internal battle washed away. He now observed this V-shaped weir, pointed downstream. Alongside his Mi'kmaw brothers, he had learned to build it from piled stones and hemlock boughs. It was holding up well. *The large net at the apex must be full by now*, he thought.

He could feel the smooth skin of the fish churning about his feet. *Plamu'k*, he said to himself, the Mi'kmaw name for these delicacies. Eagle Feather clutched the silver-coloured smolts in both hands while Bear Cub stitched a spruce root through the lower part of each mouth. One by one they were securely tied and bundled onto the spear. The women of the village had recently boiled spruce roots, splitting them to be used for baskets and canoes. Eagle Feather had snuck a few for this purpose, hoping his mother would not notice.

Once they had stitched the last of the fish, Eagle Feather tossed the bundles onto the bank of the river, then walked farther upstream to a deeper section. Bear Cub ran after him. When he waded into the water's depth, Bear Cub attempted to stab a salmon with his three-pronged spear. His brother laughed at his clumsiness and pushed him under. Bear Cub bounced up to the surface, gasping for air.

"I would starve waiting for you to catch food," Eagle Feather teased.

Bear Cub grabbed a handful of his brother's black hair, dragging him under. But his brother escaped his grip, reappearing at the shoreline.

"I'm as good as my teacher," Bear Cub called back.

"Come, my brother," Eagle Feather called. "It is time to return to camp."

Bear Cub waded back. "Leave it to you to quit when I was winning." He slapped his brother on the back.

"So you think," Eagle Feather said, as he tousled Bear Cub's blonde hair. "But you are improving."

Before gathering the catch, Eagle Feather set bits of tobacco upon the water and said, "We thank these salmon for giving themselves so we may eat. Thank you, Great Spirit, for supplying this river with abundance." The tobacco quickly disappeared with the current. Bear Cub submerged his cupped hands to scoop up water, then released it between his fingers until just tiny beads dripped one by one, returning to the river collective below. As they had done for uncountable generations before, the rivers carried not only an abundance of nourishment to the People, but also carried the Mi'kmaq throughout Mi'kma'ki. *A river shares her knowledge with anyone who listens,* Bear Cub thought.

As the two young men made their way back to the canoe, Bear Cub stopped to slice off a hardened piece of amber sap from a spruce tree and popped it into his mouth. It was crumbly at first, but as he chewed through bits of insects and grit, it gelled together into stiff gum. Eagle Feather always declined Bear Cub's offer, but not today. Instead, Eagle Feather wrapped it inside his deerskin pouch. "My mother likes it," he said, folding the flap down.

They flipped the overturned canoe upright and filled it with food.

"Maybe today, we will win," Bear Cub quipped. A friendly competition to be the best fisher or the best hunter kept the larders full. The two men pushed away from the small beach and a short time later entered a lake whose shoreline was dotted with many wikuoml. As they passed the stone eel weir built to catch the Autumn migration, Bear Cub dragged his paddle in the water to stop the canoe. Eagle Feather sat ahead of him— his wet hair sticking to his dark skin. Through the river channel, they watched from a fair distance a full-rigged British ship sailing south.

"White man's Big Canoe," Eagle Feather said.

Bear Cub did not reply. *I came to an unknown land to join the colonies under Great Britain,* mused Bear Cub, *but it was not a "new world."* His brother began to paddle away from the weir, and Bear Cub placed his own paddle in the water to assist him. *Instead, I came to an ancient land, long occupied by Eagle Feather's ancestors.*

Long before Bear Cub could see their Summer encampment, the stray smells of the open fires served as a beacon, welcoming him back into the warmth of the community. A hollow, rhythmic pounding spoke to him—*thonk, thonk, thonk.* The routine echo of Spring when the log of the tall, straight black ash must be worked immediately after it was harvested and still wet. Then the silence as the pounder peeled back a long strip following the grain of the wood. Again, *thonk, thonk, thonk,* crushing the fibres between the growth rings as they lifted from the log. Then quiet.

Villages grew much larger at this time of year, with many individual groupings spread along the coast. The sun picked up the painted animals, birds, and fish on each of the conical and oblong wikuoml that stood around this lake. Behind the dwellings a thick forest continued up and over hills as far as the eye could see.

Bear Cub and his brother beached the canoe and unloaded. Spotted dogs greeted them, pushing their long noses about the lifeless catch, curly tails wagging furiously as they nipped their way to a hopeful meal.

Eagle Feather placed the speared bundles of fish outside the wikuom for his mother to clean and scale.

"My mother, a good feed today," Eagle Feather said as he lifted the bearskin door-blanket to an empty dwelling.

Singing Sparrow, Eagle Feather's sister of seventeen Winters, walked up from behind. With a quick, shy glance at Bear Cub, she turned to her brother. "Our mother is not pleased with you. Nor is our father. I am assuming you helped yourself to spruce roots this morning before leaving?"

"E'e, but—"

He was interrupted by his father firmly planting his large hands on Eagle Feather's shoulders from behind. He whispered, "My son, you know better…"

Singing Sparrow made herself scarce by attending to the returning children, whose moss-filled baskets cushioned harvested seabirds' eggs. Bear Cub was about to abandon his brother, but a stern glance from White Cloud's dark eyes persuaded him to stay.

White Cloud turned Eagle Feather around to face him. "You know your mother well. She used up the roots for that canoe."

Bear Cub squinted against the sun's brightness. The seams of the canoe were already sealed with hot pitch.

"Perhaps you thought the ones you borrowed were of no consequence, but your mother and sister needed them to finish that wikuom," said White Cloud, gesturing to a bare frame of eight spruce poles lashed together at the top where a hoop of moosewood braced the supports.

"E'e," Eagle Feather said sheepishly.

"Your mother had only a short supply." White Cloud sighed. "Her wrath is over now, but you need to speak to her immediately."

"Right away, my father." Eagle Feather turned to go.

"After, you are both to forage for more. Gather as many as you can carry." White Cloud glanced at Bear Cub. "I leave now for the seal hunt." Hundreds of seals had been spotted on a nearby beach, Bear Cub remembered.

Eagle Feather answered with a nod. "I will not be long, Bear Cub," he said, and left.


EAGLE FEATHER SAW HIS MOTHER, Morning Dove, glance at him before entering a wikuom that was to be used for the Acadians. The floor had been recently cleaned out, and a new layer of fir and cedar boughs had been laid down and covered with several caribou skins. Outside the door lay a well-worn reed mat.

The fresh aroma of evergreen greeted Eagle Feather when he entered. His mother stood, ageless, before him. Her long black hair, untouched by time, was tied back with a string of deerskin. A narrow leather band fit snugly about her forehead, decorated with bright beads they had received from the French in exchange for furs. Her buckskin dress, which hung just below her knees and was belted at the waist, displayed dyed quills of blue and red in a geometric dove design. She preferred to wear the clothes of her ancestors; she said that through contact with her skin, she embodied the spirits and strength of the animals whose skins and pelts she wore. There was no such bond when dressed in cloth and wool.

Eagle Feather presented the spruce gum to her. "My mother, do forgive me. I was wrong." He wrapped his arms around her; her head just reached his chest. She was of average height, but he took after his father.

She gently pushed him away. "Did you not remember we have guests arriving in two sunrises? I thank the Great Spirit it is not sooner."

Eagle Feather nodded.

"And still you took them?"

He nodded again.

"I hope you made good use of them?"

He smiled down at her. "We harvested many fish."

Her eyes twinkled and she reached up to stroke his smooth face. "I cannot stay angry with you." By the look in her eyes, Eagle Feather knew of what she would speak next—how he came to be known as Eagle Feather. "After Ma'li died, five Winters before I gave you life, our Great Spirit delivered a message to me in a dream, from the Land of Souls."

"E'e, my sister and many others died of the black sickness. You called her your Apje'jit Mimikes—small butterfly."

"In my dream, Apje'jit Mimikes was a young woman with an eagle perched on her left arm. It flew up high into the sky, then swooped back down to Mother Earth and landed beside her. Brother Eagle changed his shape to become a warrior. The following sunrise, the puoin explained there will be another child—a son. When the salmon-run filled the rivers once more and the geese shed their plumage, my prayer was answered. One day, your aunt and I were picking berries. Before we returned, we stopped by the river to give our thanks." Morning Dove reached into the beaded mink-skin pouch that always hung from her waist. It had once belonged to her great-grandfather. She withdrew an item and unwrapped the cloth. "When I looked down, I found this small eagle feather on the ground between my feet. It was a message to me from the Land of Souls. The following Winter, I birthed you."

Eagle Feather never wished to interrupt his mother when she related this story. Nothing ever changed in its telling. And surprisingly, he never tired of it. But he never knew she had kept the feather.

As she carefully tucked it away, he promised to replace the harvested roots before the sun went beneath the earth. "Watch for your sister," his mother said.


ONCE BEAR CUB AND HIS brother had gathered muskets and cartridge-filled leather pouches, they left to find a location best suited for spruce roots—someplace boggy.

The farther they walked along the footpath, the younger the trees. The unkempt understory and the more open canopy above were ideal. Spruce needles and rotting bark grew more pungent with the heavy humidity. Chipmunks and red squirrels scattered at their presence, and a sudden drumming of grouse wings vibrated nearby.

Bear Cub knelt on the spongy forest floor and peeled back moss to find rotting bark from a dead tree. As he was taught, he followed the log to its roots. When he dug his fingers into the soil to search for tubers, the fresh, musky smell wafted up to greet him. He carefully traced the length of the tubers with his hands, then cut them with his knife. Only the ones that were long, straight, and no wider than his thumb were harvested

"You stay—looks like a good area to collect more. I will explore that way and meet you back here," Eagle Feather said. "You know the call to use if you are in trouble."

Bear Cub nodded. An owl call would alert the other of any imminent danger.

"Watch for Singing Sparrow," his brother added. "She might be foraging for medicines in this area as well." Eagle Feather moved in a northward direction.

About two hours had passed and Bear Cub had not ventured much farther than where he had started. Unfamiliar voices wafted through the trees. Bear Cub grabbed his musket and scrambled down over a river embankment and waited. The words, though muffled, were clear enough for him to know they were German. Branches snapped underfoot. Barely raising his head, Bear Cub could see three men approaching. Their dress was familiar—knee-buckled breeches, stockings, and linen shirts. When he ducked, he hooted the signal. He peered over the embankment to see one man motion to the others to go ahead. The two left while the third one relieved himself. When the owl call was answered by Eagle Feather, the remaining male looked up, alert. Bear Cub's musket was already loaded and half-cocked. The intruder looked around until he fixated in Bear

Cub's direction. Perspiration began to drip along Bear Cub's forehead. He dared not breathe.

A shrill wail scratched the stillness. The outsider ran just as Bear Cub bolted, both racing toward the noise. Bear Cub ran faster through the forest, dodging trees, jumping deadwood—his only thoughts were of Singing Sparrow. He slowed his pace to crouch behind a tree. His sister struggled vigorously to free herself from her two captors, one of whom had his hand clasped over her mouth.

The running German appeared a few yards away. To Bear Cub's surprise, the dishevelled runner aimed his firearm at his companions and yelled, "Let her go!" But the order fell on deaf ears. Singing Sparrow howled in pain when her head was wrenched backward.

Bear Cub lunged closer, pulled back the doglock, and stood up. He rested the butt plate against his shoulder and moved from the shadows. His body trembled and his heart started to pound as he aimed the gun at the two thugs. He was not sure if it was his fear or his rage. He had never killed anyone. With one eye closed, Bear Cub stared along the barrel, about to press the trigger, when Eagle Feather appeared, musket aimed.

"Release her! Now! Or I will kill one of you myself and let my brother finish the job on your companions." Eagle Feather pointed his weapon first at the terrified small group, then at the one who stood alone, not far from Bear Cub. The musket and the tone of his voice spoke volumes, even if the Mi'kmaw words were not understood.

In a flash of courage, Singing Sparrow kicked one of her assailants in the groin as her brother shot a warning over their heads. Howling, she covered her head with her arms. Eagle Feather ran to his sister while the two assailants disappeared into the forest. Sobbing, Singing Sparrow collapsed into her brother's arms.

Bear Cub pointed the barrel of his gun at the chest of the remaining intruder, who stood rooted with his arms in the air. "On your knees!" he ordered in German and kicked the man's gun into the underbrush. He briefly looked back at his brother. "Singing Sparrow?"

Eagle Feather replied, "Shaking but not hurt." To Singing Sparrow he said, "Shh, you are safe now."

"Christian?"

Bear Cub turned to the voice. "How do you know...?" Bear Cub stared at the man, dumbfounded.

"Do you not know who kneels here before you?"

Bear Cub dropped his gun at the sudden realization.

The German lowered his arms, got to his feet, and smiled.

Despite the growth of the beard and shoulder-length, straggly hair, the voice was unmistakable. "My God! Peter?" Bear Cub rushed to embrace him. "You're alive!" he sputtered.

Bear Cub had not seen his friend since they had been ambushed on the Pisiguit River. He had seen Peter escape just before he slipped into unconsciousness.

Eagle Feather and Singing Sparrow looked extremely perplexed. Bear Cub introduced his friend and was surprised when Peter spoke to them in Mi'kmaw.

"It is best we return to camp," Eagle Feather said, still holding his sister.

"Moqwe," Peter replied quickly. "No, please sit. Christian's brothers and sisters are mine."

Eagle Feather smiled. "Wela'lin, but it has been distressing enough. Your friends may be looking for you. Please have your time with Bear Cub without us."

"You needn't be concerned about the other two. You have frightened them off," Peter assured them.

Bear Cub said, "I'll bring the remaining roots, my brother."

As Eagle Feather and Singing Sparrow turned to leave, Bear Cub heard his sister ask, "Is our brother safe?"

Eagle Feather readjusted the weight of the roots looped through his arms. "Just as safe as when he was found by us. As our father teaches, little one, do not judge a whole People by a few corrupt ones."

As they sat together on a fallen tree trunk, Bear Cub and Peter slipped back to their mother tongue. In all his dreams, Bear Cub never foresaw ever meeting any of his family again, let alone his nephew's father. They quickly caught up on the past four years in snippets of information and quick replies. Bear Cub learned that his mother had succumbed to her illness in Dartmouth soon after he had paddled up the Shubenacadie in the late fall of '52. He was then chilled by the news that Jakob was killed in the Lunenburg insurrection, though he was not surprised he had met such an end.

Bear Cub changed the subject. "Who are those men you were with?"

Peter scoffed. "Deserters from the Lunenburg militia. Under a Lieutenant Jessen, they told me. I only joined up with them yesterday."

Bear Cub raised an eyebrow. "Oh?"

"I was hungry and they had food. Nothing else."

"You speak Mi'kmaw." Bear Cub squinted at him. "How…"

"Two years ago, I was captured near Pisiguit. I was bounty to them. They were about to turn me in to the French, but I convinced them to let me stay." With one hand on his knee, Peter leaned closer. "I had witnessed the Acadians' extraordinary camaraderie with the Mi'kmaq. My perception of the natives has been transformed. I learned their tongue—enough to get by—and hunted and fished with them. And you, my friend? What of you?"

"My memory is cloudy. If it wasn't for Eagle Feather, I wouldn't be talking to you now."

"Did you make any attempts to escape?"

Bear Cub shook his head. "I was very sick through the Winter. It wasn't until Spring I recovered fully, thanks to Eagle Feather's mother. By then, I couldn't be sure if my own family had followed the other settlers to Lunenburg."

"But you knew in all likelihood they would not be in Dartmouth. They had talked about making the move before you left." Peter sounded bewildered. "Almost four years have passed. Were you being held against your will?"

"Nein."

Peter stared into his eyes. "Your family thinks you are dead, Christian."

"How do you know this?"

"At times, Elisabeth has allowed me to visit Petie—in secret and only when her husband is away. Georg knows nothing of this, and as far as my little boy is concerned, Georg is his father. Before they sailed for Lunenburg, they heard talk of an ambush on the Shubenacadie, so they assumed the worst. At first Elisabeth insisted that you might still be alive, but over time, her hope was challenged."

It hurt Bear Cub to hear it. "There are moments when I wish to return, but only brief ones. When we first arrived in Dartmouth, my relationship with Papa was, at best, tolerable." He shut his eyes to regain his composure.

"You can't pretend your family doesn't exist."

"The Mi'kmaq are my kin now." Bear Cub paused. "They

are a good People, abuse is unheard of among them." The word *abuse* hung loosely between them. Peter was aware of the misery Bear Cub had endured with his uncle. Avoiding his friend's eyes, Bear Cub massaged his rough hands together. "I don't need to tell you. You must know this, having lived among them."

"I do. But, the recent raid near Lunenburg says otherwise. It's getting worse."

"I don't blame them. Their lands have already begun to shrink as a result of our greed." He clenched his teeth so hard his jaw began to ache. "When they speak of this, Peter, they're talking about us." He looked away and cleared his throat. "Deep down, I know Eagle Feather would never think of me that way." Bear Cub stared back at his friend. "But when I hear 'white man,' it cuts into me."

"But, Christian, your papa and sisters are blood. You belong with them. You need to at least try to—"

"I cannot. They wouldn't understand." Bear Cub stood to leave. "I don't need blood to recognize the tenderness of family. Just as wolves nurture and adopt other pups that are not their own, so my Mi'kmaw family has done with me."

Peter left the subject alone and begged Bear Cub to stay longer. Resisting at first, Bear Cub finally complied.

"Governor Lawrence hates the Mi'kmaq as much as he despises the French, maybe more," Bear Cub said, not quite sure if he was just trying to get a rise out of Peter.

His friend replied, "The colonists are grateful for his support; he knows the Germans to be good permanent citizens. He has had their back, even after Lunenburg's insurrection."

"That may be so. But at what cost to the Mi'kmaq? The English can't plant their flag here, claiming the land is theirs to keep."

"I know, Christian. I was just stating a fact. We took it on good faith when we signed those papers for this land. It was only after we left Rotterdam that the crew spread the horror stories of Indian attacks. We did not know why they were happening. Just who are the deceivers here?"

Bear Cub changed the subject. "Has Lunenburg seen good harvests?"

"Elisabeth told me there have been crop failures, and sickness."

"Was my family afflicted?"

"Right now, I'm not sure. It has been a while since we met up…" His voice faded. Bear Cub could see sadness creep into Peter's eyes. "You know how headstrong your sister can be," Peter continued. The heat of the day intensified, and beads of perspiration appeared on Peter's flushed face. His shirt was adhering to his skin. "Your papa and Hanna are southwest of the town, on the other side of the harbour, just before the start of an area they call Middle Range. Elisabeth said your father received a cow and one sheep. I do not know if the animals survived. Up until that raid, there had been no attacks on or near the town."

"The Mi'kmaq have their quarrels with the English, not the Germans or French," said Bear Cub. He stood up. "I need to head back to camp. Eagle Feather will be worried. And so will his parents. Are you living in Lunenburg?"

Peter shook his head. "The authorities know me. I'm still a deserter, since I refused to work for my passage here. I'm putting my life at risk to see my son."

"Come with me. At least to fill your belly, then you can be on your way. You look like you could use a meal or two. First, I need to collect the roots." Bear Cub started off in that direction, then turned around. "Or you can stay at our camp until you're ready to leave. Where will you go from here?"

"I may head back to Louisbourg."

"Oh?"

"I wintered there a year ago. It has seen a great deal of trade with New France and the West Indies. Even illegally with New England."

"We were informed France sent two more battalions to strengthen the garrison." Bear Cub recalled the morning a runner brought the good news.

"It needs more than additional regiments if the French wish to hold onto it—they need to rebuild the fortifications. Cannons are misfiring and the walls are crumbling. If the Mi'kmaq are to survive, the British cannot take that fort," Peter said as he followed Bear Cub through the woods and back to his home.

# Chapter Two

When they arrived at camp, a few heads followed Peter as they crossed the compound.

"I need to see Singing Sparrow," Bear Cub said, as he dropped the roots on the ground.

Peter laid down his bundle. "And I will be in good hands. Eagle Feather has spotted us."

Bear Cub was relieved to find his sister working with the women to finish the wikuom. He caught her looking his way while she submerged the dried bark in water. As he walked toward her, she lowered her eyes. Peeled and split spruce roots were lying loosely around the women's work area. The women worked from the bottom up, layering and overlapping each piece of bark and guiding the small hands of the children, who soaked up the lessons they were being taught.

Bear Cub knew that Singing Sparrow usually ignored her own distress so others would not fuss over her. "You need to rest," he said, staring down at her hands. "You're trembling."

"I need to keep busy." She raised her head, and their eyes briefly locked. "Please go. Do not worry," she said before returning to her task. Then women crowded around her, jostling Bear Cub away.

The talk around the village was of the morning trauma. Peter was initially looked upon with suspicion until Bear Cub explained how his friend had aided in Singing Sparrow's safety. Peter mitigated any further fears when he spoke Mi'kmaw. Of course, with their camp near Lunenburg and Mahone Bay, the Mi'kmaq had many questions for him—the new habitation was restricting their movements, making it more difficult to gather food safely. To continue trapping along the familiar trails and fishing by the rivers was treacherous. Sneaking around their own hunting and fishing grounds was inconceivable, but slinking they were. And they'd had to find different routes to the seacoast.

The LAST OF THE CANOES arrived. White Cloud dragged his onto the shore and helped unload their catch of seals, still dripping with blood. He lifted his harpoon and greeted his wife with a wide grin. "For this, there will be a celebration to heartily thank the Great Spirit," he said.

"Of course." Morning Dove smiled back. "We cannot forget the hungry dark days of Winter." The mammals were a good source of food, fat, and oil, as well as skin for moccasins.

Morning Dove motioned White Cloud inside their wikuom. She gently placed her hand on his back. "My darling..." He turned to her. She carefully chose her words to describe what had transpired and how their daughter's safety was entirely due to her brothers and Peter. As she described the trauma, White Cloud paced in front of the circle of stones around their firepit. He did this often when faced with difficulty.

Morning Dove concluded, "She will recover."

White Cloud inhaled sharply, running his hands through his hair. "She is not to venture alone into the woods again," he ordered. "Her life is in peril." Then, "This cannot continue!"

His wife read his meaning and the consequences of it. "Are you now bowing to the Elders' pleas to retaliate?"

White Cloud grunted. He stopped pacing.

"I vow to avenge this nightmare." He held his wife's tiny hands up to his face, pressing his lips against them. "I will speak to our council of Elders before the celebrations. The usual meeting of the districts will be in session soon." These meetings brought together all the local Nikanus and Saqmawit from each district.

"E'e, that is in eight nights. Calm Water will be attending?"

White Cloud did not reply. Morning Dove studied her husband's distant eyes. "Is it wise to ruffle feathers with talk of war? The last time you met with Saqmawit Kopit, the offer was extended to Governor Lawrence's table for peace, was it not?" Morning Dove would always attempt to pull him back. Even if she agreed with him, reason compelled her to examine all sides.

"E'e, and where has that gone? If you remember, our hand of friendship was conditional," he said.

"But Kopit stated that the People were willing to negotiate if the governor thought our requests unreasonable."

"That is not a compromise! They give us land only they deem fit, regardless of our livelihood. For the past three Winters, Merligueche and now east of there are occupied with Germans and French with no consideration of what our needs are. Where we are camped *now* is in peril." White Cloud was silent for a moment. "As I remember, we have not countered Lawrence's reply to our offer. But the British are pitted against the French, most Acadians are expelled, and these hideous scalping bounties have terminated any concept of further discussion."

"Our disputes are not with the settlers."

He sighed. "I know." He turned his back on her. "As much as I push for a compromise, I feel trapped between the two factions in this very community. I have not changed my mind, but…" He faced her.

Morning Dove noted the change in White Cloud. "You frighten me with this talk. Has our daughter's anguish moved you to a path of destruction and loathing?"

"I am not so swayed as to put our People in further danger."

"But you are doubting now?"

He did not answer. "I must go to our daughter." His immediate withdrawal left Morning Dove feeling desolate and helpless. As she watched him cross the compound, she wondered if he was reconciled to the idea that there may be no other course of action but to retaliate.

The village was active, so she abandoned her worries to focus on what needed to be done. The women were shelling and cleaning portions of the bounty. Fish were slated to be sun-dried and smoked for leaner times. Many were already hung from racks over smouldering fires, and the seals had already been removed. She would boil their fat at sunrise. For now, she would cook the eggs—the rocks were hot enough to place inside the kettles. The children were roasting their fish on split sticks.

Morning Dove was not hungry.


THE CELEBRATIONS WERE POSTPONED AS White Cloud called an unexpected meeting of the community. Within the sharing circle, Bear Cub and Peter sat cross-legged, next to Eagle Feather. Bear Cub saw Singing Sparrow glance at him, but she turned away and sat by her mother. The smaller children sat in front of their parents, and the sacred fire burned as everyone took their place around it. The sun sat low on the horizon, ready to drop beneath the earth. The whispers spread when the runner arrived three sunrises ago, and Bear Cub wondered if there was any more news of the Maliseet raid at the time of the gaspereau run.

Elder Calm Water walked around the inside of the circle, cradling a large sea snail shell, within it a braid of smouldering sweetgrass. With a large eagle feather, he fanned the smoke to cleanse all negativity and allow only positive energy to flourish. He called upon the spirits to help those gathered to enter the sacred realm. The smoke was waved to four directions—north, south, east, and west—above to the Great Spirit, and below to Mother Earth. Then to the spirit within.

When Bear Cub had first arrived, his brother had taught him that the smoke cleanses our eyes to see the good in people, our ears to listen to others, our mouths so good words are spoken, our minds for good thoughts, our feet so they are guided on good paths through life, our bodies to respect ourselves, and finally our hearts to remain pure and respect all creation.

The Elder placed the shell in the centre and spoke. "Bless and purify this circle, O Great Spirit. We seek wisdom to know what is good. We seek truth and, above all, humility—no one is superior to the other." He took his place beside White Cloud and picked up the talking stick. "My brothers and sisters, the runner carried a message from the Maliseet Nikanus, Grey Wolf of the Siknikt District." He passed the stick to his left, giving it to White Cloud.

"Thank you, my brother." White Cloud looked around. "We can all be relieved that Singing Sparrow was not mortally harmed this morning." White Cloud cleared his throat to collect himself before continuing. "As to the runner, we have news of the raid on Rous and Payzant's Islands at the last moon. Vaudreuil, the Governor-General of New France, gave orders for Captain Boishébert to attack all British settlements. The captain complied by sending a Maliseet detachment to Merligueche.

Direction did not come from Grey Wolf. The French are still hiring Maliseet who are willing to do their bidding. Grey Wolf is deeply distressed." He paused. "The Jesuit priests not only bring their teachings to the People, but they instill in others their own hatred for all Protestants—English and French. Any Maliseet who will listen is encouraged to keep attacking in the hopes it will force the colonies to surrender, thereby restoring the French Catholic territories." White Cloud paused to let his words sink in.

He continued, "Britain has declared war on France. My brothers and sisters, I ask the Great Spirit to keep this war short. The loss of lives on all sides, especially of the innocent, is never justified." White Cloud passed the stick to the person on his left, who in turn passed it to the next until one started to speak.

"Why do the Maliseet fall for this manipulation?"

White Cloud replied, "We are all caught up in it—a war that is not ours but into which we have been drawn. Like us, the Maliseet are rewarded with food, clothing, and guns. But also rum and brandy. Good or bad, we are becoming dependent on these supplies."

Another person, sitting farther away, stood up. "Governor Lawrence has increased the values of the scalping bounties on our People. He is dangerous!"

"I do not see any compromise," said another. "If we do not retaliate, we will be pushed from Mi'kma'ki like our Acadian friends."

Neither of these men was in possession of the talking stick. Bear Cub eyed Calm Water, who started to rise. The Elder would never allow this to pass uncorrected. But White Cloud pressed his hand on the Elder's arm, saying, "Moqwe. Let them speak."

"With this recent raid, things will worsen for us. We are not safe."

"Think of the consequences if we attack," one female Elder implored. "Over half this village is women and children."

Many nodded.

Those who had been standing now sat down. One said, "The governor eyes this land like a bear watches salmon. He hates us for protecting the Acadians; he knows we have sided with his enemy."

The talking stick moved to the left. "The British have violated the last Treaty. When any one of them is killed, we are prosecuted. They kill for profit and are free to go. Where is the justice?"

The anger energized people to speak out of turn. "They do not know the meaning of it. They say one thing in their Treaties but mean another. They are deceitful!" The speaker's eyes widened. "They managed to recruit a few Acadians to keep them informed of our movements." He stood. "The French need us to win against the British. We need the French to regain our land."

Bear Cub was uncomfortable and chose to remain quiet. Everyone had befriended him. He knew well they would never think of him as a threat. But right now, it was difficult not to feel alienated.

White Cloud interjected. "Like us, there are many Acadians who do not wish to take sides. Like them, we want to be left alone to live our own lives." White Cloud addressed the last person who spoke. "You are right. The threatening situations are growing." His eyes scanned the circle. "Our own People are not without their quarrels, but our ancient stories tell us that we have always managed to work through disagreements to promote peace, not war. Do not fall to defeat or narrow-mindedness. Let us keep our minds open to the possibilities for healing wounds. Consider our children's future and that of their children." He looked to each one, beseeching them to reconsider. But more frustrations were vented—the loss of respect and freedom, and diminishing livelihood.

It was obvious to Bear Cub that they *would* strike to gain back what they were losing.

White Cloud continued. "I plead with you to think again. The well-being of all here comes before our individual desires."

The stick was passed around a second time and made a full circle with nary a word. Dusk crept in and the sun dipped below the earth.

"It pains Jikeyulkw, the one who watches over us," White Cloud stated.


The gathering slowly dispersed. The remaining braid in the shell was left to burn itself out.

"At times, my father, there is no alternative," Eagle Feather stated. "We cannot sit idly like ducks and watch our People die."

Bear Cub lingered with Morning Dove, listening.

"How is your way going to keep them alive?" White Cloud said. "If we counterattack, more will be slaughtered. As it is, there are not enough of us to ensure we will win."

"Together with the French, we can succeed. As it is, the English do not need a war to murder us—their bounties do that. If we allow them to push us from our food sources, we will die anyway."

"We know this land best. Our chances of survival are better if we stand firm."

"Need I remind you, we almost lost Singing Sparrow!" Eagle Feather blurted in anger.

Bear Cub knew his brother had gone too far when he saw White Cloud's face fall.

"My father, I—" Eagle Feather stopped when White Cloud walked away.

Morning Dove placed her hand on her son's shoulder before she followed her husband. When they reached the wikuom, they held each other. White Cloud kissed the top of her head.

Morning Dove looked up at her husband. "In the circle, I am surprised you allowed them to speak out of turn."

"They were angry. It would serve no purpose to correct them." White Cloud turned away. "Am I delusional?" he asked.

She shook her head. "Moqwe," she said, and sat on the woven mat, motioning to her partner of thirty Winters to come by her side. "They are defeated. They feel there is no recourse but to fight now."

"I have known their feelings for quite some time. I did not wish to believe it. Why cannot both sides compromise so we can all exist peacefully with these newcomers?"

"Their ways are not our ways," she said simply. "You are a good man. You have the courage of a bear and seek the truth in all matters. You want only the best for the People. You have managed to stay the inevitable. Maybe it is the only choice now. Those in other camps have realized this fate."

"In the eyes of the Great Spirit, we are to live together in harmony, in diversity, to share. No one can own!" His voice rose. "I do not wish to pick up my musket yet. But I believe I stand alone."

She placed her hand over his. "That is untrue. Six Winters ago, you did what was necessary, by attacking the British military and shipping. You turned over British soldiers alive to collect bounties. The innocents were left untouched." She paused. "There will be a consensus. In the past, you have changed others to see your way. You are well-loved, my husband. We will continue to extend our hands of friendship until everyone agrees."

"Maybe it is too late. Vaudreuil goads the priests to keep the People at war with the British."

She studied her husband's eyes—his suffering was hers.

White Cloud laid his hand over hers. "I need to be alone."

Morning Dove stood and quietly left. She overheard her husband's words. "O Great One, I come before you humbly with bowed head, with tears in my eyes…"


The last moon of Spring was giving way to the first of Summer. With each passing sunrise, the warmth of Na'ku'set lingered long into the night. Everyone now slept outside—the fires were extinguished inside and the door-blankets pulled back. The village was asleep as Bear Cub and his brother lay near the warmth of the fire.

Eagle Feather pointed to Muin, the bear in the sky. "The appearance and habits of animals on Mother Earth mirror the same as their ancestors in the sky."

Bear Cub looked at the group of stars high in the northern sky. "In my homeland, we call it *Großer Wagen*, Great Cart."

Eagle Feather continued. "The three stars resembling Bear's tail are the first of seven bird hunters who have started their chase of Bear across the sky. Bear is pursued throughout Summer until the first moon of Autumn when the other four hunters, Blue Jay, Saw-whet Owl, Screech Owl, and Pigeon, grow weary. One by one they lose the trail and drop below the horizon. Only Moose Bird, Chickadee, and Robin are left to continue hunting. At last, Bear grows weary of the chase and is overtaken by Robin when he pierces Bear with his arrow. She falls on her back and lies thus in the sky. But her life-spirit enters another Bear that is sleeping in her den on Earth. Then, the cycle starts over when Spring touches the sky and the Bear awakes, comes from her den, and descends the steep slopes of the sky, again to be chased by the hunters. It is the circle of life."

Bear Cub remembered how he was named by his Mi'kmaw

family. At the last moon of Autumn, his brother had found him lying on his back. But, as Eagle Feather had told him, his heartbeat was strong. His new family restored his health, and his life-spirit returned in the Spring. Hence he was named Bear, and *Cub* soon followed because of his stature.

Eagle Feather sat up and gazed at the lake. The rising full moon now illuminated the darkness, outlining the maple trees and spruce along the shore. "I sensed your despair in the circle. We look here first, my brother," he said as he gave his bare chest a hard pat over his heart.

Bear Cub propped his head on his arm. "We are not all dishonourable."

"No need to say such words," Eagle Feather said. "But greed and power corrupt, turning otherwise good people into beings with no conscience. They lose sight of what is vital for living."

"The missionaries are indifferent to your needs when they manipulate the People to war," Bear Cub said.

"Things have gone too far. The only answer now is to gain back our land, even if it means force."

"White Cloud doesn't see it that way."

Eagle Feather shrugged and glanced back at his brother. "In this matter, my father and I do not see eye to eye."

Bear Cub sat up. "The missionaries shouldn't interfere. When they converted the People to Christianity, did you not lose sight of what is vital for you?" He had learned about Kisu'lkw, that which created us, the one who breathed life into all who moved, who created Mother Earth, the Sun, the Moon, the Stars. Every living thing, each rock and waterway, has spirit.

"To respect the newcomers, we listen to their stories," replied Eagle Feather. "If the missionaries think it important for us to believe, and it can promote peace on both sides, the mode of worship is purely incidental. Christianity does not strip us of our traditional beliefs. It adds to it. Jesus's teachings are not unlike our own."

"In German society, some think the earth and certain people should be tamed and mastered," Bear Cub said. "You have taught me that we are all tied to Mother Earth. As the water gently follows the course of the river, I have come to know my journey. It is no longer a constant struggle upstream."

Bear Cub moved his bare forearm next to his brother's. The light of the moon shed a glimmer across their skin, and Bear Cub's was pale in comparison. He knew his brother's heart, yet a childish yearning bubbled up to make him dig deeper for reassurance. "Does the obvious matter to you?" he mumbled.

His brother's eyes widened in bewilderment. He shook his head. "Remember the spirit moose."

This moose was sacred. The Elders had described the rare sightings of this animal who appeared dissimilar. In the old country, Bear Cub had heard the term *albino* coined for such anomalies in other species.

Eagle Feather turned to him, and Bear Cub could see that his eyelids were becoming heavy. The corners of Eagle Feather's eyes crinkled. "He is still a moose."

Eagle Feather lay down and drifted into slumber before Bear Cub had a chance to respond. Tomorrow night, celebrations would commence.

Four distinct beats on the elk-skinned drum sounded outside the circle, breaking the trance of the storytelling. Calm Water had been teaching the children about how, when animals give of themselves to the hunter, nothing can be wasted. White Cloud appeared at the head of a long line of people, colours, and movement. Decorations made of porcupine quills in varying hues of red, yellow, white, and black with hints of blue were woven on vibrant headbands and in the clothing down to the fringes. Shells, bone, and tiny copper cones rustled against each other in the night air. White Cloud's head dropped forward as the line of men and women behind him moved up and down and side to side in unison, each person with their hands on the shoulders of the one in front of them. With heavy feet they stomped on the ground in time to the drumbeats. The chanting rose above the beats. "Het, het, het," they sang. "Het, het, het." The children scurried to the end of the line, adding to the consistent descending of height from the leader. The hypnotizing movement of twisting left to right, up and down, resembled a serpent. They wound back and forth until they reached the opposite side of the dance circle. The beat slowed. White Cloud stood in the centre while the line of dancers circled around him. When the rhythm increased, the leader emerged from the centre again, twisting back and forth to reach the other side with the line in tow.

Bear Cub and Peter stood apart from the scene. Eagle Feather added himself to the link just behind his father. Bear Cub could not take his eyes from Singing Sparrow. She danced with such grace. *She does everything with fluidity and poise*, he thought. She had always teased him mercilessly in her sisterly affection, but her playfulness was now pulling at his heartstrings. When had this changed? He had crossed some sort of line from just being siblings to something more tender. Something White Cloud might not approve.

Singing Sparrow suddenly broke from the other dancers to move toward him and Peter. Bear Cub's smile faded when she gently pulled Peter into the serpent.

"Well! This is a surprise," Peter called back to Bear Cub.

*That may be, but must you enjoy it so much?* Bear Cub frowned. As for Singing Sparrow, she was likely just extending a courteous hand to a guest. After all, not only was the celebration gratitude for Mother Earth's provisions, but also indebtedness toward his friend. Or was there something more? Singing Sparrow could very well be attracted to Peter, now clean-shaven. A pang of jealousy pricked Bear Cub.

The dance wound its way down, and all dispersed. But Peter continued talking to Singing Sparrow. Bear Cub turned away. The sun had dipped farther from view below the streaks of orange and red that stretched across the sky. Eagle Feather tapped him on the shoulder and tried to convince him to play waltes, a dice game. He said a few others, as well as Peter, were joining.

"We will need to teach Peter though," Eagle Feather said. "Are you well, my brother? You seem distant."

"I'm fine," Bear Cub said. He could not reveal his feelings for Singing Sparrow to his brother. "E'e. It's high time I finally beat you, my brother." Bear Cub was not good at the game, but at least it would pull Peter from Singing Sparrow.

The three marched into the largest of the A-frame wikuoml set up for the night's event. Inside, most of the men were in separate groups of three or four with a wooden burl set in the middle. There was a collective noise of caribou bone dice clattering and banging at different intervals. Calm Water and two Elders welcomed them. The rules were quickly explained to Peter.

"The more dice you flip up the same way, the more points you score," Eagle Feather chimed in. "And these sticks tell you how many points you have earned."

Peter slammed the wooden bowl down and the six dice bounced upward.

"Not with so much vigour." Calm Water laid his hand upon

Peter's arm. "You will wake our ancestors. Gently tap the bowl on the ground, like this. Any dice that land outside the bowl cannot be counted."

"Ah, maybe these ancestors would like to play with us," Peter said.

Calm Water let out a hearty laugh. "I will not be responsible for the consequences."

Time melted away and Bear Cub excused himself. He was losing anyway. Peter, on the other hand, had the most sticks piled in front of him. "Luck is on my side," Bear Cub heard him say as he stepped outside. The night air was warm and muggy, and the moon had not yet risen. Except for the game activity, the village was very quiet. In the dark, early fireflies intermittently flashed their tiny glints of light. As he strolled toward the lake, he thought of Peter. *Maybe he is right*, Bear Cub thought. *I should return to my family. Why am I so afraid?* Love or obligation, it made no difference—he did not wish to stir up old wounds again with Papa. So maybe he should just let sleeping dogs lie and let them think he was dead.

When a wolf howled in the distance, he identified with the animal. Maybe the two of them were crying out to Kisu'lkw for an answer. Soft humming mixed with the animal's lament, and Bear Cub caught movement out of the corner of his eye. It was his sister, unaware of his presence. He stared, admiring her before she disappeared inside the wikuom. He turned back to the blackness of the forest. The howl echoed again and the half-moon glowed as it finally rose above the canopy. In time, he would retire to the family wikuom where Singing Sparrow slept. But not yet. He would remain with only himself for company and try, if he could, not to think of his sister in that way again.

Bees buzzed as Singing Sparrow walked about the tall blades of sweetgrass and mixed meadow grasses that grew as sisters. As she carefully moved along, she kept Bear Cub in her sight. Her hand shook slightly as she ran it along the pointed tips of various reeds. She could not keep her mind free of the assault. The worst was the groping, the weight of the calloused hands as they moved roughly across her skin. She shuddered and thrust the memory into a dingy, dark corner. Her eyes scanned the meadow, searching for the best patch. *Never take the first that I see.* It was a lesson never forgotten. She again caught sight of her brother, who smiled back at her.

More than any other place—even at ceremonies—it was here the ancestors spoke to her. *Ah, this is it!* She whispered to her grandmother's spirit and sprinkled tobacco around the sweetgrass. Its musky aroma always calmed her. She asked for permission to harvest, then pinched a long shiny blade at the reddish base, careful not to disturb the roots. As she continued to gather, Singing Sparrow hummed a French song she had been taught by her Acadian grandmother, who had long ago passed on to the Land of Souls. It was about a love between a young Mi'kmaw boy and a French girl. She wondered as she picked her way through the grass if the story was about her grandmother and grandfather. She glanced over at her brother. It was low tide and he was digging through the wet sand for clams. His basket was half-full of the mollusks, as well as mussels he had found around the black rocks, still dripping with seaweed. She stopped.

E'e. There was a precarious yet precious bond between the two of them. Unspoken but there, nonetheless. Every time she was around Bear Cub, she could feel it. She caught the occasional sidelong glances from him. Singing Sparrow had sensed his disappointment when she had chosen Peter to dance. Her instincts never failed her. She always remained sensitive to them to guide her to the truth in any situation. But her shyness often overpowered her instincts when it came to the hidden matters of young men. She laid the sweetgrass in her basket before moving to another part of the meadow.

Bear Cub suddenly but quietly appeared by her side.

"Shh, get down," he whispered urgently. He took the basket from her hands and pulled her to the ground. "I heard German voices."

Singing Sparrow's body tensed, her heartbeat quickened. They were not camouflaged well enough to remain completely undetected. But to attempt an escape now would be perilous. The sound of footsteps and the swishing of grasses around the meadow grew uncomfortably close.

Bear Cub pulled his musket toward him and cocked it. He slowly raised his head. "It is the same two we met in the woods," he whispered. "They are heading this way." His basket of shellfish lay in the open.

Tears stung Singing Sparrow's eyes. She desperately tried not to panic. She could taste blood where she had bitten her lip. The intruders were very close. *Do not breathe*, she admonished herself. *Keep still, do not move. Do not cry out.* But her instinct to run screamed inside of her.

"Well, well, Len. Who do we have here? Two frightened natives," one of them mocked, then kicked Bear Cub hard in the side, knocking his gun to the ground. "Correction: only one." Singing Sparrow froze when her brother moaned.

"Stand up! Both of you." The man called Len spit and latched onto Singing Sparrow's wrist to drag her up to his level.

Bear Cub propelled forward to claw at Len's legs, but his companion hit him hard with the butt end of his gun and pinned him down. Bear Cub gasped for air.

"We'll take them prisoner, Kasper," Len said. "They'll be worth more alive than dead."

Kasper yanked Bear Cub to his feet. Behind their assailants, Singing Sparrow spotted Peter within close range. "Kasper!" Peter hissed. "Let them go or I'll shoot Len through the head. You are both worthless, so I have nothing to lose."

Kasper slowly slid a blade to Singing Sparrow's throat. A loud crack echoed as puffs of smoke arose from Peter's gun. Len fell backward and Bear Cub retrieved his gun, which he aimed straight at Kasper's head. Singing Sparrow's legs gave out beneath her. Her brother had a twisted expression of disgust on his face as he pulled the trigger. The sudden close attack propelled Kasper's body backward, eyes wide with surprise. Singing Sparrow sobbed hysterically. She could barely feel Bear Cub's arms around her, but his repeated pleas to forgive him were heart-wrenching. "If you were taken from me…!" he cried.

Peter's Mi'kmaw words rang. "We need to bury them." He ran to the dry part of the beach and began to dig into the sand with his hands. "If the British discover the bodies, they will retaliate on the Mi'kmaq."

The tide was still out. Bear Cub and Singing Sparrow followed. "It was in defence!" Bear Cub yelled. "Justice—"

Peter cut him off. "Justice? You of all people know it means nothing."

Bear Cub stared at him.

"Wake up, Christian. Where the Indians are concerned, justice doesn't exist. Our actions here will be an excuse for more attacks from the British, or for anyone to take matters into their own hands. Vengeance has no boundaries."

Peter was on his hands and knees, feverishly scooping to make a burial pit.

Singing Sparrow forced herself to follow his lead. She raised her head to Bear Cub. "He is right. I am scared for my People. This can come to no good."

Bear Cub crouched beside her and began to scoop out handfuls of sand as fog started to roll in.

# Chapter Three

JULY 1756

Hanna Heber tossed in her bed and unknowingly threw the covers onto the floor. It was the middle of July, and the heat of the previous day had trapped itself in the loft where she slept. As she settled, Hanna slipped further into a deep slumber. She could hear the ocean waves breaking along the shore. As a heavy grey mist curled around her, a cold sweat beaded over her arms. In the distance, a man buried what looked like a human body. Grains of sand collected between her toes as she tried to catch up to him. Hanna caught a glimpse of his face. "Christian!" she called. Her brother's hand grasped for hers, but he became one with the fog and disappeared. She panicked.

"Hanna. Hanna!"

She jolted awake. She stared up blankly and saw her papa looking down at her.

"You were dreaming, my liebling," Michael whispered.

She blinked hard to force her eyes to focus. "It was Christian." This was only one dream of many dreams about Christian that she had experienced in the last few months.

"We will talk about it during breakfast. I have just stoked the embers. Get yourself dressed and draw up some water." Her father clambered back down the ladder. "I was up long ago and did the milking." From the doorway, he said, "Go to the chicken coop and see if there are any eggs this time. I don't know what's wrong. Maybe the hens are too old, or this heat's too much for them." He grinned at his daughter who was leaning over the bed to look at him. Then, he left. She rested her chin on her arm and watched stray sunbeams reach for the dark corners of the kitchen.

"Ja, Papa," she answered to the empty doorway. After splashing her face and arms with water, she quickly dressed and made her way to the kitchen. Outside, wispy spiderwebs glistened on top of the grass. They predicted another scorcher. Hanna could hear the clatter of Papa adding more logs to the outside hearth. As soon as he and Georg had built it two weeks ago, the oppressive summer heat had descended upon them. The stone structure was not large by any means but was big enough for their household of two.

Hanna stared across a carpet of sky blue—they had planted the flax three months ago with seeds they had brought from their homeland. Potatoes were growing to the east of that, with wheat and oats farther down from the house. Turnips would be planted later. Forest still stood, sparse in some areas and much thicker in others, on the entire back half of their parcel of land. They had planted their crops where it was easiest to tackle the land—the section abandoned by Acadian families. It had been overgrown with thickets of alder, wire brush, and Indian pear. Neighbours helped each other when they could, but there was very little progress on the removal of the large stumps and roots from the felled trees, as oxen were scarce. To make matters worse, they were not able to grow the necessary feed, and most of the distributed livestock had not survived the winter before last.

Hanna checked the two hens they owned and ja, they had

laid. Just two though, one each. Chickens were scarce in the settlement. She gently gathered both eggs, patting the hens' bottoms as a thank-you, and headed toward the well.

"Guten morgen, Papa," Hanna chimed, reaching up to kiss him on the cheek.

"And a grand one it is. I see we have struck gold this morning," he said, taking the brown eggs from her. Michael wrapped his arms around his youngest and planted a kiss on top of her head.

For four years, it had been just the two of them. She was eleven now and well beyond her years, according to her sister, Elisabeth. Papa and Hanna now lived on South Division A, from which it took a good couple of hours to walk overland to Georg and Elisabeth's place on the First Peninsula. Initially, Papa drew a lot on the LaHave River, but for safety, he was allowed to forfeit it for his deceased son's property. Jakob's lot was much closer to town. With two sawmills nearby, their cleared trees soon became hewn lumber for their small log house. It stood sturdy with a thick thatched roof. Doors and shutters were made of two-inch planks fastened with iron hinges and bolts. Glass windows were very dear, so they used oiled sheepskin, which allowed some light to penetrate.

Hanna carried water inside the house and was setting the table when Papa appeared with bowls of potato soup leftover from the night before. He broached the subject of the dream as he tore off a piece from the loaf of heavy bread that lay between them.

"It was different this time. Christian was pleading for me. I know he is alive. I just know it, Papa."

"I want to believe, but I'll not get my hopes so high only to be disappointed." Papa studied her. "You are not the first one in the family to have the sight, you know, and you probably will not be the last."

Hanna smiled. Maybe her papa was coming around. Elisabeth said he was almost back to the old Papa, the one they knew before Margaretha had died. Their sister was twelve years old when the light dimmed from Michael's eyes, the year before they crossed the ocean. Like a dark shadow, her death sailed with them to this new land.

"Mama said her sister was able to foresee things."

"Ja, your Tante Catherina. You probably don't remember her. You only met her once, you were two years old."

His eyes stared blankly and she knew his mind was in the old country. Hanna thought of her youngest brother, Stefan, who died on the crossing. He would have been six years old now. Hanna laid her hand over his. "I will not give up on Christian."

He cleared his throat and stood up. "If we intend to get to Elisabeth and Georg's on time, we best be on our way."

"We plan to visit Frau Born. Maybe she has a new shipment from Halifax." Hanna was excited to be going.

Michael stepped into his bedroom off the kitchen as Hanna cleaned the dishes. She could hear him fiddle with the key in the blanket chest. Returning with the small tin box where he hid what money he had, he pressed two farthings into her hand. "Here. You will be twelve in September. Something for your hair, maybe?"

Money was hard to come by, and she knew this offer was from his heart. Last summer, some of the settlers left temporarily for Halifax where there was much more opportunity for employment. But Papa refused to abandon her for that length of time. What money he did have was from Philip Knaut, who operated one of the mills. Herr Knaut paid a fair price for the wood from their felled trees. Hanna put the coins in her pocket and kissed her papa. "Come on, we had better get a move on," she said, stroking his soft beard.

Hanna smoothed down her calico dress and placed a cotton cap over her head. With no hint of a wave or curl, her black hair hung loose down her back. The cap was the same unrefined material as her dress, unbleached, and not nearly as fine as the muslin the wives of the British officers wore. She stepped outside to join Papa, who was wearing his large-brimmed hat.

The roads were no more than roughly cut trails along the baseline of each range of farm lots. They followed along the edge of their land, then a small part of the Middle Range where many of the lots were swamp and uncultivated. Next to a brook, Herr Knaut owned a row of lots just for the trees. Establishing a sawmill proved crucial and advantageous for building locally as well as having enough to supply Halifax. Herr Koch owned the other mill, located at the mouth of Grimm Brook in South Division B, which was farther south. As Hanna and her father picked their way along past Reverend Moreau's land, the rhythmic sound of the sawmill could be heard in the distance.

Papa stopped. "Do you hear that?"

Hanna stopped beside him. "It's a woodpecker," she replied, searching through the trees for a sighting.

"That's no ordinary one." Michael pointed to a large balsam fir. "Can you spot him now? See the red head?"

"I do!" Hanna rang out excitedly. "It is a pileated woodpecker." Remembering the name pleased her, as they had never seen them in the old country.

Hanna had a love of nature that mirrored her papa's passion for it. One morning last week, he had awakened her just before sunrise to show her a beaver dam on a nearby river. As the sun rose, the two of them sat quietly together among the bulrushes and observed as the creature built his home. The closeness they shared since her mama's death had grown to a level of endearment and comfort only the two of them understood.

As they continued toward town, Michael occasionally bent down to show Hanna how to differentiate between edible and poisonous mushrooms. Despite the rough terrain, observing nature on their long journey made for an engaging time, when two hours could easily melt into three.

Past the common range where the land had been left for pasturing and propagation, an eight-foot palisade skirted the west side of town and joined the back harbour to the front harbour. Lunenburg was situated on a neck of land between the two. Blockhouses stood out at each end of the picketing. Hanna admired the British soldiers in their red tunics, white breeches, and black shoes. The wide leather belts strapped across their chests carried cartridge pouches, making their uniform appear cumbersome. Muskets glistened in the sun as they marched, keeping step along the tall fence. Hanna and Michael walked between the picketing and the large pentagon-shaped fort. All five bastions, angular in form, were flanked on both sides with guns. She took hold of Papa's hand as they passed the recently dried ditches that lay around the structure.

Elisabeth Gessler wiped beads of perspiration from her brow, inhaled, then blew a welcomed bit of cool air up to her forehead. In the humidity, kneading the bread dough with such fervour defeated her attempt to keep cool. The front and back doors were both open, but a cross-breeze was not in Mother Nature's plans this morning. Elisabeth's sister and papa would be arriving shortly, and she was quickly preparing the dough to rise. So, sweat she must. It was the last of the flour ration, but she would pick up more when she and Hanna went to town.

Through the soldiers' fear-mongering about possible raids, everyone was anxious, but since the inception of Lunenburg three years ago, there had been no such attempts. Until the raid on Rous and Payzant's Islands two months ago, fear caused sporadic clearing of everyone's lands. After heavy spring rains last year, sickness, and the loss of most of the cattle, Governor Lawrence had sent wheat and oat seeds to compensate for the settlers' distress. Victuals had resumed but not to those farmers already doing well on their own. Thus far this year the land was proving to be more fruitful, with the right amount of rain and sun. There was hope in the settlement. Elisabeth put more muscle into her dough and thought of Papa who was burdened with regret for bringing his family here.

She heard a tiny rustle and glanced up. A brown mouse skittered across the bulky wooden beam from which hung a small assortment of dried herbs.

"Mama! Mama!" Petie hollered from outside. Whimpering quickly followed before it escalated to an outright sob. She wiped the flour from her hands and ran out the door. She gathered her son onto her lap and tried to kiss his sorrows away. His hand was only scraped from his fall, but the wailing denoted something much worse. Through his hiccups, he explained in incomplete sentences the loss of the mouse he had found and wished to keep as a present for her. His green eyes welled up again. She could see the tail end of the mouse skitter through the tall grass.

"I know, my liebling," she said, feeling his plight. "But we have enough of those little creatures in our house without you bringing in another one." She squeezed him closer and refocused his attention on a toad hopping amid the dandelions.

Looking down the slope of their land to the edge of the back harbour, she could see Hanna and Papa making their way toward them. She waved to them and placed her son on his feet. "Tante Hanna and Opa are here!" Petie ran as fast as his five-year-old legs could carry him. As she watched her son leap into her papa's arms, she could imagine Stefan doing the same. *Foolish to wish it*, she thought and shoved the image away.

Elisabeth returned to the kitchen. After a quick examination, which showed no mouse in the resting dough, she laid it in an iron pot to rise and covered it with the lid.

"In this humidity, those loaves will be rising in no time." Hanna chuckled and hugged her sister from behind.

"Ja, and probably well before we return from town." Elisabeth laughed and returned the embrace. She held her sister at arm's length. "Except for Papa's blue eyes and his compassion, I see Mama in you." But Elisabeth and Jakob were the only ones who had inherited their mother's stubborn, domineering, hotheaded ways.

"You always say that! How are you feeling these days?" Hanna asked.

"Much better. No nausea for a week now. I have just missed my third monthly course."

"So, you are sure now?"

"As best I can be. Looks like January." Elisabeth beamed.

"Does Georg know?

Elisabeth nodded. "He is ecstatic! Hush now, Papa's coming," she said.

His grandson in his arms, Michael kissed his eldest daughter. "Our little one here has more freckles than the last time I saw him. And the energy—just keeping up with him is testing my stamina."

"Do you think you can handle another one?" Elisabeth tried to keep a straight face but lost the battle.

"Ach!" Michael bellowed. "Do not tease an old man like this. Truly?" His eyes welled up through his grin.

Elisabeth raised her eyebrows with a quirky smile.

Petie, who had no interest in having a brother or sister, managed to wriggle down before the hugs and kisses started. He grabbed his opa's hand to steer him back outside, all the while rambling about a mouse and a toad.

"Tend to your grandson. Go, we will talk later," Elisabeth said, ushering him out.

Through the doorway, Elisabeth could see her husband returning. She nodded in Georg's direction and turned to her sister. "He must have seen you two coming. I'll only be a minute."

Elisabeth changed her dress and tucked away stray strands of blonde hair that had made their way out of her braid, then wrapped it around the back of her head before putting her cap in place. When she caught up to Hanna, Papa and Georg were conversing together. "Petie will be with us," she said to Hanna. "Georg may be called out to the Mosers'. Barbara is long past her due date, and Dr. Erad is in Mahone Bay for a few days. His assistant, Dr. Phillips, is not yet experienced enough, and they are expecting complications."

"Cannot one of the midwives help?"

"If you remember, there was a problem with her last pregnancy. Forceps were needed and the midwives have no knowledge of them," Elisabeth replied.

Her attention was sidetracked by Georg's conversation with her papa. "Since May, another blockhouse has been erected at Mahone Bay with more reinforcement," her husband was saying.

"That is all well and good. But what if the raids spread?" Michael replied.

"Colonel Sutherland just received authorization to build a blockhouse halfway between Mahone Bay and the LaHave River, as well as one on the Northwest Range. The sawmills at Lower and Upper LaHave already have blockhouses, not to mention those built in town."

"Herrs Kuhn and Feder have no qualms about abandoning their farms unless more safety is assured. Who knows what is lurking nearby? And those on the inland lots are much more isolated," said Michael.

"And I have my own apprehensions. But daylight is even more comforting when the British soldiers are about." Georg changed the subject. "About the cattle drive, are you still—"

Michael quickly shook his head to refrain Georg from continuing.

Elisabeth and Hanna had been standing back, listening quietly. "And on those thoughts…" Elisabeth kissed her two favourite men.

Georg answered with a nod and squeezed her hand.

"If I finish early enough at Herr Born's tannery, I'll meet you at the fort to help with the rations," Michael said.

The sisters walked as briskly as possible with Petie, eager to get to town and within the protection of the palisade. The Borns lived in a log house near the top of the hill at Fox and Duke Streets, looking over the front harbour. Frau Born would be alone with Rosina, as Martin was at the tannery today along with his partner, Kris Metzler. Elisabeth rapped hard on the knocker.

When the door opened wide, they were greeted with Frau Born's usual kindness and enthusiasm.

"Come in, come in," she said, gesturing, then caressed Petie's face. "My, he has grown much since we last met! I will not tarry here and keep you waiting. Follow me."

"And you, my son, are not to touch a thing. Do you hear me?" Elisabeth whispered.

When he nodded his assent, Frau Born smiled and guided

the boy to a small wooden rocking chair just the size for his age and handed him a few colourful wooden blocks to entertain himself. "Now, you two come with me across the hall. Petie will be fine. My little girl can sit there playing for hours."

Inside a smaller room, Frau Born opened the birch trunk about five feet long and two feet high with two cumbersome, rust-spotted iron hinges. Inside was an elaborate display of calicoes, ribbons, sewing needles, and buttons—everything a haberdasher would carry and more. "My sister sent quite a replenishment to my little store," Frau Born explained. "Barbara Moser was in earlier this week and said my prices were affordable, she who complains about every price in town. But imagine, her being here and past due with that baby. I don't know how she manages with that brood of hers. Seven children was the last count. This one makes eight." Her eyes sparkled when she spoke. "Martin and I have not been so blessed and only have the one. Don't get me wrong, we love her dearly. Except..." Elisabeth was aware of Frau Born's miscarriages and knew she had been warned by both Georg and Dr. Erad that she might not survive another.

As Elisabeth scanned the treasures, Hanna nudged her. "Elisabeth," she said softly, fingering a silky ribbon of the loveliest green, "this is exquisite." She held it up to the light streaming in through the glass window.

"Do you like it, my dear?" Frau Born asked.

"Oh. Ja. But how much is it?"

"What do you have?"

"Papa gave me two farthings." Hanna smiled, then half-frowned. "But I fear it is worth much more."

"You guessed the exact price, two farthings. This must be your most glorious day to find such a bargain." Frau Born gave Elisabeth a sidelong glance. "Shall I wrap it for you?"

"Oh. Bitte, please," Hanna answered, digging for the coins in her pocket.

"And can I interest you in anything, Elisabeth?"

"I'm looking for a sewing needle, as my old one broke two days ago. I have carried it with me since leaving Hohctorf. It was Mama's."

After paying for the purchase, Elisabeth joined Petie who was now playing with two-year-old Rosina. "Would you like to stay for tea?" Frau Born asked.

"Danke, but no. We still have our rations to pick up. And I'm sure my bread is now over-proofed."

Frau Born kissed all three warmly, and they were on their way.

When Elisabeth and Hanna had walked past the fort earlier, there was a long line of people winding its way from the open door and around the corner. It had since dispersed, leaving just a steady flow of people moving in and out of the front room of the barracks. The tiny cool area was welcome relief from the heat. Except for a large table with a chair behind it, on which a soldier was seated, the room was devoid of any furniture. Uneven stacks of flour and casks of beef in brine filled the perimeters of the room. There was a much shorter line in front of the table. In no time, Hanna and Elisabeth found themselves giving their names and handing over their ration cards.

The soldier was very young, maybe eighteen. He had a sharp, angular face and prominent cheekbones. His dark brown hair was parted in the middle and tied back with a coarse piece of cloth. His black cocked felt hat hung on the back of his chair. Elisabeth gave Hanna a stern look when her sister smiled at him. He turned a few pages in his leather-bound logbook, running his finger down each one until he came to the name Gessler. He twisted the book around, dipped the pen nib into the ink bottle, and handed it to Elisabeth. "Please sign here, ma'am." Then, eyeing Hanna, "Sign here please," he said, showing her the correct spot at the bottom of the next page. "Usually Michael is here for the weekly victuals. Is all well?"

"Ja, sir, of course. He had business at the tannery," Hanna replied handing the pen back.

"Ah, I see," the soldier said, initialling their ration cards before passing them back. "I am sure there will be discussions on the journey Captain Steignfort is leading for the cattle drive in a couple of weeks. I believe Michael put his name forward a week ago to volunteer."

Hanna was about to protest when Elisabeth jumped in. "It is certainly kind of you to speak our tongue. You speak it well."

He turned to her and smiled. "When stationed here for three years, one tends to learn quickly."

Elisabeth said, "So, I am assuming nothing has changed. It is still seven pounds of flour and one pound of beef per person in a household?"

"Ja, that is correct." He gestured to a soldier who retrieved the supplies for them.

Elisabeth glanced at Hanna, who was rooted to the floor in a state of shock. Elisabeth could read her sister's thoughts well. She knew Hanna didn't want Papa to go on the cattle drive. She thanked the soldier and started for the door.

"Frau Gessler," he called. "Do you realize you only have two weeks remaining before you are removed from the list?"

Elisabeth turned back to the desk. "There must be some mistake. Most of our land is still forested. You must know that my husband has been very busy with patients since the fever epidemic. Last year, the victualling continued after Colonel Sutherland sent our petition to the governor. I am confident it will resume." Elisabeth spoke with conviction. But the soldier shook his head, so she continued. "I am aware we have received more than the government originally contracted to supply. But these small improvements to our land don't allow us to support ourselves with the little produce we are harvesting. If the rations stop, most of us will have to leave. Then all the results from these years of labour are for naught."

"I am well aware of that, but the colonel says otherwise. He feels prospects are looking up this year, so much so he wishes to implement a regular public market every Saturday."

"Then the colonel is premature. We are accomplishing so little, especially with the threat of attacks." A sharp jab from Hanna irritated her; but Petie was squirming to leave, and Elisabeth knew her voice was rising, especially when she voiced "the colonel" with contempt.

"Rest assured, Governor Lawrence will heed the colonel if matters have turned for the worse. But the Board of Trade in London can only approve the continuation by recommendation from the governor."

"Maybe the governor embellishes too much of our circumstances here. The Board of Trade has no idea what is involved in breaking in new lands."

"That is not for me to say. I cannot speak for either one of them."

"We will stage another protest." The year before, Elisabeth had marched with other women and their children as they made known the hardship any loss of rations would cause.

Hanna's face turned red. "You are embarrassing me, sister. He is only passing on information that was written in the log." Hanna grasped Elisabeth's elbow to steer her away. "There is nothing we can do here. And the line behind us is growing."

Elisabeth stood her ground. "Who's in charge of the

supplies? I would like to speak to him." Elisabeth refused to move. Hanna released her arm.

"Thomas Saul, he is the Commissary for Stores and Provisions. He is not here today. He is also an agent for the army contractor, William Baker. Very busy man, he is, very busy," the soldier said, shaking his head. "Herr Saul does not only keep provisions for the settlers here," he said, sarcasm creeping into his tone.

"When is he back?"

"Unknown," he replied. Then, looking over her shoulder, he cried, "Forgive me, I will be with you shortly." And to Elisabeth he added, "Try tomorrow."

Elisabeth could see a lengthy line behind her now. Her sister looked distraught, and Elisabeth's posture slumped in defeat. "Danke," she said briskly. She took hold of her son's hand. Hanna gathered a portion of their supplies and headed out the door.

"Next!" the soldier called.

The sun had peaked and their stomachs were growling. With their arms full and Papa nowhere in sight, they started their hike home.

"He was insulting, Hanna."

"Not so. You kept prying and pushing him. I sympathized with him."

"Ach, nein. I meant he should never have mentioned that Papa had volunteered."

Hanna stopped in her tracks. An ocean breeze whipped a bit of dust around her skirt. "Wait! Did you know about this?"

"I thought Papa had discussed it with you," Elisabeth fibbed.

Then, a sight for sore eyes. Papa came from behind, greeted them both with a kiss, and grabbed a few items.

"Papa," Hanna started in, "are you leaving for the cattle drive?"

He appeared to be taken aback. "We will discuss it later."

"Nein. I wish to talk about it now!"

"Hanna! Take that back." Elisabeth could not believe Hanna had spoken to their papa with such disrespect. Hanna lowered her head.

Firmly and tactfully, he replied, "It will be later, young lady. I will not discuss it here like a couple of ill-mannered urchins. People are turning their heads. Wait here," he demanded. "I'll get the remainder of the rations."

When he returned, the foursome walked home in silence.

# Chapter Four

JULY 1756

*I*t was midmorning and the sun poured through the clear glass windows. Sitting in church made Hanna fidgety. She played with the new ribbon in her hair, twisting and untwisting it around her finger. It was all she could do to concentrate on her prayer to keep Papa safe. Everyone who had volunteered to retrieve the Acadian cattle was leaving in five days to meet others in Mahone Bay. She glanced sideways at her sister, who sat still with closed eyes, head bowed, Georg beside her, with Petie between him and Papa. A few sleepless nights and many tears had ensued after Papa elaborated on the journey to Hanna. He had tried to alleviate her anxieties but with little success. All she could think about was the old, dark Acadian trail to Pisiguit. The dense forests along the way occupied by hundreds of natives, shadowing and scrutinizing their prey for the first opportune moment. Dwelling on it only increased her tension as her mind spun like a mill wheel. Hanna could not stop it, nor was it a simple task to even try.

The dull drone from an insistent, deeper voice drilled its way into her thoughts. Reverend Jean Moreau had ministered St. John's Parish since Lunenburg's inception. Hanna peered up at him as he stood like an impregnable fortress, preaching his sermon from the second level of the triple-decker carved pulpit. His eyes caught hers as if he knew full well she had drifted from his oratory. And no wonder! The service was usually spoken in English, which was fine for the few members who spoke it. On occasion, he would do the service in French but rarely in German. However, all baptisms, marriages, and burials were predominantly spoken in her tongue. Communion as well, which the minister had just announced would now commence.

Hanna studied the water stains along the ceiling and down the wall behind the reverend. Her eyes scanned above and below the galleries. The stains were much worse where the squared windows were situated. The Board in London had provided money to have the church built, and it now catered to about fifty-six families, seating about two hundred. It was situated in the centre of town. The builder, who was too lavish on the decorated intricacies of the structure, ran out of money. It was nowhere near finished and was nowhere near watertight. After the consecration of the bread and wine, Hanna followed her family to the front to receive the Eucharist in silence. When the service ended, everyone milled about outside, with the main talk being the drive.

The Mosers, Knauts, Metzlers, and Kuhns had been invited to Georg and Elisabeth's home, so they naturally congregated together. Hanna freed Frau Moser of her loaves of bread so she could more easily carry her newborn. The Knauts brought a jug of molasses, and most every couple brought their spare eggs and salted beef. Elisabeth had potato soup to serve. All set out together, chattering, the women leading the small group while the children delayed the trek somewhat to examine anything that flew, buzzed, or crawled.

Hanna laid a basketful of juicy strawberries on the table in front of her sister and Anna as they busily prepared the noon meal.

"Ach!" Anna Knaut shouted. "Lovely!" Waving away flies from the fruit, she added, "These strawberry leaves will make a delicious tea. Danke!"

"I wondered where you got to," Elisabeth said to her sister as she bit into a strawberry. "The table is set up outside. Help us carry some things." Hanna was handed the butter and a plate full of sliced bread.

"Did you notice the beef we received last week, Elisabeth?" Anna queried.

Elisabeth nodded, making a face. "Ja. Old! The grain was too rough-looking and spongy. The dent remained when I pressed my finger on it."

Anna shook her head. "It certainly wasn't fresh. Mine is hanging in the smokehouse. Not quite sure if it is fit to be eaten." She covered the strawberries with a square of cloth, carried the basket outside, and announced everything was ready.

After dinner had been eaten, the men formed their own discussion groups outside while the women sat around the wooden quilting frame. The cross-breeze blowing through the kitchen was a relief.

"We can use these few patches I cut from an old, tattered blanket," Rosina Metzler said, laying the colourful squares in the centre of the partly finished quilt. "I picked through and brought the best ones." All agreed.

The room quieted as each person threaded her needle. The soothing songs of robins and finches drifted in from the open door. After placing the cotton squares at right angles along the backing, they created tiny stitches to attach them. Elisabeth had taught Hanna two years before, and everyone patiently offered their own hints and suggestions. Hanna welcomed all of them.

Eva Kuhn started the conversation. "Another petition will be ready soon for the governor."

"Is that for the German pastor?" Elisabeth asked. "If it is, that must be the third one."

"Ja. I can't help but nod off during the service. My Joseph is always elbowing me," Eva said.

"Reverend Moreau speaks French well." Barbara Moser smirked.

"And that serves us no purpose. We are the majority here, and his German is quite unpredictable and difficult to follow," Eva replied. "We need our own separate Lutheran church and pastor."

"That's not going to happen anytime soon. After receiving the church bell from Admiral Boscawen last year, a steeple is needed. Has anyone heard if there has been any headway on that?" Barbara asked. All shook their heads in bewilderment.

"In any case, let us hope this petition will be successful," Eva said, as she finished attaching one yellow square and grabbed another.

"Herr Knaut said the British government is not at fault." Anna nodded in agreement as Elisabeth continued. "Both a German minister and English schoolmaster have been in the parliamentary vote for the past two years. He thinks London can't find a Lutheran pastor anywhere, not even in Europe. No one is willing to accept an offer to come here."

Barbara shook her head in disbelief. "The so-called English school we have now is making little progress. My children don't know any more of the language than I do. For heaven's sake, the teacher, George Bailly, speaks French with a smattering of English to teach reading." She stopped sewing and sat back in her chair. "Most parents I have spoken to want their children to be taught in our mother tongue so they learn religious instruction right away. The majority of us are German—English can come later." As she resumed her stitching, she added, "Frankly, I agree."

"I would not be one of those parents," Eva opined. "It is good for the children to learn the other language first—all the soldiers speak it." When she raised her head, all eyes were upon her. All hands were motionless, except hers. "Ouch!" Eva's finger immediately found her mouth when a tiny spot of blood surfaced.

Elisabeth voiced her agreement. "What we need is a schoolmaster not affiliated with the SPG."

"Pardon me?" Barbara said.

Elisabeth glanced at her. "You know, the Society for the Propagation of the Gospel in Foreign Parts. That is where our Anglican ministers and schoolmasters come from."

"Ah. That is most likely why we will not get a Lutheran minister," Barbara said, shaking her head.

This said, there were a few grumblings.

Anna leaned close to Hanna and whispered, "Making your stitches a bit smaller will allow ten stitches per inch." She demonstrated on her patch. "See. This will ensure the quilt lies flat with nary a bump."

"I don't think I will ever be as good as you, Frau Knaut." Hanna sighed. She knew Anna to be a superb seamstress; her stitching was always so even and uniform.

"My little liebling, you will in time. It takes lots of practice and even more patience. You should have seen my first quilt." Anna half grinned. "I could not give it away."

One of the children burst into the room and ran toward Anna. "Mama! Mama!" It was her four-year-old daughter.

Anna wrapped her arm around the child. "Shh, quietly please, Catherine."

"Mama," she panted. "Petie fell out of a tree. I think he hurt his leg."

The chair tipped over when Elisabeth leapt to her feet. "Where is he?"

"Near the edge of the forest." Catherine pointed in the direction of where the children were playing. Elisabeth ran.

"I'll come with you," Hanna cried after her sister. She grasped Catherine's hand. "Show us."

By the time Hanna and Catherine arrived, Elisabeth was soothing her son in her arms. "Nothing looks broken that I can tell. He has a cut here on his calf." Hanna could see his torn breeches soaked with blood.

"What happened?" Hanna asked.

"He was trying to climb a maple tree." Elisabeth pointed. "One of the children lifted him to the nearest branch. He will be fine as soon as I get him cleaned up and a poultice on it. I'll see you back at the house."

The children all ran back as well, but Catherine remained to show Hanna just exactly how it occurred. "I told Hans not to give Petie a boost. His hands slipped on that branch."

"Why were you down here anyway? You know you are not to be playing near the woods."

"Hans heard a noise, then he thought he saw Old Labrador through the trees there, so we ran after him."

"Scoot now! Your mama will be looking for you." Hanna shooed her back, and off the little girl ran.

Paul Labrador was a Mi'kmaw who had lived with his Acadian family at the head of the front harbour long before the new settlement. Hanna's brief encounter with Old Labrador a year ago had been profound. An inexplicable familiarity had floated between them, and his second glance at her only further fused their connection. It was uncanny. His spirit beamed at her from his dark eyes when he smiled.

Standing in the safety of the open field, Hanna searched the pine forest for any movement. Suddenly, a doe walked from behind a broken tree trunk. She raised her head at Hanna, ears perked up. Her white underbelly stood out against the reddish fur that ran smoothly along her back and sides. When the animal darted farther away—her tail upright—Hanna felt compelled to follow. She wound her way through the woodland, careful to keep sight of the animal. The creature would stop at times, then leap deeper into the woods, beckoning Hanna to follow her.

When Hanna reached a brook, the doe had disappeared. The sound of the rushing water overtook any hope of hearing the animal through the brush. She stopped to look around. "It's magical here," she said to herself. Water bubbled around the terraced rocks, each coated with tightly woven moss. Large ferns stood guard in the dappled sunshine. The doe reappeared with two others, and the three bent their heads, eagerly lapping to quench their thirst.

Then a voice spoke—a soft voice, from behind. When Hanna turned around, Paul Labrador stood before her. Each wrinkle of his weatherworn face hinted at a history to be told. A small, crude wooden cross hung from a piece of leather cord tied around his neck, and shiny black hair hung above his bare chest. The leggings he wore were made of unknown material. His shoes were made of animal skin. Out of the side of his mouth, Paul sent up puffs of smoke from his pipe.

His first words were foreign to her. He made a second attempt, perhaps in French, which she knew Paul spoke, but Hanna still did not understand. At first, she was nervous— should she run? But her heart spoke differently. He gestured for her to sit with him on a large flat rock. For a few minutes, she watched as he pointed to different plants, speaking of what, she did not know. Paul laid aside his pipe and picked at a handful of leaves. He tasted them and encouraged her to copy him as he gently placed a few small pieces in her hand. His hands felt like soft leather.

The spell broke when she heard her papa call out, "Hanna! Hanna! Answer me!" Then silence.

She panicked and ran first in one direction, then another, becoming disoriented. Paul waved his arm for her to follow him. Again, the voice rang out, "Hanna!" When a clearing came into view, Paul vanished.

"Papa! I'm here," she called, breaking into a run when she saw him enter the clearing.

Michael ran toward her and hugged her as if he would lose her if he let go. "Never do that again. You have frightened everyone." He squeezed her tight. "What possessed you to go into the woods alone? You know it is forbidden."

"I followed a deer to a brook," was all she offered, glancing back from whence she came.

At the house, Michael bent down to kiss Hanna. "We'll start out for home shortly."

Hanna disappeared inside.


"The stray has been found," Philip Knaut said. "She's no worse for wear?" He laid his hand on his friend's arm.

Michael nodded. He did not wish to dwell on what could have happened. He steered Philip away from the topic. "What was the last count for the cattle drive Friday?"

"Fifty volunteers," Philip replied.

"You're still going?"

Philip nodded. "Jakob Konrad and his eldest can keep an

eye on the farm. The mill is silent for the moment—the river is too low."

"We're to meet Captain Steignfort at the north corner of the fort," Kris Metzler said. "Martin Born will look after the tannery."

Joseph Kuhn had not volunteered, as he refused to leave Eva alone. What happened to the Payzant family had shaken him so badly, he was ready to take his family back to Halifax. Louis Payzant had been murdered in the raid and his wife and children taken prisoner. Michael doubted Joseph would waver in his decision. Heinrich Moser was also staying behind.

"It'll be hazardous across the peninsula. The Acadian trail can't be fit for driving cattle," Joseph warned. "And the Indians! Not to mention that a few of our men were killed last December when Lawrence sent a party from Halifax."

"We know, Joseph!" Michael snapped. "Bitte! Do not repeat it again." Everyone stared at him, and he wished he could take it back. "Forgive me. I'm just a little apprehensive about the journey," he said, rubbing his temples.

"We all are," said Philip, and others spoke of their anxieties as well. Philip remarked, "The cattle were healthy and alive this spring because they fed on partly harvested grain left by the Acadians. But next winter will be a different story, so we need to bring the cattle here now. It is worth the risk." He surveyed the men and said, "There are more of us this time."

"This should not be! The Indians signed a peace treaty," Joseph said.

"As a collective, they didn't," Philip said. "It was only signed by Chief Kopit of Shubenacadie, who only had a small band under him. Kopit was expected to convince other chiefs to sign on, but the treaty angered the Louisbourg governor so much that he persuaded them not to sign it. To have the Mi'kmaq allied with the British is a death knell for the French."

"Weren't there more negotiations last year?" Michael asked.

Because of Philip's liaison with the governor, everyone assumed he was privy to all that happened in the province. It was known Philip had accompanied Governor Cornwallis on his expedition to Nova Scotia seven years ago and had set up a fur trade with the Acadians. He had won Halifax's confidence and received the small positions of Justice of the Peace and coroner. Last year, Governor Lawrence paid for his sawmill's entire output just to encourage and attract more entrepreneurs to the area. Speaking both German and English, Philip Knaut was a great asset to the settlement.

Philip answered, "There were, but Lawrence rejected the Mi'kmaw requests of specific territories."

"Maybe it was too extravagant," Joseph said.

Philip disagreed. "It is the least the government can do."

Joseph cut him off, his eyes narrowed. "Careful where you step, my friend." And he moved closer to Philip.

Georg pulled him back, calmly saying, "Ach, let him finish, Joseph."

Philip finished his thought. "The government is swift to bring the axe down upon their heads, are they not?"

"And so they should be!" Joseph was seething.

"The treaty was clear in stating it would protect the Mi'kmaq in court, prosecuting anyone who caused them harm. Has this happened? Nein! This is good enough reason for them not to sign. Do you think it fair that we do not punish our people for killing an Indian, but it does not go unnoticed when an Indian robs or murders? In my opinion, Lawrence's hatred has blinded him to reason."

"The way you speak sounds disloyal to me," Joseph stated. "Lawrence has always been overly persuasive with the London Board. I just heard that the victuals will be continuing until next year."

"I'm not saying he doesn't have faith in us. My point is we're the ones who have intruded on Mi'kmaw territory, not the reverse," Philip said, trying to reason with him.

Joseph snorted derisively, and ugly, twisted glares of disgust grew on Heinrich's and Kris's faces. Michael wondered how far Philip would go with this.

Philip continued, "The only white allies the Mi'kmaq have are the French, who have been friendly with them for decades."

Up until now, Georg had been quiet. He jumped into the conversation. "Philip, do you think the '52 treaty was signed under duress? Was it corrupt?"

"Duress, you say? Nein, I think not. I'm sure the Mi'kmaq desire peace as much as we do. Corrupt? Maybe. Chief Kopit knows only a little English, which was the language used in the document. I don't think he would be familiar with the legal terminology either. Just like previous treaties, land has never been addressed. You tell me, Georg—do you think it is right?"

"When you put it that way, no!"

"Lawrence is confident that when the French military posts are eradicated and the ammunition is cut off, the Indians will submit to the Crown and pledge their obedience to the King."

Georg said, "From what you've told me, the Mi'kmaq won't submit to a conditional allegiance, just as the Acadians did not."

"And they were expelled from the province," Philip commented.

"When this town was a French settlement, wasn't Cornwallis told the Mi'kmaq were friendly and not to be feared?" Georg asked.

"Ja. Then five months later, he ordered an attack here and had the French village destroyed. It left only Paul Labrador and his family."

"I see," Georg said.

"And scalping continued." Philip stopped and looked to Joseph. "You ask what side I am on. I would like to think I am on the side of justice."

"The governor must have had good enough reasons to impose such bounties." Joseph's voice was shrill.

"Bounties are no answer to a people who are defending their lives, Joseph. I have learned much. We are living on their territory," Philip answered adamantly.

"You are bordering on treason, Herr Knaut." Joseph glared at him, then stomped away.

Philip said, "At this point, it doesn't matter who did what to whom first. This is our war now, whether we want it or not. The British have attacked French positions west and south of here. France could very well attack us and any other British settlements by sea. You may hear talk soon that Lawrence wants to build a road from here to Halifax."

The road raised more questions than answers, and another hour melted away.

Michael said to Georg, "We must take our leave now. I'll see you Thursday. Elisabeth asked that we stay here the night before the early morning departure."

"Of course, you must."

Michael collected Hanna from the house, and with cordial farewells to all, the two of them were on their way. As with most gatherings, when one departed, it was only a matter of minutes before all headed for home.

EVERYONE WAS GONE. ELISABETH WAS glad of the solitude. She tried to cool herself with a frantic flutter of her apron. In the distance, a billowy mass of dark clouds foretold an approaching storm. As the sun slowly descended behind the curtain, stray sunbeams shot upward and around.

"We need the rain to break this humidity," Georg said, hugging his wife from behind. "How is Petie?"

"Sound asleep. I'll change his dressing in the morning. He likes the smell of the sap and says it makes his leg feel good."

"Balsam fir?"

She nodded. "There is little left. I need to stock up again."

"Whew, the house is very warm. Come, let us go outside." Georg grabbed her by the hand. "Sit here," he said, patting the pine bench he had built over the winter. "So, my dear, what news went around the quilt today?"

"Anna spoke about a new cookbook called *The Art of Cookery Made Plain and Easy*. Hannah Glasse had it published in London about nine years ago. It has become quite popular."

Georg laughed and kissed her hand. "You don't need one. Is it in German?"

"English. I wasn't thinking of it for me but for Hanna, as I'm not always with her to teach her. Anna brought it with her from Halifax, and as she knows the language, she offered to lend it to her. She will help Hanna through parts of the book."

"You have taught her well, Elisabeth. She is almost as good as you." Georg grinned at her, wrapping his arm around her shoulders.

Elisabeth leaned into his embrace. She relished the new closeness they had found over the past two years. Before then, it was quite different. Her papa had forced her to marry Georg, who was nine years her senior, and she had called him Dr. Gessler for a very long time. His love for her was initially unrequited, but in time, through his enduring patience and undaunting love for her and Petie, Elisabeth's respect for Georg had grown to such a dear tenderness and desire for him. On her wedding day, her mama had assured her she would learn to love him, but on that day, Elisabeth had been filled with such anger and remorse. Now, the first child from their union was growing within her.

Thunder echoed as it rolled and growled across the bay.

"Then most of the talk centred around the petitions. And, of course, Eva ruffled a few feathers about what the children should be taught."

"But she has no children," Georg quipped.

"Exactly, but you know Eva. She has an opinion on everything, even when it doesn't pertain to her. And what did you talk about?"

"The usual—politics." Georg sat silent, then added, "I still feel it's my duty to go on the drive. "

Elisabeth sat straight up. "Is that guilt talking, or loyalty to our friends?"

"A bit of both, I believe."

"In this case, your loyalty to Dr. Erad and your patients must come first. Dr. Phillips is still green around the ears."

"But he is improving. He's a fine surgeon."

"You forget, you each have your own territory in assisting Dr. Erad. It would be unfair to put more pressure on his new assistant. You also have an obligation to the governor, as he is the one who pays your three shillings a day."

"I don't believe Johann Erad will be with us much longer."

"Is he still coughing?"

"Ja. He doesn't have any loss of appetite, nor is he coughing up anything. But I still suspect consumption. I'm sure he knows, but he will not openly admit it."

The threatening clouds were moving closer. Elisabeth

watched a stray hummingbird hover as he pushed his long beak into a sunflower. He finally rested, wings motionless.

"I have no further news about us being dropped off the victual listing. This is the last week," she said.

"Joseph mentioned the rations are now continuing for everyone and will not be reduced. It was decided not to leave anyone out—especially those who cannot work on the land yet."

"That's a relief." Timidly, she added, "In town, there was some talk of another raid." Did she really want to know? She heard her husband take a short intake of breath.

"Philip heard of one in Oakland on the other side of Mahone Bay. So far, no one has been able to confirm if it's true. Warburton's Forty-fifth Regiment is stationed there, and if it was so, we would have heard by now."

Elisabeth shivered. Not even the warmth of her husband's arm could relax her misgivings about living outside the palisade. Losing herself in the daily workload of the farm, she managed at times to forget it. But when darkness came and Georg slept soundly, the dread of her not being able to protect her children when he was not home would invade her mind. Last month, she had convinced Georg to teach her to load and fire their musket. He showed her the secret place where he kept the ammunition.

"It's starting to rain. Looks like a deluge is coming," Georg said, standing up to stretch. "We best be retiring." He kissed the tip of her nose and bowed in jest.

She smiled up at him.


THE RAIN HAD STOPPED AS suddenly as it had begun, then several flashes of lightning announced a tremendous clash of thunder, and a second downpour began. After finding a comfortable spot that did not needle or scratch him, Georg lay still on the straw-filled mattress while Elisabeth slept soundly beside him.

When he had built their oak bed, he had made sure the bordering sides were deep enough to hold more than the normal amount of straw. With the cotton covering Elisabeth had made, it was somewhat agreeable to his body.

He could hear the rain muted on the thatched roof above, then a steady stream of runoff was amplified by the spatters and droplets below. It was soothing.

His mind wandered to the conversation earlier. It was true—there had been a raid. Dr. Erad had confirmed it today at church. Three bodies were found in the field. Ever since he had found out that he and Elisabeth were expecting their first baby, he was in the habit of filtering the truth.

Was it a dream? Hanna's encounter seemed a ghostly memory. To tell anyone would undermine the essence of her secret bond with Paul Labrador. To tell of it would break the spell. Paul's whereabouts were safe with her. She would tell no one, especially not Papa. Her love for her father ran deep, but their codependence ran even deeper. He would not understand. Her new-found acquaintance with Paul transcended all her fears and all she had learned thus far about the natives.

Hanna closed her eyes to the sound of her Papa's rhythmic breathing, which lulled her to sleep.

# Chapter Five

MID-AUGUST 1756

After pouring hot water into the large wooden tub, Hanna cooled it down with well water. Just enough to temper the heat to immerse her hands.

"Nein! Nein!" Elisabeth squealed. "Do not cool it. Tsk, tsk. What has Papa been teaching?" She disappeared into the house and reappeared with freshly boiled water, dumping it into the tub. "Here," she said, handing over the stick to her sister. "Now, agitate." With that she returned to the kitchen. Then she quickly popped her head back out the door. "The other two tubs you can cool down—one to scrub and the other to rinse." Elisabeth grinned, then withdrew.

Hanna was exasperated, to say the least. For the past two weeks since Papa had left, her sister's moods swung due to her pregnancy, or so she assumed—maybe it was just having another person underfoot. Hanna was unsure which but was certain she had to adapt by helping Elisabeth where she could.

Papa had left Hanna amid her many fears about what might happen. She had permitted the stories to control her imagination, playing with all sorts of scenarios. No reassurances of precautions, that they were all well-armed and with experienced soldiers, alleviated her suffering. It was still fresh when Papa hugged her goodbye. It was early morning, before the sun raised its lazy head, but the dark clouds and light rainfall that followed matched the dreary mood of everyone as they gathered to see the men off.

Hanna pushed the scene away and continued scrubbing the clothes in the second tub. She gave them a good rinse before hanging them on the line that Georg had strung from the outside kitchen wall to the tree. Back inside, Hanna checked the chicken roasting above the fire. She twisted the twine again, hanging from the mantel. The smell of the sizzling drippings made her mouth water. Cooling August temperatures allowed for the use of the inside kitchen. Unless the heat returned, the outside hearth would not be used for another year.

"The bread there has risen. You can shape the loaves," Elisabeth said, pointing to the end of the table. "There are not enough loaf pans, so the last bit will have to go into the bake kettle. And those over there have had their second rise and are ready for the fire."

Hanna lifted the iron kettle and placed it into the hearth to warm up. She would never forget when she had put partly risen dough into a cold kettle. After heaping large quantities of hot ash on top and underneath the covered kettle, the bread had burned outside and was raw inside. Alas, her first experience of baking bread. She could laugh now. At the time, she was devastated.

The intense fire that had burned in the hearth earlier was now reduced to glowing remnants of the logs Hanna had laid when she rose that morning. The hearthstones would now radiate heat for hours. The bread was always baked first when the heat was at its hottest. To the left of the hearth Georg had built a separate oven at eye level for baking. Hanna threw a bit of white flour onto the floor of the heated cavity to see how quickly it would brown. "It's ready," she said, turning to Elisabeth.

"You know me, I prefer this way." Elisabeth leaned her full arm into the oven, counting to herself before the heat became too uncomfortable for her skin. "Ten seconds. You're right." She smiled. "Here, tuck your dress hem in so you don't injure yourself." Elisabeth grabbed a goose wing and brushed embers off the hem of Hanna's dress, then pulled it up and tucked it into the waistband of her apron.

The smell of baking bread had filled the room by the time Georg walked through the door. "I'm going now to help Heinrich harvest oats. Ours can wait a couple more days. Hanna, most of the flaxseed heads have turned gold. You would be a tremendous help if you could gather what I have just swathed and bring them up here to dry out."

"Of course. First, I need to gather potatoes for Elisabeth."

"I'll go with you," her sister offered.

"I'll take the loaves you wanted Barbara to have, and I'll be on my way," Georg said.

"The fresh ones are not ready yet, but these from yesterday are fine," Elisabeth said as she put two into the basket along with a raspberry pie also baked yesterday. "With the new baby, it'll be a relief for her. And bayberry root powder. She was complaining of pain in her hands. I have extra balsam sap now," she said, and added a stoneware jar to the other items. "God only knows the scrapes those children of hers get into."

"Anything else, *Doctor* Gessler?" Georg quipped.

Elisabeth made a face. "I'll see you for supper."


GEORG HAD PULLED UP THE flax by their roots, and to Elisabeth and Hanna's surprise, he had tied it into bundles, leaving very little for them to finish up. They gathered what they could handle and carried the stooks to the south side of the house where they stood them up to dry. They returned for more sheaves, repeating the trip several times with Petie running behind. He helped where he could until he discovered a patch of wild blackberries he wished to devour. Tying what was left of the stray pieces of flax, Hanna nudged Elisabeth. "I see we have company."

Elisabeth was puzzled. "Philip? Should he not be with Papa?"

"Guten tag," Philip called out as he climbed the small hill to greet them.

"What happened?"

"The colonel requested I stay to assist him in other matters."

"Is one the reason why you are here?"

"Somewhat," he said. "As I speak, people are gathering at the fort. Everyone is demanding to speak with Colonel Sutherland." He looked around. "Where's Georg?"

"At Heinrich Moser's. Is anything wrong?" Elisabeth asked.

"Not at the moment but could be. Joseph Kuhn is going to see Heinrich now, so Georg will know soon. The crowds are demanding better protection."

"Hanna, could you stay with Petie?" Elisabeth lifted her son into her sister's waiting arms. "If Georg comes back here, tell him to meet me there."

Elisabeth and Philip made their way into town. The jumbled mess of voices grew louder the closer they got. Elisabeth recognized some of the faces in the crowd, but many she did not, and there did not seem to be any one specific person speaking for all. The words were indiscernible until the chants merged into one calling for Sutherland to appear. Elisabeth spotted Anna at the edge of the crowd and stepped in beside her just as Philip made his way to Colonel Sutherland, who was standing outside an open door. Sutherland's buff-coloured waistcoat was open, revealing his linen shirt. The black knee-high leather boots stood out against his white-grey breeches. His sleeves were rolled up above the elbows, and his dark brown hair hung as one braid down his back with a limp, muted red ribbon tied at the end.

Although the throng of citizens, men and women alike, were pressing in toward the colonel, there were no outright displays of vexation.

"We're not safe here," one called.

"More blockhouses need to be built," called another.

A sea of heads were nodding in unison, then the chanting began. "Blockhouses! Blockhouses!" Sutherland raised his arm to settle the crowd, and Philip shouted for order.

One man wove his way closer to Sutherland. "Colonel, unless you send an urgent message to Governor Lawrence to make good on our requests, most of us are ready to desert to Halifax. There isn't enough protection here. Even with the voluntary detachment of twenty or so who man the little we do have, we are being attacked."

A woman spoke beside the man; Elisabeth assumed she was his wife. "I have five children and my husband willingly takes his turn for the required week of militia duty. Some of us have husbands who have volunteered on the cattle drive, a few have already deserted this colony, and then there are the men who died from the fever last winter. The male labour is dwindling. When I'm alone, I fret for my safety and that of my children. I pray we're not scalped in the middle of the night."

Her husband held her close under his arm. He added, "There are some here that live close to the security of a blockhouse, but what about the others who live in other ranges who have nothing—Oakland, First and Second Peninsulas, Clearland? The Northwest Range is eight miles long. This alone requires more than one blockhouse. We appeal to you, sir."

Philip translated all that was said into English. Sutherland's face displayed compassion and concern as he stared out across the masses. Then he spoke directly to the two standing before him. "What are your names?"

"Zwicker, sir, Melcher Zwicker, and this is my wife, Sophie."

Sutherland smiled at them. "After the May raid, there is another blockhouse to be built in the Northwest and the LaHave. I—"

"That is still not enough! There have been two more attacks since," someone shouted back.

"Please! Allow me to finish. I agree with you and I wholly understand. You're all greatly discouraged and under tremendous distress. I know there are not enough troops under my command. There has already been an urgent request to the governor for another detachment to be employed here." A quietness settled and the colonel continued. "Lawrence approved these extra blockhouses to be built."

"We need more than the two extra. Most of us who are not living near any blockhouse are terrified. Some have no food except for their rations. Now there is talk they are ending again!"

After Sutherland listened to Philip's translation, he answered. "That will not happen while I am in charge. The victuals are continuing for everyone. Commissary Saul is already aware of my orders. You have my word! And for those on rotation standing guard, I am aware that some of you prefer an extra weekly ration over and above the normal allotment, instead of the sixpence salary. That option still stands for anyone. And you will be given plenty of advance notice when you are on militia duty so it will not interfere with your work in the cultivation of your land." He paused while Philip translated.

"A sixpence salary for duty is too little, and I have told as much to Governor Lawrence. He has agreed to double this to a shilling." After Philip translated, there were surprised but elated murmurs throughout the crowd.

"What about the blockhouses, Colonel?" Herr Zwicker raised his voice so the crowd could hear. "We have had some discussion, and we all feel there should be one erected between every ten families."

Sutherland raised his eyebrows in amazement when Philip translated this for him. He paused. "Ten families? I will send a message to Halifax with your plea; however, I cannot promise you the outcome will be to your satisfaction. I'll do the best I can."

The colonel rested his hand on Philip's arm and raised his voice even further. "As you know, two shots are fired within the minute if anything untoward has been discovered in the settlement. There was much confusion and misinterpretation when the last attack occurred. Please! Do not fire your weapon unless it is directly upon an enemy. When you hear the two-shot warning, stay inside your homes and remain on the defence until the cause for alarm is known. To fire your musket indeterminately is putting yourself and your neighbours at risk."

"Did I miss much?" Georg whispered into his wife's ear.

"Quite a bit. I will explain later. Where are Joseph and Heinrich?"

"In the crowd somewhere, I suspect. They went on ahead of me. Just worried about you, thought you were still at home. Hanna filled me in."

Georg acknowledged Anna with a nod. "I see Philip is interpreting?"

"Ja," Anna replied. "And it looks like the colonel is continuing the conversation with Philip privately. You two go on without me." She made her way toward the door where her husband was engaged with the colonel.

As Elisabeth prepared to leave with Georg, she noticed that only a small handful of people had drifted back to their homes.

The majority remained. In the company of the commander and within the confines of the palisade was the one place they were less vulnerable, shielded from the outside uncertainties in their lives. A woman started singing, "Be still my soul, the Lord is on your side. Bear patiently the cross of grief and pain." Voices joined her and sang in unison, "Leave to your God order and provide; in every change God faithful will remain." Georg and Elisabeth were drawn in. For the first time, the clouds of isolation she was feeling were banished by the spiritual closeness and fortitude of the colony.

Philip and Anna had decided to talk with others about the results of the meeting after Georg and Elisabeth left for home. "What you heard openly, Elisabeth, was the complete gist of it. I assume you talked it out with Georg?"

Elisabeth nodded.

Hanna half-listened to the conversation as she placed a second bowl of blueberry grunt on the table, then rescued her nephew's hands from a dumpling. When she wiped them clean, Petie burst into laughter, revealing his tiny blue teeth.

Philip chuckled, then continued. "What you don't know is that Sutherland is attempting to get approval to build sturdy houses at key points in various farm districts. They would be large enough to have sleeping quarters to accommodate anyone who wishes to be together under one roof in case an alarm is given. He is hoping Halifax will supply the wood and nails. Same as the extra blockhouses asked for today."

"And the labour?" Georg asked.

"No change there. All men required, just as we do for the blockhouses. Roads also will have to be cut between each one."

"But that will make it more difficult to cultivate our own lots," Elisabeth complained.

"Victuals will be reviewed again next June," Philip explained. "You underestimate Sutherland. He is practical and a truly considerate commander. He will go to battle for this colony, and so will the commissary."

"Thomas Saul?" Georg asked. "Not too long ago, the rations were set to stop altogether."

"If it were not for Saul, the rations would not have resumed. It was his creative paperwork that got us through last winter. Baker, the army contractor, had a surplus of provisions from the governor."

"Does Baker normally provide for the troops as well?"

"Yes, and when handling the large quantities, allowances are always made for losses. Lawrence has relied heavily on Saul, especially when no budgetary provision had been made through the Board, or when the supply ships were delayed getting into Halifax."

"And the Board is aware of this?"

"I believe so. Last winter, it was by order of the Board that provisions were only for three-quarters of the colony, those who were industrious enough but not self-supporting. The remaining, less diligent ones were to be struck off, until Sutherland had a say—he had no wish to lose those people. They had already threatened to leave if not put back on the victualling list. The colonel believes they are good and valuable settlers."

"I agree. I'm sure we're all doing the best we can under the circumstances."

Hanna suddenly spoke up—she found the conversation boring. "Elisabeth, I would like to pick some blackberries for our supper. I'll be back soon." She took a worn wooden bowl from the shelf and excused herself from the company. "It was nice to see you again, Herr Knaut," she curtseyed, "Frau Knaut."

"Don't be long, and stay within the clearing where I can see you," Elisabeth called after her as Hanna bounced out the door.

Hanna's mission was more than the berries. It had been at least three weeks since she had last seen Paul, and she was missing him. She watched for him daily, but she could only count two times she had dared to venture away from the house without questions arising. Running to the end of the clearing where most of the berry bushes were, she eagerly filled her bowl. There were plenty for picking. A whoosh of wings and a deep-throated *kwawk* alerted her to a raven landing on a tree branch above—the wedge-shaped tail beneath bobbed when it spoke. The shaggy throat feathers quivered.

It was eyeing her appetizing morsels. "Come," she called, throwing a few on the ground near the base of the trunk. The bird dove down and pecked away at the black bits. It downed them in its long, thick beak, then spread its large wings to return to the pine. Hanna did not mind ravens, although others considered them to be omens. They were mysterious. They seemed secretive and cunning, yet wise and kind. Cocking its head to observe her one more time, the raven flew farther into the woods. When the bird disappeared, she heard a familiar voice and followed it. It was Old Labrador, coaxing the bird with his own unique calls.

"Paul!" He turned, smiled, and waved his hand for her to approach him. He grabbed a handful of berries and threw a few on the forest floor. The bird swooped down and devoured them. Paul held out his hand with the remaining berries. To Hanna's amazement, the bird perched itself upon his arm and looked at her with curiosity. Paul gently stroked the bird's head, then down its back and nodded to Hanna to come to his side. Paul's rich, throaty chuckle lured her to come closer. She gently ran her small hand down the bird's glossy body, the feathers tightly enclosed against it. Sunlight briefly broke through the forest canopy and caught the pitch-black of the plumage, giving it a blue tinge.

Paul spoke to the bird, "Kwe'," and the bird bounced its head. "Kwe'," he said again. Not knowing what he was saying, Hanna said to her feathered friend what came naturally, "Hello." The raven lifted off to a nearby tree to observe the two below.

Paul squatted down with a small twig and started to trace a picture in the dirt. Hanna deduced that his squiggly lines winding through primitive-looking trees was the brook. At the end of it was a lake or clearing, and beside that he drew a structure that was wide at the bottom and tapered at the top. He then drew two stick people and a bird. When he pointed upstream, she assumed he was indicating where he lived. *Maybe the raven lives with them*, she thought. Paul peered up at the bird. "Kjika'qaquj." Hanna knit her eyebrows together and awkwardly attempted to repeat it. "Ook-chee-gah-hah-hootch," she said. The result was Paul's infectious laugh.

She laid her hand upon her chest. "Hanna." She repeated, "Hanna."

Her friend cupped her chin and sounded her name. "Ana," he echoed.

# Chapter Six



One distinct shot echoed into the night air. Hanna heard her brother-in-law in the next room say, "Wait!" Seconds later, a second musket shot. Georg said, "Another warning." Hanna's heart started to pound as she lay still in her bed, counting the minutes. When she heard her sister stir, she ventured into the kitchen. Hanna found Elisabeth blowing against the log buried within the hot ashes. "Help me here," Elisabeth demanded. A mouse, surprised by the sudden nightly movement, skittered underneath a closet door.

"Nein!" Georg remarked in a loud whisper. "If they are close by, do you wish to be detected?"

Hanna grabbed an iron ladle to help her sister scoop the ashes back over the log. "Petie is still sleeping," she said. Hanna shared a room with her nephew.

"Best to leave him as is." Elisabeth paused, eyeing her husband. "Now, we wait." She handed him a box of paper cartridges.

Hanna shivered and wrapped the blanket tighter around her shoulders. Georg tore the paper with his teeth, poured gunpowder into the musket barrel, and with his finger pushed the paper inside. After he inserted a lead ball, he removed the ramrod and tamped the paper and ball down. Time seemed painfully slow as Hanna watched him go through the motions. Her mind drifted back to Hohctorf when a difficult time was whether to tease her brother Christian.

All at once, another three shots, one after the other. At least an hour passed before two hard raps on the door broke the silence. "All is safe. Open!"

There were two soldiers—their presence even more chilling as they stood in full uniform with guns at their sides. A third soldier searched outside around the house.

When the soldiers entered the doorway, they removed their hats.

"The danger has passed?" Georg asked.

"Yes," said one soldier. He glanced at Hanna and Elisabeth and lowered his voice. "We spotted two Indians near the back harbour and followed them here."

"No need to whisper, sir. It's obvious we are all aware of our circumstances," Georg said.

The soldier shuffled his feet. "My apologies, ma'am," he bowed his head to Elisabeth. Then, to Hanna, "Mademoiselle." Hanna recognized him as the same soldier who managed the rations. He cleared his throat and repeated his explanation.

Elisabeth stiffened and inhaled sharply. "Here?" She was barely audible.

"Not in the immediate vicinity but about a mile west of here, at the side of your farm lot. We fired but it was too dark to follow through the woods. Possibly one was injured."

*Paul!* Hanna thought. Her stomach knotted. Was he injured?

The third soldier returned. "Nothing. All clear."

Georg thanked them and bid them farewell, closing the door behind them.

HANNA LET THE BUCKET FALL with a splash to the bottom of the well. Retrieving the second load of water, she attached it to the other end of the wooden yoke and carried it to where the flax bundles lay. She and her sister had laboured since yesterday to remove the seeds from the remaining stooks on the ripple. Collecting the seeds was paramount to ensure another crop next year. Her sister drew the last of the flax bundles through the coarse combs.

"We need to take those to the stream where there is continuous running water," Hanna complained as she lowered herself to remove the yoke from her stiff shoulders. "This is too slow to finish retting the flax in time." For two weeks there was no humidity and no rain to expose the flax to any bit of moisture. The first bunch had been harvested three weeks ago.

"Much too dangerous. The brook runs through the woods."

"Not at the lowest end, Elisabeth," Hanna said, pointing to the end of the property. "Down there, the stream opens to a clearing before finally emptying into the harbour. Besides, they won't attack in broad daylight."

Elisabeth let out a heavy sigh. "I suppose," she said, throwing the last few stalks to the ground. "Pile it up in that small wagon."

Hanna was relieved. "The faster the retting, the quicker we can dry it out in the fields if this weather continues."

Elisabeth laughed. "So, my baby sister can tell me a thing or two!"

"Once in a while," Hanna jested, as she threw the stooks into the wagon.

The next day dawned as bright and dry as the previous morning. Georg left immediately after breakfast. His usual house calls had patients ranging from boils, broken bones, and rheumatism to consumption, typhus, and dysentery. The mysterious fever that had raged last winter had petered out in the spring with no new cases. But it took many to their graves during its run.

The hearthstones were fiery hot. The flames were now burned down, leaving only the glowing pieces of charred wood. Quickly, Hanna lay the beef into the bake pot and covered it with cold water. While waiting for it to boil, she swept the floor, then damp-dusted ash deposits around the kitchen. Outside, she grabbed a few stalks dripping wet from the tub. As Hanna wriggled the now darkened flax back and forth with her fingers, the fibres separated more easily from the straw.

She went to find Elisabeth, who was working in the garden. Petie grabbed the leafy crop with both hands, revealing small potatoes dangling from the root. "Elisabeth, the beef is simmering. You might need to adjust the crane a bit if you want it to boil more."

"I hope you didn't add hot water to the beef. You know—"

"It will make it too tough," Hanna interrupted. "I know. Starting it in cold water will make it tender," she said, then grinned sheepishly. "The potatoes are now in the root cellar."

"Danke. Are you going now to the brook?"

"Just on my way. And ja! I will be careful. And yes, I will help you with the stooks," Hanna said, pointing to the flax soaking in water. "You were right, they are ready to be grassed." The flax now had to be dried before scutching, and she hoped the weather would hold out. She turned to go.

"Oh! Hanna!" Elisabeth called after her. "Did you notice if the cream is ready to be skimmed?"

"It is. Love you," Hanna replied over her shoulder and was on her way again.

Hanna knelt beside the stream where the bundles of flax were left. The cool water bubbled over her hands as she manoeuvred them slightly to ensure they remained stable. The repeated tapping of a woodpecker announced its presence. A raven landed near Hanna, bobbing its head at her. Then it lifted off again and flew erratically in and around the forest, then upstream, before it returned, closer to where she stood. *Is this the same bird who fed on my berries?*

"Do you want me to follow you?" Again, the same performance was replayed as the raven disappeared upstream and into the woods and returned, all the while calling to her as it receded back into the shadows. Hanna ran after it, following the stream as it edged the farm, but where the brook wound its way deeper into the forest, Hanna suddenly stopped. She had never ventured this far.

The raven circled above in the distance. She could hear someone crying, "Aide-moi!" Hanna followed the voice until she spotted an elderly woman with a man's head cradled in her lap. Hanna's heart sank. *Paul!* He was breathing but unconscious. His arm was covered in dried blood. *So, the soldier was right*, she thought. Bunches of now red leaves were stuck to his left shoulder where the woman had presumably tried to stop the bleeding.

"Puis-tu m'aider?" the woman pleaded.

"I'll go for help," Hanna said. She frantically mimed for the woman to stay put. She ran as fast as could, following the brook downstream, almost tripping over protruding stones and roots. *Please, Georg, I beg to God that you have returned.*

As she neared the house, Hanna yelled as loud as she could, "Georg!"

Elisabeth raced to her sister. "He hasn't returned yet. What is the matter?"

Hanna blurted, "I need him." What followed was a torrent of words that were barely sentences. She relayed as little information as possible about an elderly couple—the man was gravely injured.

Elisabeth drilled for more answers, but Hanna would not divulge anything for fear of Paul's safety. "I cannot...," she said, and walked away. She could not think about the possible repercussions if her sister knew who Paul was.

Elisabeth caught up with her sister. "Maybe I can help."

"You cannot!" Hanna insisted.

"There is no way to know when Georg will be back. You say this man is seriously injured..."

Hanna caressed her sister's hand. "Bitte, forgive me, Elisabeth. I should not have barked at you like that."

"But is it not imperative we help now? I can leave Petie with Barbara..."

"I'm afraid there is nothing you or I can do. He is unconscious, and there is a lot of blood. Only Georg can help. Please do not press any further," she pleaded.

It was at least another hour before Georg appeared. Hanna was equally reluctant to give him all the details. Thankfully, he only pried to receive enough information on Paul's condition to ensure he had the correct medicines. Georg had planted many seeds of various medicinal herbs he had brought from the old country, and he was very much at home with the native herbs Dr. Erad had introduced to him. Hanna recognized the poultice made from anise hyssop. He placed that, more balsam fir resin, and witch hazel into his shabby bag. He hurried into the back garden to cut fresh sprigs of thyme, then closed the leather flap.

"Ready, Hanna."

When they reached Paul, the woman was nowhere to be seen. Georg carefully removed the leaves from Paul's shoulder, washed the skin, and cleaned around the ragged wound to remove as much dirt as possible. All the while, Paul lay motionless.

"It's bleeding again." Hanna's eyes welled up.

"That is good for a little while to clean off the dirt. Here, press firmly now," he said, handing her a cloth.

A sudden wave of nausea overtook Hanna. "It's very swollen and red."

"Infection has set in." Georg dug into his satchel and opened a folded cloth containing some large leaves. He tore them into smaller bits and moistened them with water. "As it is so deep, the plantain will be much more effective than the thyme." He covered the gash with the poultice.

There was a commotion upstream. The woman returned and was frantically running toward them. "Paul!" she screamed. She stopped short. In her arms, she carried a large brown blanket bordered with red and blue stripes.

Georg gestured her to approach. Large strands of her hair hung from an unusual looking red-and-black bonnet. It was pointed like a hood, the material dropping down around the neck to her shoulders. It was decorated with a motif consisting of straight lines with curly ends. The woman had white-grey hair, but her face barely revealed a wrinkle. She cautiously reached into a cloth sack and handed a clay jar to Georg. He opened the lid to sniff the contents.

"What is it?" Hanna asked.

"Not sure. Some type of bark and leaves mixed with fat." The woman pointed to Paul and gently urged him to apply it. After repeated failed attempts to say otherwise, Georg gave in and applied her ointment.

The woman then spread out the blanket on the ground, motioning to Paul.

"I think she wants us to help carry him," Hanna said.

"And we should. He can't stay here." Georg helped her lift his patient.

Hanna held the woman's hand. "I am Hanna," then she pointed to Georg and said his name.

"Ah, je m'appelle Magdeleine."

It was a long trek to their camp beside a lake. It was an entirely different world. One with beached, overturned canoes and cone-shaped structures built of poles and tree bark. Smoke escaped through a hole where the poles met. There were two other smaller formations, but there was no evidence of anyone else living there. A hollowed-out log lay on its side beside the firepit. Fish hung from a wooden bar within a small A-frame, and an unknown animal skin stretched across another larger framework. Single-headed and three-pronged spears stood upright against a birch tree. Hanna swept her gaze across the compound, catching sight of a musket and everyday items of survival—pots, kettles, and tools.

Inside the conical structure, the fire glowed within a circle of stones. Hanna stared up at the opening that the smoke curled through. Over the firepit, soup was simmering in a metal pot. Inside the door lay a woven mat. Fragrant fir twigs were scattered around the dirt floor. Georg and Magdeleine laid Paul down on the left side of the dwelling, and Magdeleine covered him with an enormous black-furred animal skin. He had briefly regained consciousness before falling back into a deep slumber.

Georg handed over more plantain and thyme leaves. He tried to demonstrate how often to change the dressing. "You are failing miserably," Hanna said, smiling.

"S'il vous plait, rester," Magdeleine said, offering her guests soup.

"Ja," Georg replied. "Danke."

Magdeleine showed her guests where to sit, at the back behind the fire, and served the soup in clay bowls. She settled on the right side. After their meal, Georg gestured with two fingers walking on his upward facing palm. "Time to leave," he said to his host. "We must go."

Hanna stood over Paul. "Will he live, Georg?" Her eyes filled again with tears. Magdeleine lightly touched Hanna's wet cheek.

"We'll see. I'll come back tomorrow," he replied.

"Merci," Magdeleine bowed, handing Georg an intricately decorated box. Hanna lifted the lid—the creamy white contents appeared to be fat. Magdeleine scooped a small bit on her finger and ate it. Georg did as well. "Mmm," he said and motioned to Hanna. When Hanna politely declined, their host's laughter depicted there was no offence taken, and she embraced her young guest with a hug.

Georg held Magdeleine's hands. "Danke," he said.


"You cannot force me to stay!" Hanna's anger got hold of her. When she and Georg had returned to the house yesterday and told Elisabeth where they had been, Hanna's sister had not kept any feelings in.

"I cannot make you do anything. What I said was if you no longer visit Old Labrador, I will not tell Papa."

"Don't call him that. His name is Paul and he's harmless. Everyone here either knows him or has heard of him."

"Why did he suddenly disappear a year ago?"

Hanna shrugged her shoulders. "Our communication is not with words." For some reason, she chose not to even try to go down that road with her sister.

"Then how would you know he's not an enemy?"

"You don't understand, Elisabeth!"

"Oh? I grasp things quite well. I know Old—," she paused, "Paul's sudden disappearance is suspicious. If he never signed allegiance to the Crown, that makes him an enemy."

Georg walked in on the standoff, clearing his throat to announce himself.

"How much have you heard?" Elisabeth asked.

"Not much, but I can imagine," Georg retorted.

"Well, your sister-in-law has emphatically stated, in no uncertain terms, that she is going with you this morning to see Paul."

He looked at his wife with compassion. "There is no danger. It's just the two of them living alone. What do you think an old man on his deathbed and an elderly woman can do?"

Elisabeth's breathing calmed somewhat, her eyes shifting to the musket in the corner. "And outside dangers?"

"You know I always carry it, Elisabeth. There will not be an attack in the daylight."

The look she gave her husband was enough to say she did not wish him to go either. But Elisabeth knew that Georg was compelled to administer aid wherever needed.

Hanna was relieved when Elisabeth nodded her consent and wrapped her arms around her.


When Georg and Hanna arrived, Magdeleine greeted them with kisses upon each of their cheeks. Paul was awake, but barely. Following his examination, Georg complimented Magdeleine. "I see you've been changing the dressing." He pointed to the bandage and smiled at her.

"Ana," Paul breathed. Hanna knelt beside her friend. His limp hand lay over hers. "Kwe'," he said, staring at her.

"Will he be alright now?" Hanna asked Georg.

"He's not out of danger yet. I'm not sure what herb has been put on his wound, but I will change it to the plantain I used yesterday."

Magdeleine touched Hanna's shoulder. She was holding an unfinished basket and motioned for Hanna to come outside.

They left Georg to treat the patient. Magdeleine sat down and placed a partly finished birchbark bowl into Hanna's lap. "Je t'enseigne," she said.

Magdeleine placed another bowl beside Hanna. It was full of porcupine quills in warm water, some white with black ends and others of yellows, blues, and reds. There was a design on the water-soaked bark, outlined with tiny holes. Magdeleine guided Hanna to insert a blue quill into one of the holes. She then poked a threaded needle through the bark, leaving a small loop to bend the quill through before tightening the thread around it. The thread was a thick substance unknown to Hanna, sinewy but flexible. When Magdeleine formed another tiny circle, she bent the other end of the quill through the loop and tightened it again. She left it to Hanna to continue. This went on for many minutes, inserting, looping, and securing. Hanna enjoyed the closeness with Magdeleine by her side.

Magdeleine offered her guests some tea. The taste was completely foreign to Hanna and Georg but very flavourful. Paul fell back to sleep again, and Georg explained to Magdeleine that her husband was now feverish. Magdeleine understood. When he handed dried yarrow to her, she nodded.

Before they reached home, Hanna and Georg could hear rustling, loud voices, and the familiar sound of mooing. They quickened their pace. When they reached a small clearing near the trail, there were men herding cows and oxen, manoeuvring them with switches. It was slow moving as they headed toward the common located west of town and south of the First Peninsula Range.

"What a sight for sore eyes!" Georg exclaimed.

"Oh my!" Hanna stopped. "Papa!" She waved frantically and ran across the meadow.

# Chapter Seven



Other than the haunting call of an owl, it was quiet while the current carried them downstream. The moon shed enough light that Bear Cub could see the fast-moving bats skimming across the water. He tried to breathe life into his numb hands. They were hunting during the moose rut, and he hoped to kill his first moose. Even with the dogs this past summer, his attempts to down one failed. Maybe tonight would be different. Eagle Feather sat straight-backed at the bow; White Cloud was seated behind Bear Cub. They lagged behind the others, which left them the lone canoe in this part of the river.

All paddles rested as White Cloud signalled to Bear Cub again. For the fourth time, he scooped the cold water into a bowl. He stood up and steadied himself as he slowly drained it back into the river. Because it mimicked the sound of a cow-moose urinating, it would attract the bull-moose to the river. Their canoe hardly left a ripple as they continued along the river's bank. Bear Cub listened for the slightest sound of the animal, but nothing. He pressed the moose call to his lips. Two months ago, his brother had helped him make the birchbark cone. The nasal sound of a female bellowed loudly.

"Shh," White Cloud whispered.

From afar, twigs cracked. Bear Cub blew again. Then, a third time. A sudden rush of snapping brush and rebounding tree branches created a crescendo through the forest. A pair of broad brown antlers emerged. From the size of his butterfly-type antlers, Bear Cub pegged the bull-moose to be in his prime—six years.

Bear Cub held his breath as the beast waded into the water. The moose lowered his head to drink. Bear Cub now had a clear view of his side. His hand was steady as he aligned his shot and followed the back edge of the front leg up to the middle of the chest cavity and aimed at the lungs.

"Shoot," Eagle Feather urged. He had his musket ready just in case.

Despite the cold air, Bear Cub could feel perspiration beading along his forehead. A sharp crack blistered in the wilderness. The smell of gunpowder hung about him as the moose fell with a splash. Bear Cub lapped up the warmth of praise from White Cloud's hand on his back.

"I am proud of you, my brother. You did it!" Eagle Feather grinned back at him.

They paddled toward their prize and lifted the canoe onto the embankment just as the other canoes returned. A trump line was tied around the antlers, and they dragged the animal to higher ground. They broke branches to mark the kill so the women could find it, then made their way back to camp. It was no great distance to their village, so they did not need to build a shelter for their wives. It would take the women a few days to field dress the animal.


When the men returned, the women left immediately with torchlit canoes to flay, dress, and carve the carcass. It was Singing Sparrow's Moon Time. Her body was purifying itself, preparing to receive life. Each month, she spent her four to five days separated from the regular living area to be attended only by the female Elders. The men would not come near her, and touching any sacred objects was strictly forbidden—not because she was unclean but because of the powerful energies flowing through her to Mother Earth during this time. The portal through which a spirit comes to Earth to be born among the People was a sacred gift from the Creator. To be able to give life was key to her People's survival. Her role as a life-giver had its imposing rituals, but this one was particularly tiresome. She disliked the separation. She would much rather be a man and only take several hours in a sweat lodge for purification rather than several days.

In this moon, Singing Sparrow was alone. No other females yet had joined her in the Moon Lodge. Not even her dear friend Brigide. She and her father had come to the village when Singing Sparrow was a small child. Brigide's mother had died of smallpox—a white man's disease that almost ravaged the entire village in which they lived.

Brigide's Acadian father was killed seven Winters ago, when the village he was visiting was attacked by British soldiers, who murdered most and took others hostage, burning what was left. Growing up together, Singing Sparrow and Brigide were rarely apart, entrusting each other with their most private of thoughts. Brigide had recently married Calm Water. She had missed her last Moon Time and suspected the Great Spirit had blessed their union to bring them a gift next Spring. Brigide now had only seven moons to go.

Singing Sparrow shook two long strips to free them from a pile of flattened reeds. She sang the Song of the Stars as she continued weaving the mat into a twill pattern. When her eyes began to tire from the firelight, she wove in the last one then readied herself for bed. Tomorrow she could join everyone in the activities. Her cycle had ended.

She opened the door-blanket and sat on the stack of firewood. The celebration of song and dance for the moose kill had just ceased. A small group sat around the sacred fire. Bear Cub was among them, as well as her brother. Those two were very tightly bound together in friendship, just like she and Brigide. Singing Sparrow smiled to herself as she watched Bear Cub. Her innermost feelings were private, so intricately hidden in her heart, she dared only scratch the surface to reveal just minuscule pieces to her friend. She may be dishonouring Brigide's trust, but she could not betray whatever spark she and Bear Cub might have between them.

Singing Sparrow yawned and closed the flap. *The women will return soon*, she thought. She could feel the fir boughs beneath the moose skin as she crawled under the warmth of heavy bear fur. Lying there, Singing Sparrow stared at the walls of her temporary prison. Fire shadows created lively images around her. She caught the sweet spruce scent just before drifting into another realm of existence—her dreams.

Singing Sparrow awoke soon after to loud wailing and the clatter of canoes. It was still night. When she pushed aside the door-blanket, men were racing to the shore, and women were carrying two bodies. She ran toward them, then stopped suddenly. Blood dripped from the necks of the limp bodies.

Her father lifted one of the dead women, took her to the nearest shelter, and lay her by the fire. He commanded the others to lay the second on the mat beside her. "Who did this?" His voice echoed with anger.

Her stomach in knots, Singing Sparrow moved to her mother, whose dress was covered in bloodstains.

Morning Dove was shaking. "We know not their language—

not French. The moose carcass was skinned and cut—most of it in the canoes. 'We will make a second trip,' we said. Marie and Running Doe stayed on shore to gather what was left of the tools. Three men suddenly came upon them with knives." She choked. "S-Slit their…" Singing Sparrow grabbed her mother's hand as Morning Dove tried to compose herself. "They pulled back their heads to scalp them. All of us rushed screaming with our knives and killed two. The third ran into the woods." Morning Dove sank to her knees. "Ahh!" she screamed in pain, rocking back and forth. "Ahh! Forgive me, Great Spirit. I am as low as the ones who murdered our sisters." Tears streamed down her face.

Singing Sparrow knelt beside her mother. She held her tight, rocking her, hoping to suppress her torment.


White Cloud had left at sunrise the next morning with a dozen men. They could not find the dead bodies of the attackers, and there was no sign of the one who had escaped. The men were gone for three sunrises, but their search turned up nothing.

The celebration began after three days of weeping, during which friends and relatives, their faces smeared black, brought gifts for the spirit world. Each person had spoken as part of the funeral oration. Now, the festival of joy was a rejoicing of the deceased's journey to the Land of Souls to see their relatives, friends, and ancestors.

Bear Cub stared at two graves filled with twigs and dirt and partially covered with logs. That morning, Marie and Running Doe were buried deep in the ground, their bodies swathed and tied up with skins, and their knees positioned up against their stomachs. They now rested for eternity within Mother Earth's bosom.

Bear Cub's brother walked up from behind. "Our ancestors

once made biers high enough so the animals would not prowl and feed. On this, our dead lay for twelve moons as the sun dried their bodies. They were then buried with tools, snowshoes, and skins to be used in the Land of Souls—anything needed to be comfortable in the Spirit World." Eagle Feather paused. "The ancient rituals are buried with our grandfathers and have become stories around the fire. Now, muskets replace our bows and arrows. Copper and iron replace stone and wooden tools. Cotton and wool replace our skins."

"And you trap to satisfy traders' ever-increasing desires for skins and furs. You have traded one life for another, and exchanged stability for their ways," Bear Cub said.

"The missionaries first changed our ways when they brought their beliefs. They know what is best for us."

"They *think* they know." Bear Cub narrowed his eyes and looked into his brother's. "Aren't you angry?"

"We respect the missionaries. Abbé Maillard cares for and understands the People. More importantly, he has influence over the British. We have great faith in him."

"What about the Great Spirit?"

"It watches over all of us, even our enemies. Abbé Maillard's rituals do not change who we are." He gazed down at the graves. "I am sickened at the carnage and blood that results from moving freely about our land. If we resist, more of our People will die. If we do not, we are trapped under English control. Either way, we lose."

"Do you yearn for the old times?"

"Does anything stay the same? Creation is ever-changing. Look at the tides, the animal migrations. Mother Earth changes her dress through the seasons. We adapt as we move within the circle."

"I wish I had your fortitude. You make it sound simple."

"It is not. Kisu'lkw has given all of us the right to share this land collectively. The British have forced us to fight for something no one person has the right to own. I am enraged that the British display no respect for us or our ancestors. I am saddened that we have not been given this appreciation."

Bear Cub looked across the lake. A loon glided, creating ripples upon the water, her checkered back now transitioned to the grey-and-white winter plumage. One by one, her brood of three flapped their wings, skimming the lake before flying away. He had been observing the female ever since her chicks had hatched three moons ago. *They have been taught well to survive in this world.* The call of another loon echoed from the back of the lake. "They are ready to migrate soon."

"As our village will also." Eagle Feather walked to the shore and aimed a flat stone at the water. It skipped several times before sinking. "My brother, have you thought more of going to Merligueche?"

"There have been two more attacks on Lunenburg that we know of. I am worried for my family," Bear Cub said. "I think it's time."

"This spilled blood speaks loudly in our father's decision to strike back."

White Cloud had the support of everyone in the village, and the villages were banding together with the French. France's king continued to supply the Mi'kmaq with guns, powder, and shot. But there was fear they would be pressured into peace by signing allegiance to the English king.

The prospect of unmitigated war preyed on Bear Cub's mind. "Peter must go with me. He knows where my sister lives."

"I will go as well. I know the territory better."

"I can't jeopardize your safety for mine. Your parents won't allow it."

"I will discuss it with them. There is talk that Winter camp will not be in the same place as the last two Winters but the one of three Winters back. Your memory will not serve you well. You will not find your way back. I will wait for you."

Behind them, a singular voice rang out in song, then a unified grunt emanated from the assembled crowd within the centre of the compound. Bear Cub observed White Cloud dancing alone, head bowed with hands behind his back. There were four Elders seated around the large drum placed in the centre of the compound.

Bear Cub looked down at the graves. "They are at rest."

Eagle Feather laid his hand on Bear Cub's shoulder. "Come. Our spirits need this. We celebrate Marie and Running Doe with joy." The crowd mimicked the dance of their leader, demanding the chorus of chanting be increased, "Heh, heh. Yo! Ha! Yo! Ha!" Bear Cub joined his brother within the growing circle and was caught up in the repetitive and deliberate dance steps and the hypnotizing sounds of the ji'kmaqn as the bound split ash splints were time after time hit against the knee and palm. Bear Cub feverishly picked up the pace to match the energy of his brothers, and his face dripped with sweat despite the chilled air. It drove him to the point of frenzy. Only the Great Spirit knew if his passion was caused by anger.

He was oblivious to Singing Sparrow observing the scene from a distance.

At sunrise, Eagle Feather spoke to his parents. They expressed resistance, but their fear gave way to common sense as he brought forth the possible consequences if he did not go. Eagle Feather continued his discussion with his father privately. "Hopefully we will return before you start out."

"It could be earlier. I feel danger," White Cloud said, touching his heart. "Most families will disperse before us to their Winter camps. Your mother and I will wait as long as we can. Calm Water and Brigide will Winter with us, as well as Mathieu and his family."

Two moons ago, White Cloud had sheltered the Acadians Mathieu, his wife, Angeline, and their two young boys when they sought refuge.

"No Acadian is safe, even if they pay homage to the English Crown," Eagle Feather said. "And neutrality is unacceptable. Both the English and the French demanded military support from the Acadians. When they refused, there were consequences."

White Cloud let out a quick, short breath. "With our allies in the Wabanaki Confederacy, we once were powerful against this threat. But many of our brothers and sisters have gone to the Land of Souls—the Acadians, the Maliseet, the Abenaki. Many, many." His voice drifted to barely a whisper.

Eagle Feather did not wish to interrupt. His father had never opened up to him like this.

"Now, the British outnumber us. The People cannot survive without both the Confederacy and the French." White Cloud's eyes darkened as he stared back at his son. "Cornwallis's intentions were quite clear. Surrender everything to his king. And we…we have no rights whatsoever?" White Cloud's indignation rose. It was a side Eagle Feather had rarely witnessed.

His father continued. "Many Winters ago, before Cornwallis, the British were warned. Your grandfather told me of a letter the District Saqmawit and three other Nikanus wrote with the help of the French. It was a warning to stay out of Sipekne'katik. 'The Mi'kmaq were given this land from the Great Spirit,' it said."

White Cloud paused for a long time before Eagle Feather spoke. "Who was this letter sent to?"

"Governor Phillips. He lived in Annapolis and threatened to reduce the Mi'kmaq to servitude. The letter said the Mi'kmaq will dispute with all men who want to live here without our consent. Then, our claims to Kjipuktuk, the ancestral hunting and fishing grounds, were ignored." His upper lip pulled up. "Halifax! The name sits heavy on my tongue, and the sound of it is bitter. My father took my mother, my sisters, and me there for the annual Mi'kmaw gathering after the first full moon in Sqoljuiku's."

*The ceremony that celebrates our creation*, Eagle Feather thought. Kjipuktuk was the sacred place of spirits, where many tributaries ran from the Sipekne'katik River, where the Great Spirit Fire's sparks gave birth to the original seven families of the Mi'kmaw people. Eagle Feather's own wrath surfaced. "And they stole this land to give to the Protestant settlers."

White Cloud's eyes fixated on the fire between them. "They send their surveyors to our territories to divide them among themselves."

Helpless, Eagle Feather replied, "My father, you have a peaceful spirit, but you have rightly agreed to do what needs to be done, to save what is left. You know what you must do, but I still see a battle raging within you."

"I do not like what I have become. I have this growing compulsion to..." He did not finish.

"Even the deer eventually will attack if cornered."

"Humph," White Cloud grunted, half-laughing. "Our adversary does not know how to walk beside us on a path to peace. If the governor wishes our eradication from here, he will be sorely disappointed."

THE HEAVENS WERE COVERED WITH as many stars as there were ancestors.

"Hold the torch closer to the water," Eagle Feather said. Bear Cub sat behind his brother, holding the light. Eagle Feather stood upright at the bow of the canoe, holding his harpoon high, waiting for a fish to appear. The ten-inch barbed rod was pointed at one end of the spear with a line looped through a hole at the top end. The other end of the line was tied to the bow of the canoe. Bear Cub leaned his torch over the dark water. There were five canoes at various locations along the river.

"Good." Eagle Feather was grateful when an eight-foot sturgeon curiously nosed the surface, investigating the sudden flickering light. It swam in circles, turning from one side to the other. Eagle Feather steadied himself, careful to wait until the fish showed his stomach, so he could penetrate the soft scales. He rammed the spear into the belly, causing numerous tail splashes that soaked the two of them. The sturgeon swam a good distance, dragging the canoe like an arrow. As best he could, Bear Cub kept the canoe from overturning before the fish finally weakened and his brother drew the line in. When the sturgeon came alongside the canoe, it was dead. Together, the brothers passed the cord with a slipknot over the tail.

"Not as large as the ones we caught two moons ago," Bear Cub said. "Must be a male."

Both agreed to rest a bit before paddling back to camp.

"Our father took Singing Sparrow to empty the weirs. Plenty of salmon to smoke for Winter." Eagle Feather was deliberately steering the conversation toward his sister.

Bear Cub nodded. "They left with Calm Water. Possibly, this time, a sturgeon may be found within the mix. That circular weir doesn't look so pen-like anymore—needs fixing."

*What is the best way to approach this?* Eagle Feather thought.

"I did not tell our father the circumstances of you saving my sister's life."

"Hmm?"

"The two men who came back," he reminded Bear Cub. "On the beach, the three of you buried them." Not getting any acknowledgement, he asked, "Where are you, my brother?"

"Not where you are," he quipped. "White Cloud found out anyway. Peter told him."

"I just want you to know that you can trust me to say nothing if you disclose anything to me."

"Disclose what? It sounds like you're fishing for more than sturgeon."

Eagle Feather turned to face his brother. "Is Singing Sparrow still interested in Peter?"

Bear Cub shrugged his shoulders.

Subtlety was not Eagle Feather's strong suit. He charged forward like a moose. "Do you love Singing Sparrow?"

"Of course I do. She's my sister," Bear Cub said nonchalantly, staring up at the stars.

It was painful. "Do not play coy with me." Eagle Feather kicked Bear Cub's foot, forcing his brother to look at him. "Your secret glances in her direction are not so hidden."

"Does this upset you?"

"Moqwe. She glances as well, and not in Peter's direction. You have caught Singing Sparrow's eye."

"Do you think?"

"The whole village probably knows."

Bear Cub sat up and glared back. "Don't tell your father." Then, "Do you think he suspects?"

Eagle Feather shook his head. "The affairs of the heart are not his strong point. But, you are delaying the inevitable, as I am sure it has not passed by my mother."

"It's too hard to ask your father for permission."

"You are not frightened of our father, are you? In his eyes, you are his own blood."

"This is different. I wish to court his only daughter. The mere thought of asking him has been insurmountable."

"He may be the Nikanus, but he is also reasonable."

"What sort of gift should I give him?"

"You have hunted beaver, wolf, muskrat, fox. Pick one," he offered. Then, "Snowshoes! Winter is coming." He laughed out loud as he started to paddle along the river.

"I will ask him before we start for Lunenburg."

"Maybe my mother can speak to him first," Eagle Feather said. "Soften the news so it will not be a shock." The comment was reciprocated by a backsplash of water from Bear Cub's paddle.


HER SON CONFIRMED WHAT MORNING Dove already suspected. Eagle Feather wished her to warm White Cloud to the news before Bear Cub met with him. Outside, Mother Earth was displaying reminders of the impending snows. Fallen maple leaves were now tinged with frost, and geese announced their intentions in V-shaped migrations. Ghostly apparitions of mist moved across the cooling lakes and rivers. Inside the wikuom, the fire crackled as Morning Dove stretched strips of caribou rawhide over and through the maple frame to create a mesh. It was wide enough for the wet snow. *I will make the next pair tighter and smaller for dry snow*, she said to herself. These were the fourth pair of snowshoes White Cloud had carved for her to finish. Her son had just left to send White Cloud to see her and to head his brother in a different direction.

Morning Dove kept an eye on the crushed moose bones boiling in the kettle. She hoped to collect at least five pounds of fat. On the last hunt, she rendered six pounds for eating, as well as for gifts and for seasoning food.

When her husband lifted the door-blanket, the nip in the air swirled around her, and the aroma of smoke-dried salmon and cod drifted in. He crouched to kiss her, then sat down to warm his hands over the fire. "The beavers and muskrats are working overtime collecting hundreds of food stems. I see many freshly gnawed trees down." He blew into his hands and briskly rubbed them. "The beavers have already started building their raft to keep the good branches down beneath the ice when the water freezes. Have you seen the fresh mud they added to their lodge?"

"Are you happy to only talk of beavers?"

"Moqwe, my beloved."

Morning Dove put aside the snowshoe. It was best to come straight to the point. "Do you notice that the sibling affection between Singing Sparrow and Bear Cub has changed?"

"Is it sibling rivalry now?"

"Far from it," she said.

"Speak plainly. Should I be concerned?"

"Moqwe. But be prepared for a visit from Bear Cub."

"Ahh," he grunted.

"Do you approve?"

Silence.

"Is this a surprise?"

Silence

"Speak to me, White Cloud," she said, moving to sit beside him.

"I thought she liked Soaring Hawk," her husband said.

"That was five Winters ago. She was twelve," Morning Dove exclaimed. "She is a child no more."

"Jean-Pierre? Or Sapiyel, as you like to call him."

Morning Dove sighed as she leered back at him.

He fell silent again. Then, "He is acting on his yearnings to return."

"And so he should. Would you not do the same if you were in his position?"

"Do you think Bear Cub will come back to us?"

"I do not know. But we must trust him to make the right decision."

"I cannot give my approval knowing Singing Sparrow will be heartbroken if he does not return to her."

She leaned into White Cloud and whispered, "My beloved, we love Bear Cub. Your disapproval of the courtship does not change her feelings for him. Remember, you can accept his decision to court our daughter, but Singing Sparrow still has the final say."

"She will not have a say if I disapprove of his request."

"Then Singing Sparrow would be dispirited and inconsolable, and disappointed in her father. What if my father refused you when you asked him for permission to court me? I know you would have asked him again and again to prove you were worthy." Morning Dove caressed White Cloud's hand. "If Bear Cub does not receive your blessing, he might think the situation is hopeless, which could drive him not to return to us."

When he mumbled, "I will think on it," Morning Dove affectionately stroked his cheek, and he added, "I promise."

Eagle Feather nudged Bear Cub. "Are you ready? Our father is alone." The two brothers were standing in a vacant dwelling.

"Now?" asked Bear Cub.

Eagle Feather was holding a small pot of red ochre. "E'e, he is in a good mood. I heard him singing to himself. Here, I have mixed the ochre with egg yolk and moose fat."

Bear Cub made a face when his brother smeared it over his cheeks, chin, and forehead. "Are you sure I have to do this?"

"E'e. You want to make the best impression in terms of the Mi'kmaw rituals, right?"

"E'e, but," Bear Cub mumbled, "you said in the old times, the Mi'kmaq only wore red paint for war."

"Shh. Stand still," Eagle Feather said as he completed his masterpiece. "There. Now, do you have the gift?"

"Gifts. I am taking three. One can't be too careful."

Bear Cub stood before Eagle Feather dressed in his best leggings, jacket, and the knee-high moccasins of varying types of skins his brother had lent him to ensure his best foot was forward. He wanted to appear he belonged by wearing moose and caribou, rather than the latest trade goods of wool and linen. Over his arm, he held beaver, muskrat, and fox pelts, all of which he had hunted down. Eagle Feather pulled the door-blanket aside and gave him a gentle push to start Bear Cub on his journey across the compound.

A chuckle bubbled up from behind. When Bear Cub turned around, Eagle Feather gestured with his hands to go ahead. Eyes now on the wikuom, Bear Cub aimed straight for it. By the time he arrived, he was sweating from anxiety, his legs weak. The warmth of the afternoon sun did not help matters. *It would have been better to do this in the morning, when it was chillier,* he thought. Or not, and he slowed down to turn away. Just as he was about to turn back, White Cloud opened the door-blanket. "Bear Cub?"

The two stared at each other—one, mystified, the other, terrified.

"Do you want to speak with me?"

Bear Cub barely nodded. "E'e," he croaked. He cleared his throat and with a surge of courage said, "E'e, sir." White Cloud ushered him inside.

White Cloud stood in front of Bear Cub, arms folded, eyes narrowing as if perplexed. He looked even more imposing as he peered down upon Bear Cub, whose confidence faltered. "Sir?" he asked, hoping this one word would break the silence. When he was not shown to the place of honour at the back of the wikuom, all hopes of receiving permission were crushed. His situation remained bleak at best. All he wanted to do was drop the pelts and run. But, he waited.

White Cloud's face softened. "My son, why have you painted your face red?"

The notion that Eagle Feather was playing a prank on him was now plausible.

"Was it Eagle Feather?" White Cloud asked. "Ah, you do not have to reply. I know by your expression. He will be spoken to."

"As well as by me."

White Cloud let out a belly laugh that relaxed the situation immensely.

"I have brought you gifts to ask your permission to court Singing Sparrow."

"I can see that."

Then a plethora of words burst out of Bear Cub. "These pelts are of my own doing. I hunted them last Winter. As you know, I have just killed my first moose. This shows I am a good hunter. You can be assured your daughter's safety is of utmost importance to me. I have only the deepest respect for you and everyone in this village. I have—"

White Cloud's hand rose to calm him. "I know. You have shown wisdom in your actions, truth when you speak, and humility in situations that demand as much. You are a good son. Anyone would be pleased to give permission."

"But?"

"This situation demands honesty. Will you return here?"

"Right now, my answer is yes—my heart will always steer me back. I care deeply for your daughter. I love you and Morning Dove and yes, truth be told, Eagle Feather. I can't imagine my life without all of you. But, in all honesty, I really don't know. I can't foresee what lies ahead for me in Merligueche. My father and I parted with unresolved issues between us, and my family thinks I'm dead. To live my life in contentment now, I must face my past first. I must have no regrets."

"My only wish is to protect Singing Sparrow."

"If the situation were reversed, I would have said the same thing. But giving your permission can only bring gladness and contentment to both your daughter and me in the short time we have before I leave. Would you not wish that for both of us rather than to separate us from each other in despair and sorrow?"

Hands behind his back, White Cloud slowly walked to the back. "Come, my son. Sit by me. We will talk more."


"Do not be angry with me, my brother," Eagle Feather begged. "And slow down so we can talk."

Bear Cub stopped. "Do you realize what could have happened? You could have jeopardized it for me." Bear Cub had scrubbed his face clean of the paint, in anticipation of his meeting with Singing Sparrow.

"I knew our father would see through that. Tradition dictates that a playful prank be played when one is seeking courtship," he jested, waving his hands in the air.

Grinning, Bear Cub could no longer feign anger and slapped his brother on the back. "Well done!" He saw Peter approaching. "And I suppose you were involved?"

"Never!" was his playful reply.

"You're lucky I'm talking to either of you," Bear Cub yelled back as he continued to walk.

"Meet us at the shore," Eagle Feather called out.

"E'e." Bear Cub was joining them later for the beaver hunt.

"And we are departing for Lunenburg tomorrow at sunrise," Peter added.

Bear Cub grunted his answer as he stood still outside Calm Water and Brigide's wikuom. Morning Dove had arranged for her daughter to visit her friend, away from any possible interruptions. Nerves were getting the best of him. He wished he had a waisisl, an animal spirit helper, to give him strength. His brother's was the wolf, who helped him rid himself of weaknesses to strengthen his spirit. To survive, as in a wolf pack, each member of a community must be aware of their individual role so they can all act as one. Bear Cub had not received an animal vision, even after four days and the assistance of Calm Water to guide him through the secluded ceremony.

He could hear his intended singing, but he did not comprehend the words. His ever-expanding grasp of the Mi'kmaw language was difficult to retain at times. He was often at a loss to understand the full meaning of what was being expressed.

Brigide opened the door-blanket before he had a chance to announce himself. She was grinning from ear to ear as she ushered him in, then left.

Bear Cub stopped just inside the door. So close he was, he could feel the heavy caribou hide fall against his backside when Brigide closed it. The warmth from the fire was inviting, and he let the blanket fall from his shoulders. Singing Sparrow stood with her head bowed as if she were waiting for him— and Morning Dove, the chaperone, stood beside her. Surely, he could never imagine the unthinkable of seeing his intended alone. But he did! Briefly. Now he started to sweat—again.

It was even more difficult to move his feet toward her, knowing she was aware of his mission. Her blue woollen bodice lay flat against her black skirt. The front was cross-laced with deerskin ties, and on the collar were two small buttons made of deer antlers. Both pieces of clothing were trimmed with two stripes—one yellow, the other red. The skirt dropped mid-calf over her tall caribou moccasins. Tiny blue and white beads were intricately sewn in the shape of a dove near the toes of each boot.

*She is so petite and delicate*, Bear Cub thought. Building the courage, he said, "I assume you know why I'm here?" then silently berated himself for saying such a silly thing. Her mother was here. Of course she knew!

Singing Sparrow raised her eyes and nodded shyly.

Morning Dove settled to one side upon the floor, busying her hands with a half-woven mat. Bear Cub moved closer to Singing Sparrow. "As you know then, I have spoken to your father." *Now that sounded stiff*, he thought. "There was much hesitation over his approval. Did he speak to you about it?"

She shook her head. "Not in any detail. When are you leaving?"

"At the first sunrise."

"How long will you be gone?" Singing Sparrow's eyes were sad.

Bear Cub edged closer to her side, but not too close. He whispered, "After what happened to you, my heart screams for me to stay, to protect you. But I must first answer a deeper ache to face my past. I will understand if you decline my wish to court you." He held her small hands up to his lips. "And I promise to return to you. The Great Spirit knows how my tormented soul is weakened by your touch." Bear Cub gazed into her green eyes. "You will do me a great honour if you say yes; I will grieve if you deny me this hope."

Singing Sparrow silenced his lips with her slender finger

and motioned him to sit on the animal skins scattered on the floor. She opened a chest and presented him with her answer. She lay her handcrafted gift on his lap. The earthy odour of the deerskin pouch tickled his senses. Tiny red bird feathers hung on each side of the shoulder strap. He ran his fingers over the quilled design, worked into an image of a small black bear cub. On the flap, a line of small fish were sewn. His heart leapt. He now could carry his own medicine pouch.

"As you are to me, a treasure to be protected, my love," she said. Her eyes danced when she looked at him.

Bear Cub opened his jacket and lifted a pendant from around his neck. The chain had broken long ago and been replaced by a string of caribou skin Morning Dove had made for him. "This pendant was my grandmother's," he said. "When she had taken ill, she asked my grandfather to always wear it close to his heart to entwine their spirits together even in death. Through this, I feel his strength at times." The cameo of a tiny ivory rose framed by even tinier leaves against a beige background was carved of conch shell. He knelt behind Singing Sparrow, placed the necklace around her neck, then lifted her silky hair over the cord. "Hold onto it when your thoughts drift to me, and you will feel my love for you."

He slipped his arms around her and she leaned back into his embrace. "You're trembling. Are you sure of your decision?"

At her mother's slight cough, Singing Sparrow straightened, leaving a respectful space between them.

She turned to him and nodded.

# Chapter Eight



EARLY SUNRISE

e will hug the shoreline from here, camp near Amaqapskekek, and avoid any trails, so it will take a full day. We will rest at dusk. Peter and Bear Cub will leave at sunrise for Merligueche. I will stay behind until Peter returns with or without my brother," Eagle Feather explained as the three of them stood with the family.

Yesterday, Bear Cub had shaken out the cobwebs of the old clothes he had packed away in the chest. They hung a bit loosely on his body, but for outward appearance the clothes fit. For the past four years, he had lived mostly in soft animal skins and furs. He stared down at his moccasins, which now lay atop his deerskin breechcloth and leggings, neatly folded on the ground. He had traded them for itchy woollen knee-breeches, long stockings, and a heavy coat along with stiff leather boots. He felt confined. He wore Singing Sparrow's gift strapped across his chest with the pouch safely tucked on his right side.

This morning, White Cloud seemed apprehensive about the venture. Bear Cub knew White Cloud would never divulge his worries. Morning Dove and Singing Sparrow both attempted to hold back their tears but failed.

"I grieve to let you go," Morning Dove said as she embraced

him. "But go with the comfort that you are well-loved. You are our son and a brother to us even though you did not come forth from my womb. The Great Spirit brought you to us. May the Great Spirit carry you through your difficult journey."

Bear Cub swallowed a lump in his throat as his eyes welled up.

He and Singing Sparrow held each other for a long time. The sweet smell of her hair was all Bear Cub needed to sustain him while apart.

"Know that I will return to you," Bear Cub whispered.

Singing Sparrow breathed into his ear, "Your promise is my contentment."

Eagle Feather and Peter were waiting near the river. Bear Cub slung his musket over his shoulder and joined them. He let the two walk ahead, so he could look one last time at a scene of activity unchanged from the time he had first arrived. The men were preparing for a day of fishing, checking traps, and emptying weirs. For a moment he watched them load canoes with spears, nets, and baskets. The number of those in the village who had wished him well last night was a testament to their caring nature.

"Christian, are you coming?" Peter called.

"Ja," he answered as he waved to Singing Sparrow once more and adjusted his haversack over his shoulder.


It was high tide and Bear Cub could hear the waves crash onto the beach and feel their salt spray on his skin. The wind threatened to snap several treetops as they deeply bowed to its force. The storm arrived quickly and late in the day. There was no dusk; the rain had darkened the skies like night. After travelling for many hours, Eagle Feather was confident they were near Mahone Bay and led them to a familiar small cave far enough from the ocean to be safe even at the highest of tides. Bear Cub knew that if Eagle Feather had his druthers, he would have endured the outside elements rather than be subjected to wiklatmu'jk, four-foot-tall mischievous people, who helped or harmed and lived in caves. Bear Cub remembered the Elders' stories—used to teach children respectful behaviour—about wiklatmu'jk playing tricks to restore order within the community.

Bear Cub attempted to comfort him. "I choose to believe they are here to help us, not hinder. Besides, they may not live in this one." He wasn't sure if his ruse helped, but Eagle Feather agreed to stay, keeping to the outer perimeters of their shelter.

The tree branches that littered the cave floor were evidence they were not the first to use it. Bear Cub pulled out his tinderbox containing pulverized, dry-rotted punk wood to start the fire with scraps of dry grass and leaves he had found. Eagle Feather struck the steel and flint a few times, creating the sparks to catch it ablaze. In no time, with added wood, the fire was warming the cave.

"Not much dry wood left here. We may have enough just to dry ourselves out before we sleep," Eagle Feather said. He gave thanks to the Great Spirit before handing out pieces of smoked eel and beavertail. His mother had loaded everyone down with food. Peter passed around the luski, Bear Cub's favourite. It was made from ground acorns and yellow pollen from the male cattail flowers. He pierced his bread with a sharp twig and held it close to the fire.

"Tell me, before we arrived, was it so vastly different?" Peter asked Eagle Feather.

"Once, there was abundance for everyone," Eagle Feather replied. "We hunted only enough to feed ourselves for one day." He paused, eyeing each of his companions. "Now, we must hunt farther away. Animals have scattered to new areas. Since the white men arrived, over one hundred Winters ago, fish off the coast are not as plentiful. What you call Mahone Bay is one of our main Summer camps. It has been taken from us. Our grandfathers travelled to Merligueche to harvest clams." Eagle Feather stood up and stretched. "At one time, our People were spread over large areas for easy access to resources. With war, they must come together to survive."

"But to do so means your resources are compromised," Peter observed.

Eagle Feather nodded. "The place you call Halifax is good moose-hunting grounds."

"And to Cornwallis, it is a strategic location against French Louisbourg," Peter added.

"A counterweight," Eagle Feather said as he cut a chunk of dried caribou tongue.

Bear Cub needed to step outside. It was painful to hear how much the Europeans had changed the lives of the Mi'kmaq, and he agonized over the repercussions to the Mi'kmaq if the French lost the fortress of Louisbourg. Discomfort had surfaced when Eagle Feather and White Cloud had reached out to help him, or when Morning Dove had touched him with kind words. He shivered and ducked back inside the cave.

"It has stopped raining and the wind has lessened. We should try to get some sleep," Bear Cub said.

Eagle Feather set the eel bones aside in a pile to be returned to the ocean so more would be born.


The wind was still brisk, but the sky was cloudless as the sun rose from beneath the earth. Bear Cub was up early before the others to commit the bones to the waves. Standing on the beach with eyes closed, he imagined he could hear the ocean inhale with each receding tide, then exhale as the flow of water rolled up to meet his boots. A wave of emotion swept over him as he thought of Papa. Papa's strict traditions of primogeniture had rendered him blind to Bear Cub's hopes. On top of that, Bear Cub lived with his own misgivings for leaving the family to find Jakob. How would Papa perceive these past four years? As "wasted"? He scooped up a handful of pebbles and let the sand sift through his fingers. In a sudden rage, he threw the lot into the ocean and stretched his arms out to meet the sky. "Walk with me, Great Spirit! Help me face this burden!" he screamed. Although it was childish, he expected an answer. Incensed with himself, he walked back to the cave.

After their morning meal, the men parted ways. Eagle Feather assured an agitated Bear Cub that he was safe and would wait for him.

"Give me two sunrises," Bear Cub told him. "Then, I will return with Peter. If not, I will stay the Winter and return in the Spring." In departing, the brothers each lay their right hand on the other's chest. Bear Cub could not remember who had started this unconventional but habitual farewell between them, but it was comforting.


When Peter offered him food, Christian refused. He had no appetite. It had been hours since they had left the cave, and the trails past Mahone Bay and around the ranges were thick with stumps, brush, and dense wood. The entire journey was farther inland, away from the coast, with Northwest Range being the longest stretch. Finally, they followed a river, then skirted the end of a lake before hearing any sounds of life. They found themselves at a common where cattle were grazing. Oxen and bulls were separated from the black cows. There were a few browns mixed in the herd. Christian could see the palisade enclosing the town.

"So different from the Franconian cattle we had in the old country," Christian observed.

Peter stopped. "What?"

"Look at their beige muzzles and udders. Our larger breed was reddish gold. These are much smaller and don't seem as muscular. I wonder if they are primarily a dairy breed."

Peter shrugged. "Are you nervous?"

"Do I sound it?"

"Just a bit." Peter smiled.

"Are we close to Papa's farm?"

"His is a ways to go yet. Elisabeth and Georg are closer." Peter pointed, then shoved his hands into his pockets. "I haven't seen your father since Hohctorf when he banished me from your house, never to see Elisabeth again."

Christian raised an eyebrow. "That I do remember."

The two followed a brook through the woods to the edge of Georg and Elisabeth's land. The small cleared fields were already harvested. At one end of the farmland, newly pulled tree stumps lay scattered in sludge, the recent work of oxen hooves. As Christian and Peter approached the thatched house, only the distant squawking of seagulls could be heard. A wooden pitchfork stood propped against the house, and the barn door was open enough to show a mouldboard inside. They lay their muskets on the ground.

"Are you sure you want to be here?" Christian asked. "After all, it'll be a shock with me, let alone both of us."

"I'm certain." Peter knocked. They could hear female voices, but when no one answered for some time, he opened the door.

Elisabeth and Hanna were lifting the large iron pot from the hearth. "Peter! What are you doing here?" Elisabeth shrieked. Hanna turned too quickly and down went the pot, the contents splashing on the floor and onto their skirts. Peter rushed to their aid as Christian stood alone in the open door. Any fears of an awkward entrance were waylaid by the scene until Christian caught Elisabeth's eye. He watched her eyes widen with the realization of who was standing before her. "Oh, my Lord! Oh, my—" She stifled her cry with the palm of her hand. Christian embraced her, his own emotions unchecked.

Hanna was dumbstruck. "I knew you were alive," she said, barely audible. "Papa!" she hollered, and she ran from the house.

"Sit, please, Christian," Elisabeth said, grasping both his hands. "Papa's in the barn." Then, to Peter, "Leave that. I'll clean it up later."

Christian's stomach was turning somersaults. He had not been expecting to see Papa just yet. His sister could not take her eyes off him, searching his face as if to find answers.

"Where do I start?" she said. "So many questions!"

"Right now, I just have one. Am I to be an uncle again?" Christian raised his eyebrows.

"Ja. End of January. It has been—"

His papa's voice interrupted her. "'Tis true," he sputtered. Christian turned to see him out of breath, leaning against the door frame for support.

Physical changes were few. The bushy, red-blonde beard was longer than Christian remembered. A sun-tanned complexion highlighted the added wrinkles around his eyes, which were now only taking in his son, there in flesh and blood. Christian would always recognize his papa through those icy-blue eyes, mirrors to his prideful soul.

"I gave up," Michael said, choking back tears. "Hanna did not. She knew."

Christian stood just before his papa brought him tight to his chest. "I am so sorry, my son," he sobbed.

WHEN CHRISTIAN AWOKE, THE SUN was already up. His sister must have decided to let him sleep. He shared a room with his nephew, while Peter slept in the barn. When Georg had arrived home, it was to find an entirely different atmosphere from when he had left for his rounds yesterday morning. Christian answered the questions as much as he could. In between the laughter and joy of the reunion, more tears flowed when they shared that they had all assumed the worst—that he had been kidnapped and held hostage. Christian had not tried to change their perception, and thankfully Peter had remained silent. He knew his family, especially Papa, could never grasp the truth that he was not held against his will. Elisabeth had an early supper ready for everyone, and Papa and Hanna returned to their farm before sunset.

In all the commotion, Peter had been the fifth wheel but happily sat in the background to just listen. In time, he and Elisabeth had their discussion, and Christian could only assume with Georg as well. It was all done privately and, as far as he knew, calmly.

Once Christian stepped outside, he could see the expanse of their land. The smaller harvested fields abruptly merged into vast uncleared areas of forest. Hundreds of autumn leaves stirred up into a swirl and hovered above the empty farmland.

Peter emerged from the barn. "Ah, I see you're ready to leave," Christian said to him, then cleared his throat. "Does Georg know now of the two of you?"

"It was never discussed. However, Elisabeth no longer wishes me to see my son. It is probably for the best. Petie didn't know me this time." He rubbed his face. "I don't have my beard. He was not even four when I saw him last."

"Ah, I see. In time, she will feel differently. She usually does."

"With the new baby coming, she prefers now to just cut all the ties."

"And Papa? I couldn't help but notice you kept your distance."

"I believe it was easy for him to say nothing as well." Peter tried to make light of the situation. "Good that he and Hanna left last night."

"What will you do?"

"Nothing. Are you staying?"

"For now. Tell my brother to come for me in June, the Leafy Moon after the gaspereau run." Christian gestured toward the house. "They know nothing about this."

Peter nodded.

"I have written a letter to Singing Sparrow. Would you translate it for her?" He placed it in Peter's hand.

"Of course." Peter picked up his musket. "I've already said my goodbyes inside."

"Does Petie know yet you're his father?"

He shook his head, then set off to meet Eagle Feather.

# Chapter Nine

FEBRUARY 1757

"Off with you!" Christian yelled, chasing two dogs from the common. It was not the first time they had spooked the cattle, and regulation required that all dogs be on a leash. A fine would be issued when he reported the incident to Herr Kuhn.

After the cows and sheep settled down, Michael walked over to his son. "Same ones, I see." He scanned the common. "We need to trim out the cattle. I shouldn't have said yes to the extra animals—this area is just not big enough."

"But Herrs Pernette and Mauger paid for the privilege. It's one of the rules we all agreed upon."

"That they did. And the money is given to our poor who, like the Mosers, have large families and can't afford to pay for the pasturage of more than their rightful allotment. But I do have the final say."

They continued spreading hay over the field. So far the winter had been mild with little snow, and the first week of February was no different. In addition to the added livestock, each person had the right to pasture one cow, five sheep, a goat, and one sow at no cost. A few colonists had drawn up a proposal of regulations last September for Colonel Sutherland to consider.

120

These were approved and the rules enforced immediately, with Michael chosen to decide the number of animals the common could sustain through a season. Of the 120 animals herded to Lunenburg, only 60 oxen and cows survived the journey. The rest had perished of fatigue and hunger.

"The hay will hold us until late spring," Michael said. "And if more is needed, I'm sure New England will ship it to us."

Christian had worked with Papa in cutting trees and pulling stumps with the oxen. He had met most of the farm neighbours. There was an intense sense of community until self-supporting. The best of the cut trees were kept for the colony, while the remainder were sent to Halifax for firewood, which made Lunenburg a major source of supply. In return, the farm owners benefited with the extra cash.

There had been no more attacks, which was instrumental in the amount of work accomplished. For the moment, everyone's fears seemed to be laid to rest. Even the rapport he and Papa enjoyed was a blessing—not a harsh word had been spoken between the two. The guilt of the half-truths Christian spoke, or allowed to be believed, was still there in the back of his mind, but it was the only solution. To leave in the spring would be devastating to them, but not returning…well, for now, he pushed the prospect away.

Frantic hollering broke his thoughts. Hanna was running across the common toward them. "Papa! 'Tis Elisabeth. Her labour has started and Georg is on his rounds."

"Get Louisa!" Michael said.

"It must be Marta."

"She left earlier toward the Northwest Range. There's no time to find her. Louisa it is," Michael commanded. "Run, little one. We will go to your sister now."

Hanna headed toward town.

Elisabeth was doubled up on her side in extreme pain. An hour had passed before Papa had arrived, and he stayed with her until the midwife showed. Louisa was not her choice, as she didn't speak German and Elisabeth didn't understand French. But at that juncture, it didn't matter. With Petie, she had been in labour for more than twenty-four hours. This time, the pain was not gradual as before—it was sudden and gripping. She remembered what Georg had said on the ship from their homeland; his voice was speaking to her now. Breathe deeply through the pain, he kept repeating. *Try to relax*, she said to herself. *Inhale, exhale.*

As incomprehensible as Louisa's words were as she fussed about her, Elisabeth was sure they were reassuring. "Respirez. C'est bien." The midwife demonstrated the breaths. "Respirez."

Elisabeth could feel the warmth of a hot compress on her stomach. Her knees were up while Louisa examined her. It was happening all too fast. The contractions were on top of each other. She held her breath. *Oh! I need to push*, she thought.

"Je vois la tête," Louisa excitedly cried. "Pousser!" She made a gesture of pushing.

Elisabeth pushed again, then again.

"La voilà," Louisa exclaimed as the baby arrived in one gush. "Une fille." Then, a healthy wail filled the room.

*Was it a boy or a girl?* Once she had cut the cord, Louisa lay the newborn briefly on Elisabeth's stomach—a baby girl! Louisa gently lifted the baby and washed her in the basin of warm water before returning her to the mother's arms. Elisabeth could hear voices in the next room. Georg was home.

Elisabeth watched her daughter sleep and examined her tiny fingers. The door squeaked open. She smiled at her husband and moved the blanket edging away, so the small face was more visible. "Our daughter."

Georg settled himself beside her on the bed, beaming. "You don't waste any time, my love."

The baby briefly opened her eyes. "Ah," he said. "I think you have your mama's eyes." He wiggled his baby finger into an almost closed fist. Then, to Elisabeth, "I'm sorry I didn't make it in time, but you were in excellent hands."

"There were some communication mishaps, but Louisa and I managed."

"Lunenburg is very lucky to have her as a midwife. She studied in London under the best male midwife, Dr. William Smellie."

Elisabeth let out a small laugh. "Strange how things have changed." When her brother Stefan was born, the midwife was appalled when her mama demanded Georg deliver him. The midwife could see no good in having a man step into a woman's domain. It was the devil's dance, she had argued.

"Do you still wish to name her Marta? Louisa did bring her forth."

"I promised Marta months ago if we had a girl, it would be named for her. Louisa will understand."

"There are three fidgety people waiting in the kitchen. Are you up to it?"

"Of course. Hanna will be absolutely delighted. She very much wanted a niece."


A warm embrace came from behind with a whisper of breath in her ear. "Uh-uh, Georg, not now," she giggled. She wormed her way from his arms to lay a hot plate on the table. "Our friends will be here any minute. Are the kegs set up outside for our guests?"

"Small casks they are. Herr Mauger offered us his spruce beer at no charge."

"Spruce beer!" Elisabeth was moving quickly about the

kitchen, placing bread on the table, ensuring enough bowls and plates, and keeping Petie's small, prying hands from grabbing a morsel or two. "A far cry from stout."

"We can't grow enough barley or hops," Georg answered, guarding the food as best he could from his son, who now thought it a game. "What we have plenty of is spruce and molasses." Georg lifted Petie into his arms.

"I guess there are some traditions that must change somewhat. At least we have something for anyone who wishes to drop by. Now scoot, the both of you," she declared and tasted the soup simmering over the fire. "Lovely. It's ready. I'm so glad I could add beef before the meat rations stop next month. It adds so much more substance." She was alone now. Marta was sleeping soundly near the hearth but out of the way of any stray hot ashes that would invariably drift. It had been two weeks since their daughter arrived, and Elisabeth's recovery was surprisingly quick. Her energy had waned for just a couple of days. At birth, Marta had been healthy and suckling within the hour.

Elisabeth placed the christening candle in the centre of the table. It was still uneven at the top near the wick. The last time it was lit was for her brother Stefan. "May God rest his soul," she whispered, folding the embroidered cloth Mama had stitched.

MARTA'S WAS A JOYFUL CHRISTENING lasting into the middle of the afternoon. Most of the guests had now departed for home, leaving just Herr and Frau Knaut. Anna and Hanna cleaned up while Elisabeth nursed Marta in the privacy of the bedroom.

Conversation veered toward the victuals. Christian listened closely and decided to put in an opinion, for what it was worth. "Why not fish?" He may as well have asked them to hunt moose or bear. The foreign concept sunk to the bottom of the ocean before it had a chance to be considered.

Philip laughed. "That'll never happen. No one has any interest."

Michael nodded. "Tilling the land is in our blood. That cannot change. The Board knew who they were recruiting."

"Fishing is better than starving. And I am certain the government would think better of us if we were so industrious as to learn how."

"Most of us are farmers. Ach! Nein. I'll not continue to talk on this," Michael said, waving his hand in frustration.

"The government won't force the issue either," Philip offered in a soothing tone. "Michael's right."

"Your conviction is commendable, but with all due respect, Papa, these times demand a change. Or at least to be considered. Fishing means the colony would be self-sustaining," Christian said carefully.

"And we will be, Christian," Philip answered. "All in due time. It's just unfortunate the weather hasn't worked well in our favour. But the cattle will eventually increase, and victuals are just a temporary solution until we can stand on our feet."

"But you've been here almost four years. Fishing is the immediate and most sensible solution. There's plenty to be had. The catch can be smoked and dried for later use."

"You have spent too much time with the natives," Michael quipped.

"We would do well to learn from them," Christian said.

"Have your kidnappers become your friends now?" Michael said scornfully.

Christian stepped back. Hanna and Anna were now listening intently to their conversation.

Michael continued to probe. "They are primitive and crude—from what I have heard, uncivilized. What can the civilized possibly learn from them?"

Christian was taken aback. "Don't judge what you don't know," he retorted.

"Anna, we've overstayed our welcome," Philip suddenly declared. He took hold of Elisabeth's hands. "Danke. Your hospitality is always a pleasure. We hold your friendship dear to our hearts. You can now say your daughter is naturally a citizen of Nova Scotia," he added. "As for us, we must wait."

"Last year was your seventh year here," said Georg. "Did you not receive your naturalization yet?"

"Anna and I will be receiving our certificates soon. As it must be given to us from an Anglican clergyman, it will be Reverand Moreau officiating the ceremony. But nothing has been confirmed yet. I believe you are eligible next year?"

Georg nodded, as did Michael and Christian, who remained aloof following the sting of words between them.

Georg shook hands with Philip and kissed Anna farewell. Their guests departed and Elisabeth quietly shut the door after them. Michael and Hanna left soon after. Christian remained quiet for the rest of the evening and retired early.


As Elisabeth and Georg readied themselves for bed, Georg said, "There'll be no relief of rounds. Dr. Phillips and I have split all of Dr. Erad's patients between us."

"How is Dr. Erad?" Elisabeth asked.

"I'll be surprised if he lasts another month—he's rapidly losing weight. Since he has started coughing up blood, the medicine is no longer helping, if it ever did give him any relief. I visit him daily now, and it grieves me to see him in so much pain."

Elisabeth caressed his face. "It'll be a blessing if God takes him quickly then."

She crawled into bed and let her body sink from exhaustion, relaxing into the mattress. Georg snuggled against her.

"It was lovely having the Brissang family stop by. Their children are so polite and well-behaved. That says a lot of their parents," Elisabeth said, turning her head to see Georg smiling at her. "What are you grinning at?"

"You. I love you."

Elisabeth played with the corner of the coverlet, and her husband covered her hand with his to stop her fidgeting. She turned back to face him. "I heard the words between Papa and Christian."

"Things were a bit heated. I don't know what led Michael to make such an accusation. Christian was a prisoner."

"Was he?"

"What are you saying?"

"I have a suspicion there's more to his capture than he is leading us to believe. I never told you, but the day Peter left, I overheard Christian talk about Singing Sparrow."

"A bird?"

"A person. A woman. Christian handed Peter what looked like a letter and asked him to take it to this Singing Sparrow."

"That proves nothing," Georg said. "Do you think he has come out of captivity an ally of the Mi'kmaq, that we can no longer trust him?"

"Nein! My brother is honourable. I would never think that of him. But why, after escaping, would he communicate back to his captors?"

"You don't know that for sure. Has Peter ever confided in you? I mean, where does *he* live?"

Elisabeth just shook her head.

"Maybe it's all very innocent—nothing to get into a fluster over. It could be someone Peter knows."

"With a name like Singing Sparrow? Sometimes, Georg, you can be so naive. On the other hand, you always look for the good in everyone. That is why I love you so much," she said, wrapping her arms around his body.

"Talk to your brother. I'm sure he'll confide in you."

"Mmm," she moaned, as Georg gently stroked her back.

# Chapter Ten

MAY 1757

Who is Singing Sparrow?"

"What?" Christian fired back at his sister, then regretted the tartness of his reply. "Forgive me, Elisabeth."

Hanna spoke. "Tell us."

Papa and Petie were in the barn tending to the two calves. Of the recovered cattle, two cows had already conceived before the drive. Marta was asleep in Elisabeth's arms. Even alone with his two siblings, Christian was not sure he was ready. How would they react?

"How long have you known?"

"That doesn't matter. I said nothing as I never was completely sure. So, we are asking now. Were you truly a prisoner?" Elisabeth asked.

"In the beginning, maybe. I remember very little from that time. My brother never divulged their initial intentions, and I never asked."

"Brother? Then, it sounds to me you did willingly stay. Are we that easily forgotten? How could you…" Marta started to cry from the tension.

"Elisabeth! Allow him to tell his story," Hanna chastised.

Relieved in the telling, Christian hid nothing and spoke

129

candidly of his life with the Mi'kmaq. He even revealed his courtship. "I owe my life to them!"

Marta now asleep, Elisabeth paced back and forth in front of the cradle. She looked baffled, trying to absorb what he had said. Elisabeth was nothing if not passionate about her family's welfare. And when it came to Christian and Hanna, she had always been the mother hen, especially after Mama had died.

"To them? What about us? We are blood. They are not," she remarked. "I'll not believe this. I refuse!" Elisabeth turned toward him, and he could see the fire in her eyes. "I simply cannot believe that you actually chose those *savages* over—"

Bear Cub's voice was harsh when he cut in. "That word is horridly misplaced."

Elisabeth's face was flushed. "What on earth are you talking about?"

Christian fell silent. No amount of telling would prove to her that the Mi'kmaq were not as she had been convinced they were.

"Where's your alliance now?"

"Elisabeth! Don't speak so," Hanna said.

"I will say what I please. Is our brother now the enemy? Let us know now, Christian, and speak truthfully."

"I've no alliance. My love for my family has not changed. In fact, it is stronger than before. But I have no regrets."

Elisabeth's demeanour changed suddenly. She was looking at the door in horror.

"Georg!" Hanna screamed.

Christian turned to see his brother-in-law, his face white as a sheet, bloody smudges splattered on his shirt and breeches. His hands were smeared with red, revealing an unsuccessful attempt to scrub them clean.

"Louis, Francine. They're gone." Georg was blinking rapidly in disbelief.

"What are you talking about?" Christian helped him to the table and poured him a bit of the rum Elisabeth had just handed him. Georg's hand violently shook as he grasped the cup.

"They were murdered."

"God have mercy on us!" Elisabeth's voice quaked as she started to cry. "I just spoke with Francine yesterday. M-my…" She choked back her tears.

"I thought it strange when I arrived. It was eerily quiet. Usually, I hear the children playing. Louis was not in the field." Georg could not stop trembling as he took another gulp. "The door was wide open. Both Louis and Francine were still in their beds—scalped! The children…" He covered his face with his hands and sobbed. "I searched everywhere outside. I couldn't find them."

"Possibly taken prisoner," Christian said.

Elisabeth glared at her brother.

Instantly, an intense flush of heat enveloped Christian. His thoughts became distorted with possible reasons for this horrendous event, then impossible thoughts of who could have sanctioned it. *It certainly was not done on orders from any Nikanus,* he thought. One could not live with the Mi'kmaq and not know their true nature. Then he remembered the community circle before he had left and those who were prime for an onslaught. Did a few fall victim to the French authorities who wanted them to form a rebel militia? What about the other villages?

Georg continued. "Dr. Phillips arrived, he had planned to meet me there. He raised the alarm to the regiment at the Northwest blockhouse."

"And where were *they* when this occurred?" Elisabeth's voice was a high-pitched squeal. "Where was the militia? How could this have been allowed to happen? There was no warning shot during the night!"

"There was, Elisabeth. I heard it," Christian replied.

"And you didn't awaken me? I can't believe I didn't hear it," she said, puzzled.

"And what could you have done? Wait in the dark, huddled in fear? There were soldiers on duty."

"Obviously, they were of no help last night, were they? That could have been us—your family! Or do you really care?" The accusation hung like icicles in the kitchen.

"Take that back," Hanna yelled. "Sometimes you can be so cruel!"

"Why would you say such a grievous thing?" Georg said, dumbfounded.

"Tell him, dear brother. How you made friends with our enemies who did this. Tell him the whole sordid story," Elisabeth whispered vehemently.

Christian was angry—trapped, like a snared fox. He was being pulled in two directions. His German family was vulnerable, and he was distraught over what could happen to his Mi'kmaw family because of this raid. The British would have an excuse to come down hard on any Mi'kmaw, even the innocent.

He walked out.


"Do you remember when i used to follow you around like a homeless puppy?" Hanna asked, trying to divert her brother.

Christian glanced at his sister. "You were quite a nuisance," he said, smiling. The twig he was using to trace lines in the dirt suddenly snapped. "Do you think I was wrong?"

"In what?"

"Everything. In coming back here. In not waking Elisabeth last night."

Hanna tenderly touched his hand such as he had done so many times to calm her childish traumas, as if he were now the younger sibling to be comforted. "Don't ever second-guess your decision. These past few months have been so dear to us. As for Elisabeth, you know she is quick to anger. Her love for us runs so deep it causes her to burst out with bits of frenzy."

"Don't tell me she means well." Christian rolled his eyes.

Hanna laughed and crossed her heart. "Not I," she promised with mock solemnity. "This will soon blow over."

"Maybe not. Eagle Feather will be watching for me. I promised Singing Sparrow I would return to her."

Hanna inhaled sharply, and he saw her eyes well up.

"How soon?"

"Next month." Christian thought for a moment. "It will be hard to speak to Papa about all of this."

"It will," Hanna agreed. "Papa is another Elisabeth. You'll need to pray to the Great Spirit." She smirked.

Christian studied her more closely, and her eyes softened toward him. "Why are you so different?" he asked. "You seem to be the only one who is accepting of me. I think I shall go home with you today."

"If I tell you something, you must promise not to tell Elisabeth and especially not Papa."

"And Georg?"

"Georg was with me, he knows. He understands. As for our sister, well, she's aware but made me vow not to do it again or she would tell Papa."

"Hanna, what?"

"Promise?"

"Ja," and he crossed his heart.

Then, Hanna told him about Paul Labrador and Magdeleine.

The tension in the house was thick. The situation with Papa was no better since the last time he and Christian had spoken two days before, so Georg persuaded Christian to stay with them. Christian's presence relaxed Georg's misgivings about his absences from the family.

Elisabeth had taken the children into town that afternoon. The HMS *Albany* was moored in the harbour along with three other fourteen-gun sloops. Petie had been talking excitedly of nothing else. Christian harrowed part of Georg's field to prepare for potatoes. After the last frost in April, he had helped plant turnip seeds, which were now germinating. Small, green shoots were pushing their way through the dry soil. With little rain, he and Georg both were concerned about the crop bolting.

Christian had agreed to meet Hanna at the bottom of the creek. With no one to answer to, there would be no questions asked of his whereabouts. They moved upstream toward where Paul and Magdeleine lived. Few words had passed between the siblings before Christian saw a familiar sight in the clearing. It looked like home. He missed home.

Hanna explained, "The last time I saw them was last fall when Paul was injured. Georg looked after him until he was healed, even under Elisabeth's protests."

Christian greeted them. "Kwe'," then proceeded to speak of the beautiful surroundings. Paul replied but he was clearly bewildered that Christian spoke the language.

"Ana!" Paul said, and embraced his dear friend.

Christian removed his pouch from around his neck to gift its contents of tobacco to their hosts.

"Wela'lin," Paul replied.

They sat outside around the fire as Christian conversed as best he could, translating to Hanna when there was a pause. He could see the pride in his sister's face when she looked at him and her relief at being able to speak to her friend through him. A whole new opportunity had presented itself to explore the two cultures together. Paul and Magdeleine spoke of being the only survivors when their village was attacked. The British left a murderous trail of scalped corpses. Then Paul spoke of their relations with the new settlers.

"Please ask why they left Lunenburg," Hanna said.

Conversing in Mi'kmaw, Paul revealed his story of family members deported from Pisiguit.

"His nephew, Clovewater, claimed he had saved the crew of a New England vessel from an Indian attack. He was also expelled," Christian told her. "You see, Hanna, the Mi'kmaq will have nothing to do with the Labrador name either. They feel betrayed. And as for the war, your friends don't feel safe in town."

Hanna's face darkened. Paul rested his wrinkled hand upon her cheek, and Magdeleine wrapped her arm around her. "Mimikes."

"She called you butterfly. It's a good name for you. You are beautiful, Hanna," Christian said. "You have transformed from a caterpillar into a sensitive, mature young woman."

Hanna's face faintly flushed as she lowered her head. "What will they do now?" she asked.

Christian carefully listened to Paul's description of how the influx of settlers at key waterways was cutting off their food sources.

"They cannot stay. Their freedom of access to some of the best fishing along this coast has been disrupted by us," Christian explained. "Paul and Magdeleine need these rivers for sustenance, and we need them to power machinery. The sawmills are preventing salmon from swimming back upriver to spawn. The logs on the rivers have increased. Now there's talk of a gristmill. For that, a dam will be built."

"Can they not move farther down the coast from here, past the LaHave River?"

Christian shook his head. "The war makes it impossible to fish safely. The French might attack by water."

"Where can they go?" Hanna cried. Christian asked their two guests.

"They will travel farther inland. But they must stay away from Minas. The British have settled the Pisiguit and St. Croix Rivers. The trail is now used by the military from Halifax to Pisiguit. Paul says they will most likely go upriver on the LaHave. Many lakes and rivers feed into it."

At his own words, Christian's stomach tightened. He thought of his brother's safety. He was at a loss and had no words of encouragement. "Where the Mi'kmaq travel on these ancient waterways, now so do the British regiments."

More conversation arose, along with many more translations. Christian and Hanna thanked their hosts for their hospitality. The farewells were distressing; they didn't know if they would even see each other again.

On the way back, Hanna said, "Elisabeth says all Indians can't be trusted, but I disagree. Not all are our enemies."

"Likewise, there are Mi'kmaq who perceive all of us as enemies. We tread on dangerous ground when we allow our assumptions to control our actions. It's much easier to understand someone when you know their story, especially when they are a perceived enemy."

"Especially when that perception is a lie." Hanna changed the subject. "That is a beautiful pouch. I never noticed it before."

"Singing Sparrow made it for me," Christian replied. He draped his arm over his sister's shoulder as they continued through the woods.

"Petie! Come here, away from the water," Elisabeth called. His excitement was endless as he stared at the sloops bobbing in the harbour. The *Albany* was the largest of the four moored. All its sails, including the gaff fore and aft, were collapsed. Elisabeth could see two sailors carefully picking their way along a long bowsprit. After the recent news of four smallpox cases in Halifax, it was the last time they would see these ships for a while. There was an embargo on any vessels originating from there.

"Here, my dear, I'll take Marta if you like. Free you up a bit for Petie," Frau Born offered.

"Danke," Elisabeth said as she handed over the infant and gladly focused her attention on her eldest. "I pray the disease amounts to nothing. As sporadic as the ships have been, I feel less isolated when they are in port."

"Since the horrid attack on the Brissangs, I haven't slept. There were more shots last evening, two or three in succession."

"At least you're living within the palisade. I wish we were, but Georg will have none of it."

"Your original house is still empty," Frau Born said encouragingly. "But on the other hand, the town is now more susceptible to French invasion."

Like the other colonists, Elisabeth and Georg had built their house four years ago in town where they lived for one year before moving to the acreage. In her mind, it had been too early to leave the safety of the palisade. "Let us speak of other things," Elisabeth pleaded. "Have you heard anything more about the road to Halifax?"

"There is still no agreement. Cost, you know!"

Elisabeth kissed her friend and lifted Marta back into her arms. "We'd better be on our way." It took some effort, but she finally managed to convince Petie to leave.

"Will you be at the meeting tonight?" Frau Born asked. "I heard a patrol shot and scalped an Indian last evening."

"Not I, but you may see Georg and Christian." Elisabeth no longer wanted to hear about it. The awareness of raids was ever-present these days, and she did not need another depressing meeting to remind her.

CHRISTIAN ATTENDED THE MEETING WITH Georg. Visiting ships had passed on the news that the settlers' wood did not always reach its destination. French privateers had been intercepting the vessels.

"Once the pox threat is gone and the wood shipments start up again, Admiral Holburne will leave a large naval force at Halifax to drive off these privateers. A convoy has been suggested to escort the vessels bearing wood to and from here," Sutherland announced.

Philip Knaut was sitting next to Sutherland for any translations. Philip questioned the practicality of shipping so little wood. "There are thousands of soldiers and sailors in Halifax. We can't possibly supply them all."

"Many civilians have left Halifax for the older colonies to the south of us. And most of the troops will be leaving soon as Lord Loudoun readies his attack on Louisbourg. What's next on the agenda?" Sutherland asked his assistant who pointed to the item.

"Ah, yes. The crop bounties have now been resumed. We've accumulated a goodly amount from the duties." This statement sent up a cheer, until Sutherland finished by saying, "But only by a little."

Through Georg, Christian was aware of the price per bushel paid to the farmers for various crops. These bounties were funded by the duties imposed on alcoholic spirits, namely rum. When the bounty claims exceeded the proceeds of the duties, the farmers questioned if all the duties collected were used for the benefit of the colony. There was some suspicion that the money had gone elsewhere, but this was never proven.

Heinrich Moser stood. "Is there any hope that we will receive bounties in cash as it is in Halifax?"

"No, it will be as before—payment in the form of goods, along with various discounts."

Another stood. "On exactly which crops can we claim?"

"Potatoes is one. I believe hay another. The list is posted on the back wall there. We'll revisit this next year. So there is no misunderstanding, nothing has changed for the claimants. All of you still need to make an oath before the Justice of the Peace that the crop is yours."

"Will there be full disclosure of what is being done with the proceeds?" Herr Kuhn asked.

"I can answer," Philip interjected. "Starting next month, there'll be a report of the breakdown of the excise and import duties added to the alcohol, along with a second report of where these proceeds are dispersed. This will be open to anyone who wishes to see it."

A united assent spread throughout the room.

"The last item is about the recent shots," Sutherland stated. "A patrol fired on four Indians near the Northwest Range. The three that barely escaped with their lives were not caught."

"Did they have anything to do with the Brissang murders?" Herr Kuhn asked.

"Don't know."

"Any word on the extra blockhouses there?"

"I've written to Governor Lawrence." Sutherland scanned his audience. "Please. This all takes time. I ask again for your patience."

"I have no more patience! What about the three hundred acres we were promised?" Joseph Kuhn demanded.

"Sit down!" Heinrich Moser stood. "That is the last thing on our minds right now. Until I have self-sustainability and safety measures are put in place, I'll not be encumbered with more land."

Most nodded in agreement, and one dared to voice his opinion. "I understand, Joseph, but we don't need people like you who'll fracture this colony. Leave your pessimism at the door. Have you forgotten the reasons why we left Europe in the first place? Henrich, you came from the Palatinate. Gabe, you are from Montbéliard. Philip, your home was Saxony, correct? And, I, like many others, hail from Württemberg. We all came from different regions, but we all emigrated for the same purpose. To escape persecution. To make this work, we need to stick together. But we also need to be realistic."

"Realistic? Ach! Go to blazes, the lot of you!" Joseph Kuhn walked out, slamming the door behind him.

"He'll not be long here," Georg whispered to Christian.

"He's free with his threats but does nothing. It's probably for the best that he go," Christian said

"Joseph just feels helpless—like we all do."

Sutherland spoke up. "We've not been negligent to any of you. But the 300 acres per family are extensive—about 100,000 acres. They're outside the boundaries of this township and at present consist of all lands between the LaHave River and the easternmost head of Mahone Bay. All the islands in the bay are included, and these lots will be located behind most of the ranges you are already occupying, in all probability extending at least seven leagues farther back. Surveyor-General Morris has yet to draw the boundaries."

Georg stood. "When I left Württemberg, the notices promised fifty acres only. We all know why we received only thirty—to keep our distance from the town as minimal as possible. The three hundred is over and above what we were originally promised. The government has been more than generous, so I'm more than content to wait it out." Many clapped in agreement.

"Danke, Dr. Gessler. Well said," Philip commented.

"Does anyone else have anything outstanding to be addressed?" Sutherland asked. Only seconds passed before the colonel banged the gavel down. "Then consider this meeting concluded!"

A clatter of benches scraped the floor as people got up and formed small groups to continue the dialogue. Christian and Georg were conversing when they were approached by Philip. A taller gentleman walked beside him.

"Allow me to introduce Lieutenant Dettlieb Christopher Jessen," Philip said. "He's our new muster-master, replacing Captain Steignfort who died soon after the cattle drive. This is Dr. Georg Gessler."

"Guten abend, Lieutenant Jessen," Georg said, extending his hand.

"Most call me by my nickname, Detleff. Please feel free." He bowed his head. "Your reputation precedes you, Doctor. Though we have not met, I have heard nothing but praise. Thankfully, though, my wife and I have not needed your services."

"I can think of one service you may welcome if Frau Jessen should find herself in a delicate condition," Georg replied.

"As of yet, we've not been so blessed." Detleff smiled, then turned to Christian. "And you are?"

"Ach, please excuse my rudeness. This is my brother-in-law, Christian Heber."

"Pleased to meet you," Detleff said, taking Christian's hand in a firm grip. "Your name is familiar to me. Have we met before?"

"I don't believe we have," Christian remarked.

Georg interjected, "Christian only arrived in Lunenburg last fall. Where are you from, Detleff?"

"Originally from Holstein. I arrived at Halifax in '51."

"We arrived on the *Pearl* in September of '51. What ship were you on?" Christian asked.

"My brother and I arrived earlier on the *Speedwell* from Hamburg." Detleff tapped his forefinger to his lips. "Nein. I am thinking we met last summer."

Philip laughed. "That would be impossible. He was captured by the Mi'kmaq in '52 ."

"Ah! Then I heard your name in passing. You spent a few years in captivity then, ja? I'm wondering now if that's what happened to Leonard Gorckum and Kasper Gerhart. They went missing last year."

Christian's heart jumped. Those were the names of the two soldiers he and Peter killed. Were he, Peter, and Singing Sparrow seen? He forced a deep breath and held his tongue. If Detleff witnessed the burying of bodies, he would've made himself known and would have been armed, Christian reasoned. He could not have seen them.

"That's most likely," Georg said.

"That must have been quite an ordeal for you with no chance of escape. Sometime, we must meet again so I may hear your story, Christian. I'd be most interested. I've been told some captives are not held against their will. Have you heard of Michael Francklin? He owns two dram-shops in Halifax. He was apparently captured by Mi'kmaq and spent three months in the Gaspé, but he actually made friends with his captors. And learned their language."

Christian raised an eyebrow at Detleff. "From my experience, I would think it highly unlikely," he lied. "Herr Francklin must be one of the lucky ones." Christian's stomach lurched.

"I agree with you. Frankly, I find these stories of people not wanting to escape hard to believe," Detleff declared. "And when friendships are formed with our enemy, it is cause for concern. Do you not agree?"

Georg stepped in. "It was nice to meet you. We must bid our farewells. It's getting late."

"Indeed. A pleasure." And to Christian, "My apologies, sir, if I have made you feel uncomfortable in my request to discuss your ordeal. I must be mistaken in my recollection of you."

"No need to apologize," Christian said. Bidding their goodbyes to Philip as well, they departed.

After passing through the palisade gate, where dozens of soldiers stood guard, Christian and Georg hiked up the hill toward the farm.

Georg spoke. "You're very quiet. You seemed rattled by Detleff's conversation. Do you know anything about the disappearance of those two men?"

"Nein. Never heard of them, and I certainly cannot place Detleff," Christian said. As much as he trusted Georg, he had no intention of explaining any of the circumstances. *Better he knows nothing, to alleviate any possible ramifications for him and his family.* Christian carefully changed the subject, bringing focus on other matters discussed at the meeting.

Georg said, "I can't blame Joseph for wanting to leave. Maybe he will fare better in Halifax."

"From what I've learned, it's no better. He may be going from the frying pan into the fire."

"Possibly. I guess you could say the same."

"Hmm?"

"I mean you returning to your family nest only to find Elisabeth's wrath. Not to mention Michael's when he finds out," Georg said. "But she's over it now."

"Not completely, I think." Christian could not yet broach the subject of him leaving next month. As far as Elisabeth was concerned, her brother was now home to stay, and he allowed her to think thusly. "Our bond now is only of passing pleasantries—tolerances, if you will. She refuses to discuss anything related to the Mi'kmaq."

"Convince me to learn your side, Christian."

"If I must convince you, you are not open to it. Now, no more. Elisabeth will hear." They had arrived home. His sister sat outside mending one of Georg's shirts.

"You'll ruin your eyes. The sun has all but disappeared into the horizon," Georg said.

"I'm turning in," Christian said. "Papa has asked that I help him in the field. I'll be up early and gone before you rise." He bent over to kiss his sister on the cheek, and she returned a polite affection.

"Things are still stiff between you," Georg said after Christian had withdrawn inside.

"I need time. Time to truly forget what my brother has done to us."

"But are you capable?"

With that, Georg left his wife alone in the dusk.


*Capable!* The word kept turning over in her mind. Elisabeth sat alone in the kitchen, staring into the hearth. Everyone was in bed. She knew exactly what her husband meant. The first three years of their marriage had not been consummated. She had stubbornly refused to let go of Peter. Only through her husband's deep devotion and endless fortitude did her feelings for him grow to match his mature love for her, the love he so deserved. In time, she took her pangs for Peter to be nothing more than a young girl's infatuation. What remained of her affection for Peter was simply a tenderness toward her son's father.

The situation now was different. Elisabeth was responsible for two children, to protect them from anything lurking in the hidden corners of their new world. Where was her brother's allegiance? Disappointment soon gave way to outrage when she mulled over the words he had spoken about another family— barbaric primitives she had feared. How could he treat his own family with such disdain, being absent all that time?

Images of Mama drifted back to her. She squeezed her eyes shut to stop a fresh flow of tears and pleaded for Mama to give her guidance. As she hugged the quilt around her shoulders, she remembered the hours Mama spent sewing it for her wedding. Oh, she so wanted to lay her head once more upon her mother's lap, to feel the warmth of Mama's hand upon her forehead, to hear her comforting words, to be sheltered under her protection. These unfulfilled yearnings left her feeling empty and melancholic.

She could wish all she wanted to have things as they were before, but it could never be. Just as it could never be the same again for her and Christian. *I cannot move on,* she decided.

# Chapter Eleven

JUNE 1757

*F*og drifted in waves from the sea, briefly claiming the fields before the sun burned through. Christian gripped the handles of the turn wrest and steadied the mouldboard as it burrowed long, dusty furrows through the soil. Flies buzzed around his head as he snapped the switch above the ox's backside.

Several rows down, Michael plodded along the narrow trenches sowing the seeds. Instead of scattering seed by hand, they had been lucky enough to borrow the neighbour's seed drill two days ago. New seedlings drank what scant moisture there was from the frequent and heavy fog. Christian had worked hard with Papa the past two weeks to clear additional land for next year's crops, and for the last three nights, he had stayed overnight, sleeping in the barn. It had been a welcome relief from the mounting unease he experienced with Elisabeth, which gave Christian more reason not to approach Papa about his leaving.

As the sun climbed higher, blue sky dominated. Christian took over the sowing while Papa used the ox to pull up rotted tree stumps. Humidity intensified and the grit clung to his wet skin, his breeches growing more uncomfortable.

Philip Knaut picked his way across the field toward Christian. Michael soon joined them. "How did the meeting go?" he asked.

"Gut. Much more accomplished than at the previous one," Philip replied.

"We're about to take a break. Do you have time to talk about it?" Michael said, wiping the sweat that trickled from his forehead.

"I was hoping you'd say that."

"Come, then. Your wife and Hanna have been busy all morning with that new cookery book."

The three made their way to a bench in the shadow of an oak tree. Christian hauled up the bucket of water from the well and poured ladleful after ladleful of welcome relief over his head before handing it over to Papa. The cool drips running down his back made him shudder.

"Has Governor Lawrence changed his mind on the legislative assembly?" Michael asked.

Philip shook his head. "A group of merchants and settlers in Halifax are now supporting his opposition of it—hoping for personal office appointments under the governor. You may have seen a petition around town with trumped-up stories coercing people to sign."

Michael nodded. "Yesterday, Heinrich was approached. He was told if there were an Assembly, the victuals would stop."

Christian fumed. "That is deceit at its lowest. Bully tactics!"

"The council consists mainly of Halifax merchants appointed by the governor. It's been suggested Lunenburg would benefit from an allowance of money instead of food rations. You can see how they would gain from having no elected body. These merchants would still be in control and benefit from the settlers purchasing from them."

Michael shook his head, frowning. "But for us to have a say, an Assembly is necessary."

"Relax. The Board certainly wants to make this province self-reliant, and to impose taxes the Assembly must be established. London ordered Lawrence to go forward with it. There is to be no delay, were their words." Philip paused a moment. "Remember, one of the reasons Lawrence didn't want the Assembly was because we are not yet in a position to pay taxes."

"Hopefully our lot will improve soon," Michael said.

"Is there a date in mind for the election?" Christian asked.

"Not until more people are naturalized, " Philip said. "Michael, if the election is expected to take place after your naturalization, I wouldn't be opposed to you putting your name in as a candidate. As you know, I have officially put mine in. Two are to be elected from Lunenburg."

"You flatter me, and it's tempting." Michael grinned and reached deep into his pocket for his pipe. "Are there any new issues to be addressed?"

"Nothing new. Of course, the larger acreages could be priority."

Christian tensed up. The current government, the proposed legislative body, and the Crown were all key components of a pompous authority over land. The large-scale lot extensions just drove the point home. It was as if everyone was completely devoid of empathy as they blindly went about their business, sheltered within their own self-righteousness.

"I'll think on it," Michael said, puffing hard on his pipe.

They touched on the land topic before saying their farewells to Philip. As Christian turned to go back to work, Michael stopped him. "What are your thoughts of me running?"

"That's your decision alone and not for me to speculate. If you're asking for my permission, I can't give it."

"I'm not seeking your consent, just your opinion," Michael snapped.

"For what it's worth, I have difficulty seeing anybody's side here. I don't feel I could give an opinion anyone would really want to hear. We ask, the government gives. Do they even have that right?"

"What are you talking about, pray tell?"

"You can't see it, can you, Papa? Before Philip left, he brought up the subject of the possibility of New Englanders applying for grants here."

"Ja. To take up the Acadian farmlands."

"And to settle fishing ports west of LaHave. How the hell can the British think so highly of themselves as to gift or sell portions of Nova Scotia away from an entire People who were here centuries before we arrived? It sickens me what we—nein, *you*—have been reduced to for your own selfish reasons."

"Selfish is not what I would call making a new life for you. To stay in Hohctorf was no longer feasible. It was dangerous!" Michael raised his voice. "We put our trust in this government and worked our part as redemptioners. Verdammt! How can you stand there and say that after I built the roads to pay for our passage here? In Dartmouth, you even worked *with* me on the public works."

Christian turned and stared into the field—Papa's land.

"Don't look away from me, Christian!" Michael breathed a long sigh. "I don't recognize you anymore. What happened?"

"The Mi'kmaq happened. You say you put your faith in the governor and the Board, knowing they have done right by you. But are they behaving in a way that is just and beneficial to the Mi'kmaq?"

"I refuse to listen to such gibberish." Michael closed in on his son. Christian could smell the tobacco on his breath. "All these months, I suspected your words were not truthful to me. You turned your back on your family. Why? Answer me!"

Christian stepped back. "Remember Prince Eugen!"

"That's in the past. He has nothing to do with our situation."

"He has plenty to do with it! We were at best his peasants, his cheap labour." Christian defiantly stared back. "The past stays with us, Papa. How can you forget the rising taxes he demanded just to ensure he wouldn't lose his rich French lifestyle? Mein Gott! His soldiers threatened Mama's life if we didn't pay our taxes."

Michael flinched. "I don't see your point."

"We were prisoners in our own land. We needed a pass to travel anywhere. Trade was practically nonexistent with the imposed road tolls. When Eugen made visits to our district, I witnessed your rage as the soldiers devastated our fields just for the prince's enjoyment of the yearly hunt." Michael's eyes flashed in surprise. "Ja, Papa. You thought you were hiding your emotions from us. But we all saw it. You couldn't even benefit from what your fields produced, because they were exported. And you never saw a penny."

"That was in Württemberg."

"What's strange is we've brought our troubles to the Mi'kmaq. What we thought was left behind followed us here, did it not? Nova Scotia is now a pawn in the hands of the sovereign powers as they battle for dominance through misery."

"I still do not see—"

"Do you not see the one similarity? Eugen, devoid of any respect, rode roughshod over us with no thought of our worthiness, and now the Mi'kmaw territories are being confiscated by the same government you have put all your hopes into. Their lives are slowly being snuffed out by our greed, as we cut off their sustenance, river after river."

"You don't make any sense. The British Crown owns Nova Scotia."

"Do they? As Eugen violated the legal rights of his subjects, so have the British violated the rights of the Mi'kmaq and the Maliseet."

"Your words are treasonous! You talk as if—" He stopped at an abrupt realization. "You are dead to me and this family if your loyalty is where I think it is. Your allegiance is crudely distorted."

Christian could taste the finality and hatred of his father's remarks. "When you could not mould me to your ways, you gave up. Your faith in me has long been extinguished. For Christ's sake, you gave me up for dead!" Christian pounced on his papa's attempt to reply. "Ja! I saw the family bible. Christian Heber—died 1752."

"That is unfair!" Michael screamed at his son, just as Hanna came within earshot. "Get out of my sight. Go to where your new loyalties lie. You're no longer welcome here." Michael took a swing at Christian's head but missed as Christian fell backward to dodge the blow.

"Papa!" Hanna grabbed his arm to pull it back.

"Let me ask you," Christian lashed back. "You have said *they* murder in darkness. Did you not fight in your youth against the atrocities you endured, just to protect your young family? Did not Jakob, your eldest son, my brother, follow in your footsteps? Ja, Papa, you did as much. And now you think less of the Mi'kmaq for doing the same as you."

"How dare you speak of my integrity in the same sentence as *them!*" Michael spit onto his son's boot.

"You make it very easy for me to leave for good," Christian uttered vehemently.

When he turned on his heels to head for the barn, his papa yelled, "Why? Why do you choose those heathens over your own family?"

Christian stopped but kept his back to him.

"Answer me! Are you Indian or German?"

Christian did not turn around. "I am your son!" He walked away.

Hanna's words followed him. "Papa! Do something! Bitte, I beg you. You can't allow this to happen." She was sobbing.

Christian heard Michael stomp to the house, his sister calling after him. He gathered what little he had and rummaged through the straw for his medicine pouch. He picked stray pieces from the quilled motif before throwing the strap over his head, then grabbed his gun. His sister was waiting when he headed out the door.

"Here, I gathered bread and dried beef." Hanna handed over the cloth sack. "Before you leave, you must at least try to mend things with Papa." She was weeping.

He gazed into her crestfallen face and slowly shook his head.

"For Elisabeth! You must," she pleaded.

"I ask that you speak to her for me. If her reaction is only a tenth of his, that would still be too much for me to handle right now."

"I can't bear to lose you again. This is all too fresh for him. Papa just needs time," she pleaded.

Christian wished with all his heart he could kiss her hurt away as he had when she was little. But he would speak his heart. He held her small hand in his. "It's a delicate dance for us, Hanna. At times, the movements must take us far from each other. Remember, the tether is never severed, only stretched."

"And sometimes the best thing to do for the other person is to let go," Hanna whispered through her tears.

Christian hugged his sister tight to his chest, then left. Before he cut across the field, he glanced at the house only to see Papa turn back inside and shut the door.

# Chapter Twelve

JUNE 1757

Last night, lightning lit up the sky like a beacon. The jagged arrows ended their journey with ear-splitting cracks inside the forest. This morning, the wind had shifted, filling the sky with thick smoke. Five days ago, Christian had had no difficulty in finding the cave. Trees were now displaying their Spring leaves, and he was sure Eagle Feather would arrive soon but worried that the forest fire had cut off his path.

There had been no intruders since his first night here, human or animal. Nonetheless, last night he had heard movement; a careful, armed search revealed nothing. That sense of being watched continued throughout the night, and it left him jumpy, exhausted from lack of sleep.

There was little left after rationing the food his sister had given him, but he had snared a rabbit yesterday and foraged roots and mushrooms. When Christian first opened the sack, it revealed more than food. At the bottom lay a small wooden flute Papa had carved for him when he was a boy. Long ago, Christian thought it had been mislaid; he had not set eyes upon it since they had arrived in the new land. *Hanna must have found it and kept it for safekeeping*, he thought. He ran his hand over the smooth wood and counted each of the six holes with the tip of his finger. He chuckled to himself when he saw tiny teeth marks notched into the wood. As a child, he was forever biting down on the mouthpiece.

After he munched on bitter cress, clover, and the last of the dried beef, he watched a black squirrel sitting near him nibbling on a morsel of tree bark. "You look good enough to eat," he said, before it scurried away into the underbrush. He followed it only to be attacked from behind, knocked flat on his face. His assailant straddled him so he could not move. As he struggled to free himself, he screamed.

"You need to be on your guard, my beloved brother," Eagle Feather said, playfully holding a clump of Bear Cub's hair. He dismounted and extended his hand. "And, you shriek like a girl."

Bear Cub laughed aloud, yanking hard on the help, toppling Eagle Feather over. "As you yourself must be ready. Call me by my Mi'kmaw name! Go on, I need to hear it," he said, brushing the debris from his clothes.

"Bear Cub!" Eagle Feather pronounced emphatically. "You have been sorely missed. Singing Sparrow has demanded I give you this." With his left arm, he gave Bear Cub a rough embrace before letting go.

"You have no idea how I have longed for this moment." The two of them rested their right hand upon each other's chest. "Good to see you, my brother. The Great Spirit is truly smiling on us today."

"Not too far from here, the canoe is ready to take us upriver to our village. We are camped farther inland than our father would have liked."

"What about the fire?"

"It will not hamper our journey, the wind has changed again. It is taking the fire farther west. We will put our faith in the One who watches us to bring rain." Eagle Feather walked away, then stopped. "It must have been difficult for you to leave."

Bear Cub was still angry. "Somewhat," he replied. He placed the musket strap over his head and followed his brother through the woodland.

As Eagle Feather forged ahead, Bear Cub turned at the sound of twigs breaking underfoot but could see nothing. He looked once more but toward the cave. There was a flash of a red-coloured coat as a man scrambled down an embankment and out of view. He wore no hat. The last thing Bear Cub noticed was a large patch of white hair. Then a second man followed. Bear Cub squinted; he looked like Detleff.

Bear Cub stopped his brother. "I'm going back," he said and explained. They retraced their steps and searched where the two men had disappeared but turned up nothing.

The fact that someone had followed him weighed heavily on Bear Cub's mind. His uneasiness did not wane even when they paddled past the steep rocky cliffs that flanked both sides of the river on their way home. The jagged formations—the rock people—came to life through the stories Bear Cub had heard. While not all rocks were people, there were shape-changers who chose these forms to rest or to hide until coming alive again as powerful beings.

Throughout the journey, they could hear the faint roar of rapids. Bear Cub was thankful for his brother's expertise in navigating through the whitewater. Then, the river suddenly revealed tree-lined banks and silence, and as they continued, the monstrous rocks slowly faded away.

Now, Bear Cub could see many wikuoml—it appeared that this Spring, the village had more than tripled. He spotted Singing Sparrow holding a puppy, and his heart leapt. When they beached, they were greeted by everyone. To Bear Cub, it was the warm embraces of White Cloud, Morning Dove, and his beloved that signified home.

# Chapter Thirteen



Even though Singing Sparrow's birth eighteen Winters ago had occurred amid growing uncertainties and suspicions of the new people to Mi'kma'ki, it was over the past few moons that a sense of foreboding had gained momentum. *This menace is vastly different from the Elders' stories of our history*, she thought. *These transformations seem to be occurring more rapidly.* She sensed the uneasiness from her parents, especially in her father's withdrawals to be alone and the lowered voices with the visiting Nikanus. Within the village, talk of war became more loudly pronounced than the joyous chants of a successful day's hunt.

Their self-reliance was slowly waning to dependence. Two nights ago, the usual hatchets, clothing, and ammunition had arrived. Even more came from the French—dried peas and fruit, stale flour, and hard biscuits. With these new foods, sicknesses soon followed, something Singing Sparrow had witnessed before. In return for these commodities, they traded bags made from reeds or animal skins, and various furs. The pelts piled higher in the compound as the men began over-trapping. That left little time to hunt for their own food. The new people were increasing in numbers, and they were using the same canoe routes as the People were. Because the settlers did not know how to live the teachings of the Creator, Mother Earth was beginning to show her displeasure.

Singing Sparrow recalled the stories of the much smaller camps dispersed over Mi'kma'ki, deliberately spaced out to ensure the People had enough food. Lately, the Summer camps were becoming overly concentrated, but she understood why— her father had always welcomed the sick and the starving. The past Winter had been one with little snow, warmer and wetter. The lakes and ponds did not freeze. No beavers could be hunted, and caribou were scarce. As the villages grew in numbers, it put a strain on the surrounding land, and herds thinned.

Singing Sparrow had been taught the practice of sharing from a very young age. Her mother preached the importance of maintaining a lasting relationship with all of creation. Things must remain in balance, her mother said. *This wisdom is gathered from our ancestors.* She was baffled. *Is this not taught to the new people? Are they not disciplined to share?*

Bear Cub had returned with talk of fortifications built to protect the new settlements. Of fences built. Fences erected for what? To separate themselves from each other? To keep something or someone out? Why would they restrict people from land? Singing Sparrow was frightened of these changes. Several of the People had left for Louisbourg to defend the fort against the British. Peter was one who had readily volunteered.

She lay her unfinished basket down and listened. Musical notes danced on the cool air. *Bear Cub,* she thought, and followed the music. She found him sitting at a secluded cove. The puppy she had gifted him lay beside him asleep. Alawei. Bear Cub had named her as such because she was so small. Wherever he was, the pup was not far behind.

"Teach me!" she said eagerly and sat on a rock beside him.

The flute stopped abruptly. "You shouldn't be here alone. If your mother catches us—"

"Shh. I will be gone before she finds us." She stared down at the flute. "Please, I wish to know. I never learned."

Bear Cub placed the instrument into her hands and manoeuvred her fingers over the tiny holes. "Blow softly here." He pointed to the mouthpiece.

His flute had a much higher pitch than the larger one her father played.

"In time, I'll teach you a song," Bear Cub said.

He turned and stared at the water rippling at the touch of a dragonfly nymph skimming the surface. A fish appeared from beneath, nipped it, and was gone.

"You are sad, Bear Cub. Do you miss your family?"

"You are my family now. I am scared for you and your People." Bear Cub rested Singing Sparrow's hand in his and entwined his fingers in hers. "Our People," he corrected. "Where will this all end?"

"We all come from a spirit-driven place, the same Great Spirit. I need to believe that these are only adjustments through many misunderstandings."

"We're past that! Who will benefit from such adjustments? So far, I can only see it will not be the Mi'kmaq."

Singing Sparrow lay her hand on his arm, stroking his small bleached hairs. "I am angry. They want us to be like them at the expense of our lifeways. The treaties are lacking in Spirit and the understanding of the way we live."

Bear Cub concurred. "We all need to embrace the rights of Mother Earth. So do our enemies."

"Hearing what our ancestors have to teach us makes us

survivors." Singing Sparrow slipped her hand into his and squeezed it tight.

This was the first time they had been alone since Bear Cub's return. Singing Sparrow could still feel the warmth of his arms from when they had embraced two moons ago. She needed so much to be held again without the watchful eyes of her parents. Her eyes locked with Bear Cub's and she quivered at the unexpected touch of his hand softly stroking her hair. His fingers played with the ends of her long tresses, and she closed her eyes to relish the new sensation. Then, he tenderly touched her lips with his. The moment lingered until Alawei's wet nose nudged up between them.

"The chaperone." Bear Cub sighed, raising an eyebrow.


Bear Cub awoke to loud voices. The entire dwelling was in turmoil.

"Stay here!" White Cloud ordered before stepping outside. It was still dark, only the central fire in the compound was glowing. The promise of needed rain had not materialized.

"Where is Eagle Feather?" Morning Dove's voice screeched in anxiety.

Singing Sparrow crouched down in front of the open doorblanket. Bear Cub ventured outside, telling the two women to stay put. The dog followed him.

"Moqwe, Alawei! Stay," he commanded. Singing Sparrow reached out to hold the puppy. Most of the compound was now awake.

Quarrelling escalated to a frenzy before an assault erupted. Calm Water was one of a group of men who restrained the instigators from behind by latching onto flailing arms. Bear Cub instinctively put himself into the thick of it just when Eagle

Feather collapsed to the ground, heaving as he vomited. There was an undeniable stink of sour rum.

Two men proved to be the most dangerous. Each of them held a gun, which they fired carelessly above the crowd before one aimed at one of the Elders. A musket ball forced Sulia'n back against a tree trunk before he slumped forward.

"Grab them!" White Cloud commanded.

Bear Cub rushed at the shooter and tackled him to the ground. Others rounded up the intoxicated, shoving them into a nearby wikuom. White Cloud screamed more commands as he scooped up Sulia'n and rushed inside Calm Water's wikuom.

Bear Cub stared down at his brother. "Feeling better now?"

Eagle Feather angrily knocked away the extended hand of help. This was a side of his brother Bear Cub had never seen before.


EMBARRASSMENT, HUMILIATION, AND DISGRACE WERE all understatements for what Eagle Feather was feeling as he rapidly blinked his eyes into focus. He found himself prone on the forest floor—spruce needles pricking his skin. At a stab of pain, he rubbed his cheek to soothe the tenderness. There was an enormous bruise on his forearm. Slowly he sat upright. His mind was very groggy until suddenly last night's chaos became all too clear. The sound of familiar voices indicated he had not strayed far from the village.

One searing and prominent memory came to the forefront—those eyes. As brief as the encounter had been, when their eyes locked, the hurt in his father's glare had cut through him as a knife through fish.

He brushed the debris from his clothes and composed himself before entering the commotion of morning activities. His stomach turned somersaults at the smell of smoked meat;

nausea gripped him at the sight of oily soup scooped into a bowl. His nose wrinkled at the strong smell of cod guts used as lobster bait. Then, dread of what he would face when meeting his father took over. He was heavy-footed as he made his way home. *It is too quiet*, he thought. The door-blanket was open. When he entered, his mother was alone. Morning Dove glanced in his direction and made him sit. No words were exchanged while she fussed over his injuries. She opened the jar of boiled pussy willow bark, smoothed the thick molasses-like salve over the injured arm, and covered it with a large plantain leaf.

The look in his eyes must have spoken volumes. She spoke briefly. "Do not plead. Save your words for your father. I see him coming now." Morning Dove slipped out quietly.

Eagle Feather overheard his father—Sulia'n had died during the night. His heart sank. When his father entered, he quickly stood up. His temples throbbed, his muscles were stiff.

"What happened?" White Cloud sputtered.

Eagle Feather's stomach churned again. He really did not know. "When the sun set, I found the same Mi'kmaw men from our village you caught two moons ago. They were deep into the woods behind the sweat lodge, where the two rivers meet. They could barely stand. The others were tapping into a rum keg. I doubt if they remember much."

"And you?"

Eagle Feather averted his eyes and ignored the question. "One was arguing over the number of skins they traded for the liquor."

"How many?"

Some of the best skins held to trade for food had recently been disappearing from the village. "Six beavers. I am not aware where they hid the other skins, nor do I remember if they told me. There were none where the kegs were stored. They spoke of needing more beaver and caribou."

"Is that all you can recall?"

"E'e." Despite his extreme unease, Eagle Feather looked back at his father, whose anguish seemed to deepen the lines on his face. "I have dishonoured and shamed you," Eagle Feather said. "For you to bear this pain is unforgivable. I deserve nothing but your wrath." He paused, then lowered his head. "Show it!" It took all his energy to yell it out.

White Cloud's forehead furrowed. "And what would that accomplish? E'e, I was angry—I still am. Do you need my temper to diminish your own torment? Must I punish you as a child who has done wrong? That is not me. You are a man. A grown man who must accept the consequences of his actions. Instead, I grieve for you. My sorrow is not mine entirely to bear." He laid a hand on his son's shoulder, giving a squeeze of assurance. "I see your anguish. You do not need me to point it out," his father said, barely above a whisper.

"How can I hold my head high knowing I have dishonoured you, my father?"

When White Cloud sat down beside him, a warm breath lightly touched his cheek.

"You alone did that to yourself."

Eagle Feather could not look his father in the eyes.

After a strained, long silence, his father added, "But I understand."

"You did foolish things?"

White Cloud nodded and cleared his throat. "When you were a small boy, you wanted to follow in my footsteps."

Eagle Feather looked up at his father whose eyes softened toward him.

"You must earn the right to lead, my son. You still have

much to learn. The best Nikanus shows compassion not only to the People but to himself."

Eagle Feather's own suffering intensified. He lifted the necklace from his neck and put the caribou string over his father's head. Two bear claws now lay flat against White Cloud's smooth dark chest. "Forgive me."

"This is your most treasured possession. From the first bear you killed. I shall not accept this," White Cloud said, and started to remove the gift.

Eagle Feather stayed him with his hand. "You helped me; I was not alone in the hunt. I need your pardon. It is yours to wear."

"I accept. But you need to forgive yourself, my son."

Two sunrises passed before Eagle Feather approached him. Bear Cub accepted the apology, but he was still burdened. "My beloved brother, it is I who regret my words in making light of your situation. I must ask for your forgiveness."

"True." Eagle Feather laughed and put Bear Cub in a playful headlock. "Now, onto nourishment. We will check the fence weir at the mouth of the river. The tide is out. How many mackerel do you think the tide caught?" Most of the camp was deserted of men; they had left earlier in their individual hunting task groups.

Bear Cub climbed into the canoe. "What will happen to the one who killed Sulia'n?" He knew the community circle had met. They had agreed not to expel any from the village but to hold counselling sessions with the Elders for the two who were armed. Others refused help and left the village of their own accord.

"He and Sulia'n's family have each been assigned an Elder for guidance," Eagle Feather explained.

Bear Cub, who had previously known only of hard labour, filthy prisons, and public executions for crimes, was continually learning and adjusting to the Mi'kmaw justice system. "It seems a light sentence," he said.

"To restore their spirit to peace and harmony? Moqwe. It is not only for them but for the community. The offender and the victim's family will face each other as well. How can your prisons reform?"

Bear Cub could not think of any subjected to such lenient consequences and said so.

"It is unthinkable to ostracize those who make mistakes and leave them to their own devices. We gain nothing by your way. To punish that individual for his wrongdoing does not heal the individual nor the community. We build on healthy relationships, not fear, to foster the good in all," Eagle Feather said.

Bear Cub was deep in thought as his brother silently pushed the canoe into the water.


WHITE CLOUD RELISHED THE TIME alone, away from the hum of the village. He and Eagle Feather had checked the deadfall traps and snares earlier. Only one mink and a marten were caught, plus a few snared rabbits. *When the sun goes beneath the earth, we hunt ducks*, he decided. Calm Water's group was yet to return, and he wondered if their hunt for beaver and otters had been successful.

*How can we keep up this high demand? We are more dependent on the French supplies than I thought we would ever be.*

As he gazed across the lake, a balmy breeze sifted through his hair. She whispered about his ancestors' presence. The stirring of leaves behind him uttered their wisdom. Water ripples ebbed and flowed over his bare feet, nudging his spirit. He closed his eyes to listen. A soft hand slipped into his reality, and his wife smiled up at him.

"You left before we spoke. Our son is good now?" Morning Dove asked.

"He is troubled, but you may put your worries to rest. We have taught him well." White Cloud grinned.

"And you, my husband? Would you prefer I leave you to your thoughts?"

White Cloud squeezed her hand, encouraging her to stay. He squinted at Na'ku'set, the giver of light and heat, who had started his descent beneath the earth.

In the fading light they watched a tiny bird attack a raven many times her size to save her nest of fledglings. "As that small creature's babies are threatened, so are we," White Cloud said matter-of-factly. "And as Eagle Feather told me once, there is a right time to be aggressive." He turned to his wife.

"We all seek to survive," she said, "but often the expense is death. Such is existence. To survive, we must adapt to life's challenges and transformations."

A runner suddenly appeared in the compound and approached the two of them. He was from the next village and had started out at sunrise. He carried a belt covered in purple and white shells made from clams and sea snails. The message on the wampum belt was grim. At the last moon, a Mi'kmaw village had been attacked, leaving no survivors. All were scalped—nothing had been left but smouldering rubble. In retaliation, British soldiers had been killed along a nearby footpath.

White Cloud's heart raced as he was suddenly seized by hate. The deaths of the soldiers provided the only respite from his heartache.

# Chapter Fourteen



Three nights ago, from a dry sandy place called Oqomkikiaq, Jacques Saouque travelled to their village with four Elders. The Nikanus brought gifts of bear grease, sweetgrass, and birchbark boxes of the creamy white fat rendered from crushed moose bones. No village was without a supply of this delicacy, an excellent source of energy when eaten by itself, especially during the Winter moons.

The surprise visit was welcomed with songs and dance, and speeches extolled the virtues of both the hosts and the guests. The sonorous echo of drums continued long afterward, mimicking the heartbeat of Mother Earth. At times, the chants were like haunting pleas to Jikeyulkw. The songs, passed on from the old times, reflected the differing lyrical notes of the world around them. Bear Cub recognized the harsh cries of the seagulls and the hoots, cackles, and caws that owls make during mating.

The visit also involved discussions between White Cloud and Jacques; Bear Cub assumed they were about the massacre. Within their village of now almost two hundred, he had expected a great deal more talk of the butchery. Instead, the atmosphere was clouded with silence as everyone carried on with their work. Last night a sharing circle revealed their dread of what the future held for them.

Now, Bear Cub stood knee-deep in the river with his brother. They were fixing the linear brush weir, which spanned almost one hundred feet. White Cloud, Calm Water, and their guests were replacing damaged and missing spruce branches throughout. The weir had been reconstructed in the Spring after the destruction of the Winter ice; it had needed a repair or two since. The large wooden stakes that they drove into the river bottom now were vertical, no longer showing a severe list. Bear Cub pounded them farther into the silted riverbed while Eagle Feather held them steady and straight.

The tide was coming in and the others had gone on ahead. Bear Cub and Eagle Feather were alone as they waded through the river grasses to the canoe.

"Alawei! Come here, girl!" Bear Cub commanded as the dog swam toward him. He lifted her dripping wet onto the bench of the canoe, then ducked before she shook her fur dry. They canoed upstream then portaged to a smaller river that led to the ka't field camp. Howls of laughter grew closer. The tide had dropped behind the stone weir, leaving hundreds of trapped eels slithering about in shallow pools of water. Bear Cub had soon learned how important these fish were to the Mi'kmaq. Eel was used in ceremonies and for medicine and was often the only food source to get them through harsh Winters, eaten cooked or raw. Bear Cub favoured ka't as it tasted sweet, like lobster. He thrust his spear, and the two outside prongs sank deep into the soft river bottom. The middle spike penetrated the long slithering body. One by one, he threw the eels onto the shore to be deslimed. In thanks, pieces of eel flesh were returned to the waters. The Elders then voyaged back to the main camp while

Bear Cub, Eagle Feather, White Cloud, and Jacques remained, intending to follow the others shortly.

Alawei cocked her head, then suddenly bolted into the woods. Bear Cub whistled for her, but she kept running, her barks fading away.

"Must have seen an animal—I will get her," Eagle Feather offered and disappeared into the forest.

Scooping the eels into baskets, Bear Cub heard footsteps from behind. Assuming his brother had returned, he stood up and spun around. He was face to face with Detleff Jessen. Two other soldiers had White Cloud and Jacques at gunpoint. On the outer woodland ridges, another six British soldiers stood armed in red coats. Detleff squinted as he searched Bear Cub's face. Bear Cub's mouth dropped.

"Ah, you're a good liar. Move!" Detleff ordered.

As Bear Cub walked toward White Cloud, Detleff repeatedly pushed his pistol into Bear Cub's ribs from behind. The jarring pain jolted Bear Cub until he stood next to White Cloud and Jacques.

One of the soldiers spoke English to Detleff. "If they answer to King Louis, a substantial bounty has just presented itself."

Bear Cub didn't understand until Jacques answered in Mi'kmaw. "We answer to no one, least of all your King George."

Bear Cub translated his words into German, speaking directly to Detleff.

"All the more reason to take you in," Detleff said, "to avenge the blood the Brissang family shed in the colony."

Bear Cub translated.

"Our hands are not stained. We take soldiers as prisoners and turn them over to the French," White Cloud replied. "On our hunting grounds, British soldiers kill our women who gather food."

Bear Cub interrupted to translate again.

White Cloud continued. "Four of our people approached your fort in Annapolis Royal to make peace. In good faith, two remained as hostages. Two returned and set out with two Nikanus for Lunenburg. They were met with gunfire."

"They should have been more forthright of their purpose. We were unaware," Detleff replied after the translation.

"You make it difficult by letting your guns speak first."

"Well, at the moment, you're in no position to put us in chains." One of the soldiers laughed and readjusted his musket, aiming at White Cloud.

The translation ended and White Cloud scrutinized Detleff with contempt. "You force our camps away from the coast. Do you also begrudge us this land you now stand upon?" He looked to Bear Cub. "Tell them!"

"We stand on King George's lands." The soldier lunged forward to attack, but Detleff shoved his forearm beneath the musket, forcing it skyward. It triggered a deafening crack as it was discharged. His ensign was flung backward, which knocked his hat to the ground and revealed a large patch of white in his brown hair. Bear Cub's stomach sank. *The cave! Detleff was the second man. They followed us. Do these men carry the bloodstains of an entire Mi'kmaw village?*

White Cloud mocked him with laughter. "We govern ourselves with our own laws. You are not the master of me."

Bear Cub translated, then all of the infantrymen cocked their guns.

"Enough! Stand down!" Detleff ordered gruffly.

Bear Cub noticed a slight movement in the woods in front of him. Eagle Feather caught his eye as he quietly squatted down in the brush, holding Alawei back.

White Cloud stared down at Detleff and grunted. "Sharing

our land is one thing, but stealing it is an entirely different matter."

The ensign had scrambled to his feet. After listening to Bear Cub, he spat, "In '13, the Utrecht Treaty ceded these lands to us."

Jacques replied, "Our land was not for the French king to give away. This treaty you speak of was agreed between the two Crowns and without our knowledge."

Another attempt to rush at White Cloud was abruptly stopped when Detleff shoved his ensign back.

"The '52 treaty gave us the freedom to hunt in any place but Annapolis," Jacques said.

Bear Cub related his words to the lieutenant.

"That treaty allows us to enter these lands for our own enjoyment and with no retribution from you," Detleff rebutted. "Our colonists are living in a small portion of Nova Scotia," he added. "You can just as easily hunt elsewhere."

Bear Cub's own anger got the better of him, and he replied in German, "Why should they change?"

"Because the king rules them," Detleff said.

When Bear Cub translated, he watched the fire grow in White Cloud's eyes. He was dumbfounded at White Cloud's calm demeanour in answering.

"You can live beside us, but do not keep us out, away from our food. You do not know our ways. We hunt and fish where it is most abundant and only take what we need."

Detleff was defiant. "I'm only aware of one Shubenacadie tribe who have the liberty to do this. I'm aware of no other tribes who signed." He looked to Bear Cub. "Tell your Chief that!"

With translation completed, White Cloud retorted, "Kopit's territory is vast and includes this land you stand on. We continue to hunt and fish as before!"

Detleff ignored what was said and blurted, "We are scouting

for those who have scalped our soldiers on a trail not far from here. As well as the recent raid in—"

Jacques cut him off. "As my brother stated, our hands are clean."

Bear Cub wondered if those who had left their village had been in another drunken stupor and were responsible.

"Two others are missing—Leonard Gorckum and Kasper Gerhart." Detleff gazed hard at Bear Cub, who stared blankly back at his accuser.

"Do you wish to arrest us on trumped-up assumptions?" White Cloud asked. "Have you persecuted any who have murdered *our* people?" He glared at the soldier while Bear Cub translated. "Even if I knew those who have dirtied their hands with English blood, I could not and would not reveal their whereabouts to you, as the treaties you sign are lies. You do not know what justice is, my brother!"

"You have agreed not to molest any of His Majesty's subjects on any existing settlements," Detleff shot back.

"That does not include your Lunenburg and Mahone Bay, which did not exist at the time of the treaty," White Cloud answered.

"Is this your admittance?"

"Moqwe. You trick us with your words to justify our arrest. Look elsewhere!"

Detleff scoffed at Bear Cub. "I wonder if traitors bring in a higher price."

Eagle Feather stepped out of hiding and aimed his musket at the back of one of the soldiers standing next to his cohorts. "I will shoot to kill!" he announced.

White Cloud lifted his own weapon, pointing it straight at Detleff, as did Jacques and Bear Cub, positioning their guns directly at the two soldiers who stood behind the lieutenant.

One foolhardy soldier rushed at Eagle Feather's feet, knocking him backward. Alawei attacked the assailant, gripping his arm in her teeth. Bear Cub could see blood rapidly staining the white shirt.

Detleff yelled, "Call the damn dog off!" as the others reached for their weapons. Jacques fired his musket near the feet of one of the soldiers.

White Cloud called to Detleff in a ploy to defuse the situation. "There are other Mi'kmaq hiding, ready to attack."

Detleff looked to Bear Cub for the meaning and retorted, "You bluff."

"He doesn't believe you, my father," Bear Cub said.

White Cloud was ready to trigger the musket. "Do you want to take the chance?"

On Detleff's orders, everyone gathered their guns. Eagle Feather yanked Alawei free of the soldier she had attacked. Before the invaders walked away, Detleff leered at Bear Cub, "I'm not finished with you, Christian!"

"What do you have against me?"

"The fact that you turned to the wrong side of the fence is enough." Detleff walked away and Bear Cub was flooded with dread. He clutched his hands to keep them from shaking.

BY THE TIME THEY HAD returned, the demonstration of archery skills was underway, and others in the camp were readying the canoes for the races on the lake. White Cloud stood back, away from the crowds. He could hear the spectators urging their favourites to win, but his mind remained with the earlier confrontation. Halfway through the competition, Jacques headed toward White Cloud, his team having been defeated.

"You are off your game, my brother," White Cloud quipped.

"E'e, we needed your skill," Jacques answered, as he laid his cedar arrow atop the bow. "Can I convince you yet to join us?"

Many times, White Cloud and Jacques had entered on opposing teams in stiff competition, all the while quarrelling with each other in jest as to who was better. "I always said you would need me one day." White Cloud grinned. "It will be a while before the canoe races begin. Let us retreat."

Now alone inside a wikuom, the two sat on blankets of animal hide as White Cloud lit the pipe with an inflamed sweet-grass braid. He inhaled deeply on the long wooden stem as the flame moved over the tightly stuffed tobacco. Once it caught, he puffed small clouds of sweet-smelling smoke out of the corner of his mouth. He repeated this several times before he was assured of its stability. White Cloud released smoke in each of the four directions, sending his prayers with it.

"How can you ignore what happened?" White Cloud asked.

Jacques shrugged. "Do not be deceived—it lays heavy with me. But I need a diversion."

White Cloud remained silent.

"May your prayers be answered, my friend," Jacques said.

"You have known me for more Winters than I care to count. Have you known me to struggle in my decisions?"

"Never. When we returned, you had no problem sending out the scouting party with your son in charge."

"They will shadow that man Bear Cub called Detleff, as he is not to be trusted."

"You must be proud of your son today. He showed much courage," Jacques said.

"The act was foolish."

Jacques sighed. "Have you forgotten how impetuous we were in our youth?"

White Cloud grinned impishly. He remembered all too well how careless they both had been in their rash choices. And in life-and-death situations.

"When the bear attacked me, you rushed at him, yelling and pounding his back with your fists." Jacques tapped his chin with his forefinger. "And there was that long trek inland in Sipekne'katik. We were gone for two Winter moons. We were green in our young minds and hungry, and you tore into a beaver lodge and grabbed a beaver with your bare hands."

"He was tasty but on the stringy side." White Cloud laughed. He passed the pipe to his friend. Then, he turned serious. "Did you see the animal pelts in the compound? One hundred! And more newly trapped beavers ready to be skinned and sun-dried. This destruction is the beaver's demise. Our demise."

"There are no signs of it slowing down. The Elders speak of our grandfathers' stories of beaver trappings in disproportionate numbers. The assurance of plenty for our children has been broken."

"You heard the soldier's words. They refuse to acknowledge our rights. Their appetite for fish and furs is impossible to satisfy."

"We escaped with our lives. We may not be so fortunate next time," Jacques said, handing the pipe back. "I have heard talk of another treaty."

"I do not foresee it, let alone a successful one that will include specific lands." White Cloud pushed up to standing. "This is so foreign to me!" He started to pace, then suddenly stopped and looked down at his friend. "If we do not stop it, we will lose everything."

"I agree," Jacques answered. "The Mi'kmaw world cannot exist on newcomers' beliefs."

"I do not like this person you see before you. Hatred consumes me. The vile taste of rage rises in my throat. I feel powerless, and at times, I hesitate in my decisions."

"No one can fault you, my brother. The change you feel is not only within you." Jacques drew on the pipe. "The newcomers do not know us. If they did…" He exhaled the smoke. "I wonder, could there be *no* hatred?"

White Cloud raised an eyebrow in surprise.

"I have heard talk of more planned raids on Lunenburg and Mahone Bay," Jacques continued. "New France's governor is hoping to burn Lunenburg."

White Cloud reached over to cut off a chunk of smoked trout. He handed it to his friend and sat down again. "When Bear Cub returned, he talked of structures built where trees are cut into smaller pieces and their food harvests are ground. Bear Cub called them *mills*," White Cloud said, repeating the English word. "These are to be built at the mouths of Pijinuiskaq and Amaqapskekek where Bear Cub says they will disrupt the fish run. Lawrence now is recruiting more settlers from New England."

"We will do what we have to do and win!" Jacques declared. There was a long lull until he spoke again. "The wisdom of the ancient ones is my guide."

White Cloud's eyes lit up, and he smiled at his friend. He kept quiet as he drew on the pipe one last time and handed it back. "Their voices are not heard over my inner turmoil. Even their footsteps have been silenced."

"As my grandfather taught, only the wise continue to doubt. That is what makes them clear-sighted." Jacques lightly tapped out the remaining tobacco into the firepit. "Now, let us focus on a more pleasant and important task at hand. The canoe races are about to begin." He stood up and extended his hand to White Cloud. "I invite you to my team. Both of us will be assured to beat Calm Water." He slapped his friend's back and in all seriousness said, "For once, let us leave our troubles here in this wikuom."

White Cloud inclined his head and held open the door-blanket.

As the two exited into the bright sunlight, Jacques said, "I hear Bear Cub is soon to marry Singing Sparrow. This will be a joyous occasion." Then, the two were accosted to select their team.


WHITE CLOUD'S ANXIETY RAN HIGH while he waited for his son to return. Jacques could wait no longer and had left two nights after the games ended. Two sunrises after that, Eagle Feather returned with news of Detleff's detachment. Their camp was found a half-day's trek away. Hidden from view, the scouting party observed for three nights a small encampment of thirty but found nothing untoward. When Detleff led his men out early at sunrise on the fourth day, the Mi'kmaw party returned. They were heading east, Eagle Feather said. Still, White Cloud did not trust Detleff not to return.


BEAR CUB AGONIZED OVER IT. *I put the Mi'kmaq in further danger just by returning to Lunenburg. I should not have gone.* He walked to the lakeshore to join his brother. It was now Wikumkewiku's, the Animal-Calling Moon—the backside of Summer before the turning of the leaves—and it was tinder-dry as the Summer had been. It was also the time of the French traders.

White Cloud stood waiting as others slowly congregated. When the flotilla of ten canoes drifted in, the clatter of retrieved oars echoed across the lake. White Cloud and Calm Water waded in to steer the first arrival onto the sandy beach, avoiding any hidden boulders.

The one who alighted from the canoe was not a familiar face. His stature was short and stocky, but his swarthy face was thin under a bushy, dark beard. His cheeks were sunken, his nose sharp and pointy. In a gruff voice he gave a cheery "Bonjour," then "Kwe'" and introduced himself as André. There was a distinctive scent about him, a mustiness mixed with body odour. André was wordy as he described the carnage of the French raid on the Pisiguit post. Thirteen British soldiers had been killed.

"En route, the guerilla bands of Acadians strengthened their numbers with Mi'kmaq. They seized most of the provisions from the fort before it burned to the ground," André said.

Bear Cub surveyed the variety of wares that lay in the canoes, from copper cooking pots and kettles to weapons. Piles of colourful cloths lay beside white woollen blankets, hatchets, and knives. The Mi'kmaw parchment pelts had already been piled on the shore for trading, along with durable wooden handles to fit the settlers' tools. Axe handles and paddles that the Mi'kmaq carved from ash were always in high demand. The oars ranged from the light and narrow for calm lakes and rivers to the heavier sugar maple wood used in rougher waters.

"That musket you are eyeing is twelve pelts—six for that pistol."

"We paid Étienne ten and four," Eagle Feather said.

"I am not Étienne," André said in his rough Mi'kmaw tongue. He smiled through his yellowed teeth. "That was then. It has taken weeks travelling through rapids, danger, and near starvation to get these here from Louisbourg."

Bear Cub's ears perked up at hearing he had travelled from Île Royale. "Do you know Peter Beck?"

"E'e. Four months ago, he arrived at the fort on the brink of death, sick with a fever. He came off one of the privateer ships. Apparently, they had intercepted a British sloop bound for Halifax and captured it, bringing prisoners and plenty of provisions to the fort. He's a survivor, that one! Should be dead!" André chuckled.

Bear Cub was relieved. "Is he still there?"

"When I left, most certainly! He's working hard with the French troops that just arrived on a dozen warships. Months ago, word was received of a pending British attack from Halifax led by Admiral Holburne." André paused briefly. "Now, to matters at hand." To Eagle Feather, he said, "If you want it, the price stands."

"You and I both know the prices are greatly inflated. We will pay what you ask, but you must throw in the two ivory combs and an extra keg of gunpowder and lead balls." Eagle Feather grinned.

André thought for a moment. "You drive a hard bargain."

"I disagree," Bear Cub chimed in. "Our beaver underfur is much thicker and better quality than your European rodents—if they have any left over there…"

André extended his hand. "Deal!"

The People congregated around André. Now, three pelts bought one blanket or eight knives. The women were bargaining for awls and needles. Bear Cub overheard Morning Dove and Singing Sparrow giving André an earful, bartering for better pots and kettles. In the last trade they were cheaply made and wore out quickly. "The copper pots were too thin, they punctured at the slightest drop or bump," Morning Dove exclaimed in frustration. Singing Sparrow said, "The glass beads were flat on one side, and the axe heads were made with soft metal, which blunted easily."

New guns were always in dire need. All too often, the French traded old war supplies that broke frequently. Repairs were difficult as only the French had the skill to fix them, and those few who had that ability only sporadically drifted to their villages. André was one of them and offered to fix what needed repairing.

Among the many provisions, foodstuffs of dried peas, beans, and prunes were aplenty, along with the usual flour and biscuits. There was the prevalent lure of brandy and rum kegs, but White Cloud banned it outright before they were even off-loaded.

Hours of negotiating later, the flotilla moved on.

The village women were busy mending and stringing snowshoes and skinning rabbits. Singing Sparrow scooped up the hazelnuts she and Brigide harvested earlier and placed them in a small basket. They also had collected whatever little blueberries were now left for picking. She thought of Bear Cub when she popped a couple in her mouth. Their wedding was happening soon. Singing Sparrow was overjoyed for him to know of Peter's welfare. She went in search of her mother.

The growth of the camp, which had almost doubled the normal maximum of two hundred for a Summer encampment, had levelled off. It relaxed anxieties from the threat of attack, but food was becoming scarcer. The two parties that had left early for the eel and salmon runs on the Pijinuiskaq had yet to return.

Singing Sparrow found her mother plucking the quills of a dead porcupine. Her nimble fingers were making fast work of it.

"There you are," she exclaimed, handing her mother a small reed box.

"Hazelnuts! You know how to make me very happy, my daughter. My favourite time of the year. You and Brigide did not go alone?"

Singing Sparrow shook her head. "There were a dozen of us. We all had knives."

"But, still—"

Singing Sparrow interrupted. "If the rain spirits remain at bay, Na'ku'set will dry the nuts in very little time. Then, your taste buds will scream in delight." She giggled. "When the leaves drop, there will be much more for the picking." Out of the corner of her eye, Singing Sparrow caught sight of a dress lying across a bear pelt. "Oh!" she uttered. She had seen this only once when she was a little girl. It was her mother's most prized possession, the robe she had worn on her wedding day.

"My memory of it was faded. It is exquisite," Singing Sparrow whispered. It was a white moose hide with narrow red and black strips of ornamented leather in peaks along the bottom of the robe. Above each peak was a small deer, which represented her grandmother, and a dove for her mother. And above those was a tiny stitched sparrow that, she was sure, had not been there before.

"You like it?" Morning Dove asked, raising her eyebrows. She laid the porcupine down and stood up.

Singing Sparrow wrapped her arms around her mother. "You cannot know how meaningful this is to me."

"But I do." Morning Dove smoothed the hair from her daughter's eyes. "I cannot have my daughter marry in her everyday linen and wool, can I? Much too plain."

Singing Sparrow laughed through her tears. Her mother would never allow their ties to traditions vanish.

"Do you love Bear Cub?"

"Oh, e'e." Singing Sparrow solemnly lowered her head.

"What is wrong?"

Singing Sparrow raised her chin and focused her eyes on her

mother's face. "What if love is not enough? What if Bear Cub is not happy with me, or…"

"Nothing is for sure. Do you think of my sister and her husband? Only they can answer why it did not work for them." Morning Dove caressed her daughter's hand. "Your happiness is important to your father and me. You know no one will encourage two people to stay together if they are not content with each other. It is better to be apart. As to you and Bear Cub, allow room for growth—love matures. Listen to each other."

Singing Sparrow wanted a more definite answer, an assurance for her new life.

"You cannot know what the future holds, nor should you wish it." Morning Dove took hold of Singing Sparrow's hands. "When a river moves around obstacles, it changes its course to continue its journey with the least resistance. My daughter, we are always in a state of fluidity as we move through life, adapting to whatever falls across our path. You will adjust to each other when each situation demands it. Walk, my daughter, do not run. Every moment will have its own lesson. You and Bear Cub will grow together."

# Chapter Fifteen



Bear Cub stood stock-still before Eagle Feather and White Cloud inside the oblong wikuom. The front and back doors were open. Following the initial announcement of when the wedding would be, there were four days of ceremonies and feasting between many speeches of praise. Tobacco pipes were lit, stories were told, and the Elders spoke of the couple's ancestral lineage with examples of the groom's and bride's greatest qualities. Eagle Feather spoke on his brother's behalf as he knew Bear Cub's history best, but Bear Cub was made uneasy by the way Eagle Feather embellished his hunting prowess.

"Hmm. Good," Eagle Feather quipped, carefully examining his brother up and down.

"Good? What do you mean, just good?" Bear Cub was hoping he looked much better than mediocre, something closer to extraordinary.

"In this light, it is the best I can do. Na'ku'set has not risen from beneath the earth yet!" Eagle Feather paused, drumming his finger against his lips. "What I mean is, I approve. You will be pleasing to my sister's eyes." Eagle Feather stepped around him for a closer look. "My mother did well to fit these to your stature."

"And I thank you, my brother, for your generosity," Bear Cub replied. Eagle Feather had offered his best jacket with a caribou design of red and bright yellow quills on the back. The front flap had two small eagle feathers fashioned from white and dark-brown beads. Also in his charitable package were seal-hide leggings with triangle designs painted around the bottom and sides. Morning Dove had stitched a new pair of moose moccasins for the day, as his own were worse for wear. She had also painted his cheeks and chin with a geometrical design that curled at each end. Singing Sparrow's gift of the medicine pouch hung, as always, around his neck.

White Cloud cleared his throat. "My son can be short on praise and does not freely give it to what is obvious in my eyes. You look superb," he declared.

Bear Cub breathed a sigh of relief. He was very thankful for the cool air that occasionally wafted through the open doors.

White Cloud surprised Bear Cub when he handed him a beaded leather band with two hawk feathers sewn on one side. As he placed it around Bear Cub's head and tied it at the back, he said in a low voice, "I wore this on my wedding day. I am honoured to have you wear this, my son."

The warmth of belonging flooded through Bear Cub. He thanked the Creator for his new family. His own father was on his mind these days, but the anger was still there, and it tormented him. On this day, his heart ached that his sisters could not be with him.

Morning Dove peeked inside. "We are ready. Singing Sparrow is waiting."

Bear Cub's stomach turned somersaults. White Cloud followed his wife out the door, leaving the two brothers alone.

Eagle Feather stepped close to Bear Cub. "You are complete now." He firmly laid his hand upon Bear Cub's chest. "I am happy we are brothers."

Morning Dove popped her head back in. "Come, you two!"

As Bear Cub left the security of the wikuom, White Cloud was waiting for him, holding his white moose-skin robe, embellished from top to bottom with embroidered fish and animals. White Cloud wrapped it around Bear Cub's shoulders, and his knees buckled slightly under the weight of it. Everyone had already gathered in the compound. Bear Cub and White Cloud walked together to the centre where Singing Sparrow met them with Morning Dove by her side. Seeing his fiancée for the first time in her wedding robe melted away any tension he had been feeling. Her belted dress was wrapped around her petite body, leaving her shoulders bare. She wore two arm bracelets of blue and white, and her hair was plaited in several braids.

As the sun slowly ascended over the lake, the rays shot upward, outlining a ceiling of clouds, quilt-like in the golden glow. The warm tones of a flute joyfully played for abundant blessings echoed all about.

The drums started to beat—first one, then two. As they faced each other, Bear Cub and Singing Sparrow nervously held each other's hands. The tiny ivory rose stood out against her skin. *My grandmother's necklace now adorns my wife*, Bear Cub thought. He closed his eyes and prayed for their happiness. When he opened them, Singing Sparrow smiled.

White Cloud and Morning Dove approached them and kissed them both. Then, White Cloud lifted Bear Cub's heavy robe and placed part of it on his daughter's shoulders, symbolically joining them. The village started chanting in unison, "Hau, hau, hau." They continued as people started to dance clockwise around the couple. Alawei nipped at their feet and snuggled her way between the happy couple. They stood side by side, hands clasped, fingers entwined, as Calm Water stepped around them, fanning the sweetgrass smoke. He held the bowl in front of the couple and waved the vapours with an eagle feather. The two cupped the smoke toward themselves to cleanse their eyes, their ears, their mouths, and their hearts. Singing Sparrow thanked the Giver of Life, Grandfather Sun, "for our shadows who are our ancestors that guide and protect us." She closed her eyes and Bear Cub thanked Mother Earth for all she provided them, then prayed to the four directions. His whole being submitted to his new way of life. The road he had chosen was his to walk and his place to be.

The dancing, feasting, and orations continued well past sunset. Bear Cub was exhausted but exhilarated. Near the end of the celebration, the wedded couple was led to a wikuom that had been set up just for them.

In the serenity of their new home, they both breathed a sigh of relief. Bear Cub could smell the fresh cedar boughs strewn under the mats that Brigide had laid. Alawei sat outside the door-blanket, whining. "Shall we?" Singing Sparrow asked, raising an eyebrow. Bear Cub slowly shook his head and stepped closer to his wife. He watched her untie her braids and break apart the strands with her fingers. Bear Cub picked up the ivory comb her brother had given her and carefully untangled and combed her long tresses down her back. He could feel a slight tremor when he touched her.

He nervously started to ramble about his turn to patrol tomorrow night. "Your father insists we stay on alert. I do agree but—"

Singing Sparrow turned and pressed her finger to his lips and led him to their bed.

S‌INGING S‌PARROW AWOKE THE NEXT morning to chanting outside their retreat and the sound of Alawei lavishly licking Bear Cub's face. Discovering they had fallen asleep in each other's arms, they burst out laughing. Bear Cub leaned over and lifted the corner of the door-blanket. "They are gathering now for the hunt. The bird migrations are beginning." Singing Sparrow nestled back under the bearskin and shyly watched her husband while he quickly dressed. He leaned over and kissed her.

After Bear Cub left, Singing Sparrow dressed and stepped outside, where Brigide greeted her. Her daughter, now four moons old, was laced into her cradleboard, which was lined with soft fox skins. The little one peeked out from behind her mother's back, smiling at Singing Sparrow. "She is always happy," Singing Sparrow said, stroking the chubby cheek with her finger.

"As you are, I am sure." Brigide grinned.

"And I suppose you just happened to walk this way by accident?"

"Not really. I saw Bear Cub leave, so I knew you were alone. Well?"

"If you are thinking what I suspect you are thinking, my dear friend," Singing Sparrow scolded in jest, "what goes on between a husband and wife is sacred." Singing Sparrow tried and failed to suppress the wide grin on her face. Brigide did not need to know the particulars. Besides, nothing had happened—that is, nothing like what Brigide was hinting at. Something special did occur instead—she and Bear Cub had grown closer together last night, talking into the wee hours. She would lead her friend down the road of imagination and leave it at that.

Singing Sparrow and Brigide put their energy into making rib baskets. Plenty of long green reeds had been harvested and dried. Beach grass, cattails, as well as nettles and moose hair lay about. The quills had already been whitened with a good soak and dried, and plenty of flowers, roots, and leaves had already been collected for the dyes. Goldthread for the colour yellow, elderberries for black, the bark of dogwood for blue, and bayberry and larkspur for green. There was orange dye still left over from the bloodroot that had been harvested in the Spring, and brown from acorns.

As the day progressed, Singing Sparrow moved her attention to tanning dried rabbit skins with bird livers and oil. After the third one had been stretched, she rested a moment to massage her aching fingers. The men were now returning, carrying pigeons and curlews. The birds hung limp by their legs in orderly groupings of three and four. More arrived with geese. *It is a good hunt*, she said to herself. When Eagle Feather announced that there were more water birds left around the marsh, the women set out on foot to collect the kill. Half a dozen armed men escorted them—no female left now without protection.

Her husband said that if Detleff knew the Summer camps had greatly increased in size over the Winter villages, he would not attempt a raid. "One moon has passed—surely if there was going to be another attack, it would have happened by now," he'd told her.

After the evening meal, Singing Sparrow settled down alone. Bear Cub and her brother were on patrol with a dozen others. Dark clouds loomed overhead leaving the sky devoid of moon and stars. It was quiet except for the litany of crickets chirping in unison, then solo. *When their evening songs signal the end of Summer, it is safe to dry meat for the Winter.* The last sound she heard was the wind's breath against the leaves before a deep slumber washed over her, sending her into the spirit world.

*She was surrounded by trees, digging for roots with her bare hands. Brigide was ahead of her. The more Singing Sparrow foraged, the greater the distance between them. A voice rang out, "Fire!" She could see her friend through the trees, stepping toward the flames. Singing Sparrow screamed for her to stop. "Fire!" another voice screeched. Her feet were rooted like a tree to the forest floor. She could not move. She stared as fingers of flame teased the fringes of Brigide's robe until the fire engulfed her in an inferno.*

Singing Sparrow lay paralyzed between sleep and wakefulness. In her trance-like state, she was semi-aware of her nightmare but also conscious of her surroundings in bed. Again, "Fire!" she heard. Jerking to full consciousness, she lay there, her heart pounding. The instant awareness of brush crackling behind the wikuom and pandemonium in the compound brought her clambering for an escape. Outside, people were frantically running, women clutching their children in a desperate attempt to flee. Alawei howled and jumped against her legs to be lifted.

"Get to the lake! Everyone!" It was Bear Cub. Over his shoulder she could see her mother racing toward them. "You'll be safer at the shore. Listen to what they say," Bear Cub said, out of breath. "Your father's there, getting as many of the women and children into canoes as he can."

Singing Sparrow looked behind her—a rim of fire embraced the outskirts of the camp. A stiff breeze fed the flames, which leapt from one tree crown to the next. She heard piercing cries as several wikuoml quickly caught. Singing Sparrow covered her ears to shut out the noise.

The loud, sharp firing of muskets sounded amid the chaos. "Go!" Bear Cub cried, then he disappeared.

A flash of her dream—*Brigide!*

"Here, take Alawei." Singing Sparrow pushed the dog into her mother's arms.

"What? No! Come now!" Morning Dove grabbed her daughter's arm, tugging hard.

"Moqwe, I must find Brigide."

Morning Dove pleaded, "Don't be foolish. Her wikuom is farthest away. You'll be killed!" Tears were coursing down her cheeks.

"I won't be long. Please, go now!" Singing Sparrow pressed her mother away and ran toward the village outskirts.

The flames were edging closer. Singing Sparrow appealed to Jikeyulkw. And her prayers were answered when she found a small area of woods bereft of the burn. Smoke crept closer, wrapping its ugly fingers about the trees.

She ran into the woods as far as she dared and hollered for her friend as loud as she could. She stared from a safe distance as the fire edged closer to Brigide and Calm Water's shelter. The birchbark curled from the heat. She bolted when she heard a baby cry. "Brigide! Calm Water!" she cried. Singing Sparrow suddenly stopped when she saw their bodies—both face down on the forest floor, shot. Calm Water had been scalped. She dropped to her knees and turned over Brigide. Her eyes were open, staring blankly. Singing Sparrow fell backward and dug her heels into the dirt to push herself away from the lifeless body. From their wikuom came a muffled whimper. "Lise!" she called. Crawling on her hands and knees, she found the little one hidden underneath a caribou skin. The heat of the fire made Singing Sparrow's skin burn as she wrapped the baby in a blanket and escaped just before fire ravished the wikuom. She covered the small, tear-stained face and ran, gasping for air as the smoke clawed at the inside of her throat. By the time she reached the main compound, her eyes were burning—her chest ached with each breath.

Singing Sparrow saw her mother running toward her. They embraced without words, then hurried to get into one of the waiting canoes. Alawei raced ahead.

They were helped into an ocean canoe and were shoved out to deeper waters where others were waiting. Singing Sparrow coughed uncontrollably as Morning Dove pulled her daughter toward her in a tight embrace. When Singing Sparrow lifted the blanket from the baby's face, she wept a release that flooded her entire being. She listened to the distant cries and the gut-wrenching screams. Trembling, she watched the flames reach higher as the inferno encroached upon the main camp. Through the sounds of destruction, Singing Sparrow could hear gunfire.

A SOAR OF EAGLES SILENTLY flew above, hunting the salmon that were returning to spawn, but the scene went unnoticed by the group below. The hours seemed to drag on as the many canoes travelled upriver on the Pijinuiskaq. Two portages had to be made before they silently paddled into Jacques Saouque's village. They were welcomed with open arms.

Sleep was unknown to Singing Sparrow and her mother. White Cloud, Bear Cub, and Eagle Feather were among the many men who had stayed behind. The distress of wondering whether they or anyone else had survived was too much to bear. One morning numbly melted into the next, and still no word. On the fourth night, Singing Sparrow sat alone with Lise nestled on her lap. Darkness closed in early when rain clouds gathered. Large drops tapped on the sides of the wikuom, and the fire sizzled as a few leaked from above. Her mother entered, picked up an unfinished mat and the strips of reeds, and sat down beside her. "This is difficult," her mother said. "Waiting does not come easy for me."

Suddenly, her mother seemed old. Singing Sparrow reached

over to clutch her hand and rested her head on her mother's shoulder. She had no comforting words to give her. Outside, the rain increased from a steady drumming to a heavy downpour.

The next morning, a light coating of frost covered the compound. Singing Sparrow had just placed Lise in her cradleboard when the cry went up.

"They are coming!"

She looked up and saw her mother pointing at the river. Five canoes were heading toward the shore, and dozens of people scattered to greet them. Singing Sparrow choked on a sob when she saw Bear Cub waving.

"Go!" Morning Dove cried. "I'll bring Lise. Go! I'll be right behind you."

Singing Sparrow ran.


Everyone now knew that the fire had been set deliberately. The men had tracked down British soldiers and militia, killed some, and taken others prisoner to be turned over to the French. Neither Bear Cub nor Eagle Feather had encountered Detleff during the attack, but one familiar footman was found dead, recognizable by his unusual patch of white hair. Bear Cub had refused to talk further on it. Singing Sparrow knew that Bear Cub blamed himself for the decimation of their village.

Everyone was frightened of another ambush, worried that any surviving British might come with reinforcements. A few wanted to return to the burned village for the scalps of the dead soldiers. As Singing Sparrow half-listened to their frantic opinions, she watched the tall columns of smoke from afar. Even after the rain, the fire was still burning.

Her father spoke. "I cannot foresee any of the British continuing their onslaught. They did what they came for. As for the dead soldiers, they would be burned beyond recognition."

The circle prayed for the wind not to change direction.

*It is too sordid and grotesque to barter the dead*, Singing Sparrow thought. All her energies would now be on Lise. The child's parents had no surviving relatives; therefore, it was natural that she and Bear Cub adopt her. White Cloud concurred whole-heartedly to their taking in his new granddaughter. Lise would now be treated by the community as though she were their biological child. Several women came forward who had recently birthed children to act as the baby's wet nurse, and Bear Cub joyfully stepped into his new role and made a rattle for Lise from fish skin, filling it with tiny pebbles and sand.

Over the next few days, White Cloud and Jacques met privately on numerous occasions, and each then led his own sharing circle. Then came an announcement for the entire community to meet. The topic: relocation west on the Oqomkikiaq. As Jacques held the sculpted talking stick, he lightly rubbed the carved head with his thumb and looked directly at White Cloud. "It goes without saying, my dearest and beloved friend, that all of you must stay with us until it is time to separate and move with Keptewiku's. Everyone has been through much sorrow and grief." He glanced partly around the circle at his guests. "However, my brother, I do understand why you wish not to tarry but to relocate now before early snows could hamper your progress. Our brothers and sisters of the forest indicate that the snow could come early." He handed the stick to White Cloud.

"My esteemed and cherished brother, your hospitality knows no end—it is selfless to the extreme. But your newly increased numbers here will put a burden upon this land and all its creatures. It is not viable for us to stay. This decision weighs heavily on my mind, bringing many sleepless nights." He now fixed his eyes on those of his own village. "If any of you prefers to stay, I do not begrudge your choice."

With the cradleboard strapped on her back, Singing Sparrow quietly stood and walked outside the circle to obtain some relief. Bear Cub followed and helped her to remove it.

"There are some who will be staying with Jacques," Bear Cub said. "But most want to put as much distance as possible between the new camp and the old."

"I as well." Singing Sparrow wondered if her father's decision was in any way linked to Detleff's discord with Bear Cub. She knew it placed a heavy burden on her husband's mind.

No time was wasted. By early sunrise and after saddened farewells, the canoes paddled with just over a hundred Mi'kmaq up the Pijinuiskaq then onto connecting tributaries. Once into the Kespukwitk District, they spent time with the Saqmawit who allotted hunting and fishing areas for the district. That meant their numbers would decrease into the next moon as their village split into smaller groups to set themselves up on specifically designated base-camp sites. The arduous journey was wrought with many narrow portages through forests of red spruce and hemlock to traverse waterfalls and rapids. As they were travelling up the Oqomkikiaq to Kejimkuji'jk Lake, some set up Winter camps on the main river, while others stayed along the brooks and streams that fed into it.

For White Cloud's and two other households, the consensus was to camp along a smaller river that flowed from Kejimkuji'jk Lake. There were only four bare-bones, framed wikuoml and a cold firepit of charred acorns where Bear Cub now stood. Dark evergreens stood out between the bright red colours of the sugar maples. As he watched the current steal away the falling leaves from above, Bear Cub could hear the churning rapids downstream.

The site was level with a sandy beach large enough for

keeping many canoes aground. In the bend of the river was a large treeless area edged with river grasses; cattails, their brown heads now fuzzy white, had already burst their seeds. Upstream, the river continued out of sight amid evergreen trees. Their site was far enough away from a clean water source that there was no possibility of it being contaminated by charcoal or human waste.

The men split into groups to hunt for food. The women off-loaded canoes, started the main fire, and then commenced unrolling sheets of birchbark to cover the frames. Jacques had given them the supplies and plenty of spruce root and strips of eel skin. Some of the women foraged for hemlock deadwood to build more wikuom frames. With winter coming, they would have to gather enough spruce boughs to thickly cover the outside of shelters to prevent cold drafts from entering.

The hunt was long. The men were gone for most of the day, returning just before dark. Fires had now been lit inside the wikuoml with the sacred fire burning briskly in the centre of the compound.

Bear Cub watched Singing Sparrow clean Lise and refresh her bottom with moss before tucking her under the fox skin. As they laid back on their bed, a night owl broke the silence. The lonely hoo-hoo-hoo was clear as it cut through the chilly air. Alawei perked up her ears then closed her eyes again.

Singing Sparrow lay with her head on his bare chest; her hot tears stung his soul. He hugged her closer. Lise was a daily reminder of their loss, and time was not kind to his wife's grief.

"Did I tell you about the dream I had about Brigide that night?" Her voice was quaking.

"Moqwe," he said, surprised.

"The spirits were warning me, but I could not help her."

She explained her dream, which was followed by a fresh flow of tears.

"You couldn't have saved them, my love." He paused, stroking her hair. "You'd get along with my sister."

"Hanna?"

"Uh-huh. Hanna has dreams like yours. In our family, we say she has the sight."

"I would like to meet her."

"That would be nice," Bear Cub answered, just before he drifted off.

# Chapter Sixteen



Singing Sparrow adjusted the woollen blanket over her head to darken the ice hole. The brilliant sun above infused the surrounding frozen surface, illuminating the cold water beneath. A puffy breath cloud escaped her mouth as she exhaled. "There you are, little one," she muttered and speared the greenish-brown tomcod. She held it in both hands and gazed into his eyes. "Wela'lin," she said to her tiny brother. "I thank you for putting yourself in my path."

She sat up and placed the fish into her half-filled basket. Lise was wrapped in furs and still sound asleep, safely strapped in the cradleboard. Singing Sparrow noticed that her mother had already started a second container. After her many years of ice fishing, Morning Dove made it appear effortless. Their companions were scattered along the shoreline of Oqomkikiaq. When Singing Sparrow hugged the bearskin snuggly around her neck, she could barely feel the coarse fur brush against her numbed chin. Her woollen peaked hat protected her ears, while the buckskin leggings tucked inside her tightly laced knee-high moccasins kept her dry.

Singing Sparrow immersed her tiny carved decoy back in the

water and jigged the line to attract more spawning brothers. Though Winter had arrived early with blizzards and deep snow, the temperatures had not shifted to the usual bitter cold. They fluctuated to varying degrees as the top of the snow melted during the day, then left a frozen crust on the surface when the nights grew colder. That crust made it easier for the dogs to travel when tracking caribou and moose.

Singing Sparrow was now chilled to the bone. A sudden blast of wind blew great swirls of snow against her cheeks, and her teeth chattered. It was none too soon when everyone decided to pack everything onto the toboggans and start back. As she pulled her toboggan up the small embankment, she stumbled and landed on her backside, letting out a shriek of surprise which caused Lise to cry out. More astounding was the sudden appearance of four men, out of nowhere. One lifted her onto her feet, while another gathered up the spilled fish.

Morning Dove hurried to her side and removed the cradleboard. "Are you hurt?"

"Moqwe," Singing Sparrow replied and laughed at her clumsiness. The strangers were relieved there were no injuries, and she thanked them for their concern.

"I see you have a whole contingent coming to your aid. You are in good hands," an old man said.

He spoke Mi'kmaw, the other three were French. He introduced himself as Paul Labrador. He had been hired as a guide and interpreter. "We are on our way back to Port Rossignol." Singing Sparrow knew the port as a long-time French Summer base for fishing. Her father traded furs there, but she was curious to know why they needed a guide in Winter. Paul did not venture to say where they had been, nor did she ask.

The sun had almost disappeared, and a full moon was cresting. Darkness would soon be upon them, so Morning Dove invited the men to join them in returning to the women's field camp. Her invitation was readily accepted.

Once the fires were lit, the fish were cleaned and roasted on sticks. Paul was doing most of the talking, translating back and forth with his clients. Singing Sparrow listened to their tales and any bits of news they shared. She peeled away the hot white flesh of the fish, chewed a small bit, and placed the pulp into Lise's mouth. Her chubby hand hungrily reached out for more, but she was distracted when one Frenchman made faces at her. She eagerly grabbed his finger when he touched her hand. When his face lit up, he rattled on in French.

Paul translated. "Claude has a family in France whom he gravely misses."

"Please tell him he can hold her if he would like." Singing Sparrow lifted Lise into his arms. The lavish attention he now poured over her daughter made her glad she had offered.

"When was the last time Claude saw his family?" Singing Sparrow asked.

"Last Spring." Paul explained they had set sail at King Louis's orders with weapons for Louisbourg's defence. "They sailed first to Rossignol to barter for skins with what stores they had and hired Mi'kmaw guides. The ship left without them and set sail for the fort, but it never returned. When the end of the Harvest Moon showed no sign of it, all hopes faded for returning to France. Now, they are just hoping it will return for them in Summer."

"Do you know what happened?"

"They can only surmise. Might have been a sudden storm, or privateers."

Singing Sparrow read the unease on the women's faces as they sat around the fire. What would happen if the French were defeated? She thought of Peter aiding the fort's defence.

Glancing at her daughter, now innocently sleeping in Claude's arms, she worried.

Paul turned the conversation to Beausoleil, who recruited Mi'kmaq for guerilla warfare. Whether Beausoleil willfully incited the People with his talk of victory or simply reignited the hidden fire of hatred that many harboured, Singing Sparrow could only guess. Before the ice had formed, Paul and his clients had met such a band on the river farther north. They talked of a British detachment of about one hundred who had been attacked by such a group of Acadians and Mi'kmaq. The English had suffered a high number of casualties before retreating to Annapolis.

The talk of war was enough to dilute any responses to it, and Singing Sparrow was glad when Paul quickly changed the topic of conversation. In time, the fire dimmed and everyone eventually retired. Before Paul turned in, he indicated they would leave before the sun showed and thanked everyone for their hospitality.

True to his word, they were up and gone before Singing Sparrow rose. The women had planned to clean and smoke the catch before returning to the base camps, but thick snow clouds quickly formed a heavy blanket over the rising sun. In that narrow cloudless window on the horizon, the illuminating light grew to a brilliant red. The consensus was to move on.


WHEN THE BLIZZARD HAD ABATED and the Tomcod Moon waned, the men returned from their seal hunt. It was the last of the storms. Even the Snow Blinder, which was typically harsh, came in unusually mild and stayed as such into the Spring Moon. When the snow began to melt at the base of the trees, the women selected the maples to tap and cut an opening into the bark. Almost immediately, the clear watery sap started its journey down the grooved stick and dripped into the birchbark bowls and iron kettles that hung below.

*It is good medicine*, Singing Sparrow thought as she drank it, preferring it before it was boiled. She stirred the contents of the kettle over the fire, then grabbed the awl and punched a final hole through the caribou skin from which she was making a pair of moccasins. She was now ready to sew the seams together at the top.

Bear Cub squatted down beside her and kissed her cheek. "You do wonderful work."

"You are very hard on your moccasins. I will need to doubly reinforce these." She winked back.

"I'll miss you terribly." He leaned into her and nibbled at her ear.

Singing Sparrow playfully recoiled from his advances. "They will not be ready in time if you continue like this." Then, "Will you know how to find Paul?"

"Your brother is more familiar with the area than I and has offered to be my companion. We're taking the furs as well to trade at Port Rossignol, so I'll return later than I promised."

The needle stopped and she rested her hands on her lap.

Bear Cub placed his hand over hers, and she well knew he was attempting to appease her. "Nothing will happen," he said. "It's a French trading post. And since the war, most of the fishing vessels from New England have stopped. Besides, it's too dangerous to sail up near these waters this time of year. The storms alone—"

"You attempt to pacify me, my husband." Singing Sparrow was curt in her reply. "It will not work this time."

"The military concentration is in Halifax, not Port Rossignol. There must be thousands of British soldiers wintered there."

"If you wish to relax my fears, your decoy has failed. Do not—" She was stopped by a kiss on her lips. She groaned.

Bear Cub briefly removed his lips from hers. "Everyone here will be starting to move anyway—closer to the port—for the Spring migration. Soon, we will not be far apart." And he resumed his affection.

Singing Sparrow moaned.

# Chapter Seventeen



For Hanna's sake, Bear Cub had intended to spend time with Paul and Magdeleine to ensure they were both well. What Eagle Feather and Bear Cub found was unforeseen. Five scalped Mi'kmaw bodies scattered around the compound—two were women. The air was thick with a sickening buzz of flies.

Eagle Feather's legs weakened and his shoulders slumped as he dropped to the ground. He stared at the carnage, trying to digest it. *How much more must we bear!* He wanted to scream it at the top of his lungs. But his spirit denied him the luxury of weeping—his spirit would not succumb to defeat. His brother's hand pushed hard upon his shoulder.

Bear Cub walked toward one of the wikuoml. A pair of legs protruded outside the open door. "It's Paul."

When Eagle Feather neared the body, he saw that Paul had been shot between the eyes. Eagle Feather crouched to feel his skin. "Cold. Judging by the bloating, this happened about four nights ago."

"One of the women is Magdeleine. Hanna will be grief-stricken," Bear Cub replied. He curled his nose up and gasped. "He smells."

The earth was soft under the thin layer of Winter snow, so they began the arduous task of digging a pit. Eagle Feather gathered as many skins as he could find to wrap the bodies. Five now lay side by side within the grave. The last one put to rest was Paul, who now lay atop a caribou hide. They covered him with more skins, tied him securely, and lowered him into the cold earth. They filled the cavity with twigs and soil until only an inconspicuous mound was left. After they had placed stones of various sizes on top, Eagle Feather lit a braid of sweetgrass.

As Bear Cub played his flute, a curious thing happened. A raven gently landed on top of the grave. With a ruffle of his feathers, the bird stared up at them. "Kwawk," he called, then flew away.

DARKNESS HAD STARTED TO DESCEND, and Eagle Feather's warm fire was welcoming. They roasted hares, which they ate in pro-longed silence.

Bear Cub described his first meeting with Paul Labrador and his wife.

"Hanna had a soft spot for both of them. They seemed to have a special connection." He looked off into the distance and did not speak again for the longest time.

"You have drifted from me, my brother."

"I'm thinking of Papa. If I had no sisters, I would never return."

"In time, your feelings may change." Eagle Feather looked upward. The sky was freckled with twinkling stars, and Muin stood out; the bear had emerged from her den and had already started her ascent.

Bear Cub followed his gaze. "I've been thinking of all the senseless deaths. Then I remembered the recent mid-Winter feast giving thanks to all spirits." He turned to his brother. "We acknowledged the blessings of life, health, and community and marked the end of the old year and the beginning of the new. But we have death that is so final, so cold."

"Not so. Nothing is constant. It is the present form that changes. You may not see Paul as he was, but he is here. Death is simply another door that opens."

Bear Cub could not answer. He wanted to believe it.

Just as they were about to leave the next morning, Eagle Feather noticed a caribou string caught between two rocks. When he retrieved it, he held it up to Bear Cub. The cross twisted back and forth in the sunlight.

"It's Paul's," Bear Cub said.

Eagle Feather handed it to his brother. "I am sure he would want Hanna to have it. From what you have told me, she will cherish it."

Bear Cub placed it into his medicine pouch. "Wela'lin."

Bear Cub and Eagle Feather paddled along two tributaries before continuing downstream on the Oqomkikiaq to Port Rossignol. As they navigated around a collapsed beaver dam, they heard geese noisily honking overhead and saw mallards drifting with the current. Yellow beaks and shiny green heads dived for food, and their feathered bottoms pointed skyward. Sunning turtles slipped off river boulders into the cold water and disappeared beneath the ripples. The last section of the river was wide and tidal. After passing a stone weir and another fenced structure, they arrived at the mouth of the river at mid-tide.

"This is unusual—there is no activity," Eagle Feather said under his breath.

There were three canoes and one shallop resting on the shore. In the distance, Bear Cub could see a brigantine anchored on the ocean.

They left the furs in their canoe, armed themselves, and set off for the two-storey wooden building that sat atop a hill. Outside on the steps stood a tall, lanky man. He removed the clay pipe from his mouth and gave the back of the bowl two sharp cracks on the door frame. He nodded for them to enter. Bear Cub laid his hand on the knife handle neatly tucked away in a leather sheath. They could hear nothing from within. Eagle Feather opened the door.

BEAR CUB AWOKE FROM A stupor, face down in grain—bits of it stuck to his sore cheek. In the darkness, he could hear water lapping against his ear as his eyes rapidly blinked open. Rolling over was a labour of excruciating pain, which radiated over his back. His head throbbed. His wrists were raw, tightly tied in front, but he managed to right himself and rest his back against a pile of stuffed burlap bags. A tug pulled him back. Eagle Feather was bound with the same rope, a short tether between them. His brother was sitting upright but was barely conscious. Bear Cub heard loud voices and heavy footsteps from above.

Someone lifted a hatch overhead, and daylight streamed down a steep set of warped steps. Aware now that they were on a ship, Bear Cub could see a half-dozen bound Mi'kmaq and French lying opposite him and his brother. Bear Cub's knife was gone, but his pouch still hung around his neck.

A middle-aged sailor brought hardtack, and a much younger tar carried a cauldron of watery porridge. When Bear Cub got a whiff, memories of the voyage to Nova Scotia flooded back.

"It's this or nothing," the sailor said in English. He stared down at Bear Cub—a few strands of his unkempt hair dangled over the bowl. He chawed on tobacco and spat on the creaking floor then laid the bowl beside Bear Cub's feet. The sailor ducked to avoid low beams and kicked the other captives awake.

Eagle Feather was now fully conscious. "Where are we?"

Bear Cub repeated his brother's question in German on the extreme off-chance the sailors understood. The elder sailor frowned at them and left, quickly climbing out of the hold.

"I wish I knew," Bear Cub replied in Mi'kmaw.

One of the Mi'kmaw captives repeated Eagle Feather's question in English, shouting at the young sailor as he headed for the stairs.

"Sailing to Halifax," he answered, then looked around to see if any of his fellows heard him speaking to the captives, as though fearful he had given too much information.

Before the hatch closed in on them, Bear Cub heard the familiar name, "Jessen!" Then, "Yes, sir!"

"Detleff?" Eagle Feather asked.

"Could be."

Bear Cub drifted in and out of sleep. The only knowledge of night and day was the opening of the hatch. Awakening again to the increased groaning of the vessel, Bear Cub could not deny the food rations any longer. He ate the hardtack and gagged on the miserable cold porridge.

It was morning when he was rudely kicked from sleep. Detleff stooped down and held a lantern near his face.

"You survived."

"Wha'?" Bear Cub was groggy and didn't know what he meant. He attempted to lift himself up.

Detleff forced a smile. "When your village burned."

Bear Cub clawed at Detleff's shirt, but he was too weak to latch onto it.

Detleff pulled back and straightened up. "You're mine now." He left. Eventually, the young sailor returned. The Mi'kmaq attempted to ascertain what was going on. The sailor revealed that an approaching storm had cut the journey short—they were now sailing into port at Lunenburg.

# Chapter Eighteen

APRIL 1758

While trillium and mayflowers still slept, bloodroot was on the verge of showing its tiny white petals. But the return of robins had prompted Hanna's walk in the woods. She was hoping to visit Paul and Magdeleine. Walking among trees with barely protruding buds, Hanna was thankful the smallpox had run its course in Halifax and had not reached Lunenburg. The sailings started again between the two towns but always with a guard ship against French privateers. Warburton's 45th and Lascelles's 47th returned to Halifax to prepare for a new attempt to capture Louisbourg. The previous summer's attempted attack was a complete failure. Lord Loudoun had called off his land forces after learning the French forces were too strong to defeat, while Admiral Holburne's squadron was caught in a violent storm that disabled many of his ships.

Numerous fields had been scorched by last June's forest fire. Joseph and Eva Kuhn had given in to their fears and moved to Halifax. Those who refused to surrender were determined to remain on their farms even after the Och family was killed on the Northwest Range along with Herr Roder's wife who was visiting at the time of the raid. Now, under increased pressure from the farmers, the council willingly granted assistance of boards and nails to erect blockhouses between every ten families.

As Hanna followed the creek, she thought of her friends, and of Christian. None of them gave her any promises they would be back, but Hanna's dream a few nights ago was telling her differently. Paul was calling for her, and she held onto that as she skirted the last bend in the stream. The clearing by the lake was deserted. Their home was a shell of birch poles—the bark coverings gone. She searched through the forest for a possible glimpse of their faces and scanned the lake for a canoe but saw no sign of them.

She sank into a state of desolation and sat gazing across the water. A large trout jumped into the air. Tiny beads of water dripped from his fin before he disappeared back into the lake. An osprey swooped down, wings folded back and legs thrust forward. He entered the water with a mighty splash. Then, just as quickly, a large expansion of wings frantically flapped to take him airborne again. He worked through his struggle, claimed victory, and flew higher with his wriggling catch firmly hooked onto his talons.

A sudden hush descended. Every birdsong stopped and the breeze ceased its movement. She heard a whisper from behind. "Ana," the forest breathed. Goosebumps raised on her arms and Hanna turned—there was nothing to see. It eerily echoed again. A sudden tenderness washed over her as she thought of Paul. Her eyes welled as a bewildering sense of contentment settled around her like a warm blanket.


"He's her brother. To do such a cruel deed is incomprehensible." Elisabeth tried to remain calm.

"I, cruel! Your brother's the traitor," Michael said, clenching his jaw in defiance. "If you think I'll change my mind, you're badly mistaken." He examined his daughter closely. "I'm surprised at you. For someone who was at odds with Christian, you have altered your tune."

"It's for Hanna." Elisabeth took a deep breath. "You do as you wish, Papa, but I refuse to watch this family be ripped further apart." She set the mixing bowl firmly on the table and let out a long sigh. "This decision is not yours nor mine; it is Hanna's. She's not a helpless child anymore. She'll soon be fourteen." She stared at the bulging vein on the side of his neck. "If you don't tell her, I will. She has the right to know."

"Know what?" When her sister walked in, Elisabeth turned back to her papa, pleading with her eyes for him to speak of it.

"What's wrong?" Hanna asked.

Michael turned his back on his daughters to face the hearth.

"Hanna, Christian has been taken prisoner." Elisabeth stepped closer to her sister. "He's here at the fort."

Hanna paled. "But why? What has he done?"

"Nothing."

Michael turned to Hanna. "Allow me to elaborate," he said sarcastically. "He has shamed this family. He and others of his kind are now rotting in their jail cells where they belong."

"Remember the Indians brought in the night before that storm?" Elisabeth said to Hanna. "Papa just told me Christian is one of them."

"But that was over two weeks ago!" Hanna looked to Papa, then her sister for answers. "I must go to him."

"I forbid you!" Michael's fist crashed down on the kitchen table.

Hanna did not flinch. "And if I go against your wishes?"

A stiff and painful unease hung over the tiny room. Elisabeth waited for the thunder clouds to burst, to spew forth a torrent of words.

Instead, Michael stormed out.

When Hanna awoke, it was quiet in the house. There was none of the typical chatter from the children, nor from Elisabeth. She was glad of it, to be alone with her thoughts. She had not returned home with Papa the night before. He was on militia duty for the entire week, today being the first day, and the protocol of her staying with Elisabeth and Georg during these times was now the norm.

When she appeared in the kitchen, her sister was busy stoking the fire. Petie and Marta were outside.

"This isn't right, you should have awakened me earlier," Hanna said, noticing the bread dough already mixed for the first rise. She could not fathom how she had slept through it and quickly grabbed the cloth sack of oats.

"You needed your rest this time. I had help," she said, eyeing the children through the open door.

"Ja. I can just imagine. Where's Georg?"

"In the barn," Elisabeth said, straightening her back. "Hanna, you and I are going to visit Christian. My mind is set. With Papa away at the LaHave blockhouse, this is the perfect opportunity. Barbara always said she would look after the children anytime if need be."

Hanna was startled. She laid the sack on the table to hug her sister. "You're so good to me. Do you think the guards will allow us to see him? We have no proof he's our brother."

"We shall see."

"Maybe it would be better if we took the children with us. It would show them we're not a threat."

"You could be right. And Georg doesn't need to know. I'll explain to him later, if all goes well."

They set out after the breakfast dishes were scrubbed and put away. There was still the wool to be carded, and the annual spring wash of the entire house needed to be undertaken to rid it of the winter dust and cobwebs. Hanna idly protested that the flax must be scutched, but she was glad when it fell on deaf ears. Her sister declared Christian took precedence. Elisabeth had told Georg that their trip to pick up their flour ration would be a nice outing for Petie and Marta.

When they arrived, Elisabeth and Hanna were led across a courtyard to a large two-storey complex with eight rooms on each level. Two sentries patrolled—one above on the balcony and another below. Their little group was ushered into a small room on the ground level. The striking young man sitting behind the table was familiar to Hanna. He looked at both of them with skepticism. "Can I help you?" He took a second glance at her.

Upon hearing him speak, Hanna's memory was jarred—Elisabeth's heated confrontation when picking up their rations two years ago. He now had a moustache, an oddity for the British infantry. Hanna thought he was quite handsome with the addition.

"We have come to see our brother," Elisabeth said, setting down the squirming Marta. Hanna held Petie by the hand.

"Which regiment is he in, and of what rank?"

"Neither. He was captured two weeks ago, on a New England brigantine, I believe."

"With all due respect, ma'am, I don't think you'd want to associate with the men in these cells. Try upstairs at the other end of this building. You'll be escorted," he said, then called for the guard.

"We are well aware whom you have here, and one of them is our brother."

Hanna added, "His name is Heber. Christian Heber."

"My apologies, ladies. There's no one here by that name."

When the guard entered, he happened to be accompanied by an officer. The young lad immediately stood at attention.

"Ach, one with authority," Elisabeth said brazenly.

The officer's right eyebrow arched upward in surprise. He bowed to her. "Guten tag. How can we be of assistance, ma'am?"

"Sir, I believe these ladies are in the wrong place." It was the young lad, his stature still rigid with eyes straight ahead.

"At ease, Ensign Irwin."

"With all due *respect*," Elisabeth focused on the lad, before turning back to the officer, "we are in the right place. You are holding our brother captive."

"They say his name is Heber. We do not have—"

"Bitte! We call him Christian," Elisabeth interjected.

Hanna knew her sister's patience was wearing thin and hoped the ensign's opinion of Elisabeth from the last visit would not influence his decision to allow them to enter.

Upon hearing the name, the officer's demeanour changed to one of recognition. "Are you Dr. Gessler's wife?"

"Ja," Elisabeth sighed.

"My apologies, Frau Gessler. We've not formally met, but I know your husband, and I did meet Christian briefly at a town meeting last year. Herr Knaut introduced us. I'm Lieutenant Dettlieb Jessen."

"Ja! My husband spoke of you, Lieutenant Jessen. He said you are called Detleff?"

"I am, ma'am. I'll allow you entry, but only because of my acquaintance with Georg." He turned to the guard and dismissed him. "Ensign, please take the young ladies."

Elisabeth turned back to Detleff. "What does my husband have to do with your leniency?"

"There are things better left unsaid, ma'am."

Hanna's head was spinning, but she was relieved. She picked up Marta, then took hold of Petie's hand again. The ensign turned the key in the lock, and the door opened to a long hall that ran along six cells, all with tiny openings in the heavy dark doors. Hanna heard Elisabeth say in a low voice, "He also goes by Bear Cub."

Ensign Irwin suddenly stopped at the first cell on the right. "Ah," he said, now aware of who the prisoner was. "He's not alone."

Detleff gave him a nod, and the ensign unlocked the cell. Hanna's stomach began to crawl with butterflies.

"Would you like me to take care of the children while you visit?" the ensign offered.

"Nein, Petie knows his uncle."

The door creaked ajar. Two dishevelled beings were sitting on the dirty floor, shackled at the ankles and wrists. A thin, dusty sunray filtered through a small window above their heads. Christian was wide-eyed with surprise—his companion seemed bewildered.

The sight sickened Hanna. She cringed at their raw, red skin from the chafing and let out a gasp. Elisabeth crouched to her son. "Go with this nice man. Your aunt and I will only be a few minutes." Petie hesitated, and she said, "We'll be right here if you need us." Hanna handed over Marta to the ensign. When they disappeared into the next room, Elisabeth lit into Detleff. "Lieutenant Jessen, surely this isn't necessary! They're behind two locked doors!"

Detleff stood in the doorway eying Christian before he disappeared and returned with a key. "This is against my better judgment. I'll only release your brother," he said as the iron chains of the shackles at their feet clanged into a heap on the wooden floor. Then, he freed Christian's wrists. "Knock when you're ready to leave," he said, and closed the door behind him.

Hanna overheard the lieutenant say, "Ensign, keep an eye on them and let me know when they leave."

"Yes, sir," was the reply.

Christian tried to stand, then collapsed. Elisabeth rushed into her brother's arms, crying. Hanna stood back and wept. "Do you not wish to hug your big brother?" he asked. She choked a laugh and ran to him.

The Indian sitting with his back against the wall squirmed in their presence and spoke.

"Hanna, Elisabeth, this is my brother, Eagle Feather."

Hanna noticed her sister fidgeting nervously. Elisabeth acknowledged him with a hasty nod then turned her back on him to knock on the door. "I need warm water and cloths," she called through the opening.

"Why were you captured?" Hanna asked, kneeling in front of Christian.

"Because we are Indians. Because there's a war on." He looked up at Elisabeth. "Need I say more?"

Elisabeth stared grimly at her brother. "And what will become of you now?" she asked.

"If we're lucky, we could be released in a prisoner exchange."

"If not? Then what?" Hanna searched Christian's eyes for reassurance.

The ensign returned, and Christian remained quiet.

Elisabeth crouched down to her brother and washed his wounds. Hanna sat on the grimy floor and attended to Eagle Feather.

Before the ensign left again, Hanna pleaded, "This man has an infection on his ankle. Bitte! Please unshackle him." She surprised herself with her curt authority and was more startled when the ensign returned with the key.

"Danke," she said. When Hanna heard the door click behind her, she turned to her patient and gently washed the dirt away through his wincing. *He should be crying out*, she thought.

A red streak had moved up from the festering sore. "We need to come back with medicine."

"I agree," Elisabeth replied. "Tomorrow morning. These abrasions are very inflamed," she said, examining Christian. "I don't see any red streaks, but they could easily worsen very quickly."

"The sooner, the better," Christian said. "One of the guards who brings our food has been more lenient than he should be with information about our fate. It could be tomorrow, next week, or next month."

"And?" Hanna said.

"We're only here by the grace of God. We should be in Halifax. The guard said the fishermen received their bounties for our capture, then promptly returned to New England when the weather cleared. We're told a ship, when it comes in, is to transport us. As to when, it's anybody's guess."

Elisabeth lowered her voice. "What does Detleff have against you? He only allowed us entry because of Georg."

Christian did not reply.

"Pray, tell me. If luck stays with us, Detleff may be our only way in here. I need to know."

"Suffice to say, we didn't see eye to eye."

Hanna was half-listening to the conversation. She finished cleaning Eagle Feather's wounds. When she looked up at her patient, his head had fallen forward. She placed her hand on his forehead. "A fever."

"We've been away long enough. Georg will be worried," Elisabeth said and stood up to knock on the door.

To Elisabeth's relief, Barbara Moser willingly agreed to look after the children. Hanna gathered medicine and packed the strips of linen bandages Georg gave her. Last night, Elisabeth had told her husband about their visit. At first, he was against them returning, but in time he relented.

"Here," Elisabeth said, handing Hanna the hackmatack poultice, "you forgot this. Georg said it heals better."

Hanna tucked it away and closed the lid on the basket. "I believe that's it then."

Ensign Irwin was on duty again. "Allow me, Fraulein Heber." The ensign smiled, taking the small basket from Hanna.

Elisabeth gave Hanna a stern look when her sister's face flushed. She turned to the ensign. "Ja! Danke. It is very kind of you," she said, and forced the startled soldier to take her larger basket. The ensign walked ahead and she pulled Hanna back. "This is not the time to display affection," she hissed.

Her voice hushed, Hanna said, "Believe me, I'm not in the slightest interested, but we need him as an ally."

Once inside the cell, Hanna asked Ensign Irwin to bring hot water. Eagle Feather's fever had not broken, and the red streak had crept higher up his leg. After she cleaned the weeping wound of pus and smoothed the poultice over it, Hanna carefully wrapped his ankle. Her patient spoke. "Wela'lin."

"He's thanking you," Christian said.

She nodded. "Paul taught me this word." Hanna noticed her brother's expression changed to one of sadness. "You can warn him, he may not be thanking me after I ask him to drink this." She smiled, holding up the contents. "It's very bitter. I don't like it."

"Is it yarrow? I never heard of it being used by the Mi'kmaq."

Elisabeth nodded. "Mama used it for everything, remember?

The one thing I regret her bringing from the old country were the yarrow seeds." She laughed. "As of yet, I haven't seen it grow wild here. I don't have a salve already prepared, but the tea will be just as beneficial, for the fever."

Hanna looked again at Christian. "What's wrong? Your expression quickly changed when I mentioned Paul. Do you know anything?" Then eagerly, "Have you seen him, dear brother?"

"I have something from Paul." He paused. "Hanna—"

"Oh please, can I see? Do you still have it?"

With his good hand, Christian pulled a pouch out from inside his jacket and handed it to her. "Hanna, before you open it, I need to tell you—"

"Where are they now? I miss him so much. I would love to see them again." Hanna pulled out the wooden cross and was transported to her last visit with Paul and Magdeleine. She stared at her brother who no longer looked her way. She knew. Tears wet her eyelashes. She stood and banged on the door with her fist. "Guard!" She banged again. "Open now!" she choked.

Elisabeth called after her as Hanna ran from the cell.

OVER THE NEXT WEEK, HANNA continued to see Eagle Feather and Christian daily. Elisabeth joined her when she was able. Into the second week, Papa was off militia duty and home, which hampered Hanna's visits. Eagle Feather's fever had broken, and the wounds had slowly shown signs of healing. But not as quickly as they should have, in her opinion. Their meagre meals of bread, water, and thin broth only made things worse. Lack of substantial nutrition eventually caused extreme havoc on the health of both men, leaving them tired and weak. With the help of her sister, Hanna had taken it upon herself to bring thick stews and nourishing soups when she could. In time, there was a noticeable improvement in the two men's strength.

She was now on a first-name basis with Ensign Irwin. When he began to bend the rules more often than he should, she was sure Patrick had grown compassionate. It was a constant concern not knowing when her brother would be transported out, but in the interim, Hanna hatched ways for them to escape, digging for information to devise the best time to engage in such a scheme. There was always a guard outside the building and two soldiers on duty inside. But there were two night shifts a week when there was only one at the desk. The escape would have to happen on Patrick's watch, so she kept a close eye on the exact timings of his shift and that of the guard patrolling outside.

When she first spoke to Christian of the plan, he immediately raised red flags without asking questions as to how. And Elisabeth, of course, had agreed with him. But now Hanna was impressing upon her sister that there would be no peril involved to either of them.

"You will not be able to conceal a weapon. We're always searched," Elisabeth argued.

"Only in discreet ways—the medicine basket and the food we bring. I can easily conceal a knife inside my blouse. Safer still, strap it to my leg. They would not dare to search a lady in such private areas." Hanna gave an impish grin.

"You make light of this! It's not funny, dear sister. Christian could be killed."

"You forget Eagle Feather. Remember, this will all be played out the night Patrick is alone."

"Patrick! You're now on a first-name basis? What you are doing is improper. You're leading him on. Mama would never approve of you taking such liberties."

"Shush. I'm using it to our advantage. It's because he likes me that he has given me such allowances to enter."

"There're just too many nuances to consider. They can't just disappear into the woods without different clothes. When Christian's disappearance is discovered, that is the first place the search parties will be."

"Then a boat."

"Ach, nein! Where are—"

"Bitte. Please hear me out," Hanna urged. "After Herr Kolp's daily passenger runs, he ties his boat every evening near Paul's old farm. Christian and Eagle Feather can use it to cross the harbour to the farthest south lots—in behind Herr Waite's farm. Then traverse over the land to LaHave River."

"But that's stealing." Elisabeth wagged a finger at her. "Hanna! I'll not be a part of this."

Hanna grabbed her sister's finger and pushed it away. "I call it borrowing. If you like, we can put two pennies in his jar for the one-way fare. That is the rate, is it not?" Sarcasm was not her intent, but having to convince her sister to save their brother's life was frustrating. She calmed her voice. "Herr Kolp ferries people between the south lots and the town anyway. In fact, is not Herr Waite's farm one of his stops for passengers? Once Christian and Eagle Feather reach the other side, they will just moor the boat there."

Elisabeth let out a sigh of exasperation. "I don't know what to think. And why do you always speak of Eagle Feather? I said before, I'll not allow an Indian to escape. If I consider this at all, it will only be for Christian."

Hanna's voice started to elevate once more. "Can you not find enough mercy in your heart to reciprocate?"

"Give me time to think on it, Hanna. At least give me that."

# Chapter Nineteen

MAY 1758

*I* beg you, please come. Katharina is in great pain, and the midwives are nowhere to be found."

Elisabeth could hear the commotion in the kitchen. By the time she reached Matthaus Fausel outside, Georg was in the midst of asking Hanna to look after the children. "Come with me," Georg said to his wife. "Katharina trusts only you with the twins."

"Of course," she said, wiping her hands on her apron. "My heavens, she still has two months to go. And who's looking after the twins now?" she said to Matthaus. The girls were just fifteen months old.

"Herr Baltzer was helping me with the plowing—he's looking after them until I return."

"Oh, good Lord!" she remarked. "We must hurry." A terrifying picture formed of that bachelor looking after toddlers he knew nothing about.

She could see the horse and cart that she surmised must belong to Herr Baltzer, as he was one of the very few who was privy to such a transport. Dr. Phillips had one as well, which helped Georg on his rounds to the more distant farms like the

Fausels on the Northwest Range. Matthaus and Katharina lived near Detleff Jessen.

The trail was tedious and painful, as the cart jostled horridly the whole journey. It left Elisabeth regretting she had taken the ride when she could have walked the five miles.

It was well into evening when the hard and agonizing delivery brought forth a tiny boy. He did not survive the night. After a makeshift christening to give him a name, they immediately buried the infant. Though Georg left early, Elisabeth decided to stay on until Katharina regained her strength. Keeping busy with cooking meals, cleaning, and watching over the twins, she thought often of Hanna's scheme. The silent deliberation bantered back and forth in her head. Of course, Elisabeth knew, deep down, she would have no choice but to stand by her sister rather than have her enact her plan alone.

After supper, on the last night of her stay, she milked the Fausels' two cows. With the bucket almost full, she started humming a new hymn she had sung on Sunday. Elisabeth was absorbed in her work when something dropped with a crash. The cow turned its large head back at her and gave a low moo.

"Is that you, Matthaus?" she called. Nothing. She grabbed his musket, which he had given her before she left the house. Wondering if it was a bear about, she gingerly moved out of the stall—she had never encountered one before. A couple of months ago, a fox had carried off one of their hens.

Elisabeth stood motionless, waiting. Then, a distant shot broke the silence. Through the open barn door, she could see Matthaus's shadow walk past the house window. Was it the warning shot from the blockhouse?

An open hand grasped her mouth from behind, and her head was wrenched backward. The odorous smell of sour liquor spilled from her assailant's mouth when he spoke. The gun was ripped from her grip, and instinct triggered her. She latched her teeth onto his hand, then screamed just when a second shot rang out, warning the farmers to stay inside. When Elisabeth ran for the door, another intruder blocked her, shutting it tightly before she could escape. Elisabeth was trapped.

The barn door jiggled as Matthaus yelled for her.

She screeched. "Here! Matthaus! He—" A hand stifled her cries, and her assailant dragged her into an empty stall. The second Indian held a large knife and remained near the door. His nostrils flared and his upper lip curled as he waited for Matthaus to enter.

Her captor's tight grip forced Elisabeth to crouch down in front of him. He knelt behind her and pressed a cold blade to her throat. Elisabeth shook uncontrollably, and the tip of the blade pricked her skin. She could feel a drop of blood slide its way down the side of her throat. The barn door creaked open. A single discharge of a gun blasted, then she heard a sickening crash.

"Elisabeth!"

Darkness enveloped her.

Elisabeth jerked back from the entrance of the root cellar. Hanna had bent to enter after she'd handed off the eggs and milk for storage, and from the little light that shone through the doorway, she could see her sister stiffen and clench her jaw. Over the past two weeks, Elisabeth's nerves had been wound tight from her terrifying ordeal. Heightened by the least movement, her anxiety came on rapidly and suddenly. It had become a ceaseless vexation to her family. The wound on her neck had healed much faster than her mental state.

"You know not to sneak up on me like that!"

"You're right, I should have announced myself." Like

everyone else, Hanna had stopped trying to argue the point that she was not skulking. Who else would be passing her food?

"You know what I've been through. I only ask one small thing of you." Elisabeth brushed by Hanna, quickly retreating into the sunlight. She pushed the dirt and cobwebs from her skirt. "You never know when they'll return."

The family now knew who *they* were. "It's broad daylight. They'll not be…" She dropped it—it was not worth the effort. "I didn't mean it," she called out when her sister ran for the house. Hanna placed the foodstuffs on one of the empty shelves, then headed after her sister.

Inside, Georg was in the usual state of consoling his wife.

Though Hanna was ever concerned for her sister, she could not stop thinking about how to assist Christian and Eagle Feather to escape. She could no longer discuss the details with Elisabeth. The 60th Regiment had sailed into the harbour the day before yesterday to deliver Herr and Frau Knaut. It was now the middle of May, and time was of the essence. With access to a possible returning ship to Halifax, it was only a matter of a few days before the prisoners would be transported out.

Hanna switched to something more positive. "The weekly five-pound flour allowance has been approved to continue until June of next year."

"Terrific," Georg remarked. "We won't have to worry about the grain if the weather doesn't co-operate."

"Humph," Elisabeth grunted, daubing her eyes with the ends of her apron. "Indeed it should continue. *They* have continued with their merciless attempts to kill us. And we still have the two back fields to cultivate. I tell you, it won't happen. Even if we had the time to earn money, we can't afford the wartime prices for bread and flour."

"Frau Knaut says the rations are to keep us from fleeing to town. Colonel Sutherland needs us to stay working on our farms," Hanna said.

Elisabeth set herself down on the bench. "So many have left. You may see the Mosers moving." She stared up at Georg and cried, "My husband, I implore you to take this family within the safer confines of the palisade!"

"Nein! I refuse to let fear dictate our lives." He placed his hand over hers. "The Mosers aren't leaving. I just spoke with Heinrich yesterday—he agrees with me. If we run, we will have lost the battle. We cannot give up."

"Another blockhouse has just been completed not far from here," Hanna added.

Georg nodded. "And it's larger and not a typical station. Instead of moving into town, we can live with others inside the stockade for safety and still raise our grain on our own lots." He straightened his back. "No one promised the new world would be easy."

"I wouldn't have come if I'd known then what I know now! Now it's too late." Elisabeth dropped her head into her hands.

"Enough said. We're here now. Our tenacity will see us through this, and I speak for many of the families."

Petie and Marta were now vying for their mama's attention, so Hanna lifted a large cauldron of heated water to start the wash. "Allow me, dear sister," Georg said, and lifted the heavy pot by the handle.

Once in the bright sunlight, Hanna helped pour the hot contents into the cold water tub. A mass of steam billowed up between them. When she bent over, her wooden cross, which she had hidden safely from view, slipped from beneath her blouse.

Georg rested the cross on his fingers as it dangled from her neck. "Where did you get this?" He squinted. "It looks like St. Anne is engraved here. Are you now of the Catholic faith?"

Hanna took the cross and tucked it away. "You have no need to worry. I don't wear this for Catholicism but strictly in honour of a friend."

"Paul?"

Hanna didn't reply.

"Ach, I see. You must have seen him then. When did he return?"

Hanna shook her head. "He and Magdeleine were both killed." She tried hard not to become emotional. "I'm surprised Elisabeth didn't tell you."

"You know this through Christian?"

Hanna glanced at her brother-in-law, then off to the field behind him. She couldn't be sure if Elisabeth had spoken to Georg about the escape. Silence would be her best defence.

But Georg read her thoughts. "Elisabeth explained everything to me. I know of your visits. And your scheme!"

"I wouldn't call it that. You make it sound so underhanded."

"Elisabeth may think that way of your idea, especially when you want Eagle Feather mixed into the plot."

Hanna folded her arms in front of her. "He's my brother's brother, therefore mine, blood or no blood. My conscience won't allow me to leave him behind. And I can just imagine what my sister told you. She was dead set against it from the start."

"Can you really blame her after what she's been through?"

"Well, it's no matter now. I can't do this alone, and Elisabeth was my only hope."

"You know, Hanna, your plan does have some merit. I think it can work. Just a few tweaks to be ironed out about the boat and the timing."

"What do you mean?" Hanna said, uncrossing her arms.

"So there are absolutely no questions of where the two will be running to safety, that boat needs to be returned to the harbour shore. I can do that. The authorities will then be scouring the forests on this side of the harbour and be oblivious to their run for the river. By the time the soldiers changed their course of action, Christian and Eagle Feather would be long gone. Your brother also needs to meet the river farther upstream to avoid the LaHave blockhouse. I can help there."

"You? You will help me?"

Georg nodded. "Heavens! Your papa will never forgive me—this can't fail."

"Papa can never know! There's only one window of opportunity. It must be done immediately. Papa will be home in less than a week."

Georg added, "His next militia shift is the end of June. We need to get weapons to Christian and Eagle Feather and a signal when it's safe for them to put everything into action. We will talk more of this when I return. I'll be back in time for supper." He kissed her on the forehead.

Hanna was flush with a new burst of energy.

TODAY WAS THE APPOINTED DAY. Bear Cub was grateful for Georg's involvement. He could now relax knowing Hanna would not be involved. She assisted in other ways by giving the opportunity for Georg to examine the prisoners all the while becoming familiar with his surroundings. Her last deed and tearful farewell occurred when she slipped two knives into the cell while wearing two shirts and breeches hidden underneath her dress. Bear Cub kept them out of sight beneath their mattresses.

The time was set. At eight thirty tonight his brother-in-law would return. Ensign Irwin would not question the lateness, as he knew the medical rounds required long days. Georg had feigned a reoccurring infection in Eagle Feather's leg to require him to come again. But this morning, bluffing had not been required. Eagle Feather awoke with inflamed, watery eyes and a dry cough that disturbed Bear Cub.

Bear Cub moved to their cell door—he had heard raised voices. He cranked his neck to see two officers a few feet away.

Bear Cub heard, "They will pay, Jessen!"

"With more scalps, I suppose."

Eagle Feather whispered from behind. "Who is it?"

"Detleff and what looks like his superior," Bear Cub replied.

The older officer replied, "In war, no one's life is sacred. You'll get used to it."

"Tell me that again when you've held a scalp that once belonged to a child. It matters not which side—an innocent is an innocent." Detleff straightened his back and glanced back at his superior officer. "With all due respect, sir, if you can say that, your blood no longer runs. It is ice, and I can't wish that on my worst enemy."

"Problem?" Eagle Feather asked.

Bear Cub walked back to his brother. "I just heard a side of Jessen that I never would have suspected."

The ensign walked his usual cell check just as the sun cast an eerie red illumination onto their stone prison. Heavy footsteps approached their door. As usual, his eyes peered through the iron grill, scanning side to side to ensure the civility of his charges. Upon his departure, the last clang of a door sounded, then silence.

Minutes passed before the same door reopened and they heard a familiar voice.

"You have ten minutes," the ensign firmly stipulated as he unlocked the cell.

Georg, nodding, stepped inside with his medical bag. The moment the soldier departed, Bear Cub and Eagle Feather started to change their clothes while Georg kept a watchful eye.

"Hanna was correct, outside there's only one soldier on duty," Georg whispered. "I can easily distract him. Remember there's a set of stairs to the ramparts about thirty feet on your left. That area has the least distance to the ground below. I could only see two guards up there."

With his brother complaining of the onset of head pain, Bear Cub questioned whether he was strong enough to proceed. Eagle Feather gave his assent with a nod as he tucked his medicine pouch inside his jacket and lay on the bed beneath the blanket. Bear Cub hid his own pouch and flute, and took up his position against the wall beside the door.

"Ensign!" Georg yelled urgently, banging on the door. "Open up! This man is dead." The soldier turned the key and was quick to check on Eagle Feather. Bear Cub clutched the hilt of his dagger and thwacked the ensign on the back of his head. He collapsed.

Eagle Feather threw back the blanket to help his brother.

Bear Cub rolled the body over and fumbled for the key. Georg tied the ensign's ankles, then his hands behind his back while Eagle Feather stuffed his mouth with a cloth.

Bear Cub moved in behind his brother-in-law. "Tell Hanna she will meet Singing Sparrow one day."

"What?" Georg asked.

"This is for your own good, Georg." Before he turned around, Bear Cub knocked him senseless and he slumped over.

Eagle Feather stared up at his brother. "Why did you do that?"

"So Georg won't be implicated. Help me tie him."

The two left the cell, closing the door behind them. Eagle

Feather opened the front entry by a crack, then carefully closed it. "The guard is at the other end now," he whispered. "We can slip out before he returns."

Eagle Feather reopened the door and they headed for the stairs. It was now dark, the night sky peppered with bright stars. It was a godsend; there was only a sliver of a moon casting very little light. *The plan seems too easy*, Bear Cub thought as they stealthily moved up the stairs. Near the top, they ducked low, waiting for the sentry to pass, then they moved over the rampart and jumped to a grassy mound below.

Upon hearing a voice, they sank back into the dark shadows. Two guards disappeared in the opposite direction. Eagle Feather and Bear Cub left the fort and skirted the palisade before moving away from it entirely. The welcoming murmurs of water lapped at the shore, and they waded in to push the boat from its mooring.

Taking turns with the oars, they navigated their way across the harbour. On the other side, Eagle Feather steered into an inlet between two farms at the South Range and beached the boat at an uncleared and deserted isthmus. Bear Cub jumped out while his brother waded as far as he could to push the boat back onto the open water, setting it adrift.

Guided by the stars, Eagle Feather forged ahead on a well-trodden Mi'kmaw path through hardwood forest that led to the LaHave River.

Eagle Feather's symptoms worsened throughout the night as they travelled to get to the mouth of Pijinuiskaq. He refused food and his stamina weakened considerably, making it impossible for him to walk any distance. Bear Cub kept his thoughts to himself when the alarming chills and fever made themselves known.

Bear Cub left his brother safely hidden by the trees so he could prowl about. Not knowing how close he was to the LaHave blockhouse, he approached a small beach with caution. He could hear nothing but the seagulls above. At the mouth of the inlet lay the ocean. On the horizon, a grey blanket of cloud was stretching to seal off the clear sky in the early twilight.

He could not believe his luck when he spotted a small shallop. It lay amid stringy seaweed and strewn pieces of brown kelp. Its discoloured hull showed the telltale sign of tidal flows. Oars lay inside and the sail was furled on the single mast. There were no markings to indicate whether it was from a British or French ship. He scrutinized the area again, hoping there was no one to see him.

He rushed back to his brother. "Good fortune is upon us. There's an abandoned boat and the tide is going out. We must leave now. It's not far from here. Can you make it?" Eagle Feather grunted an affirmative, and Bear Cub helped him to his feet. Eagle Feather leaned on him heavily, and they slowly made their way toward the river.

Eagle Feather lay down inside the vessel, and Bear Cub pushed it out to deeper waters, then climbed in. As Bear Cub rowed, he watched his brother's breathing. Thankfully, he was sleeping now. Bear Cub suspected measles, but it could be the more deadly smallpox. Both had similar symptoms, and he wouldn't know for certain unless he saw the familiar pus-filled blisters.

Hours passed as they floated downwind with smooth waters. Darkness closed in and Bear Cub could only hope it remained so until they reached Oqomkikiaq. The stars were out to help him navigate. He would follow the coastline as he rowed southwest until the morning.

Long into the night, the warm breezes, once their companion, quickly turned. Earlier Bear Cub had unfurled the sail, giving him a needed rest with the oars. But now, given the stiffer winds, the choppy waves, and his little experience of handling a boat, it was an arduous task. The rain that had started lightly was now driving sheets, and the more he tried to tame the boat, the angrier the ocean became, unleashing its watery fists against them. Bear Cub panicked.

Eagle Feather, long since awake, tried to steady himself as the vessel rolled violently from side to side. Lightning lit up the overcast skies, and thunder answered with her rumbling replies. In the storm's fury, the loud crack of the mast was grimly muted. It crashed and was instantly swallowed by the mountainous waves. With the bow into the chaotic wind, Bear Cub took up the oars with Eagle Feather in a futile attempt to heave to, or at the very least to stay afloat.

Any words spoken were swept away in the pandemonium. The land lit up before them in spasmodic flashes. Barbed streaks of lightning flashed repeatedly until one pierced Mother Earth with the force of a deadly spear. Now, it was apparent—they were dangerously close to the rocky shoreline.


BEFORE HE OPENED HIS EYES, the sun warmed Bear Cub's body. He could hear the ocean swells peaking before they collapsed to a low roar. His muscles ached as he attempted to sit up. Half the shallop lay lopsided against a sand dune. His mind tried to make sense of his circumstances.

*Eagle Feather!* Bear Cub tried to recall their last moments aboard. He called out. No sound but the now dormant sea, her waves kissing the sand for absolution.

"Bear Cub!" It was a sweet sound, and the vision sweeter when he noticed a body stirring near the wreckage. He carried his brother to higher ground, then collapsed.

Eagle Feather scratched his forehead and face. When Bear Cub wiped the dirt from his brother's skin, he saw the red rash that spread down to his neck.

"By the way you look at me, it is measles," Eagle Feather declared.

Bear Cub swallowed hard and nodded. He would not say anything about the possibility of smallpox. In the next few hours, he'd know.

"I will leave you to find food. Do you know where we are?"

Eagle Feather looked around. "It is familiar. I have been here, as a child."

"Let us hope if I meet anyone, he's a friend." Bear Cub stood up, took his shirt off, and formed a sling to hold any berries he might find.

While he foraged for food, Bear Cub came upon wikuoml in a clearing. He crouched down to watch the women busily attending pots that hung over the fire.

"Kwe'."

Bear Cub fell back, spilling most of his forest harvest. "Ach! Verdammt!" He looked up at the person who had spoken to him from behind. The elderly stranger stood with ease, musket at his side. A simple wooden cross hung from his thin neck. His long hair was tucked neatly behind his ears and hung loosely at his shoulders. He gazed down at Bear Cub and held out his hand. When Bear Cub quickly rose to his feet, he swayed, feeling faint.

"Are you not well, my brother?"

Bear Cub thought of Eagle Feather and staggered several steps back up against a tree. "Do not come any closer," he said in Mi'kmaw. He raised his hand when the stranger attempted to approach. Bear Cub explained.

The stranger asked no questions and told Bear Cub to wait.

He returned with a basket of food, disappeared again, then came back with blankets, a gun, and medicine. "Show me." When Bear Cub resisted, he said, "Do not be concerned. I will walk at a distance. You are too weak to carry all of this."

"You could still be a danger to your family."

"I will be careful. Come, we go."

Bear Cub was deeply touched. He picked up some of the supplies and walked ahead a few paces before he heard footsteps following him. The stranger called, "I am called Ambroise."

He turned back. "And I Bear Cub."

Before Ambroise left, he helped by building a wikuom. Bear Cub gathered spruce branches to make it as comfortable as possible. After that, a day did not go by without their new friend bringing more food and medicine.

It was not smallpox. For the next couple of days, the rapidly spreading rash did not manifest to open sores. The only food Eagle Feather could manage was warm liquids and medicine. His sore throat was too severe for anything solid. In time, the rash slowly disappeared, but the fever and cough stubbornly hung on.

Bear Cub spent less and less time away hunting for the two of them as Eagle Feather weakened. No medicine Ambroise left seemed to relieve his cough, and no amount of cool water brought the fever down. Bear Cub had watched his brother-in-law cut into a vein once, but he knew nothing of bloodletting and was not about to attempt it.

One morning, he lay awake listening to another harsh, dry hacking. When it stopped, his brother's breathing changed. Bear Cub crawled to his side. "Shh, don't try to speak," he said. Eagle Feather's mouth was partially open, and he was labouring to catch a deep breath. His face was flushed. Bear Cub rolled up a moose skin, placed it under Eagle Feather's head, and waited for another bout of coughing to subside. He raised his brother's back and supported it with blankets until he was partly sitting up. A deep inhalation relaxed the fright that had gripped Eagle Feather. Bear Cub wiped the perspiration from his brother's face.

"I'll go to Ambroise to see about getting water from the healing spring." Ambroise had told Bear Cub of Mother Earth's gift to her People, a spring that was some distance away. Ancient stories taught that when medicines failed, the waters worked miracles. "I'll return as quickly as possible."

"When I breathe my last—"

"Stop it!" Bear Cub said angrily. "I don't want to hear it anymore." His nerves were frayed. "The Land of Souls can damn well wait for you. They don't need you. I do!"

"It is my time," Eagle Feather said hoarsely.

"How dare you give up on me! I refuse to take you home dead. Please—you can't surrender this life just yet," he begged. "We are brothers, are we not?" He placed his hand over his brother's heart. He gently moved Eagle Feather's ashen hand on top of his own. "Our hearts beat as one."

"To ease my passage beyond, do not weep for me. I will still walk beside you, my friend."

Bear Cub rushed outside—from the unbearable sorrow and morbid talk that were closing in around him. He fell to his knees, pounding his fists repeatedly onto the ground. "How dare he?" he cried. He swore at his brother for admitting defeat. Bear Cub panted heavily and pressed his palms hard against his eyes.

Before Bear Cub left their campsite, he silently offered tobacco as a gift to the sacred fire. He prayed to the Creator to watch over his brother and keep him safe until his return. He swore he would make peace with his papa if God would keep

Eagle Feather alive. He pleaded to Kisu'lkw to bar his brother's entrance to the Land of Souls—he could not go yet.

Ambroise and Bear Cub departed at midmorning, and it seemed like hours were spent traipsing through the woods, over an obstacle course of distorted, bulbous tree roots that snaked underfoot and around large boulders. Smaller-veined offshoots writhed in countless directions. If it had not been for Ambroise, Bear Cub would never have found the spring. He spoke little, wondering if the hand of death would take his brother while he was gone.

It was dusk when he returned. He woke Eagle Feather to administer the fresh water. He soaked a piece of cloth to wet his blistered lips, then let a few drops trickle from his cupped hand into his brother's mouth. There had been no instructions on how much to give or how often. Bear Cub continued to administer the healing waters every hour. He never left his brother's side, studying his patient as he drifted in and out of sleep. Every time Eagle Feather stirred, Bear Cub gave more of the liquid.

On the second day, there was no improvement and there were no changes far into the night. Bear Cub sat in the dark counting Eagle Feather's breaths. He gripped his brother's sweaty hand, closed his eyes, and prayed again. In his entire life, he had never begged for anything or to anyone with such intensity. To whom, he no longer knew.

A haunting howl drifted into their inner sanctum. He glanced at the open door to see a lone wolf staring at him. In the animal's yellow eyes he saw deep compassion. Then the wolf turned and walked out of sight. Bear Cub moved to follow him, but the wolf was nowhere to be seen. Eagle Feather called out. His voice was clear: "The circle cannot be broken."

Bear Cub jerked awake to the sun's rays penetrating the wikuom. A cool hand brush his face.

"Bear Cub."

He was groggy as he tried to make sense of what had just happened. The last thing he remembered was praying. He must have fallen asleep. Did he dream all of it?

"Bear Cub," the voice hoarsely called again.

He now gazed upon Eagle Feather, his clothes wet with perspiration. He stroked the hair back from his brother's face. The fever had broken.

# Chapter Twenty

JULY 1758

Hanna shook the dirt off the bulb before placing it in the basket along with the new potatoes. As she pulled another ripe purple-and-white turnip from the soil, she thought about Georg and Ensign Irwin. Weeks had passed since they'd been found locked inside the cell. The night of the escape, she and Elisabeth thought the worst when Georg did not return. The authorities investigated and there was no need to cover anything up with lies, as Georg was more than surprised at what had happened to him.

Posters appeared of two Indian escapees, offering rewards for their capture and causing a flurry of gossip about town. Hanna witnessed Papa's humiliation when he read *Christian Heber* written prominently in black. His shoulders slumped, and over the coming days, his vitality waned and his gait slowed. The remaining natives at the fort were promptly chained and taken to Halifax. Colonel Sutherland sailed on orders to take part in the expedition against Louisbourg. Captain Rudolf Faesch was his replacement to command Lunenburg along with his 60th Regiment.

Thus far the weather had given hope for better crops. Even though the sheep and cattle were growing, it would be another year before the settlers would be able to clothe themselves with their own wool and leather. Hanna's clothes were threadbare, and any extra money made from a surplus of crops was indeed welcomed.

Hanna stood and stretched her sore back. She watched Papa as he walked up and down the rows of oats, stopping now and then for a closer look. The back field was bursting with spring wheat, though it was susceptible to mildew if not grown with barley, as everyone soon discovered. In the early years of the settlement, these two crops had been discouraged as they needed large quantities of manure to grow, and the few cattle they had did not produce enough.

Hanna shaded her eyes from the sun. She waved at Philip and Anna coming over the rise and ran to greet them.

"Ach. It's so good to see you, Frau Knaut," she said. Her friend reeled slightly from her hug. "You've been greatly missed."

"Hanna, bitte! Be more discreet," Papa corrected. "Forgive my daughter, Anna. Sometimes her enthusiasm precedes her manners. She lacks motherly guidance."

"There's nothing to pardon." Anna returned the affections of her young friend. "I indeed have missed our times together, Hanna. Michael, I have had my fill of pompous rhetoric and insincere sentiments in Halifax. Truly, this is just the medicine I need," she said, holding Hanna close.

"It's we who should apologize," Philip remarked. "Since our return, we have been remiss in our visits."

Michael raised his hand in protest. "Perfectly understandable. I see the election notices are up."

"And a good thing. This fall, there are plans to launch a campaign to attract New Englanders."

"I think there are now fifty-eight electors," Michael said.

"There are, and the voting date is the thirty-first."

Michael nodded and changed the subject. "I'm sure Halifax must have been swarming with the military."

"You could say that! Forty-one warships and over a hundred transports were in the harbour. Thousands of sailors converged on the town. Old Dreadnought oversees the naval operations, with Major-General Amherst overseeing the expedition to Louisbourg."

"Old Dreadnought?" Michael laughed.

"Admiral Boscawen, and a well-deserved name it is. He shies from nothing. With him at the helm, we cannot lose. The entire fleet left on May twenty-eighth. It certainly was quite a sight. Even you, my dear Anna, were quite impressed."

"The officers in their full regalia just maybe left me in awe," Anna admitted with a sly smirk. "But it's very unsettling as to what will be forthcoming for both sides."

Philip grinned at his wife. "Said like a true woman who has no stomach for such things."

"And such talk bores me to tears," Anna quipped. "Come, Hanna. Let's take our leave. I've much to tell you of the officers' ball." She linked her arm through Hanna's and turned on her heels. She looked back and continued her haughty air of jest. "I must free my dear friend lest any of your glory talk of blood and gore land on her young ears."

Hanna snickered. As they walked away, she could hear dismissive laughter behind their backs. She and Anna found some shade under a tree and sat on a patch of grass among the dandelions. Hanna listened with amazement to Anna's vivid description of the ladies' ornate dresses of silk taffeta.

"Where do they hold these balls?" Hanna tried to restrain her excitement at hearing of such lavish gatherings.

"At the Pontack Inn. It is very large—three storeys, if you can imagine!" Anna leaned her back against the tree. "The main ballroom was on the second floor, where there were smaller rooms in which the officers played cards. On all four sides was this tremendous veranda where we could stroll outside." She sat up straight. "The kitchen was on the ground floor. I was a bit giddy when an officer's wife guided me down to see it. Oh, Hanna—if you'd only been with me! They had a potager stove, a masonry box but with the iron hearth at the height of my waist. No need to stoop and kneel into the hearth! On top were several holes for the pots and a built-in warming oven. Can you imagine?"

Hanna could not even picture such a thing. "Where was the fire?"

"On the outside of the box, there was a door where the fire lay. They could cook at lower temperatures for a longer time, as the temperatures can be controlled more easily."

"Did they not use the regular hearth at all?"

"They still did, and what food was finished cooking could be kept warm in the oven. The stove was used mainly for sauces, syrups, and fancy ragouts."

"What did you eat?"

"Well, Colonel Wolfe threw a party at the Pontack a few days before they sailed. Everyone who was anyone was there. There's a courtyard in the centre of the building where wagons and carriages are kept. I can still see the horses prancing across the cobblestones with heads held high, just as pompous-looking as the ones who rode them." She laughed. "I'm sure it was indeed the grandest ball given."

"The food?" Hanna prodded.

"Ach! Ja. There was plenty. Mind you, not the stews and soups we eat. Nein. They were much more delicate. *Refreshments* they were called. Things like macaroons, iced cakes, spiced cookies, and tiers of glasses, full of syllabub creams. Venison and duck.

And oysters!" Anna suddenly added. "Have you ever eaten one? No, of course not. I had not! They are distinctly slippery, to be sure. I don't care to have one again," she said, making a face.

Hanna laughed. She didn't know what a syllabub was, but she remembered there was a receipt for it the cookbook Anna had shared with her.

"Everything was served on large platters of fine china. Claret, brandy, and Madeira wine flowed throughout the evening."

Hanna could not begin to dream of what such fare would even look like, let alone how it would taste. As she listened to the descriptions of the delicacies, her stomach grumbled.

"That's enough. As much as I enjoyed it, a steady diet of those foodstuffs would not be my cup of tea. I'm so glad to be here," Anna said sincerely, entwining her fingers through Hanna's.

Hanna squeezed Anna's hand against her own. She turned to her friend. "You're suddenly so serious."

"I don't wish to listen to malicious gossip, but it's difficult to not hear it about town. Is it true your brother is willingly living with the Mi'kmaq?"

Hanna neither confirmed nor denied it.

"They're saying they were helped by your family."

"Those who speak such things should keep their wagging tongues still lest they be put in the town pillory. If Frau Kuhn were still here, I'd say she was the first to spread it."

"Hush, dear one. Do not say such things. It was said you and Elisabeth were seen at the fort many times."

"That means nothing." Hanna swallowed hard. "We did go, but only to nurse them back to health."

"Them? Who else? Did you help the Indian?"

"Of course."

"But to aid someone who could just as easily kill you in return…"

Hanna shook her head. "Nein! That would not happen. They're brothers." She started to cry. "It's Papa, Frau Knaut. We're slowly becoming estranged from our neighbours. They speak less to us now. As soon as I speak of Christian, he becomes irate. I can't bring up his name for fear of another tirade." She paused. "Bitte, don't say anything to Herr Knaut, nor Papa. He knows nothing of our visits."

"Does Michael not believe the gossip?"

Hanna shook her head.

"Do you know how they were able to obtain weapons?"

"My sister and I are absolved of any such possibility." When Anna did not speak, Hanna let the silence linger until she ceased sniffling. "I'm very much torn between Papa and Christian. My brother would never put me in harm's way, and he trusts Eagle Feather implicitly. If he does, I shall as well. Whatever love Papa had for his son has long since died. If he found out I had spent time with Christian, the consequences would be devastating." She looked intently at Anna. "No one can ask me to choose between them."

"And no one will," Anna said and put her arm around Hanna. Anna handed her a handkerchief. "And Elisabeth—how does she feel?" When Hanna did not respond, she continued, "I'm aware of what happened at the Fausels'."

"She was always timid of Eagle Feather but never prevented me from giving him medicine. When it came to Christian, she would stand up for me to Papa. Now she is in constant fear for her own family. And it has worsened since Herr Wagner was killed at LaHave River."

"It has been said Labrador shot at him."

Hanna bit her tongue. There would be too many queries into why she knew it was not Paul.

"You need to dry your tears. I see your papa and Philip coming our way."

Hanna blew her nose and patted her eyes dry. As the two men neared, she could hear them talking of the new northwest common. "Another herdsman is needed for that area," Michael said.

"Agreed. Then we can move two of the bulls and rams there," Philip replied. "We must take our leave now. Hanna, are you weary of my wife's chatter?"

"That could never happen, Herr Knaut."

"I was just about to tell her, Philip—we are much too close now. Hanna, please call me Anna."

"But I cannot. You are a mother to me."

"You touch me deeply, my dear, but I will have it no other way." Anna kissed her on both cheeks. "The matter is closed."

A WEEK PASSED BEFORE ANNA returned for a visit. As Hanna's father and Herr Knaut left for town, Hanna overheard Papa announce, "They found Wagner's murderers! There was a group of them—scalped." Then, "I heard Captain Faesch will be declaring the election results."

"Gut" was the only reply she could hear. Their voices faded with distance. Hanna's stomach ached. Was Christian among them? What about Eagle Feather? She quickly pushed such thoughts from her mind. Hanna sensed her friend scrutinizing her. She slowly moved her hand away from Anna's reassuring touch and excused herself from the kitchen table.

Anna followed her outside and sat down beside her without saying a word. Hanna was not certain she could contain her emotions, so she was grateful for her friend's silence.

"My views trouble you deeply, do they not?"

"Hanna, you have the ability to see with a second pair of eyes what the rest of us do not. You see from your soul."

"Christian has shown me another side." She started telling her friend about the baby her brother and his wife had adopted. "Lise's parents were killed when our soldiers set fire to their village. My brother and Singing Sparrow barely escaped. Others weren't so lucky." She gazed at Anna. "They have done nothing to warrant such savagery."

"You know the Indians have done as much to this colony."

"How can you blame them? Would your rage not surface if your husband was slaughtered? Anna, you know what it's like to be forced from your home."

"We arrived here amid a vicious struggle we knew nothing about."

"You're evading my questions."

"You are unique in your thinking. Everyone here sees only the blood spilled, the bodies buried, families decimated. Others say we have done nothing to provoke this. And we're in the hands of a governor who manipulates us like puppets, determining what information we deserve."

Hanna thought of Paul. "They are a loving and kind people."

"As it is on both sides."

"But does that give our soldiers the right to harm the innocent?"

"I could say the same for the enemy. In times of war, it is always the innocent who will suffer most. You know this well. Did the Brissangs and Ochs deserve to die?" Anna asked.

"It's the British audacity of ownership here that has brought all this anguish. They're the cause of our miseries, and of the Mi'kmaw agonies."

"Be careful how you speak. Never say such things where there are others to hear," Anna warned.

"'Tis true!" Hanna let out a deep breath of frustration. "At times, I can't help but think the British have no right to give us this," she opined, staring out across the fields of crops.

"Is that you talking, or Christian?"

Coming from Anna, she knew what she had said was not meant to be unkind or dispiriting. But it did trigger a moment of thought. "A little of both." She smiled.

"Only you can decipher if it is one more than the other."

# Chapter Twenty-One



Singing Sparrow draped the last pieces of raw haddock over the branches for smoking and cooled the hot coals with water. Steam rose as they sizzled. She closed the flap of the enclosure and stood watching a canoe take shape under Na'ku'set's heat. The men were applying pitch to the seams as the women mixed more hot spruce resin with bear grease and ashes. She'd been told that in the old times, canoes were made from moose skin.

Where they now lived still had an ample amount of fish, and the moose and caribou were plentiful in the forested areas west of Port Rossignol, though according to the French traders, the British were interested in the area near the port and in the land much farther southwest of Pijinuiskaq.

There was decreased access to certain ancestral coastal areas where the New Englanders continued to fish exorbitantly for profit. With the animal migrations changing and shrinking, the past Winter had seen times of malnutrition, starvation, and disease in several communities. As British movements expanded, more Mi'kmaq retreated to hidden areas of untouched abundance.

Morning Dove quickly lifted her granddaughter, who was toddling toward the firepit. Lise giggled out loud as her grandmother cuddled her tight against her breast.

"Lise did not last for the storytelling. She fell asleep mid-story," Morning Dove said. "Now, look at her."

"Ah. Drowsy eyes are the result of her active legs and inquisitive mind. She does not stop," Singing Sparrow said as she followed her mother into the wikuom.

Morning Dove laid Lise upon the caribou pelt and brushed back her hair. "Now, sleep little one." She kissed her granddaughter on the forehead then turned to her daughter. "I will stay with you if you wish," Morning Dove offered. "Your father decided to go with the others torch-fishing at the weir pools. The tide is out."

Singing Sparrow was only half-listening. She despaired over Bear Cub and her brother. Five moons had passed while she waited and wondered. Unsettling visions of their fate continuously plagued her. Even her mother's tender touch jarred her.

"You are unsettled," Morning Dove whispered.

They rarely spoke of it, and Singing Sparrow looked away to hide her tears.

"Come." Her mother took hold of her hand. Outside in the cooling air of early evening, Morning Dove placed logs upright over the hot embers, and the tiny flames grew as they licked their way upward. "Sit beside me."

Her mother was Singing Sparrow's pillar of strength, kind in her approach but tough when Singing Sparrow needed it most, even when the truth was hard to swallow. Never judging, only guiding, Morning Dove was patient in her teachings. Singing Sparrow remembered her own fumblings as she learned which spruce tree to pick and tried to sense whether its spirit was willing to give life for a wikuom frame. "Learn the way of the bark, and do not go against its nature," her mother had taught her. "Harvest birchbark at the right time—when the grey firefly beetles emerge during the Spring Moon—to yield the strongest sheets. Ensure the inner protective bark is not cut too deep, or the tree will die. Cut the outer bark as vertically and straight as possible—a horizontal cut around the trunk could kill it as well."

Her mother also had a gifted tongue. *Persuasive she can be of my father when she needs to sway him in her favour,* Singing Sparrow thought, smiling to herself.

Morning Dove noted the smile. "That is good to see."

"Thinking of how you eloquently convinced my father to allow Bear Cub to court me."

"His stubborn ways are a challenge, but there is always a way around them." Morning Dove chuckled. "In my case, your grandmother worked wonders to dispel your grandfather's doubts of White Cloud. As you know, your father has been known to embellish the truth when it comes to his hunting skills."

Singing Sparrow knew the story of the moose he had hunted to prove he could support a family. "You mean he did not kill it?"

"He did hunt it successfully." Morning Dove stared at her daughter straight-faced. "But he took it down with his musket, not a bow and arrow. And, the moose did not charge him in the pursuit as he so boldly describes. The animal never moved."

Their snickers turned quickly to shrieks of laughter. They laughed so hard and so long, Singing Sparrow's stomach started to hurt. "How did they find out?"

"In time, his pangs of conscience plagued him. By the time he finally explained, we were already courting, but it did not deter your grandfather from trying to stop him from seeing me. It was your grandmother who had the final word."

Singing Sparrow had good memories of her grandmother,

who had been lively and never held back from expressing her opinions. Singing Sparrow leaned over and dipped her finger in the pot of water she had boiled earlier. "It is ready. Are you in much pain?" When age brought on any twinges, her mother ignored them, always downplaying their severity.

Morning Dove shook her head. "It is nothing. The joints do not respond as they did in my youth." She sighed wearily, rubbing the liquid of the steeped yellow birchbark onto her hands. "Wela'lin—it does help. Later I will use bayberry. It will help me sleep longer."

"There will be many women netting shad downriver. You are to stay if you are not well."

"My daughter, I have seen only fifty Winters. With the same ailment, your grandmother walked upon Mother Earth for at least eighty." Morning Dove grinned. "None of us ever knew the exact number." She cupped her daughter's chin. "Do not worry so. You know this will not last. Sleep well, my daughter." With that, Morning Dove retired.

Even though it was not serious, Singing Sparrow would always be concerned. Any infirmity she saw in her mother just confirmed life's fragility. She picked through the tobacco leaves in her pouch and placed some in the fire. Then, she spoke to the flames.

TRUE TO HER WORD, MORNING Dove joined them after a good night's rest. The women were knee-deep in the tidal pool near the weir that stretched across Oqomkikiaq. The mosquitoes buzzed mercilessly around Singing Sparrow's head, and she was glad of the bear grease she had rubbed onto her face. She and Morning Dove threw their nets in a circular pattern onto the water. When her net reached the bottom, Singing Sparrow gave it a quick pull and dragged in the caught shad, coiling the net around her hand. There was an almost rhythmical sound as the other women continually cast their nets, which landed on the water's surface with a splat.

As the baskets filled and the tidal waters rose, fog slowly claimed their place on land. Singing Sparrow began to sing the wind song while placing the baskets into the canoes. More women joined in as they waded to shore. When the beat quickened, the words echoed to the river fish and farther to the animals. The rhythms of the world drifted upward as the women danced—their bare feet leaving footprints in the sand. The spirit washed over Singing Sparrow in waves of gratefulness. Her words moved to a low pulsating chant as she sensed the nurturing heartbeat of Mother Earth.

A strange sound abruptly burst from the forest just before a screech set a dark cloud of birds fleeing from the treetops. Singing Sparrow looked around the now still group. She had not noticed there were two missing. One woman mentioned that she had seen bears earlier. Morning Dove snatched a pistol and ran for the woods. Singing Sparrow followed but lost sight of her mother and stopped to get her bearings. She heard a muffled noise behind a large boulder. As the remaining women came up from behind and fanned out, she stopped one and pointed to the boulder. Singing Sparrow quietly moved around the boulder, gripping her knife. A pair of black Mi'kmaw eyes were wide with terror staring back at her. A white hand was clamped over the woman's mouth; the attacker had his back to Singing Sparrow. As she thrust the honed blade into his back, he arched backward before dropping to unconsciousness. His victim ran toward the river.

Singing Sparrow heard someone scream, "Run!" She turned. Between the hemlock trees, she could see her mother. The women, scattered around Morning Dove, were held at gunpoint by half a dozen men. Her mother was looking in the opposite direction of where Singing Sparrow stood at the rock. *It is a decoy*, she thought. *The attackers have not spotted me! I am far enough away to escape.* She thought of her father who would be returning from the fishing grounds. Morning Dove broke into a run to divert attention, allowing Singing Sparrow to disappear farther into the woods. Then, her beloved mother was struck down with one shot. Singing Sparrow stopped and watched in disbelief as two women ran to the lifeless body.

Singing Sparrow bolted, running as fast as she could. She wept so hard she could barely see where she was going. She tripped. And again. The faster she ran, the more difficult it was to catch her breath. At the shoreline, she followed the river's edge. Suddenly, seven canoes appeared from the mist like ghosts. Singing Sparrow tried to cry out, but her throat closed in. *They see me!* She kept waving as they paddled closer to the sandy clearing.

When her father stood before her, she struggled for air. Her breathing laboured into short quick gasps, and try as she might, she could only blurt words with great effort. "My...dead!" she kept repeating. Her father held her face still, forcing her to concentrate on his breath, until she calmed. "My mother...ambush. The women are with her." Amid the clattering of paddles and the scrapping of canoe bottoms, White Cloud instructed who was to stay with his daughter while the other half were to go with him. It was only then Singing Sparrow saw the sobbing woman who had run ahead of her. Everyone armed themselves.

ONLY A SHORT TIME PASSED before talking could be heard—English voices. White Cloud signalled with the call of a crow. His instructions were for everyone to stop and conceal themselves from view upon this signal, until he signalled a second time with the show of his musket.

The British were ten in total, five in front of the tethered women and five behind. White Cloud scrutinized every detail of weaponry carried by the front line. Their guns were carelessly slung over their shoulders. Of the lot in the back, two had their muskets pointed at their captives, who were seven in all. One of the two carried a bloodied scalp that hung loosely from his belt; long black hair swayed with his gait. A cold chill crept up White Cloud's spine. As he stared at each panic-stricken face, his belly tightened. His wife was not there. He could not bring himself to look again at what dangled from the waist. White Cloud signalled to his two partners, then raised his musket. He aimed at the head of the person who most disgusted him. The single shot blasted forth, sending the intended target slumping onto the forest floor. Two more shots followed—then chaos. The women screamed and dropped to the ground while their captors either ran for cover or stood their ground, shooting their weapons in no particular direction. White Cloud's reinforcements arrived, killing all. It was a quick victory.

White Cloud ran in the direction the captors had come from, hunting for the missing body. He found himself following drops of blood. He could only hear his laboured breathing as his anxiety accelerated and pounded loudly inside his head.

He pleaded for mercy.

The drops became larger stains of red on the now soaked moss. A motionless body lay face down. White Cloud abruptly stopped only paces from where her legs lay bare among the rotting leaves. He started to tremble, could go no farther. Did he want to know? As he neared the bloodbath, recognition was swift.

White Cloud pressed his fists hard against his eyes and sank to his knees. A piercing wail escaped from his lips, all his suppressed distrust and uncertainties spewing forth in a rage. Had the enemy ripped his heart from his body, it would have been less painful.

There would be no remorse in killing again.

# Chapter Twenty-Two



Bear Cub and Eagle Feather were now in familiar territory, not far from where they had been captured. On the Oqomkikiaq, a considerable distance from the deserted trading post, Bear Cub stabbed at an eel but missed. When another attempt wielded the same result, Eagle Feather gave him a furtive sidelong glance.

Bear Cub's yearning to return to Singing Sparrow left him with little focus. "Not a word, or I'll spear your foot." Eagle Feather sidestepped to safety.

Bear Cub let out a grunt, and with a determined aim, he speared one. "Aha!" he yelled. Cognizant of Eagle Feather's deafness in his left ear, a result of his sickness, Bear Cub always stood to the right of him.

After Eagle Feather had gained his strength, they gratefully left with a canoe loaded with sundry supplies that Ambroise had given them. Thus far, there had been no sign of White Cloud. The Mi'kmaq they had met along the way did not know of his whereabouts. As the late Summer turned cooler, they had kept to the main river so that there would be more of a chance to meet White Cloud, had he decided to move farther inland.

Bear Cub threw the eel into the basket. The leaves were turning, and with the increasing presence of herring and smelt, it would soon be time to harvest cod.

Paddling upstream, they met a single-manned canoe coming downriver. They were greeted with a "Bonjour" as the two canoes met mid-river. "Ah!" said the paddler, when he saw Eagle Feather. He said in Mi'kmaw, "You don't remember me, do you?"

"I cannot place you," Eagle Feather said.

"Nor I," Bear Cub added.

"About a year ago, trading near Pijinuiskaq. Good negotiating tactics when I look back. The women were even tougher."

"We know our prices," Eagle Feather said, grinning. Then, rubbing his chin. "No bushy hair. I did not recognize you."

"Just a bit of stubble coming back in now." André smiled.

"Did you reach Louisbourg before Winter?" Bear Cub asked, to which he received a sombre nod.

"I'm surprised you didn't meet any runners. The fortress fell the end of July."

Bear Cub glanced at his brother. Both were in shock.

"We were outnumbered four to one," André continued. "Over twelve thousand to our three."

"And our People?" Eagle Feather asked.

"Most became discouraged and left before the siege even began. Only a few remained." He paused, then said, "We held out for six weeks. Our food was cut off, townspeople and soldiers sick and wounded. I watched Louisbourg collapse before my eyes. In the end, both the fortress and the town were ablaze." André's eyes filled with emotion. He focused on Bear Cub. "I don't know if your Peter is alive, but I do know he was gravely injured."

Bear Cub acknowledged his appreciation of the news but

was deeply troubled by what the loss meant to the Mi'kmaq. "This is only one battle," was all he could find to say.

"You are in denial, my friend. This defeat opens the St. Lawrence for our enemy's attack on any of our settlements. I'm afraid this is the beginning of the end. Major-General Amherst has ordered all those Acadians who had escaped to Île Royale to be arrested. They'll be deported to France."

"Why not to Boston or Virginia?" Bear Cub asked.

"No one in the colonies wants them. Neither does England."

Neither Bear Cub nor his brother had any wish to continue the conversation, and they indicated to André as such.

"Well, I must be on my way." The Frenchman dipped his paddle into the water. "Before I go, I just came from a Mi'kmaw village. They informed me of a raid about three weeks ago. Is it not White Cloud who is your father?" He studied Eagle Feather. "He and others killed British in the woods just over there." He pointed eastward.

"There is another side to that story. My father does not randomly kill unless provoked," Eagle Feather commented.

"He was. He just buried his wife."

With the help of that village, they found their way back. It certainly was not the homecoming Bear Cub had anticipated. He stood at the ancestral burial ground with his arm around his wife. There were no markers, just a patch of newly dug ground indicating Morning Dove's resting place. They had respectfully stayed away from the grave to give Eagle Feather secluded moments in his sorrow.

"Lise will never feel the loving hands of her grandmother again. She can never hear her soothing voice nor see her warm smile."

"Our daughter will sense her presence through the stories you tell and the songs you sing."

"There are stories I have yet to hear." Singing Sparrow blinked back her tears. "Since that day, there is a blackness that never leaves me. I try to escape but it follows me like an evil shadow." She tightened her grip on Bear Cub's hand. "When I am awake, hatred seeps through me, then creeps further into my night dreams. I can almost taste the poison upon my tongue." She turned away. "Did I tell you of her sacrifice?"

Bear Cub smiled. "When loathing grips you again, think of her selfless act. Hold on to what she did for you." He gently edged his beloved's face toward him. He touched a flawless teardrop on her cheek, which broke on the tip of his finger. "You could have been ripped from me and Lise so easily." André's last words played over and over in his mind. "If it was you that…I could not have gone on." Bear Cub barely spoke above a whisper. Memories of his own mama had mingled with Morning Dove whom he had called Mother. It was the first time he had cried for his mama since her death so long ago. He wept more because he had not been there for either of them.

JACQUES SAOUQUE HAD JUST LEFT after visiting White Cloud. The night before, they had held a community circle that lasted many hours, ending long after the sun had fallen asleep. On top of the loss of Morning Dove, emotions had run high as thoughts were shared and harsh opinions were raised over the loss of the fortress. Two runners had informed them how many Mi'kmaq had held out to defend; Abbé Maillard had estimated two hundred. Bear Cub had learned that this priest, whose loyalty to the Mi'kmaq remained unquestionable, had been a great liability to the British. He was now living in a northern cove near Île Royale that was unknown to the enemy.

French King Louis terminated his supplies of ammunition and food as any attempts would be intercepted by British naval ships and privateers in the surrounding waters. Their muskets were old and ammunitions diminishing. Any chance of obtaining new weapons would be at the mercy of the French, should any come into their possession. With the rising demands for guns, the legal tender of animal skins continued to decrease dramatically. The ten pelts for a musket doubled. They decided they must be brutally selective of when to use musket balls and powder and to only use them on larger game.

Jacques described evidence of settlers setting clearing fires that destroyed lichen, the caribou's chief food. His village had been forced to move because of it. As far as Bear Cub knew, the area near Port Rossignol was still untouched by settlers, but it would not remain so for long.

After the circle had dissolved, there were a few young dissenters who distanced themselves, much to White Cloud's consternation. Bear Cub had seen his brother among them. This morning, he approached him just as Eagle Feather released salmon bones to the river. He thought of Morning Dove; it was the first thing she had taught him. He remembered her words: *"Pay homage to our brothers and sisters."*

"Are you going with them?" Bear Cub queried.

"Ah," Eagle Feather held up his hand. "Did you speak with my father?" He stood up after he filled the caribou bladder with water.

Bear Cub shook his head. "Did you tell him?"

"E'e. As much as he fills me with his wise objections, he knows I must do this. And neither can you talk me out of it." He turned to walk away.

"You know me better than that." Bear Cub touched Eagle Feather's arm to stop him. "Why are you doing it?"

"Jacques is right. The British victory at Louisbourg does not mean we can put our guard down. You heard him. It just means less land for us."

"Those men that killed your mother are dead. Does that not satisfy you?"

"You do not understand, my brother."

"Then explain."

There was a long sigh of despair. "I know intimately every rock, tree, and plant in this part of Mi'kma'ki. I can tell you where the best places are to catch seals and hunt bear. I know every river, each weir built, and where each ancestral wikuom imprint lies. When we move inland, our enemy thinks we have abandoned our Summer camps and that we will not return. More newcomers put down stakes in the camps we left only temporarily and use the best hunting grounds. Are they willing to sit down to learn our ways?" He shook his head. "I am confident violence is the only thing they will answer to."

"There are other ways. Your father once believed that in time our ties with the British would be repaired."

"He said that once! Understand this, Bear Cub—he is now bitter, and time has proven nothing. What good can come if the British think us inferior to them?"

Bear Cub had no comeback. He thought of Prince Eugen who plowed over people to prove his superiority.

"If you are to speak to me with empty words, do not," said Eagle Feather.

Bear Cub didn't know what to say. He heard it but did he grasp it? As deep-seated into the land as they were, could he truly comprehend when he was not born into it? He had only been a part of their lives for six years.

Eagle Feather frowned. "Remind me again why your father fled his country."

"Tyranny," he replied. Bear Cub knew where he was going with this. "Point taken," he added.

Eagle Feather nodded. "I refuse to be ostracized in my own homeland. And I will not run away."

"And if you are killed?"

"It may be the sacrifice. To not defend our land means I have turned my back on future generations. Every bird you see comes from the sky world uttering sweet music. Each animal from the stars. How can I not protect my brothers and sisters who give their own lives so we may live?" He smiled at Bear Cub. "Our grandmother and grandfather rocks do as much when they keep an eye on us to help us find our way."

"I will come with you."

"To protect me? Moqwe. You have a family who needs you." After a moment's thought, Eagle Feather placed his arm across Bear Cub's shoulder. "Do you hear that?"

Bear Cub could hear the rapid pulse of drums. "Mother Earth's heartbeat is quickening."

"Even she knows what we must do." Eagle Feather gave his brother a quick slap on the back. "I will miss you."

THE SUN HAD JUST AWAKENED when two ocean canoes, each with four men, paddled away. They were loaded with cooking pots and blankets, snowshoes and warm garments, as well as a toboggan. A third canoe came up the rear with pelts, baskets, and quill boxes. All were neatly hidden under moose skins for a possible trade. Bear Cub and White Cloud watched as Eagle Feather, sitting just ahead of the raised midsection of the canoe, distanced himself with each unrelenting stroke.

"It is wrong of him to do this," Bear Cub said to his father.

"Have you never done something with no thought of the outcome?"

Bear Cub did not answer. He thought of the consequences to the Mi'kmaq of him returning to Lunenburg.

"It is not ours to judge, my son. It was his choice and his alone. Now he must stay the path and decide for himself." White Cloud turned and walked away.

Bear Cub gazed into the emptiness that now stretched between him and his brother. The canoe became a mere dot as it edged the horizon before it dropped from view. "When all is said and done, I can't fault you either," he declared. "Godspeed, my friend."

He closed his wool coat tight against his chin and shivered against the damp, cold north wind. Then he followed White Cloud back to camp.

# Chapter Twenty-Three



Scores of privates from the 60th Regiment—the Kings Royal Rifle Corps, as they were known—made for a boisterous waterfront. Trained for forest warfare to combat the French enemy, they had adopted partial Indian attire. They walked about in moccasins and green cloth leggings fastened at the knee, milling around the civilians who had gathered along the shore to watch their departure. The characteristic three-cornered cocked hat of the officers had been cut down to a plain black head-covering with a narrow brim that resembled a crown. Their only apparel like that of their superiors were the red waistcoat and blue knee-breeches they wore. And instead of a short sword, they each carried a hatchet.

Hanna's cloak flapped open, and she pulled the hood over her head against the raw gust of wind. She waved goodbye to Philip and Anna Knaut, whose daughter, Catherine, was nestled into her mama's arms. A deep sadness crept over Hanna. She repeatedly reminded herself Anna would be back well before Christmas.

The first Assembly was scheduled to meet on the second of October. Though Papa did not put forth his name in the past election, he was confident that Philip and Herr Kedie, who now represented Lunenburg, could affect change for the better. With the new legislative body, the colony hoped this would be the end of unheeded petitions to the governor. People had also been dissatisfied at the lack of protection under Faesch's garrison. There had been four raids, with four civilians and two soldiers killed in July and August. Papa had been part of the expedition ordered to search all ranges, but they found nothing other than evidence of where the enemy had encamped. Now Colonel Sutherland was back, and there was hope that things would be better.

The brigantine rocked against the choppy waves as its two mainsails billowed out with another blast of wind. The vessel made her way out of the harbour, headed for Halifax.

As she waited for Georg to return from the cooper's shop, Hanna lingered along the shore. Loud expletives caught her attention. Two barrels had rolled from the off-loading ramp and crashed, spilling much of their contents. Of the four sloops still moored, two such vessels had docked a week ago, carrying sixty Germans from Louisbourg. Most were families with children, and of the men, many were deserters from Halifax's early years. Under the governor's instructions, there would be only a small expenditure to have them properly victualled until spring, and they were to be housed in Range H at the back of town. Most of the farmers and townspeople believed that the treatment of these people was much too liberal.

Hanna heard her name called. It was Georg. Someone was walking close behind him. "You will never guess who I met. Peter!" When there was no recollection, he repeated, "Peter Beck."

Peter was unrecognizable to her with his scruffy-looking beard and the dirty patch over his left eye. She must have looked witless with her mouth agape, but Peter lifted her in an embrace before setting her back down. "Look at you! A young woman stands before me. Your loveliness soothes my sore eye." He laughed, touching his patch. "Your papa is not with you to fend off any admirers?"

She adjusted her fallen hood back on her head. "He is mowing the meadow hay. Georg has been my guardian for the last few days."

Georg added, "With no hay crop to speak of, we found natural meadows. There are none close by, so it warranted several days away for scything. He should be back this week."

"Memories are flooding to me now of the Faterland. Chopping hay, scalding it with hot water, and soaking it for hours."

"There are many here who aren't familiar with our custom—the French in particular," Georg said. "They are more than delighted to know that such coarse fodder can be eaten by the cattle. You must join us for dinner. I'm sure Elisabeth would dearly welcome you."

Hanna glanced at Georg. *I'm not so sure of that, dear brother,* she said to herself. If Georg noticed, he did not let on.

"I'll not allow you to decline," Georg said.

On his insistence, Peter agreed.

*My sister may not—nay, will not be so receptive.* She cringed at the thought.


If Elisabeth was perturbed in any way when they walked through the door, her composure did not let it show. She was as pleasant and hospitable as if the Mosers or Knauts were visiting unannounced. Hanna was impressed. Petie showed no indication that he had met Peter before. Hanna concluded that Peter's changed looks contributed to her nephew's lack of memory. Marta immediately warmed to the stranger, allowing him to bounce her on his knee.

After a meal of turnip soup, bread, and steamed pudding with molasses, Peter relaxed into tales of his adventures. Georg asked what had been the turning point in the loss of the fortress.

"When the British landed onshore," Peter said sarcastically. "Which should never have happened. Instead of waiting until they were on the beach, we opened fire prematurely. Such a heavy haze of smoke hung around us, we were unaware of a few boats drifting on the surf farther eastward. Had we held our fire, we would have realized only a small contingent had landed because of the high surf."

"With no military experience, I'd say you are hardly in a position to comment on what action caused our side to win," Elisabeth noted. "From what I heard, the French were outnumbered five to one."

"Elisabeth!" Hanna scolded. "From where I sit, you're not at liberty to judge. That was only hearsay." She could see Elisabeth's true feelings for Peter were beginning to seep through.

Georg interjected. "We can't always depend on the accuracy of the news we receive, and the colonel only returned two weeks ago. Details have been sparse." He gave Elisabeth a firm stare.

"Two thousand of us had manned the trenches at different positions. But because we didn't know how many had landed at the time, panic took over and we fled for the fortress." Peter took two swigs of his spruce beer.

"Who was your commanding officer?"

"Governor Drucour. He stood alone, as General de Courban, who was sent to lead our defence, never arrived—most likely couldn't get through the enemy blockade."

"There lies a possible difficulty then. Lack of experience, no doubt?"

"He's an administrator and untrained for land warfare.

Under the circumstances, though, Captain Drucour was fearless and did his best to defend an already dilapidated fortress."

"And the English?" Georg queried as he set Petie onto his lap.

"I'll never forget the sight when we awoke to their ships in Gabarus Bay. The fog had been so thick, they had to have sailed in a couple of days before. On June third, it lifted. There were well over one hundred—maybe one-fifty. At least forty were warships." Peter drifted away in thought.

"And the French?" Hanna asked.

"It was humiliating," Peter said, shaking his head. "Because the French have been concentrating on a possible victory in Europe, we were a low priority. We never received enough squadrons."

"Maybe it was a lost cause," Georg said.

"In any case, it was too late. The British began bombarding us. The *Bienfaisant* was captured and the *Prudent* burned. Just a week before our surrender, three of our ships caught fire. Then, the fortress headquarters burned. Drucour surrendered on July twenty-sixth." He smirked. "I wish you could have met his wife. To encourage us, she mounted the ramparts and fired three cannons herself. She did that every day of the siege. Can you imagine?" He shook his head, smiling to himself.

"Oh my!" Hanna exclaimed. "I have never heard of such things." She gazed at Elisabeth, her mouth wide in astonishment.

"And you most likely will not again. Close your mouth, dear sister, so as not to catch a fly. Indeed! Not a respectable thing for a young lady to do."

Georg convulsed in laughter. "Actually, I can see my lovely wife being so bold as to attempt such a feat."

"Humph!" Elisabeth grunted.

"What happened to your eye, Peter?" Hanna may have been audacious in her abrupt question, but no one had mentioned the obvious, and she was glad she asked.

"Ach, I was wondering when someone would mention it." Peter grinned. "When a cannon gun fired, the platform blew into a thousand pieces. A wood fragment lodged in my eye. I now am blind in that eye."

Hanna flinched.

"It killed the soldier who fired it. I'm lucky to be here to tell you about it."

"And we're glad of it," Georg said to lighten the conversation.

"I must take my leave now," Peter said as he stood. He held Elisabeth's hands. "You and Georg have been most gracious. Danke."

Hanna noticed Elisabeth tensing at his touch.

Georg shook Peter's hand. "We're aware of the government's generosity toward all of you who have returned. It is good."

"There are some in town who don't agree," Peter said. "I now have misgivings about my decision to return."

"They can't see past their noses. They believe deserters will always be deserters. Their narrow-mindedness blinds them," Georg said.

"And the fact I fought against the British. But not all of us took up arms."

"Ach, they think as they will. Before Herr Knaut left, he stated the governor is confident that these civilian families will make useful settlers."

"You speak the language of the Indians, do you not?" Elisabeth said, grim-faced.

Georg replied instead. "Herr Francklin does as well, and he is well-respected. He has put his name forward for the election next year!" To Peter, he said, "I'll walk you across the fields, show you my plans for next year."

Hanna was ashamed by her sister's words. She pitied her.

THERE WERE FEW PEOPLE MINGLING about the new range. The area, even though still in the throes of construction, was the only sensible housing available for the new arrivals. Elisabeth had no idea where Peter lived, but in the neighbourhood she had met a young woman who knew him. Elisabeth wrapped her wool cloak around her and ran to a small rectangular house at Lawrence and Prince Streets. She should have listened to her instincts to pull her warmer petticoats and stockings out of hibernation. The red baize dress was of little help, as the brisk gusts knew no boundaries.

The house was made of thick horizontal clapboard, which, since seasoned lumber was arriving from New England, had been the preferred design after the roughly hewn, square logs of the earlier housing. The street was deserted. A lively flock of seagulls harped as they soared above her.

She stood alone in front of his door, which was fastened with iron bolts and hinges. *What am I doing here?* To make such a rash decision to see him now seemed ludicrous. The lie she told her husband plagued her mind. She'd told Georg she was going for supplies, but had she thought this through, she would have remembered that Frau Born's shop was closed and would be for another week. Her replenishing supplies had never arrived, so Elisabeth had no alibi.

She removed her warm hand from the muff to knock but dropped her hand instead. Then, the door swung open. He stood there, towering over her and now clean-shaven, she noticed. His unkempt hair was neatly combed back into a braid revealing the partial ear and scar that ran down the side of his neck. She had forgotten about it, a wretched reminder of his encounter with the natives a few years ago. She shivered.

"Elisabeth! I was just on my way to the tannery, but it can wait. Please, come in out of the cold."

"I'll not keep you," she said, stepping inside the warmth. The fireplace was ablaze, the dry logs crackled and spit against the flames. In the kitchen, she was surprised to hear a heavy object set upon a table and a child's voice.

He explained it was Frau Born and her daughter. "I have been blessed with her daily morning visits bringing scrumptious foodstuffs—to fill me out, she says."

"Ja," Frau Born answered from the kitchen. She strolled out to greet Elisabeth. "Ach, he is nothing but skin and bones." She tweaked Peter's cheek.

Peter winked at her. "So she says. She can be very persistent."

"Elisabeth, I haven't seen you in weeks, my liebling." Frau Born kissed her.

Elisabeth smiled sheepishly. "There just isn't enough daylight to do everything. I still have my spinning to do, but of late, Georg has needed help with harvesting the root vegetables. I'm afraid there will be dire consequences if this weather continues. Papa's not back yet." Elisabeth must have sounded flustered. Her nerves had gotten the best of her, and she was caught off guard to find Peter not alone. She realized she had made a mistake in coming, and said, "I have caught both of you at a bad time. I'll take my leave."

"Bitte. Please stay. I've done my duty today." To Peter, Frau Born said, pointing, "The soup is simmering over the fire, and I brought two loaves of my bread. That should add to your government victuals." She grabbed her coat and practically ran out the door with her daughter in tow.

The circumstances Elisabeth found herself in, alone now with Peter, were unnerving. She couldn't look him in the eye. Instead, she concentrated on the freckles that still scattered across his nose. "Don't come back," she blurted.

"Pardon?"

Elisabeth cleared her throat. "Georg knows nothing of your visits, and I would rather keep it as such."

"He knows Petie is my son. I don't see the problem."

"I'm embarrassed…disgraced that I allowed this to happen behind his back. And it's only a matter of time before Petie will remember you."

"I disagree. He would have remembered the beard at least. There was no indication yesterday that he knew me."

"I'm not willing to take that chance."

"It's not that simple. I offered my help in the fields—Georg will be suspicious. More questions will be raised if he never sees me. You're really not making any sense." His voice rose in anger. "The girl I used to know was more spirited than this. She would have confronted her husband."

"I have no wish to jeopardize the relationship Petie has with Georg."

Peter walked to the window. "I vowed to not reveal anything to our son, and it's a promise I will keep to my dying day." He turned to face her. "I beg of you, do not remove me from his life."

Elisabeth lowered her head.

"Things could have been different for us," Peter said. "I would be remiss to say it didn't grieve me when I saw our son upon Georg's knee. What you have…that should have been us."

Elisabeth softened. "I waited for you. Oh, how I had longed for you. For months, I refused to give myself to my husband. I stayed loyal only to you. But, those months became two years! How long did you expect me to wait, Peter? It was too late then—as it is now." Peter attempted to step closer, but Elisabeth backed away.

"Nein! Do not come so near." Elisabeth searched his eyes. "I can see your pain, but oh, my liebling, I need you to bear this while I truthfully speak. At first, it was not so, but Georg cared for me deeply enough to be patient through my dark days. We have an unbreakable bond, which neither one of us has any desire to harm. If he feels I betrayed him, I couldn't bear it." Peter turned away, and Elisabeth touched his arm. "We were too young to know such love. Our passion was real but only for those two young innocents we once were."

"For you maybe, but not I."

"Bitte! I have stayed long enough. Truly, I should not have spoken so with you."

"What about your trust in me?"

"I know you would not willingly betray anything to our son, or to Georg for that matter." And deep down, Elisabeth believed that. "But your warped sympathies are untrustworthy. I pray to God it was your will to survive the siege that caused your loyalty to be sadly mislaid."

"I fought beside them and would not hesitate to do so again."

"How can you after you almost died by their hands?"

"Things are not always as they appear, my sweet. The British have been ruthless in using the Indian raids to justify their destruction of the Mi'kmaq. We are made to believe the Mi'kmaq are the aggressors. The colony has a very blackened view of the truth. To change it, we must begin to teach our children. Petie—"

"Do not ever speak of *them* in the same breath as our son!"

"Your brother is one of *them*," Peter remarked pointedly.

It cut Elisabeth to the core, and she promptly turned for the door. "Good day, Peter!"

PETER DID SHOW UP THE next morning. *It was highly probable that he would*, Elisabeth thought, given his character. He had made a promise to Georg. However, she had kept the children busy with Hanna while she herself pulled as many root vegetables as possible. The farmers were on edge, as only a fraction of the crops had been harvested by the time the days started growing colder. Then, the frost quickly turned to freezing temperatures.

The harvesting came to a standstill when an early blizzard blew in from the sea. It lasted four days, leaving roof-high drifts, buried fences, and downed trees. Even when the sun appeared, the cold never ceased its hold on the settlement. Until then, the bounty of crops had been proving itself worthy to feed not only the colony, but to possibly make Lunenburg the main source of supply to Halifax. All hopes quickly collapsed.

Now, Elisabeth hustled about the hot, smoky kitchen, putting away the iron pots and kettles she had just scrubbed with sand. She missed Hanna, always coming to the realization whenever Hanna was away exactly how many chores her sister accomplished when she was here.

She shifted the bake kettle along the crane but farther back to a hotter spot within the hearth. The intensely hot flames made her already chapped face feel prickly. The wind whistled across the top of the chimney as she tested the potatoes and beets cooking beneath the ashes. *Mmm, they're almost done,* she thought.

Elisabeth kept a close eye on Petie as he dipped the candle rod again into the hot wax. As he repeatedly plunged the ten hemp wicks, they slowly began to resemble candlesticks thick enough to last at least one evening. Until the sun showed its face again to melt the snow-caked windows, they were running through candles rapidly.

"Mama, will the mice eat these, too?"

"Eventually. But I will wrap these new ones in the tin box and place them high above the door."

Petie nodded with enthusiasm. "Last night, I heard one

chewing a candle on the table. I shooed him away, Mama, but he came back." His lips pouted.

A tub of melted snow sat near the hearth. Bath time for her daughter was not always welcome, as Marta was particular in her play tasks and was displeased when interrupted. Elisabeth watched her happily amuse herself with pieces of straw she had carefully spread across the blanket she was seated on. Elisabeth lifted the pot of scalding water and poured enough to warm the icy snowmelt. Today, Elisabeth was in no mood for any of her daughter's antics.

The door swung open, sending a flurry of snow swirls about the floor. Georg banged the white clumps from his boots. "Just been in the root cellar. Our harvest was for naught. The tops of the carrots are dark and mushy, and some of the onions are soft. I suspected as much, given that they were frozen when we dug them up." He put his cold arms around his wife. She shivered in his embrace. "I see it is the dreaded bath time!"

Elisabeth mumbled her opinion under her breath. "It can wait," she said aloud, and she grabbed the oatmeal paste from the shelf to rub on his chapped face.

Georg talked of nothing but the repairs that were needed on certain equipment, especially the turn wrest. The iron plate was loose on the mouldboard, he said. "The oxen have outgrown their head yoke again. If the weather doesn't improve, it will be spring before Herr Bruhm gets here."

"I set aside one of the snowshoes for you to fix," Elisabeth said, taking the candle rod from her son. "It is beside the door. Rats have gnawed the rawhide again. Would you set out the poison?" She pulled the loaves of bread from the bake oven.

"Uh-huh."

"Are you listening?"

"Mmm."

"Georg!" She placed the last loaf on the table. He had his nose in some papers. "What are you into there?"

"Ah, here it is. Before Philip left, he said the survey fee for those acres is twenty shillings. But it says here," he ran his finger along the print, "twenty-five. They must have reduced it. I know Herr Metzler paid the higher price."

"We can't afford it even at twenty." Her eyes begged him again. "Our house in town is still empty."

"There have been no threats since August. Besides, we can't move the animals, and there'll be calving and lambing after Christmas. We stay here for the winter." He looked up at his wife. "We agreed."

Elisabeth sat down beside him.

"There is no room to extend here in the First Peninsula," Georg said. "If we got a larger lot, we would sell this property."

"I won't move—we could end up miles away. I'm afraid, Georg."

"I know, but I'm only thinking of our future. No real plans have been drawn up yet. From what Philip has told me, there has only been a draft submitted. Herr Morris has not even begun to survey." He now faced her and held her hand. "From what Peter has told me, the war cannot go on much longer. The Indians' supplies have now been cut off." Georg paused. "Peter has expressed interest in our house in town."

Elisabeth rose from the table to move the hot pan from Petie's reaching hands before he burned himself. She didn't know how to respond. She had hoped Peter would only be in Lunenburg temporarily.

"Did Philip mention why there hasn't been any more talk on the land grants? We're naturalized now—we have the certificate for proof."

Georg shook his head and held up another paper. "This is

all we must show in accordance with the promises made to us, though it's hard to trust when history has proved otherwise. My hopes are we never return to the way things were in the Faterland."

Elisabeth knew he was thinking of the feudalism they had left behind. "Will we receive a document to prove this land is ours and no one can claim it?"

"We only have their word. One advantage of not having a land grant, though, is that we're not liable to quit-rent payments." He gave a weak smile.

"I would rather pay those fees than be in doubt of our land."

"You're not in good company. Most I've spoken to are finding ways to prevent any grant from being registered, in order to avoid paying the fees. But I agree with you, especially if Peter is able to buy our town lot."

Elisabeth silently sent up a prayer that Peter would not.

It was Christmas Eve. Hanna quietly lay in bed, listening for the howling winds that had greeted her the last few mornings. But this morning there was silence. As December came upon them, the temperature had dropped further. She and Papa had hardly ventured into town. Hanna had found it quite lonely. Her friend Anna had not returned from Halifax, but Hanna was not surprised as there was nary a ship in the harbour these days. With high swells, it would be hazardous to undertake a sailing from Halifax.

Papa had deemed it essential to spend the most important celebration of the year with Georg and Elisabeth. It would be a surprise for them, and a journey Hanna hoped would be without consequences. To be ready to travel when the weather turned for the better, they had already packed a few items of clothing. This morning may prove to be perfect. She sat up and leaned over to open the shutters; her breath froze mid-air. She briskly rubbed her arms against the cold.

Papa was already outside by the time she had dressed and climbed down to the kitchen. She could hear him talking. *It must be the neighbour*, she thought. He had offered to see to the cows while they were gone. When Papa entered the house, he made an official, albeit humorous announcement: This was the day! To see him full of such contentment made her heart sing.

After breakfast, the bags were strapped onto the toboggan, and they started out on their snowshoes. The tiresome journey was entirely without incident. By the time they reached the farm, Papa was pulling the transport with Hanna now snuggled under the blankets. When the door opened to their call, they were met by expressions of disbelief before being greeted with shouts of laughter. Hanna and Papa eagerly sought the hearth, briskly rubbing their hands over the flames. The shock of the sudden heat sent a shudder through her body.

The afternoon was filled with singing and reminiscences of bustling Christkindl markets, of which Hanna had only a scant memory. But the visions came alive when Elisabeth described the spicy gingerbread Lebkuchen and the sweet yeast bread, Stollen, dusted white with sugar and for sale at the stalls, along with the pleasant-smelling beeswax candles that only the wealthy could afford. Petie sat attentive, listening. He knew Christkindl brought gifts on Christmas Eve and that he would soon receive a small present.

There was a sudden knock at the door.

"You came after all!" Georg said, delighted. "Come in." Peter removed his snowshoes and stood them up against the house.

"Ach," he hesitated when he stepped inside and saw Michael, "this is an intrusion." Peter stammered, "I shan't stay."

"Nein, nein." Georg shut the door behind him. "Their visit was a surprise to us as well."

As Peter entered, Hanna looked over at her sister and saw her jaw drop. *Ja, you are distraught—very much so. But, oh, Elisabeth, you hide it well.*

"This is a pleasant surprise," she said, masking any hint of her discomfort. "You're just in time for rabbit stew. Make yourself at home."

"I thought I smelled as much," Peter said, removing his hat and coat. "Danke." He greeted everyone else before sitting down. Michael was civil and acknowledged him only with a reserved incline of his head.

Peter said, "I do apologize. I told Georg I was on militia duty when in fact I was mistaken." He blew into his hands. "I don't think it's possible to get any colder. It has just started to snow," he said, then Petie promptly climbed onto his lap. The boy lightly ran his small hand down along Peter's scar.

Elisabeth was half out of her seat, about to object, but backed down.

"Well, good day, young man. Do I know you?" Peter quipped.

"Of course, sir."

"Ja, I do recall now. A couple of months ago, I believe." He grinned.

Petie nodded in agreement but said with childlike authority, "Before that, when I was much younger."

"You must be mistaken, my liebling," Elisabeth interjected and lifted him down. "Marta is looking for you. Go play with her."

"But, Mama, 'tis true."

"Come here, Petie," Georg said. "You must be thinking of someone else. You have only just met him."

Before Elisabeth led her son away, he continued his assertion.

"In the woods. I remember you and I met him." He turned back and smiled at Peter. At those words, Elisabeth paled considerably.

If there ever had been a conversation stopper, that was it. Hanna was keenly aware of her sister's loss for words as she led Petie to his sister.

It was Hanna who broke the ice. "Let me set the table. Supper must be ready." She lit a long piece of straw and gave it Georg. "Would you be so kind as to light the Advent wreath?"

By the end of the evening meal, everything was forgotten, put down to a childish whim, possibly a dream Petie had once had. Gifts were exchanged around the table. Petie was delighted by a carved horse Michael had made for him, and Marta prattled on to her new wooden doll, which he had also sculpted.

"Do you remember the one I made for you? You were five, I believe."

Hanna nodded. "Yes, Papa. I still have it." She watched Elisabeth staring blankly at the candle on the windowsill. Marta was asleep in her arms. Hanna drank in the smell of the pine boughs Elisabeth had strewn about the house. Greenery brought life to the otherwise dreary winter months. There were even a few smaller boughs at the end of the kitchen table with cones and sprigs of dried lavender nestled amid their needles. Above the table, the Christmas pyramid hung from one of the ceiling beams. Georg had made it with four poles and boughs tied together at the top. It was placed over a candle-lit base.

"Do you miss the Faterland?" Hanna asked Peter.

"Only at times like these, when I think of the family and friends still there."

"I liked to watch the moveable cribs in the shop windows," Georg said, in a dreamlike state. "The animals and three kings were set in motion by a coin. In Frankfort, the colourful nutcrackers stood like soldiers and sentinels of kings on the windowsills."

"Papa, tell me the story again." Petie stood next to Georg, tapping his knee for attention.

"Well, let me see. Ach, you know a woodcrafter made a nutcracker for your grandfather. He always kept it in the house to protect his family and bring them luck. But I didn't tell you that just before the logs are harvested from the elder trees, there's a feast of nuts and fruits. This passes on the magic and mystery of the cycle of life. As the seed of a nut falls to the ground, it grows into a sturdy tree that can live for hundreds of years, nourishing the woodcutters and woodcrafters. If you sit under one of these trees and hear the rustling of their leaves, they are telling you the German legends they have witnessed. Now—" A gunshot. Then, a second. Georg opened the door a crack.

"Close it!" Elisabeth pleaded. "That was our warning." She held Petie tightly against her skirt.

"I thought I heard a noise. There it is again." He put on his coat and grabbed the musket from the corner.

"I'll come with you," Peter said, lighting the lantern on the mantel. Michael dressed and loaded his gun.

Elisabeth begged for them to remain inside, but her pleas were ignored. Hanna gathered the now whimpering Marta and put her to bed along with Petie. When she returned to the kitchen, her sister was stacking the dirty dishes. Then she sat nervously wringing her hands before busying herself once again. When three consecutive discharges fired, Elisabeth collapsed on the floor, her back tight against the wall. Hanna crouched down to hold her.

Hanna listened for footsteps. She heard the crunching of the snow underfoot before the door opened. It was Papa. He spoke of Indians, and Elisabeth stiffened and yelled for Georg.

"Everyone is fine." Michael added, "Two are dead." He bragged he had killed one. "Georg said the third one is injured."

When the others returned to the house, Peter gazed at Hanna uneasily. Marta started to cry, and Hanna went to attend to her. Even when she turned into the bedroom, she could feel Peter's eyes upon her.

Hanna sang softly to her niece until Marta slipped back into slumber. As Hanna tucked her under the quilt, an eerie presence in the room made her jump "I know the injured one. He's Christian's brother." Peter's hushed tones floated in the darkness.

Hanna drew in a sharp breath. *Does Peter know Eagle Feather?* "Why are you telling me this?"

"He will have news of your brother. He'll not hurt you. I'll go with you after everyone is sleeping."

"I cannot. If Papa found out—" Hanna said in a whisper. "Please, leave this room."

Everyone eventually bedded down. Elisabeth was the last to go to bed, after Peter and Papa had settled with blankets in front of the hearth. Hanna heard her sister and Georg speaking in the next room, then finally there was silence in the now chilled house. Her mind was crowded with thoughts of Eagle Feather. For Christian's sake, it was her obligation to see to Eagle Feather's wounds. She decided she would chance it. Hanna waited until she could hear the sounds of sleep from everyone.

She quietly dressed, then opened the bedroom door. She watched for any stirrings from Papa or Peter. Assured they were asleep, she tiptoed into the kitchen. She was thinking of Peter's words when her eye caught sight of Georg's medical bag. She picked out a poultice jar she had seen him use on Paul's wound and pushed it deep into her pocket. Lastly, she lit the lantern while keeping a close eye on the pair in front of the hearth.

Before closing the door, Hanna saw Peter raise his head. She shook her head at him and slipped outside. The flame flickered rapidly when a raw, icy blast curled around the house. Lifting her cloak to protect the light, Hanna waited until the wind abated. When she neared the barn, the light picked up two half-buried bodies. She covered her mouth with her hand to stifle a scream. Closer to the door, she spotted a barely visible animal pelt. She kicked away the snow that had drifted on top of the pelt and pulled it inside.

The cow mooed as she held up the light, and Hanna caught sight of Eagle Feather, awake. A piece of rope tied his wrists together with the long end below lashed at his ankles. Hanna hung the lantern on a hook and helped him to a sitting position. While she dressed the wound on his arm, she noticed a flash of recognition in his eyes, but he spoke only Mi'kmaw words. Remembering where Georg had hidden a knife, she retrieved it and grabbed a coat hooked on a peg. As she untied him, Hanna tried to communicate that she wanted him to leave and placed the fur pelt, coat, and a pair of snowshoes at his feet. Into his hand, she placed the weapon. Eagle Feather squeezed her hand. "Wela'lin," he said and left.

Dawn broke, revealing that the snow had stopped. The house was in a turmoil when Papa and Georg went to the barn and discovered their prisoner had escaped. Surprisingly, Peter had left for home before anyone rose, and Hanna was paralyzed to speak out when the others immediately thought the worst of him. "I always knew he couldn't be trusted. He fought against us," her sister said, and repeated it to reinforce her point. Hanna was sure of Peter's intention. His act was altruistic, to divert from her any blame.

Soldiers arrived at their door; they had been ordered to investigate the night shots. With a stern glare at Elisabeth, warning her not to say anything untoward about Peter, Georg spoke to the ensigns only of the dead bodies.

"You are being unreasonable and stupid in your thinking. As much as it appears to show Peter's iniquity, we can't lay blame until I speak with him." Georg was angry and exasperated with his wife.

"Sometimes you are too relaxed in your convictions. It blinds you to the obvious," Elisabeth shot back.

"If I care to give someone the benefit of the doubt, leave me to my misery. I have no wish to be a man who indiscriminately points fingers without all the evidence."

"When you brought him into our home, I just knew the moment he spoke that—" Her stare met his. "He's not to return here again!"

"Is my wife ordering me?"

Even though she knew Georg was bluffing, Elisabeth backed down. Georg had never been the typical husband, reprimanding a wife to the point of abuse. She had heard stories in the Faterland of wives who stood up against their husbands and were whipped into submission.

"Why are you so furious over such a matter as this? You have been highly strung ever since Peter returned." Georg took a hold of Elisabeth's hands and kissed them. "Has this anything to do with what Petie said yesterday?"

Elisabeth swallowed hard and averted her eyes.

"It does. Am I right?" Georg held her face in his hands, forcing her to acknowledge the truth. "What?"

"You won't be pleased."

"It could not be that bad. What happened? Did the two of you meet by chance in town one day? This is not a crime…"

"Initially, I did run into him. Petie was with me. Three years ago, I arranged a meeting place for Peter to continue seeing his son. I only have deep regret for my actions."

Georg turned away. "You went behind my back! Why didn't you tell me?"

"I tried many times, but things were so good between us. I was frightened of your reaction. Before I knew, it was easier to keep you in the dark than to reveal my shame."

"Leave me be. I need time alone to sort this through."

"I know it was wrong of me to do such a thing! I am so ashamed. Bitte! Don't turn away from me. I can't bear it," Elisabeth implored.

"How long did this go on?"

"Just a few months. We met only four times. Then, I put a stop to it."

Georg drew in a long breath before letting it out with a sigh. "Does Petie know who he is?"

"He thinks of him as a friend." Elisabeth turned to go.

"What hurts me the most is your thoughts of me, Elisabeth. Surely, you must know I would never refuse a father to see his own son. Have you so quickly forgotten that I was aware of your circumstances before we married?"

"I did it only for Peter, so he could watch his son grow. I didn't think you would approve. I know now it was wrong."

"It didn't even cross your mind that I would understand?"

She did not reply but put her hand on the door latch.

"I'm not resentful, Elisabeth. I am disappointed…and hurt that you had a secret between us."


WHEN PETER OPENED THE DOOR of his house, Michael kicked it back with a crash. He shoved Peter up against the wall, braced his neck with his arm, and screamed, "You are a bad seed!"

"Michael! This is not the way," Georg reasoned, trying to rein in his father-in-law.

When Michael released him, Peter dropped to his knees, trying to catch his breath. Michael stared down at him. "Why? What manner of evil, pray tell, possessed you to let that Indian go?"

Peter stood up and faced Michael. "It was Christian's brother," he said. "Plain and simple."

Michael swung his fist hard against Peter's jaw, and Peter fell to the floor.

"Michael, bitte!" Georg helped Peter up. "That was uncalled for."

Michael rubbed his fist. His face was red as he attempted to slow his jagged breathing.

"I don't condone what Peter did, but you're letting your long resentment over what he had done to Elisabeth get in the way," Georg said. "Am I right?"

Michael seethed. "I am through with you, Peter. If you ever cross my path again, I will not be responsible for my actions." With that, he left, slamming the door behind him.

"There was no talking him down. He was hell-bent on coming here," Georg said.

"It was a long time coming, I'm sure."

"Maybe so." Georg turned to go. "If I were you, I would pick my allies more carefully."

"If you speak of Eagle Feather, don't be concerned. He is a true brother."

"Now, I wonder. Why would he come back?"

Peter shook his head slightly, wrinkling his brow. "What do you mean, *come back*?"

"About eight months ago, Christian and Eagle Feather were

captured. They sat in the stockade for a bit. I was called to mend their wounds." Georg left it at that.

"Then you recognized him last night."

Georg nodded. "And I don't think you set him free either." Not getting a response from Peter, he added, "I awoke during the night and saw Hanna leave the house. You must have told her who was in the barn. No one else could have."

"Why didn't you stop her?"

"And wake the house up? Hanna knows him as well. She and Elisabeth visited them in jail. You covered for Hanna, did you not?"

Peter said nothing.

"I applaud your valour. You may not confess, but Hanna will."

Georg was about to close the door when Peter remarked, "When it comes to Eagle Feather, I wouldn't be concerned of any danger. I would stake my life on it."

"I want to believe that," Georg replied.


When Georg returned to the house, Hanna found solace in the bedroom alone. From the kitchen, she could hear her papa's booming voice, saying that he was done with Peter. When her father and her brother-in-law had left this morning, she mainly kept to herself.

Georg entered her room and said in a low voice, "I know. As I cannot force you, you can choose to say nothing."

Hanna hung her head.

"But think on what you are doing to Peter." He left her.

Hanna's stomach was in knots, her hands started to shake. Peter's selfless act was her salvation. *But how can I confess? It would kill Papa. Nein, I cannot.*

But when she returned to the kitchen, Hanna heard Papa admit he had hit Peter. The guilt crushed her like a heavy stone. "P-Papa," she stuttered. He looked at her. She swallowed. "Papa…"

THINGS WERE VERY HUSHED AS they travelled along the sculpted snow-covered trail on their journey home. The beauty of it was wasted on Hanna. She watched Papa from behind as he hauled the toboggan. He had been tight-lipped since they left her sister's house. The home, blissful just two days earlier, was now in an uproar. When Hanna had confessed, Papa was at a loss for words, so stricken by what she had done. Her sister was in such a state, she was inconsolable. Georg had inflamed the situation when he had announced to Elisabeth that he had thought about it, and Peter would always be welcome in their home, to which her sister took immediate exception. But Georg was as unshakeable as Elisabeth was stubborn. From Hanna's standpoint, Georg won out.

*Papa, though,* Hanna brooded, *is trapped in his own world of unrelenting torment concerning his family, compounded by the doubt over his decision to bring us here.* Now his daughter had confessed to aiding, in his mind, an enemy.

# Chapter Twenty-Four



Bear Cub crouched behind a snow mound to calculate a bull-moose standing in front of him. Calm Water had told him if a moose showed his weak side, the animal was offering his life. The moose was clearly fatigued, as he had sunk deeper into the snowdrifts. Large puffs of steam billowed from the bull's nostrils. After hunting for days, Bear Cub and White Cloud had caught a hare, grouse, and marten to keep them barely alive to hunt for larger game. Now, it had been two days since they had eaten, and Bear Cub's hunger clawed his belly raw.

Not one caribou had been sighted. Beaver lodges lay empty in frozen lakes. The food preserved in Autumn just for these times was low, and they had seen no replenishment of ammunition nor food from the French in moons. As for their muskets, most were in a bad state of repair, and those that shot straight were only somewhat reliable.

Apïknajit proved to be a typical fierce month. Bear Cub had never experienced such a Winter. Vicious snowstorms and bone-chilling weather had hampered many of their hunts. They put in long days to find where moose had yarded together for protection from predators and easy access to suitable forage sites.

On this day, White Cloud had spotted the tell-tale signs where twigs of wood had been eaten. Bear Cub rested on his heels and aimed to kill. He held his breath and sent up a quick prayer that the musket would not misfire. The moose dropped, creating a white snow cloud, and Bear Cub exhaled with relief. He crawled on his belly to the body, then stood above the food. A deep reverence for the moose welled up within Bear Cub as he looked down at the magnificent beast. He remembered how Morning Dove had taught him to place the bones of slain animals in rivers to prevent the dogs from gnawing on them. That would honour their souls and encourage them to be reborn near their bones, she said. White Cloud joined him next to the large animal. Truly grateful, Bear Cub knelt and placed tobacco near the carcass.

White Cloud spoke. "We thank the moose spirit for giving his life so we may eat. We thank Kisu'lkw for creating the animals on Mother Earth."

In the distance, musket fire startled Bear Cub. "Ach, this is good."

Minutes later, six men returned. They had also killed a moose. Behind them was a toboggan laden with four hares and a lynx. One of the hares still had an arrow lodged in its side. They covered the dead moose with spruce boughs and headed back to their field camp to eat before setting out for the base camp before dusk. The women could start out at sunrise to dress the kill.

"He is the only one left from the village," White Cloud explained. "He is called Tma."

Bear Cub could not help but stare as the man ravenously devoured some meat. He had never seen anyone so emaciated. Tma's pallid face was very thin and drawn. On their way back to their own village, they had come across an empty Mi'kmaw camp. Apart from the frozen bodies, it had been deserted. Tma had wandered incoherently from the woods.

Half-buried limbs of men, women, and children were exposed as if animals had uncovered what they could for food. But with no teeth marks on the flesh, in all probability the weather had revealed what he now was witnessing. There was also no evidence of a massacre. Reality set in. White Cloud demanded everyone to leave everything as it was and not to bring any items with them. Tma was clearly untouched by whatever disease had taken everyone else.

Bear Cub unloaded the toboggan and made a bed of their blankets, then White Cloud lifted Tma and laid him on the transport. They arrived back at their base camp just as darkness fell. Singing Sparrow, running with Lise toward Bear Cub, was a welcome sight.

Over the following few weeks, Tma gained strength and was looking much younger than when they had first met. His story was revealed in bits and pieces according to his memory. When they found him, he had just stumbled onto the deserted compound. He didn't know how long he had been walking. He was running from his own suffering, after disease had run its course in his own community. He described how his family had been weakened by a lack of food then succumbed to a rampant fever that took everyone. From the symptoms described, Bear Cub knew it was typhus. Recollections of his own family's passage, when he had witnessed thirty-one bodies drop one by one into their watery graves, flooded back.

Si'ko'ku's, the Spring Moon arrived; the cold did not abate. Winter still had his bleak grip on the white landscape—snowdrifts stubbornly clung around the little shelter. Bear Cub cradled a dead mockingbird in his mitted hand. The dark grey feathers were frozen, the eyes closed. From a tree branch above, his mate cried out to him.

"The birds are returning and food is scarce for them." Singing Sparrow knelt beside her husband and dug deep into the drift. As he covered the bird, she sang a song to the mockingbird's spirit. She remained in quiet reflection before rising.

"Have the women packed everything?" Bear Cub asked. The night before, Jacques had given a sorrowful description of many of their people debilitated by hunger. Women from two other villages had already journeyed to aid them with what food could be spared. Still more was needed. It had been several moons since André had made an appearance.

"E'e. We will be leaving soon," Singing Sparrow said, gazing toward the sky. "The sun is high—we will arrive before it goes beneath the earth."

"There'll be no rest for me until you are safely back in my arms."

"Jacques will be with us, and I am stronger now."

"You had a dizzy spell this morning!" he exclaimed in an irritated tone. Bear Cub was extremely uneasy. In his absences to hunt, he knew that when there was not enough to eat, most of it would be given to Lise. There was little left over for Singing Sparrow, and it had Bear Cub sparring with her more often than not. He thought she was sacrificing her own life for Lise, but Singing Sparrow did not see it as such. "Don't leave," he pleaded.

"I cannot put my needs ahead of our People," she said, and gently pushed strands of hair behind Bear Cub's ears. The women, now clad in snowshoes, were gathering in the centre of the compound with toboggans of food and blankets. "We are each other's strength."

"And Lise?" Bear Cub made a sore attempt to feign helplessness.

"My husband, you have all the women still here to help attend to our daughter." She smirked. "You are in good hands." Then in a solemn tone, "We will return as soon as we are able."

Many sunrises passed and Singing Sparrow did not return. Bear Cub's only solace after the long, sometimes empty hunts were Lise's giddy laughter and effortless tiny hugs.

Winter finally showed signs of relinquishing in the middle of Pnatmuiku's, the Egg-Laying Moon. The top layers of snow began to melt, and the nightly freezes allowed the dogs to move with ease on the hunt. Alawei was now leading eight of those brothers to sniff out beavers through the ice. Throughout the many moves, the village had endured, following irregular food sources. Hope never diminished.

The cold seeped in as Bear Cub lay on his belly. He plunged his arm through the ice-hole in search of the beaver's lodge opening. He could feel a family of beavers lying against each other. Just as White Cloud had taught him, he repeatedly and gently passed his hand over the back of one, slowly moving toward the tail. At the last waning moon, White Cloud had said, "Your hand will not feel strange to them. They only think they are touching each other." When he touched the rough, leather-like tail, Bear Cub took hold and with all his might drew up sixty pounds of food from its home. He immediately struck the head with his axe for fear of a ferocious bite. Alawei sniffed her way along the trail of blood, licking it as it oozed over the icy surface. Bear Cub's hand was now cramped, and his arm, red from exposure, ached. As the sun warmed it, his skin began to burn.

White Cloud was standing thirty paces away near the second hole, with his bow at the ready. When a beaver surfaced for air, he drew back to release the barbed rod into the rodent. The cord attached to the small harpoon sunk as the beaver disappeared back into the depths. White Cloud pulled the cord to draw the catch back through the hole. After they sprinkled tobacco into the ice-hole, they walked farther down the lake to join the rest of their group before heading back to camp.

When they reached home, there was a group standing at the forest's edge. A tall man, dressed in furs, spoke from the wooded area. He acknowledged White Cloud's greeting and explained he had travelled from the village where their women were. "Do not approach me," he commanded. "A sickness has come upon our community."

Bear Cub's heart raced as he listened to the story of the many who had already succumbed. Jacques had perished.

The visitor waited while White Cloud and Bear Cub gathered supplies. One of the Elders, Elen, would be travelling with them. She brought her medicine pouch, which held balsam, juniper, hemlock, and goldthread that she had recently harvested through the snow.

Bear Cub watched his father-in-law assemble food for the journey. *I do not want you to come*, Bear Cub decided. *Too many hardships have already descended upon the People.* He thought of the man with the white patch of hair he had seen when their village was burning. Eagle Feather had found him dead, but no one knew that his demise was at Bear Cub's hands. He could still feel the man's pulse weaken as his hands gripped tighter around his neck and the life drained from his body. No one had seen him do it. White Cloud had always protected him, but Bear Cub fell short.

"Your old friend is gone." Bear Cub heard the coldness in his words. He found himself not able to look White Cloud in the eye, so he focused on loading the toboggan. "You are safer here."

"My daughter is in danger. The choice is not yours." Bear Cub did not respond, and White Cloud placed a firm hand on his son-in-law's shoulder, squeezing it for attention. "Blaming yourself for the fire serves no purpose unless you are the wiser for it."

Bear Cub hastily turned to face him, baffled. "Singing Sparrow must have…" he started. "No matter, it was careless to return when we did. Worse still was my decision to go to Merligueche in the first place."

"And the fire still could have happened. We are in a war. We cannot foretell the future, my son."

Bear Cub half-turned, realizing he would not be able to convince his father to stay behind. "Let's go then, there's no time to waste."

"Good!"

# Chapter Twenty-Five

APRIL 1759

*I* will get it, Papa. You tend to the lambs." As Hanna left the barn for the rake, she counted their new blessings. Papa was ecstatic when in February, four of their ewes had birthed seven lambs, and March had seen two new calves. Since Christmas, Hanna had tried many times to talk to Papa, but he dismissed her efforts, going about his days in feigned ignorance of what had occurred.

Hanna stepped outside into the twilight; the red sky promised a fine day tomorrow. The day's sunlight had started its spring melt, but in the fields, the snows were still knee-deep. Papa was chomping at the bit to till his land. With the enormous loss of root vegetables, it had been announced at the town meeting that Governor Lawrence would be writing to the Board for more assistance.

There was a fleeting movement toward the back of the house. Hanna ducked behind the side of the barn and waited.

"Hanna! What's taking so long?"

She delayed answering. Nothing. *My mind is playing tricks,* she decided. Hanna lifted the rake and turned back toward the barn door. She was grabbed from behind—a hand firmly pressed against her mouth. A blade flashed across Hanna's eyes.

295

"Come, daughter."

She looked on with horror when Papa appeared. His sudden rush toward her was blocked by a native armed with a gun. Papa stared at her, unblinking. The colour in his face drained to a pale grey, and he fell to his knees. She and Papa were shoved inside, to a dark corner of the barn. They lay there holding each other tight. Hanna could feel Papa's body tremble as she pressed closer to him. A quarrel erupted among the three captors; two left. When she gazed up to the remaining one, her eyes widened in disbelief. Eagle Feather! She choked in an attempt to call out to him. *Did I say it aloud, or merely mouth his name?*

He seemed fixated on her—his thick dark eyebrows knit together in what appeared to be a painful recognition. He hurriedly buried her and Papa with mounds of hay. Before he moved the last few pieces over her face, he gazed down—his face softened, his eyes moistened. Hanna heard the barn door creak, then it shut with a bang. The lambs bleated in the darkness.

She and Papa huddled together, listening for the slightest of movements. Outside, muted voices suddenly became louder, nearing the barn. It sounded like arguing, which soon died off into the distance. They waited long into the night before digging themselves from their prison.

Elisabeth was completely beside herself. After Reverend Moreau buried three members of the Oxner family in March, there was another raid—three members of the Trippos family were killed. The raids had prompted more people to abandon their farms, but Georg and Papa were among the still many who refused to give up.

It was against Hanna's better judgment, but she had told her sister anyway, knowing Papa would never have let their ordeal pass in silence. Hanna thought once her sister knew their survival was attributed to Eagle Feather, it would relieve her qualms, but it only fuelled her desire to alienate herself more from Christian and live in town. Elisabeth rattled on about the perils of Papa having a farm so close to the isolation of the Middle Range. "You must move closer to us," she would say, over and over.

Papa, on the other hand, was puzzled as to why they had not been killed. Hanna could not tell him about Eagle Feather, but that meant no amount of explanation could ever steer him to the good that had come out of it. Papa said divine providence had been the only source of their survival.

THE WARMER SPRING RAINS FINALLY blew in from the sea, doing their hasty work of melting the tiring snows. After Papa had burned the land in May and tilled the soil with the plow, Hanna broadcasted the grain and turnip seed by hand and buried seed potatoes with the hoe. She left him working with the ox as it dragged the harrow to cover the seeds with soil. From the house, Papa could not be seen, which allowed her to steal away. After filling the basket with food, she adjusted the straps on the wooden pattens over her shoes to keep her elevated above wetness and muck. Late in February, she had happened upon starving Mi'kmaq. Thrice, Hanna had left meat and a few loaves of bread. No other opportunity had presented itself for her to slip away undetected, and she thought of them often. Had they survived?

She had not far to walk to reach the spot where the brook looped back into the woods, the place where she had first met them. When Hanna arrived, the basket she had left in the winter lay empty. The tilted lid was partially lying on the ground. She shooed a tittering brown mouse away, placed the food inside, and replaced the lid so it was secure and tight. Hanna squinted to scan the woods for any glimpse of Mi'kmaq. But it remained tranquil and hushed. No branches crackling underfoot, not even a trill or a warble from the songbird eying her from a tree. Wondering how many times the women had returned for more, she chastised herself for not filling the basket more often. Had they assumed she'd abandoned them? *By the grace of God, if you are still in need, may He lead you back*, Hanna pleaded. She kissed the cross that hung around her neck then neatly tucked it back inside her dress.

Hanna headed home. From a distance, she could see someone standing by the front door. She couldn't believe it. Anna was back! She hurriedly removed her pattens, which would only slow her down, and ran to greet her.

"When did you return?" she said, hugging her.

"Last week and I do apologize for not coming here sooner. But, as you can see…"

"Oh my!" Hanna exclaimed. "When are you expecting?"

"Not until August. By looking at me, one would think much sooner. I certainly hope it is only one. My mother was a twin, and the stories my grandmother told would turn your hair white." Anna laughed. They linked arms and strolled to a shady bench. "If truth be told, though, Philip would be truly delighted, and for his sake, just maybe a little bit of me is wishing for it to be so, but…" She hesitated, screwing up her face, then shook her head.

"Where's Philip? Did he not come?"

"Oh yes! He spotted Michael, so you can imagine the talk they're having about the Assembly and other riveting political topics only they could take pleasure in. Catherine is with him. She's in such a state these days when her papa leaves her, always wanting to be by his side. Now, my dear, I have plenty to tell you. I brought a copy of the *Halifax*," she said, lifting the cloth from her basket. "Spices from the West Indies, sugar, as well as raisins and currants." Such that Hanna had never seen.

Hanna remembered the two-page newspaper from when they had lived in Dartmouth. "Is Herr Bushell still the printer?"

Anna nodded. "His daughter, Elizabeth, works with him. Although many believe a woman should not be working in a print shop, it is good to have a female perspective. Her typical political stories are here in this paper. At Christmastime, she also published a receipt for a plum cake. I have made it. With the additional spices she has added, it is much more delicious than the receipt in Glasse's cookbook."

"Come then," Hanna said, nudging her arm, "let's begin."

The two chatted as they started the arduous work of preparing the cakes. Anna prattled on about the entertaining parties she had attended, the tedious politics she would rather forget, and the gruesome war.

"So your papa still knows nothing of Eagle Feather?" Anna said after Hanna explained how Christian's brother had kept them from harm.

Hanna shook her head. She wasn't proud of it and wholeheartedly wished it to be different. She didn't relish keeping anything from Papa; it tormented her.

As they stood over the kitchen table, voices drifted up from behind them. A sudden thud made Hanna jump. Michael had dropped two heavy loaves of bread on the table. "For what purpose would you leave these near the woods?"

Hanna couldn't take her eyes off the bread and the black ant crawling across the top of one. The sinking feeling in the pit of her stomach made her legs weak. She leaned into the table.

"Sit, my dear." Anna touched her arm and pulled the chair behind her. "What is this all about, Michael?"

He said to Hanna, "I followed you." His voice was steady

and firm. "You do not leave this property without my knowledge of your whereabouts. Of all times, and with what we have just been through. Why?"

Hanna trembled as Anna gently rubbed her back.

"You think us so rich as to carelessly throw food to the wolves?" Michael turned away in frustration.

"What was so important that you put your life in danger over this? Who were they for?" It was Anna's soothing voice she heard.

"They're starving."

"Who, my liebling?" Anna asked.

Hanna's reply was barely audible. Knowing in her heart she had done nothing wrong, courage suddenly bubbled to the surface. Her voice didn't even sound familiar to her as she repeated it. "The Mi'kmaq."

"What?" Michael started pacing back and forth, his face suddenly flushed. "How long?" he started. "You are to cease this nonsense immediately!" He didn't spit forth his usual wrath. It was just his natural firm order.

"I will not, Papa."

"You are abetting an enemy of the Crown!"

"You didn't see them. Their sunken eyes, dark with despair. Whatever help I can give them, I must do." She couldn't keep her emotions in check any longer. Tears ran down her face. "I don't even know if they're still alive. I won't stand by and do nothing." Hanna stood up to face Papa. "Don't you see? We caused this to happen."

"Ach! Another one! First Christian, now you." He threw up his hands and stormed out.

"Michael!" Philip called after him.

Anna snatched Catherine's hand before she could run after her father. "Stay here with Mama."

Hanna was crushed. Her back was now against the wall and she had nowhere to turn. She stood alone and exposed.

Anna sighed. "You know I would never encourage you to go against your papa's wishes. But…," she said, "you need to do what you think is right."

Hanna hastily swiped her hand across her eyes to dry her tears.

"I should have told you sooner," Anna added, "the Assembly received a petition in March, just before we left Halifax. It came from quite a few concerned citizens here, complaining of finding Indians destitute. Dr. Phillips initiated it."

"Oh?" Hanna sniffed. "Georg must know about it. Maybe he signed it."

Anna inclined her head. "Then I am surprised you didn't hear of it."

"I wouldn't. He would never broach the subject, not with the state Elisabeth has been in these past months."

"Since our arrival back in Lunenburg, Philip has been made aware of increased interest to send another petition."

"This is good, Anna! More signatures mean added pressure upon the governor to at least do something."

"Try not to set your hopes too high. We're speaking of Governor Lawrence."

Hanna felt a door had opened. "Now, with the Assembly in place, the province must be autonomous and not responsible to the Board." She paused. "Nein, as small as it is, I need to trust in this bit of light you have given to me and have faith that the right thing will be done."

"And I will help you."

# Chapter Twenty-Six



*I*t was high tide. Effortlessly and swiftly, the Water Spirit carried them downriver.

Bear Cub glanced down at Singing Sparrow just as Eagle Feather stopped paddling to look back.

"She's dreaming," Bear Cub said. He forced a smile as he replaced a corner of the bearskin over his wife's bare arm. He was hoping the waters from the healing spring would heal his beloved—the ancient medicines had been of no use against what he was now sure was measles.

Once the pink spots were visible, they had left the camp before the next sunrise. The situation he and Elder Elen had found quickly deteriorated. They went from nursing the sick to burying the dead. From the onset of Singing Sparrow's illness, White Cloud had refused to budge from his daughter's side until Eagle Feather finally persuaded him to return to the village. Now, as Bear Cub guided the ocean canoe down the Oqomkikiaq toward the open sea, he thought how quickly the disease had spread, leaving very few survivors.

Eagle Feather had returned from his long Winter absence with a peculiar reticence. No amount of prodding from Bear

Cub uncovered what had happened during those moons away. It left Bear Cub feeling nonplussed.

As they paddled over the ocean swells, Bear Cub was persistently bothered by the stories the Mi'kmaq told about "black measles." Could it possibly be the same disease his brother had spoken of, one that afflicted the People before Cornwallis arrived? The same plague White Cloud had spoken of many times that killed over a thousand Mi'kmaq?

They steered into the cove and leapt into the cold salt water to drag the canoe onto the beach. The remains of the shallop were gone, most likely claimed by the sea. Above the ridge of sand, the solitary wikuom still stood fully intact. Except for sand drifting up on one side, it could have just been abandoned yesterday, as nothing was out of place. It gave Bear Cub an uncanny sense of belonging. Carefully, he lifted his wife and carried her inside.

"You stay," Eagle Feather said as he grabbed the birchbark container and spear. "I will return soon."

Bear Cub agreed. He gathered scraps of dry driftwood for kindling, and once he had cleared the smoke hole of debris, he started a fire. When his wife became restless, he kneeled beside her to brace her back against him. He laid a cool cloth upon her forehead, put his arms around her, and rocked her slowly, all the while humming a lullaby. Her skin was hot, the rash now spreading. When her body shivered, he cried. And he cried, thinking of her life slipping through his fingers.

Singing Sparrow slept into the afternoon. Shadows lengthened. Where was Eagle Feather? Did he remember the whereabouts of the spring? As a child, Eagle Feather frequented the area with his father, but many moons had passed since then. Had his memory become clouded?

When Eagle Feather finally returned, he brought with him

not only the water medicine, but also salmon and alewives, which were strung over his shoulders. He dropped the fish into a heap by the fire. Bear Cub grasped the container of water, but his brother stopped him.

Bear Cub nodded. Singing Sparrow groaned when Eagle Feather raised her head. Her eyes briefly and partially opened as the liquid passed over her lips. Her body rejected it in a fit of coughing, and it bubbled from her mouth.

Bear Cub sat next to his wife and held her hand tight. "Come on, fight!" he said.

"You must, my sister. You must," Eagle Feather cried. He wiped her mouth, laid down the cup, and waited. Her lips opened slightly, like a baby bird. Eagle Feather soaked a cloth and squeezed droplets into her mouth. He grinned when there was no adverse reaction. "Good. Drink," he mumbled, as she extracted more of the goodness. Singing Sparrow's eyes closed and her body eased like a limp puppy.

Bear Cub watched his brother. Eagle Feather gnawed at his bottom lip, frown lines appeared on his forehead. He seemed to have aged. Eagle Feather glanced across at him. Each one eyed the other as if buried under his own private gloom.

Bear Cub jerked awake to his brother's voice. "Ach! Must have nodded off." Unsteadily, he stood, blinking at his brother. The sun shone through the open door.

"My watch. You rest," Eagle Feather ordered. They had barely slept for three days. They were both in a stupor, going through the motions of healing and praying, which at times seemed futile.

Bear Cub disagreed. "I'll get more food," he said, and he picked up the sickness bowl to clean it.

"There is enough for today. I will check the weir later." Eagle Feather stared down at his sister. "Any change?"

"A little. She's not as agitated."

Bear Cub left and walked along the beach. His eyes wandered across the sand to the edge of the woods. On their first day, Ambroise had approached but they had not seen him since.

When Bear Cub waded into the shallow water, his toes sank into the wet sand. He stopped to allow the rush of the incoming tide to flow over his feet. As the ocean reclaimed the beach, Bear Cub's tension washed away with the sand that eroded beneath his feet.

After he buried the contents, Bear Cub cleansed the bowl in the salt water and tossed it onto the dry sand. The current tugged at his legs as he waded deeper through the waves. Above him, black cormorants sounded off their deep, guttural grunts. Gulls floated silently upon the sparkling water before diving for food. Invigorated, he immersed himself completely. He instantly came up for air at the shock of the frigid water. His body was numbed, but he felt alive.

In the distance, a bowsprit sailed into view around the farthest end of the cove. Bear Cub squinted into the sun as two more ships came from behind. He kept his eye on the edge of the barren rocks that jutted into the ocean. One by one, another two ships slowly appeared.

During the rest of the morning, four continued north, but one dropped anchor in the cove itself. Then, silence. No sounds or movements from aboard the ship as it sat like a sentry upon the water. Eagle Feather kept watch. Night fell, and Bear Cub took his turn. When the sun rose, the ship left the inlet and veered north.

"British!"

Bear Cub turned to find Ambroise standing ten paces away.

"We have seen them anchor farther up," Ambroise said. "That is the first one I have seen come this close."

"Strange they didn't come ashore."

"A good thing. Our ammunition is near depletion." Ambroise walked closer to Bear Cub. "How is Singing Sparrow?"

"There is still a fever, but she is conscious."

"Come with me, more spring water." Ambroise walked ahead.

For some time after, Ambroise kept his distance but habitually left a supply of the healing water. Singing Sparrow's fever broke on the eighth day, and the rash began to fade. By the following week, she had recovered her strength.

The ships did not return, but their presence was confirmed when Eagle Feather and Bear Cub discovered fish flakes in nearby inlets. They spied on the strangers and witnessed heaps of fresh ocean cod in various stages of curing under a heavy spread of salt. Two flakes, built of poles and spruce boughs, stood tall. Shallops were beached high and dry while buoys, ropes, and grapples lay in heaps upon the sand. Men were busily laying salted cod flesh-side up; others had already been flipped to sun the backside. The catch was neatly laid out—side by side, alternating heads and tails—where the fish would remain until it was ready to be shipped to Europe.

Eagle Feather had slowly resigned himself to the presence of the British, who seemed to spread without limit. But loathing still consumed him. As long as he breathed, he refused to bow to their arrogance. He looked to his brother, his alter ego. The one whose hands he confidently rested his life in. The convictions of each strengthened the other's fortitude.

Ambroise, who knew the needs of the People, stood with Eagle Feather and Bear Cub. He understood. *So why is he not more combative?* Eagle Feather wondered.

"We will build our traps and weirs elsewhere," Ambroise said.

Eagle Feather clenched his jaw. "Until they crowd us out again."

"My brother, you would do better to put your energy into survival."

"To fight *is* my survival. I cannot shut my eyes to this."

"You are young and full of passion. Battles have their place, but we need to walk away. We are too few."

Eagle Feather watched the fishers trample upon the rocks, upon the shape-changers. He pointed angrily. "We are enough against them."

"For now, until more arrive behind them. Remember the innocents." Ambroise hesitated and lowered his head. "Our old guns cannot go against theirs. And we gather fewer pelts to trade."

Hearing these words only infuriated Eagle Feather more. In his travels seven moons ago, he had met only two Frenchmen, and they had had no gunpowder to barter. He was enraged that the newcomers kept the People from their ceremonies on the very spot where these fishers now milled about, where Kluskap had walked.

"But Ambroise, how can we just do nothing?" Bear Cub asked.

"The scales are heavily tipped within this circle of life. They are not welcome here," Eagle Feather argued.

"But there is no existence outside it, my friend. The same circle in which they belong, we belong, and any amount of friction affects the whole. Harmony must be restored within," Ambroise remarked. "For now, we leave."

"The fish are now spawning—we are ready to renew our relationship with Mother Earth. How can we conduct our grandfathers' ceremonies in the very place where they sang praise if we simply walk away? Moqwe!"

"Think upon your sister," Bear Cub asserted. "Your mother was struck down in hate."

Eagle Feather thought back to the naked ground his mother lay beneath. His suffering had taken on a life of its own until he knew himself no more, and his burden had weighed him down till he drowned in his own agony. His only desire when he had started for Merligueche was to make someone's blood run cold at the mere sight of him, to paralyze the settlers with fear so they would run from this land and sail away. The thought of killing when justified had eased his mind—until he laid his eyes upon Hanna. A newcomer who walked the same land but had looked upon him with solicitude.

A hand caressed his shoulder. It was Ambroise. "We are all spirit. This is what binds us together into relationships. What we decide here affects our children's children."

Ambroise fixed his attention on Bear Cub. "The spirit never dies. It merely transforms with each cycle within the circle." He inspected the strangers at the flakes.

"Maybe the circle will right itself with our children," Eagle Feather said.

"But only through our connections and what we decide at this moment," Ambroise replied with conviction. He knelt beside a pink moccasin plant. "We are as much rooted as this plant and as this tall spruce that reaches for the sky, and all the insects that dwell within it; they are all different but equal in the eyes of the one who created us." With his wrinkled brown hand, he gently touched the flower. "Our sister here depends on the shade of these trees to survive and on their nutrients from the moist soil. The flower relies on those insects to fertilize her. The People need the threads from her roots for medicine. We need each other." He stood up and leaned against the tree. "Bear Cub, look around you. What do you see when you gaze on that rock, on that owl who quietly watches us, or on the worm that crawls at your feet?"

Bear Cub did not reply.

"Msit No'kmaq," Eagle Feather whispered.

Bear Cub knew it to mean "all my relations." He said, "Through creation, we are all dependent upon one another."

"And the fishers?" Ambroise said. "Even in death we are not apart."

"Then this is a complex relationship," Bear Cub replied.

"Indeed." Ambroise bent down to pick up his musket and left the two.

AT THE FIRST QUARTER MOON, Singing Sparrow had fully recovered, and they decided they would return to their village. It was a bleak day with a colourless sky above, and Bear Cub left Eagle Feather to finish loading their supplies. He followed a cheerful song in the wilderness—there was no mistaking it was Singing Sparrow. As he reached the waterfall, he caught glimpses of her dark skin when the water parted with her movements. He stopped momentarily to observe. He thought of his old life, which now was completely alien to him. His place was as solidly defined here as if he had been born into it. Their life was his life.

Bear Cub stripped off his clothes and dove in—the water was chilly against his warm body. He surfaced near her but she playfully immersed herself, hiding from view. Bear Cub followed her below the surface of the water, then up onto a rocky ledge behind the falls. His mind quieted when he surrendered to her touch. They embraced within the cascading shower. To openly display such intimacies normally left to the confines of their wikuom was inconceivable. Both were nervous. But with each gentle stroke, the shackles loosened and fell away.

Merging within the down rush of water, their bodies sculpted by the continuous flow, he dared not break the spell with words. Her wet, smooth body pressed against his, and the uninhibited desire grew between them. The act was honest—freeing.

# Chapter Twenty-Seven

JUNE 1759

*P*hilip waved to Hanna and Michael as they walked along Montague Street. They had just loaded their wooden cart with victuals. Anna was not with Philip, which was not surprising. Because of her tremendous weight gain, she had difficulty getting about. With Anna's time quickly approaching, Georg had ordered her to rest.

Philip was nothing if not direct when conversing, which nearly always steered into politics. "Guten tag! I was hoping we would bump into each other. The House will be dissolving!" he said to Michael. Then he held Hanna's hands and greeted her with a hurried kiss upon both cheeks. It was a very warm day, and his skin perspired against her own.

"This is rather sudden."

"Not really. The province is rapidly changing. Lawrence has just proposed four more communities running along this shore toward Cap de Sable Island."

Hanna boldly asked, "Why is it necessary to dissolve and start over?"

Papa was clearly taken aback, as it was not her place to ask. Philip hesitated, then sidestepped Michael and grinned at her boldness. "The council is proceeding to divide this province into counties."

"And in what county will Lunenburg be bound?" Hanna gained confidence. Philip treated her like an adult. After all, she was almost fifteen.

"Nothing has been finalized, but the draft shows the north-west boundary halfway through the province. Then southwest to the River Rossignol. Each county will return two members, as well as two from Lunenburg Township. The election's in August."

"These counties you speak of—what about the Mi'kmaq?" Hanna asked. Papa stiffened and he squeezed her hand for silence. Her stomach churned but she had no intention of acknowledging his reprimand.

"What about them, Hanna?" Philip drew his eyebrows together.

"By your face, I can surmise the petitions were for naught. If they were delivered, the governor refuses to help the Mi'kmaq. Am I correct?"

Papa gave her hand a jerk, and Hanna withdrew from his grasp.

"I hope you will find it in your heart to overlook Hanna's impertinence as a careless whim of her youth."

"Of course, Michael. Hanna, I personally handed them over to the governor. Unfortunately, I can't control the outcome. We can only hope."

"Danke," she said, smiling. "If you still represent us in the next Assembly, I know you well enough to feel confident of your support in this." Hanna truly meant what she said and curtsied to her friend. She could have stretched the conversation as to the consideration of the Indian lands they were divvying up, but Papa's exasperated sigh stopped her.

After Philip left, Michael scolded her. "If you display such insolence again, I will…I…"

"What, Papa? Anna and I aren't the only ones who signed the petition. And no, I haven't left any more food. They didn't return." She turned to walk away, then stopped. "Christian could be suffering as well. If the Mi'kmaq are your enemies, what does that make your son?" Hanna waited for a reply. Nothing. "I'm not angry with you, Papa. Just sad. Sad because you're not the person I knew so well."

Michael lifted the handles of the cart and moved on. *He carries such a weight*, she thought. There had been a time when she could always break through to him. But not now.

"Not a chance." Hanna was sitting on a stool, milking, half-listening to Papa and Philip— something about limited land ownership in the colony. But the tone had changed when the voices lowered outside the barn. Hanna leaned her forehead against the cow's side and released her hold on the teats. She walked quietly to the open door. "The Act has passed. It is deemed the fixed form of worship in this province."

"They are fools if they think this will not cause a riot! We are mostly Lutherans here, not Church of England. Why, the Mosers are Calvinists."

"There is no danger, Michael. As long as no one is a practising Catholic, all Protestants are safe. And we are autonomous as to our buildings and service. We are excused from paying any taxes to support the Church of England. Of course, Lawrence could do nothing less if he wants the New Englanders to settle here. They would demand religious freedom."

"Funny, the tide has turned in our favour. We're in the right church, just a different pew. I have no love for the Catholics, but to force the priests to leave is repeating the intolerance we escaped."

"Any priest still found in the province after the twenty-fifth of March will be imprisoned. Anyone caught harbouring a Catholic priest will be fined fifty pounds *and* set in the pillory."

Hanna shifted her weight to a more comfortable position and placed her hand over her mouth. She had inhaled the pipe smoke that had drifted her way, and it almost made her cough. Papa's muttering was not clear enough when he answered.

Philip spoke again. "The government wants to control the Indians. What better way to cut off their allies than to be rid of the priests as well?"

"I agree." Hanna heard an intake of breath as Papa puffed again. "Will this impact Reverend Moreau? He is a missionary to them."

"I doubt it'll have any bearing on him. He has made it his life's ambition to convert all the Catholics, which includes the natives, over to the Church of England."

"I don't trust him. He baptizes their children when his duties should be to this flock alone."

There was a long pause.

Their voices drifted as they strolled from the barn. Hanna held Paul's cross in her hand, then ran for the house. Thus far, she had kept it well hidden. Papa would never understand why she kept a Catholic religious symbol. Was it best to hide it for good? There was a box under her bed she kept locked with small memories of Mama. She blew the dust away and opened the lid.

"Hanna!"

Papa suddenly appeared, popping his head into the loft. Her back was to him. She banged the box shut and scraped it back under. The cross was tightly enclosed within her fist. "Ja, Papa."

"Where have you been? You have not finished milking, and the cows are telling us so. Schnell—be quick about it." His head lowered from view.

Hanna thrust the necklace into her pocket and climbed down.

The day flew by. After she finished the milking and scoured the floor, Hanna hilled the potatoes, while Papa removed more of the rotted tree stumps.

"Shoo!" she scolded, with one push of a broom to guide the mouse out the door. One last thrust had it running for the tall grass. "And don't come back!

Papa was returning but with a blood-soaked rag poorly wound around his hand. "What happened?" she asked.

"Stupidity with an axe. Took a nasty chunk out. Looks like it has almost stopped bleeding," he said, dabbing at it.

But when Hanna brought a bowl of warm water, it instantly turned to red when he immersed his hand. She pulled a piece of cloth from her pocket and wrapped it tightly. "Keep the pressure on it. When it stops, I'll apply the salve. You must be more careful, Papa."

"Hmph. You sound like your mama. She always berated me as if the accident had been avoidable."

"Well!" Hanna smirked and returned inside.

"You dropped this," he called after her.

"Supper is almost ready," she said. When Hanna reappeared at the door, Papa had the necklace dangling from his fingers.

"Where…"

She caught her breath and felt the inside of her pocket.

"Is this yours?"

Hanna nodded.

"Verdammt! Why?"

If she spoke, she would only stutter.

"For Christ's sake! Answer me!" He stared back at her.

Hanna swallowed hard to force away the lump in her throat. "It was a gift."

"And?"

First the tears, then a broken explanation of how she had befriended Paul. She went on to tell Papa how she and Georg nursed him back to health.

"You are never to see him again." Michael stomped inside the house.

Hanna followed him. "He's dead."

"Then you won't be needing this." He threw it onto the hot ashes that were scattered about the hearth.

Hanna lunged forward and retrieved the singed cross before it became engulfed. "How could you? You care nothing for me, Papa, if you are so heartless as to toss this away. Paul was a beloved friend."

Michael grabbed for the necklace, and she hid it behind her back. "Nein!" she cried. "Don't come near me. It's the only thing I have left of him." Papa raised his hand to her as if to strike. Hanna flinched but stood her ground. As she waited for what seemed an eternity, she saw someone who was not her papa.

Michael dropped his arm. "There are not enough people here that you need to resort to befriending an Indian?" He paused, breathing heavily. "That night in the barn—you knew him, didn't you." He waited. "Ach, I understand all too well, my daughter."

"It's not like that…" But she spoke to no one. He had left in a huff.


It was the middle of the night. Unable to sleep, Hanna lay in bed mulling over their words. When Papa had returned at dusk, he avoided her and went to bed. He looked haggard and old.

She heard him moving about, then their tiny home quieted. She lay listening to the rain against the window, debating whether she should go to him. She rose from her bed to search the kitchen below. The lamp was almost out, and Papa lay with his head on the table, his hand across the open bible.

He was deep in slumber and didn't notice her presence. She leaned over to the partially lit page listing the family deaths—her grandfather, her siblings, and Mama. Christian's name remained unchanged beneath Jakob. The calligraphic words distinctly stood out in black ink. Papa stirred. Hanna held her breath as his warm hand covered hers. That same protective hand that loved and guided had been very close to harming her in a rash moment of anger.

"I can't lose you," Michael said, raising his head. Hanna knelt by his side. She laid her head onto his lap and waited. "There is you and Elisabeth. 'Twas only you who never left my side when your mama died. You were the lifeline that raised me from my grief," he said, lightly stroking her hair. "One by one, God saw fit to recall my children for reasons conceivable to Him alone."

Hanna sat up. She wanted to scream that Christian was dead to no one but himself. But when she saw his eyes glistening with emotion, she realized his pain at the idea she could be taken from him ran very deep. The losses only prolonged his self-reproach. "Look at me, Papa," she said sternly. "No one blames you for bringing us here. If you had changed your mind, it could have meant death for all of us. Papa, there's no knowing what life deals each one of us. That is beyond our control," she said, holding his hand. "You know the time will come for me to leave this house. But I'll never be so far from you that you can't reach for me. For now, Papa, we are together. I'm not leaving you." Hanna could taste the salt of her tears upon her lips.

He took a deep breath, and when he spoke, his voice quaked. "I don't deserve such leniency. I was about to strike you," he lamented.

The two held onto each other, neither speaking more of it.

"Do you know him?" Michael whispered.

She could barely hear him, but she knew who he meant. Hanna no longer could continue the deceit and revealed the story of Christian's brother.

# Chapter Twenty-Eight



The war continued with no end in sight, and an increase in privateering off the coast contributed to great losses of valuable cargo. To get through the days, Elisabeth relied heavily upon her husband's perseverance and strength. But amid the insecurities, life still marched on with the growth of calves and five kids from two nannies on the Gessler farm. The flock of sheep increased with seven lambs in the spring. Two ram lambs were now at about sixty percent of their mature weight.

The farm produced a small surplus of cabbage, potatoes, and oats to send to the Halifax market—Elisabeth and Hanna had worked long hours tying oats into sheaves. The wheat again fell to mildew. Here, it never grew as high as in the Faterland, and the resulting breads were much darker. Georg had lagged in his decision to sow it with barley despite knowing the results from his neighbours, but this time he decided he would follow suit for the next crop.

"Mama! Mama!" Petie screamed, excited. "Onkel Peter is here."

With the passage of time, an unmistakable bond had grown between them. In Georg's eyes, Elisabeth was unjustified to think of Peter as a betrayer, let alone dangerous in any way.

"You've not given me a good enough reason that would warrant keeping him away from our son. It's absurd," he had said. Elisabeth had quite a different slant on things, but for her son's sake she kept her true feelings hidden. At times, she found it difficult to be civil. She could never regain her trust in Peter, but to keep peace between her and Georg, her approval of the situation was one she had to maintain. So when Georg had recently suggested Petie call Peter onkel, she didn't resist.

Peter was walking up over the rise in long strides. "Guten tag," he said, when he caught up to her.

"When did you get in? We weren't expecting to see you until next week."

"Yesterday." He wiped his forehead with his shirt sleeve and let out a whistle. "Whew!"

"Petie, run and get some water. The fresh lot you helped me draw from the well this morning will do just fine." After he scampered off, she asked, "Was your business in Halifax satisfactory?"

He nodded, then drank the water. "Danke, Petie. And by a bit of luck, I met up with Silvanus Cobb." When Elisabeth questioned who he was, he said, "Captain of the *York*. John Doggett was with him. They're on their way to Port Rossignol; they have a tract of land there."

"Is that where the New Englanders are expected to settle now?"

"Ja, with fishing and the lumber trade, it's more to their liking. The area offers great stands of pine and plenty of sea life. I've been told salmon practically leap into boats, there're so many. Captain Cobb believes there's also much interest at the mouth of the LaHave River."

"Why they'd wish to settle down there is beyond me! They must be running from something?"

Peter shrugged. "They're poor. Any land they already own has been split up to give to their sons. New immigrants keep arriving, which leaves no unclaimed land in New England. Lawrence has dangled the carrots. Free land, and a lot of it if one has a large brood. It may not entice you, but many will jump at it no matter."

Petie, who had gone to the house, came skipping back toward them. "Tante Hanna can't get Marta to nap."

"Would you like to see a ship with me?" Peter asked him.

Elisabeth hesitated. "Maybe another time."

"The *York* and *Halifax* are sailing tomorrow, and I'm sure the captain would love to see a future seaman on board."

Elisabeth stared down at her son's face, which had brightened up with a large grin. She relented. "Then you better change your shirt. It's filthy. Tante Hanna will find a clean one for you. Scoot! Before I change my mind."

"Elisabeth. I'm leaving on the next ship."

"When will you return?"

"At this point, I may not." Peter sat down on the bench out of the sun. "Come sit with me."

Elisabeth was taken aback. "What will you tell Petie?"

"The truth—that I will miss him terribly, and if I do return, he'll be the first one I seek out." He stared straight into her eyes. "There's nothing here for me."

Elisabeth fidgeted with her apron. "What do you mean? All the deserters have been absolved, and the government is giving you land in Mahone Bay. And you were interested in our town lot."

"There's no need. With the new announcement, I also own the place I have in Range H. For now, I'll keep it. However, a gentleman by the name of Rudolf has expressed interest in buying it." Peter paused. "I'm grateful for Georg's acceptance, but this situation has made my feelings for you grow stronger. For all concerned, it's best I leave."

Elisabeth averted her gaze and stood up. "Then leave you must. Georg will be back soon, and I know he would wish to speak with you. He's so grateful for your help in the fields this past summer. For his sake, can you not delay and take the next ship?"

"Nein. I signed up for crew on the *Halifax*, a privateer ship. It's heading back to His Majesty's Dockyard to be refitted with cannons and the stores needed."

Elisabeth had no words. A jumble of thoughts entered her head. She wouldn't see him again. It's what she had wanted, but why was there a slight pang in her stomach? Any feelings for him had been long buried—she loved Georg.

"This will be very hard on Petie. He worships you."

"I'll explain it to him this afternoon. It's good we will spend it together."

"At least it's a British vessel."

Peter knit his eyebrows together. "And your meaning?"

"You've made it quite clear where your sympathies lie. So I was surprised, that's all."

"To some degree, my support still lies with the Mi'kmaq. But I have also resigned myself to the belief that the British will in all probability prevail. The longer this war goes on, the greater the suffering for the Mi'kmaq. I'll do my part here to weaken the French to shorten the war."

"And if we win, the Indians will be suppressed."

"You should not be so quick to wish such a travesty." Peter now stood. "I've witnessed hundreds of scalps carried by rangers." There was silence as he paced. "When I was in Louisbourg, two Abenaki and two Mi'kmaq arrived. Governor Raymond paid them for the dozen British scalps they brought from Halifax. They spoke of a raid in Virginia where villages were burned. Six hundred scalps were taken, and five hundred women and children taken prisoner."

"Then, all the more reason to strike them down. I won't rest—"

"With each Indian recruit the French have, the British ships send more regulars from overseas to join the local militia. For a while, the French have been able to thwart their advances. But now…now, I believe the British are gaining hold." Peter paced again in slow strides. "When will it end?"

"Hopefully soon," Elisabeth answered.

"Precisely!"

She could feel the cold prick of the knife and the warm breath on her skin as if it had happened yesterday. She had no compassion for them.

"Ach, you're ready!" Peter said as his nephew ran from the house. Petie kissed his mother on the cheek to say goodbye.

"Come, Petie. Have you seen the *York*?" Peter asked.

"Nein."

"It was employed to take troops and supplies to Fort Anne and Fort Edward," Peter said as they started to walk away.

Petie stared up at him. "Did it ever capture any French ships?"

"A few. One was called the *Marguerite*. You will like Captain Cobb, Petie. He knows every harbour, creek, and cove along this coast. Do you know what a privateer is?"

They were now out of earshot, and Elisabeth continued to watch as their backs became mere dots in the distance.

Elisabeth felt her sister's warm arm encircle her waist. "I overheard the conversation," Hanna said. "What's wrong? You should be overjoyed."

"Strange, I actually feel a tremendous loss."

"That is the young girl in you speaking," Hanna said.

"You think?"

"She's finally letting go of a deep-seated hurt."

"Ach, a foolish girl she was to hang on to it!"

"Nein. I imagine it's impossible for us to forget the first to steal our heart."

HANNA WAITED AT THE KITCHEN table while Anna tended to her new son, David, now almost two months old. Catherine stood by her father outside. Papa and Philip were both puffing on their pipes. The next Assembly was scheduled for the fourth of December, and Philip was anxious to return to Halifax. Their delayed departure only made him more jittery to get back to the business of making concrete changes in Lunenburg, even though the lopsided Assembly still mostly consisted of Halifax merchants.

Hanna sat alone with a written document Philip and Papa had been discussing. It concerned the land that no longer belonged to the Acadians. Her eyes glanced over the words as she discreetly edged the paper in front of her. Except for the odd word, English was still foreign to her. *Lands* and *Crown of England*, she knew. And *legal right*. But in what context? She was baffled.

Anna returned with the infant in her arms. "Interesting reading, nein?" She rocked David gently as his eyes closed once again into slumber.

"Um," Hanna started, "I'm not sure about this section. Right here."

Anna picked up the paper. "Of course." Running her finger along each word, Anna translated to German. "The governor is assuring the New England settlers that the French cannot reclaim the lands they left."

Hanna traced her finger over the words *right* and *belong*, to which Anna said, "All bits of waterways, every speck of soil is in another's hands to do as they will."

Hanna said, "If the British are this insolent, then those relief petitions will be blindly put aside. It's of no consequence to them if the Mi'kmaq are barely surviving!"

"I'll not give up and neither should you, my liebling. Both Philip and Sebastian will do their best to push the issue. And remember Archibald and Joseph. So there are four representatives now in the House siding with us."

Papa and Philip strode back inside.

"Hanna, I've just been told of thirteen new townships that will be established for those emigrating here. Exciting news, it is!" Papa said. "Charles Morris will be responsible for the boundaries. Each future township will be one hundred thousand acres."

"Convenient," Hanna remarked, which caused Papa to give her a wary look.

"Both Doggett and Cobb have been granted land in Liverpool. There are forty-one grantees in all."

"Liverpool?" Anna asked as she lay David in his cradle near the fireplace.

"Port Rossignol was renamed after a town in England," Philip said. "If all goes well, the hundreds could become thousands to settle along the bay from Annapolis to as far as Pisiguit."

"The Mi'kmaq will be displaced!" Hanna exclaimed. "Why not just expel them all at once." She glanced at Anna. "It's a slow death as it is." Her cynicism didn't go unnoticed.

"They are nomadic—they'll find other areas," Papa snapped.

She bit her tongue. Papa would certainly have no qualms about displaying his wrath later if she did speak up. She circumvented the issue.

"Forgive me, Papa. I was only thinking of Christian."

This time, Michael forced a smile, then to Philip said, "We must take our leave. I'm sure there's plenty of packing still left to organize."

"The ship sails on Thursday morning. Oh, Hanna, I do not like it when we say goodbye," Anna said, giving her a hug.

"There'll not be a day that goes by without thoughts of you—especially when I'm baking." They both laughed.

"Michael," Philip began, "I can't thank you enough for taking on our cattle and sheep. Herr Metzler was finding it too difficult to manage my sawmill as well as my livestock and still oversee his tannery. Upon our return next spring, we'll discuss the matter of ownership."

"I don't understand."

"Anna and I have decided to sell and move into town. With the time I must spend away, it's much more favourable for us. Anna won't always wish to travel with me, and the farm is too much for her to handle. I would like to keep them for your benefit."

"This is much too generous," Michael argued. "I cannot accept such a fine gift."

Philip grunted in jest. "I know better than to quarrel with you on this. For a tradeoff, would you be interested in helping me at the sawmill? I need the help and it would mean extra income for you and Hanna."

Michael was stunned. "I don't know what to say."

"Say nothing. Think on it over the winter, and we will talk more."

# Chapter Twenty-Nine



The northeasterly gale slammed unrelentingly against the side of the house, which creaked and groaned at the assault. They had sheltered the livestock well before the barrage of rain flooded the lower pasture. Hanna pushed the last of the dry cloths against the bottom of the door as Papa wrung out the wet ones to hang over the iron crane. The storm had raged most of the day, and there was no end in sight. Autumn had always been a time of rains, but never to such a degree.

At the sound of a crash, Papa kicked the cloths away and braced himself to open the door. "Stay here," he ordered. Hanna crouched down against the wall as the door flew ajar with a whoosh, allowing a wall of warm muggy air to rush in before Papa forced it closed behind him.

Hanna hugged her knees to her chin to stop herself from shaking. Her eyes were frozen to the latch as she waited for the metal bar to rise, any movement at all to indicate Papa was back. Minutes ticked by but she could only hear the wind's fury, demanding entry.

The longer Hanna stayed, the more her muscles screamed from the tension and the more her agitation heightened. *Why is Papa taking so long—is he unable to call for help? What if the house collapses around me?* Unable to contain herself, she suddenly found herself outside. Soaked to the skin, she held on to the side of the stone well to keep upright. At the storm's brief respite, Hanna ran for the barn door, which flapped furiously against the fence. One final crash broke it into dangerous wooden shards that flung past her. She screamed just before making it safely inside.

"Papa?"

"Here!" he yelled from behind the stall. "Help me with these goats!"

Sheets of rain blew inside the barn. In one corner, a steady stream of water gushed down upon the bleating sheep. The cows mooed in protest as the jittery goats climbed onto their stalls and onto haystacks. Hanna stroked the animals, doing her best to calm them while she settled them back as safely as possible.

Papa pulled his daughter to him. She clutched at his wet hand and pressed it against her face. She squeezed her eyelids shut and prayed hard. Suddenly, without warning, the rain just stopped and the wind died—an unearthly calm. Hanna warily stepped outside, following Papa. They stood among the cracked boughs and clumps of saturated leaves. They were surrounded by sticky, thick air and the overwhelming smells of the earth. Above, stars twinkled against the dark sky. Thick clouds raced across the path of the full moon.

Hanna hurried to the house, but Papa called, "Nein, Hanna! It's not safe!" The crown of a tree had partly cracked and was leaning over the roof. Hanna ran back to him, and he pulled her toward the barn. An eerie glow startled her—a pair of eyes revealed a black wolf blocking their path. Papa's hands pressed down hard upon her shoulders. As her eyes locked into the animal's gaze, Hanna could feel Papa's fingers dig deeper to keep her still. In the distance, the wind groaned as it began reclaiming its control. Heavy raindrops splashed upon their faces. The storm's reprieve closed its curtain, and the night sky blackened even more. The animal glanced into the barn. He fixated on them once more before running off.

EVENTUALLY EXHAUSTION CLAIMED HANNA THAT night as she lay beside Papa. She awoke to glorious sunrays reaching inside where there once had been a barn door. It was cold. The storm was gone, and so was Papa. Hanna wrapped her coat tighter around herself and found him moving the debris that had once been their fence. Near the house, two trees had toppled over. The massive root system of one of them was exposed, and the ground was littered with broken branches.

"Ach!" Papa cried when he saw her. He held her tight and kissed her. "I haven't been in the house yet. The thatch on the roof is in shreds."

Together, they entered to find the parchment windows lying on the soaked floor. The kitchen table and benches were overturned, and the fireplace, of course, was stone cold.

"I'll do my best to start a fire and clean up," Hanna said, setting the bench upright.

"It's Sunday. We will walk to church after breakfast."

"You think there will still be services?" Hanna shook her head and almost laughed aloud.

"Maybe, maybe not, but I'm certain there'll be many who are looking for guidance. We will go."

On their way to town they saw large areas of forest that had been flattened. When they arrived, most of their neighbours were there, standing outside the church. The sight of the town was more than Hanna could take in. Waves had crashed ashore, flinging rocks and mounds of seaweed and kelp up past

Montague Street. Two schooners were beached, masts snapped like twigs. A sloop had miraculously survived fully intact but drifted aimlessly in the harbour. Wharfs had been destroyed, and buildings stood with damaged roofs or none at all. What few glass windowpanes that existed in Lunenburg were now shattered, leaving voids to the empty homes. Hanna overheard one gentleman state that the salt and sugar that had been in stores near the beach were almost entirely ruined.

The town was noisy with troops. Soldiers and rangers marched by them. Lieutenant-Colonel Jessen instructed those who had shown up to investigate the isolated farms on the Northwest Range, and Papa congregated with the other members of the militia. Anyone who was present that day had come with information about their neighbours' welfare. The inside of the church gradually filled. As they learned more about the extent of the destruction, Reverend Moreau helped organize the many stepping forward to assist in the repairing and rebuilding. By noon, scant reports had come in of families with varying degrees of damage, while others were in dire straits with injuries.

There had been no sign of Georg and Elisabeth. Hanna thought the worst, until Papa said, "I just spoke with Herr Moser. Elisabeth and Georg and the children are safe but for a few scrapes and with some damage to the house and barn. I must go now," he said, and started to walk. "Heinrich is heading a group of us to meet at the Fleck farm. From there, we'll start with South B and C Divisions before dark. There's no time to waste."

After they arrived home, Papa loaded a musket for Hanna then left. He had hugged her with the explicit instructions not to stray far from the house and definitely not without the gun's protection. Hanna studied it as it stood in its brown wood and metal majesty against the kitchen wall. She hoped she would never use it. She had only fired it once, and Papa had stood behind her. She would never withstand the force alone when firing. If she ever had to wield such a weapon at an intruder, Hanna could only hope the mere look of it would be enough to scare them off.

Hanna saw to the livestock and thought of her brother. It had been over two years since he had left them, and Hanna was still cautious in speaking Christian's name in Papa's presence. Whenever Papa became incensed at the sound of his son's name, hopelessness would wash over her and she would have to walk away.

Movement in the woods brought her back to the present. She reached for the gun before she saw a Mi'kmaw woman and her young child standing just a few yards from her. They were the same people Hanna had seen so long ago. And again, there was no man with them. The woman looked thinner. From what she remembered, they were wearing the same clothes as last time except now, the woman clutched a heavy woollen cloak around her shoulders. Both wore a peaked hat that covered their ears.

Hanna motioned for them to wait and retrieved a basket full of foodstuffs from the house. She lay it a few feet away from the woman. They hesitated. Hanna smiled at them and pulled out her cross to show she meant no harm. Carefully, the woman and her daughter moved closer.

"Wela'lin," the woman uttered.

"Weliaq." Hanna remembered the greeting. She reached to touch their hands and was reciprocated by theirs. She wished she knew more words.


Papa came home at dusk with a light step. Quebec, the capital of New France, had fallen on September thirteenth. Both the British and French commanders-in-chief, Generals James Wolfe and Louis-Joseph de Montcalm, had died in battle. The French had retreated to a vulnerable Montreal, which was now cut off from receiving reinforcements and supplies from France.

Wondering what the defeat could mean to Christian and his Mi'kmaw family, Hanna carefully listened over the next few days to the sporadic information as it drifted in. The talk had been mainly of the fourth-rate British warship, the *Mary*, which had briefly docked in Lunenburg en route to Halifax. French prisoners from Cap de Sable were on board, she had heard.

Papa and Georg attended the Tuesday evening town hall meeting, where the bone of contention was raised again—fishing. Colonel Sutherland strongly encouraged everyone to fish for the profitability of the province, especially Lunenburg, much to the displeasure of Papa and many like him. The province still depended on annual grants from the British government, and it was imperative that Nova Scotia soon become a lucrative member of the empire. The Indians were mere obstacles to overcome, Papa had said yesterday. What better way to push them back than with more settlers? Hanna loathed his argument but had begrudgingly kept silent.

Her mind never strayed from the woman and her daughter. Would they survive the oncoming winter? Two weeks passed before she saw them again, carrying the empty basket. Papa was working in the barn while she loaded it up and quickly returned. A man was with them this time. Up close, Hanna noticed the woman's lip was red and swollen. Behind her stood the man; he was wearing a fur robe. He held a gun at his side and spoke words Hanna didn't understand. She attempted to say her name the way Paul used to say it. "Ana," she said, pressing her hand to her chest.

When an ear-splitting crack sounded behind her, Hanna instinctively ducked. The child shrieked when the male collapsed, and the woman pulled her daughter to the ground, covering her body with her own. The Indian struggled to stand. His hand turned red as blood oozed down his arm.

"Papa! Nein!" Hanna screamed when she turned around. He was reloading. Her attempt to shove the gun away was blocked as he seized her by the wrist. "You have defied me. Get back to the house!" He released her, and Hanna stumbled as she tried to run. But not in the direction he had ordered. She stood between Papa and the Indians. "Run!" she said, and pushed at the woman and the man. Hanna did not move until they were hidden deep in the woods. Papa pursued them. There was another shot. Hanna covered her ears to deafen any screams that followed. Anger pushed her to chase after him, but she stopped when she caught sight of his black jacket between the stands of trees. "How dare you!" she shouted at him.

When Papa turned to her, he said, "You'll be glad to know I missed. Your *friends* are safe…for now." Without another word, Michael hurried back to the house.

The evening meal was taken in silence, and Hanna turned in early, distressed by what her father had done but happy to know the Mi'kmaw family had escaped. She couldn't sleep, wondering whether the man would be alright. Hanna tossed restlessly until fatigue eventually took over and a sense of falling jarred her. Below her window, the mournful cry of a wolf filled the bedroom. The familiar sound lured her, and she found herself suddenly standing outside the house. It wasn't cold, and the warm sun beat down upon her. Just ahead of her, the wolf sat still beside a pup. It was the same black wolf she had encountered the night of the storm. Those amber eyes! It was as if she could reach in and touch his soul. His spirit was her spirit, but he seemed to contain a deeper wisdom than her own. She could smell as he smelled, see as he saw.

In a blur, the animal's body moved like a spectre, drifting and reshaping before her. It gradually shifted into a human. Both the adult wolf and the pup had disappeared, and Christian arose from the fog, carrying a baby. A strange sensation overcame her, which Hanna identified as Papa's dread of losing her, his overprotectiveness and deep desire to keep her safe.

"Don't go," she called when her brother walked away. But it was too late. The wolves returned as Christian and the baby gradually faded.

Hanna awoke in her bed. Her pillow was wet from her tears.

# Chapter Thirty

DECEMBER 1759

"Marta!" Petie yelled. He gently moved his sister from the kitchen table where her reaching fingers almost overturned the kettle of hot water. "Do not touch," he said in the same firm tone his mother used, and he placed a wooden doll into her arms.

Elisabeth ran from the bedroom. As she moved the kettle into the centre of the table, she breathed a deep sigh of relief. "Danke," she said, hugging her son. "You're a wonderful big brother." He had proven himself many times over in keeping a watchful eye. At almost three years of age, Marta had certainly become a handful. Of course, Marta was never far from Petie—always on his heels and he at her beck and call. Much like Hanna had been to Christian. Where you found one, you found the other.

Since Peter had left, Petie's inquisitive eight-year-old mind had soaked up every bit of information he could get on the ships that sailed in and out of Lunenburg. He knew every schooner, sloop, and snow that docked. When warships anchored on occasion in the harbour, he could tell the ratings by the number of decks and guns, from the smaller fourth rates to the larger seconds and firsts. His infinite imagination took him on a

335

three-decker with his onkel as he dreamed of manning the cannons lined up along the sides.

"Now that we captured Quebec, will Onkel Peter come home?"

"Not yet." Georg had just come in the door. He lifted Petie up.

Elisabeth shuddered as she closed the door with a bang and the latch locked back in place. "It feels like snow is coming."

"We'll be ready. I just finished the last repair, and everything is snug and dry for the animals." Georg set his son down. "And it's time for you to milk the cows again," he said, nudging his fingers into Petie's neck. Georg burst out laughing as his son squirmed.

"Papa, is the war not over?"

Georg's forehead puckered. "The French still have Montreal as far as we know. But things change."

"Do you think he could be on the HMS *Somerset*? Did you know it has seventy guns?" Petie's eyes widened.

"I did not. You're very knowledgeable about such things. I'm glad I have someone to turn to," Georg said, grinning at his wife.

"Ja, Papa," Petie said in a serious tone. He took Marta by the hand, contented now to play with her in the corner.

Georg leaned over and kissed Elisabeth, who was in her own little world. She let out a short grunt. "It says to bake it! Like all my puddings, I will steam it instead. There should be no adverse effects."

"Is that Hanna's cookbook?"

"Ja." Then added, "Nein. Ach, what I mean is, Anna Knaut loaned it to Hanna to use while they are in Halifax. Anna wrote some of the receipts in German." Elisabeth poured the mixed contents into the bowl and draped a cloth over the top, securing it in place with a piece of twine. "Hanna had enough raisins and spices left to make this. So, hier! Oat pudding," she said triumphantly. She set the bowl into a kettle of hot water, which she hooked onto the crane. "There. Now we wait." She laughed, crossing her fingers.

Elisabeth had a sudden onset of weakness and quickly sat on the bench. She wiped her face with her apron. "Do you find it warm in here? Don't fuss so, Dr. Gessler," she said, dodging his hand. "I'm fine, just a bit fatigued."

"That's right, I am a doctor—your doctor." He laid his hand across her brow. "Maybe you're coming down with—"

"Nothing! There's no cure for this. I wanted to be completely sure before I told you." Seeing Georg's eyes crinkle in the corners, she said, "Ja, you have guessed correctly. I missed another monthly." Elisabeth started to giggle as her husband picked her up and swung her around. "Oh my, a brother or sister for our children. It's the first time I've said it aloud." She stroked his face once he set her down. "Are you pleased, my husband?"

He laughed again. Georg danced his way around the table—feet kicking outward and arms outstretched. He leapt and stomped, slapping his knees and ankles. The children gleefully joined in the merriment.

Elisabeth watched with great contentment and was transported by visions of her parents escorting her to a long-ago dance. She had spun around the floor with Peter that night, but she first partnered the Kisseltanz with Georg. She had been unaware at the time of Georg's love for her, nor could she have begun to imagine that life had plans for her other than with her childhood sweetheart. The blue ribbon Elisabeth had worn in her hair was for Peter alone. It now lay buried in the bottom of her wooden chest, long since faded.

She looked to her family and clapped to their beat as they

joined hands into a circle of gaiety and rejoicing. Elisabeth would not have had her life any other way.

THAT AFTERNOON, THE AIR WAS extremely stuffy as people crowded into the town's community building. Everyone sat shoulder to shoulder on benches that were now wet from their snow-clad coats. The smell of damp wool hung in the air as the fire began to dry out the clothing, though the heat emanating from the burning logs was oppressive. The room was predominantly filled by men, but there were also a few wives with children.

Hanna had gone to one other meeting two weeks ago and regretted it. Not only were the translations long and tedious, but she had noticed neighbourly greetings were now coupled with pitiful looks, which made her angry. She knew why they looked upon her and Papa so. Initially, some did not associate with Papa because of Christian's alliance, but after they heard Papa had disowned his son, their sidelong glances had suddenly turned to sympathies. As she scanned the room, Hanna greeted everyone she knew with a nod and a feigned smile. She would like to tell them what she really thought. She kept silent as Papa conversed with Herr Moser seated ahead of them, and Georg squeezed her hand. He knew exactly what she was thinking.

Colonel Sutherland strode in coughing, his face red from the cold. He removed his hat and coat, threw them onto the bench behind him, and took his seat at the front table. With the creation of the County of Lunenburg, he was now the Justice of the Peace. Hanna did not recognize the small grey-haired gent who knocked the gavel hard to bring the meeting to order.

The possible extension of crop bounties was first on the agenda. Hemp and flax would remain at one penny per pound.

Oats would be added at a tuppence per bushel. A hay bounty would be offered at two shillings per hundred weight.

Time passed very slowly as the translator stated the elector rules of voting for the upcoming election. A Protestant male must own land having a yearly value of forty shillings or more, and Catholics still could not vote, regardless of ownership. Hanna watched the colonel meet a few attendees with a stern eye as he spoke. *Based on the last meeting, he has reason to believe there will be discord*, she thought.

One large man stood up with a question Hanna was sure was on most people's minds. "Just how much power does the Assembly have?"

"Not enough to ignore the governor, who can still veto or at best prepare a memorandum to London for additional consideration."

"So the London Board still has Nova Scotia on a tight leash. Shouldn't this Assembly bypass this extra step?"

"That's all I know at present. Bad weather, no ships. The *York* that docked yesterday was fortunate to arrive; it won't be returning to Halifax anytime soon." He then quickly went on to talk of the vast majority of New Englanders delayed until next year. "The recent storm that destroyed many dykes in Minas and Pisiguit caused a great deal of salt water flooding to farmland."

"It doesn't surprise me, as the dykes have been left to deteriorate," a ranger remarked, raising his hand. "The handful of New Englanders don't have the knowledge to rebuild, I'm sure."

"It's been requested to have the Acadian prisoners, held at Fort Edward, help with the repair and maintenance." Sutherland left an appropriate space for more questions. None forthcoming, he asked if all the storm repairs had been completed in the town and surrounding divisions. Papa announced they had.

"Then, all in all, I wish to thank everyone for their hard work to ensure all dwellings were repaired and made livable in time for winter." He turned to his aide. "Are there any more items to discuss?" The aide shook his head. "Then the floor is open."

The same large man spoke up. "Is it true a tax act is set to pass to defray the costs of this government?"

"Not now. Lawrence dismissed the notion; he didn't want to lose more colonists to New England. For now, rum duties, fines, and other fees will suffice. Any more questions?" Sutherland scanned the room.

"Ja!" Herr Kurtz spoke loudly but stayed seated. "Where is this truck house being built on the LaHave?" That sent an instantaneous buzz throughout the room. "It isn't welcome. I have a family to protect."

Sutherland looked to his aide, who shrugged and turned the gavel around in his hand. "In the first place, the prime purpose downriver would be for the Indians to trade furs for new supplies. In the second place, you're not any safer without the post. They don't need a designated area to attack! Besides, truck houses are usually built near a fort, and there's a blockhouse there now. And the land to the west of the river will soon be settled by the New Englanders. Tinmouth, I believe the township is to be called."

"I tell you, it's not safe."

Georg piped up. "With all due respect, Herr Kurtz, a government-run trading post can actually be a deterrent to attacks. And having said this, the British have already pushed the Indians farther back. So, it's only a matter of time before they'll surrender. With the establishment of the new townships, the only means of survival for the Mi'kmaq will be the fur trade. The supplies they buy at the truck house are regulated, keeping private traders from cheating them. Frankly, it's the least the government should do to keep the relationship at best tolerable."

A man rushed at Georg, screaming, "Traitor! They need to be obliterated from the province!"

Georg grasped Hanna's arm, stopping her. The heat rose from her neck.

Sutherland banged the gavel several times for order as a ranger grabbed the attacker and dragged him outside. "I declare this meeting adjourned," Sutherland announced, and he motioned Georg to the front. People talked among themselves as they departed.

Hanna waited on the bench with Papa, watching the colonel calmly speak. As the aide translated, Georg nodded in agreement. To what? She wished she knew. Sutherland handed Georg what looked like a sealed piece of paper. When Sutherland left, she walked to the table.

"He received this from the captain on the *York*," Georg said. "It's for you."

Taking it, she turned it over. "Ach, lovely, it's from Anna," she exclaimed. "I recognize her stamp." Then, she asked Georg, "Were you severely upbraided for your opinion?"

Georg shook his head. "Just a warning for my own safety. I would appreciate neither of you mentioning anything to Elisabeth," he said, raising his eyebrows.

"Ah, 'he that increaseth knowledge, increaseth sorrow,'" Hanna quoted.

"We best be going. It's started to snow," Papa said and assisted Hanna with her coat.

"You know, Michael, we will remain British. This will not change."

"Hmm. Then the new settlers will be woefully disappointed, as they are a chartered colony, am I correct?"

Georg nodded and held the door open for Hanna.

At the earliest opportunity, Hanna broke the seal on Anna's letter. Papa sat beside the hearth, puffing on his pipe and carving wooden spoons to replace her old ones. She moved the candle closer for better light. At the top of the page, Anna had written *Halifax, October 25, 1759.*

*My Dear Hanna,*

*My apologies for not writing sooner, but as you can imagine, my hands were busy with getting the house in order and giving instructions to the maid and cook, both of whom I am truly grateful to have in our employ. We are expected to entertain on countless occasions, which at times can be quite tiresome. Abigail is our new cook, and we feel extremely fortunate to have her with us.*

*The children have settled in quite nicely after such a treacherous journey from Lunenburg. Poor Catherine was struck severely ill by the motion of the waves. Thank the Lord, David slept the entire way. He is such a happy baby and a joy to have around.*

*As the House sits almost daily, the children and I don't see Philip as much as we would like. However, the Assembly meets at Walter Manning's house, which a mere walk from our residence on Holles Street. Governor Lawrence lives across the street from him.*

*You have no need to be distraught over the relief petition, as Philip was very particular to ensure it was delivered. However, I'm not privy to its exact whereabouts nor if it has been discussed yet.*

*How I miss you and wish daily you were sitting beside me taking tea. I yearn for our talks and baking—mishaps and all. I smile as I write this. Near St. Paul's Church, there's a vendor who sells the most scrumptious gingerbread. Just the thought of it sets my mouth to watering.*

*There is an area near the waterfront neither safe nor desirable for ladies. The fish market is near the ferry, and it attracts the most unsavoury individuals. The gaol, which is near Horseman's Fort, is mercifully far enough away in the south end so as not to pose a menace to the town's citizens.*

*Even though Halifax is an exciting town, a term I use loosely, my druthers are the calmer existence of Lunenburg. Nighttime noises can be quite disconcerting here.*

*Almost four weeks have passed since I first began this letter to you. It's with great sadness that I share the news that our darling, sweet David has passed from the living and is now in the arms of Our Dear Lord.*

Hanna stifled a cry.

Papa looked up. "Hanna?"

Her voice quavered as she spoke. "It is…David has died." She continued to read but aloud.

*He had difficulty swallowing. Upon the doctor's examina-tion, there was a thick film in his throat. This caused David to labour in his breathing, which steadily worsened. Days went by but the fever would not abate. To watch him suffer was utterly horrifying. He was afflicted with the Strangler, a disease my sister died of many years ago. There was nothing the doctor could do. One morning our precious son did not awake. Philip was excused from the House but returned soon after the funeral, hoping to keep himself busy and distracted from the grief. I, myself, have not known such despair. My heart breaks as I now touch the soft linen shift he once wore.*

*I must stop writing now, as I am unable to see my words through my sorrow.*

*May all comfort and satisfaction be upon you and Michael. I beg of you, keep us close to your hearts as we bear this difficult trial. I am, beloved Hanna, yours affectionately,*

*Your trusted friend and confidante, Anna Knaut*


Hanna meticulously refolded the letter. She sat quietly trying to take it in. Her voice quavered. "I-I cannot imagine…"

Papa was at a loss for words. He reached his hand across the table to console her.

On the windowsill, a candle flickered as the wind whistled around the drafty house. The snowstorm was increasing in strength.

# Chapter Thirty-One



PUNAMUIKU'S — FROST FISH MOON
JANUARY 1760

*I*s he alive?" An abrupt whiteout eddied and biting snow cut across Bear Cub's face. He was grateful for the bear grease protecting his skin. The blizzard that had raged the last two days was now on the backside of blowing itself out. Following their return from the seal hunt, the decision to stay at the field camp had been a wise one.

Eagle Feather rolled the stranger over. Snow had caked to his long hair and beard, his exposed skin was pale, almost blue. "I cannot tell," Eagle Feather muttered. He removed his fur mitt and placed his hand on the face, then bent over him. "He's alive, barely. His breathing is slow." He looked up at his brother. "He could have come from that direction." They stood on the west side of Oqomkikiaq, and he pointed to a densely wooded area where the bent boughs were barely withstanding the Winter onslaught. When they paddled downriver at the beginning of the Frost Fish Moon, they had spotted a lone dwelling. Now, on their return trip, Bear Cub had detected the smell of burning wood from that same area.

Eagle Feather pulled on his mitt and started walking away.

"Where are you going? Help me lift him onto the toboggan," Bear Cub demanded.

Eagle Feather stopped knee-deep in the snow. "It is too late for him. He is almost dead," he said, as he plucked his snow-shoes from the drift.

Bear Cub could not believe what he had just heard. He charged at his brother's legs, knocking him over. "Is that what you said when you first found me?"

"Moqwe," Eagle Feather said, struggling to get up. "That was different."

"I don't believe you." Bear Cub stood and extended his hand to his brother. "The Eagle Feather I know would never have turned his back on the helpless. What happened to you? You returned to us shouldering a heavier burden than when you left all those moons ago."

His brother was unresponsive.

"Didn't Ambroise make any sense to you? He is right—brutality isn't the answer." Bear Cub was annoyed. "I, for one, am not leaving him here." He dragged the man to the toboggan and stared up at his brother. "Well, are you going to just stand there? Fine then, go back to the path you've chosen. I don't like it."

Eagle Feather relented.

The stranger was still unconscious when they reached two small log houses, one of which was dimly lit. Christian banged on the door. When he got no reply, he banged again.

"Go in." Eagle Feather was behind him, his gun poised to protect his brother.

As Bear Cub slowly opened the door, the wind ripped the handle from his hold. A thin woman, her face pinched and drawn and her eyes bulging, stood in the centre of the room, aiming a firearm straight at them. Bear Cub held his hands up and spoke to her gently.

"Put your gun down," he said to Eagle Feather.

The woman could not be understood. She only lowered her weapon when Eagle Feather carried the dying man inside. "Hallett!" she cried.

The woman knitted her brows in confusion when Eagle Feather covered Hallett with his own bearskin robe. She pressed her lips firmly together and gave her intruders a stern look as she pointed to the door with her gun. Once they stepped outside, she pulled the door closed behind them. The metal latch clanged shut.

"We will bring food," Eagle Feather stated.

"What?" Bear Cub couldn't believe his ears.

"Something Ambroise said." He walked ahead, pulling the toboggan.

Bear Cub hurried to catch up. "Not so long ago, you were ready to let him die."

"My anger is not with him."

"Your wrath lies somewhere," Bear Cub said, hoping his brother would divulge. He pulled at his arm. "Hey, what happened to you when you were away?"

Eagle Feather stopped in his tracks. "We will show them where to find food."

"But—"

"Do not dig deeper, my brother. Leave things be."


When Bear Cub awakened, the landscape was stark white under a vivid blue sky. Nature had sculpted windswept peaks and valleys that looked like an airy goose-down quilt. The snow softened the jagged edges of this harsh world. Small black-headed birds gathered on a weathered bough. They were chubby, puffed-up balls of warmth, all perched in a line. Bear Cub set down a food offering to Apiknajit, which would soon be upon them.

He and Eagle Feather left soon after they had eaten. His brother was still reticent to speak of his time away, but Bear Cub was relieved by his sudden change of heart. When they arrived at the settlers' cabin, they unloaded blankets, snowshoes, smoked fish, and seal outside the door. Hallett appeared from the side of the house, and if the woman had not opened the door in time, they would have been shot. She spoke in a sharp tone to her husband, who gave a nod to Bear Cub and Eagle Feather. He propped up the weapon against the house.

"They are in unfamiliar land. We need to teach our hunting skills, where to find food," Eagle Feather said to Bear Cub.

"But how? We cannot forcibly take Hallett—" Bear Cub stopped and squinted upward. "We have our answer, my brother." He pointed to a nearby tree branch.

"Ah!" Caught by a breeze, the porcupine's quills blew upward.

Eagle Feather laid tobacco atop the snow, then climbed the tree and clubbed the animal on the head. The porcupine instantly dropped, *thrump!*, into a cloud of white, then almost disappeared beneath the snow. Eagle Feather picked him up by the two front paws and lay the carcass near the woman. In a quick demonstration, Eagle Feather hand-stroked the quills down, grabbed the ends, and pulled upward to release them from the body. The woman nodded, then repeated until she had discarded most of the quills.

Bear Cub scooped his fingers to his mouth. "Food," he said.

Eagle Feather persuaded Hallett to follow him. The three of them tracked a hare to his resting bed. Except for his dark, round eyes, he was camouflaged beneath a low-hanging evergreen bough. Hallett shot it just before Eagle Feather discovered smaller footprints. "Ermine," he said, showing Bear Cub and Hallett the five-clawed toes around a V-shaped paw pad. Though the weasel had changed to its Winter white, Bear Cub spotted his black-tipped tail. Throughout the morning, Hallett remained attentive to his surroundings as they hunted.

Eagle Feather showed the best place where caribou gathered and where they dug through the snow to eat lichen. When one was spotted at a distance, Hallett instantly aimed at the target. Eagle Feather pressed down hard on the barrel. "Enough!" he said firmly, and loaded the last carcass on the toboggan. "For now, you have enough."

When Bear Cub pulled on Hallett's arm, he obeyed and fully lowered his firearm.

Eagle Feather started the trek back.


THERE WAS NO MORE AMMUNITION, no powder nor lead balls. This news was not greeted well at the base camp when the group arrived to unload the seals.

Bear Cub was met by his wife and daughter while Alawei repeatedly leapt up against his leg for attention. Singing Sparrow kissed her husband. "My father is back. Many of the People are unable to hunt, as the weapons are of no use to us. Down, Alawei!" The dog sat obediently, whimpering. "I see Eagle Feather entering my father's wikuom now."

"I will go later." Bear Cub lifted Lise into his arms and danced to a tune only he could hear.

Back in the solitude of their wikuom, Bear Cub hugged his wife. "Ahh," he murmured. "It's good to hold you again."

"Did you feel that?" she said, sounding surprised. "The baby moved. Four moons, my beloved."

"When we hear the frogs croaking, so then our daughter's voice."

"Daughter? *She* could be a boy."

"I suppose so! For now…Lise is outside, and…" With each breath, he slowly kissed the nape of her neck, entranced by her sweet scent. His coat and shirt slid down from his shoulders. Singing Sparrow's fingers lightly stroked his back, sending a shiver up his spine. Bear Cub could hear the popping of the fire, then the intense flames teased from behind.

There was a little tug at his leg. "Cannot find Alawei."

He glanced down at his three-year-old daughter, and the innocence stared back up.

"Come, we will find him then." To his wife he said, "Don't move. I will solve this crisis and be right back."

"I have nowhere to go," she said, laughing.

"I am weary of the hostility," White Cloud insisted. "Battle is unwise against such an enemy, and the losses are unforgiving. I have nothing left to give."

"You do not give up that easily," Eagle Feather said.

Bear Cub watched the flames of the firepit around which they were seated.

"My father told me stories of the battles we fought against the Iroquois," White Cloud said. "When the death toll became intolerable, a temporary peace was declared to choose a different solution to settle the discord. One alternative—have only the leaders combat each other for victory."

"Was it a satisfactory conclusion?" Bear Cub asked.

"At times."

"You startle me! You are not telling me you wish to go one-on-one with Lawrence?" Eagle Feather's eyes widened. Bear Cub suppressed a smile.

White Cloud looked at his sons and laughed aloud. "That would be foolish. The British leader lacks honour and scruples. There would be no winning." He cleared his throat. "I returned from two villages that are in dire straits. One from sickness and the other hardship."

"Measles?" Bear Cub asked.

"Rum! The men do not hunt but instead bow to their weaknesses when they crave this drink. There is no initiative to survive but for their own selfish purposes. When they do hunt, they come back with nothing. The women and children are here in this camp now."

Eagle Feather frowned. "And the second village?"

"They rely mainly on the food supplied to them, which is nothing, as the French have not visited. Fevers and coughs weaken many so they cannot hunt. What little they hunted was not enough to sustain everyone. Caribou and moose are no longer in areas where they were always found. This is the story the Nikanus told me."

"Now our muskets are useless," Bear Cub said.

Eagle Feather shook his head. "My father, you have taught us to keep the old ways. We do not need guns to live. We hunt as in the old times."

"Not all things the newcomers bring us are bad, and I lay no blame on any who abandon the old ways to embrace these new ones. They are only doing what their fathers taught them."

Eagle Feather said, "The French will return! I am confident"

"Moqwe. The situation is irreparable. It will not happen," White Cloud said. "Abbé Maillard will be our hope."

Bear Cub perked up at the mention of the brave, stalwart missionary.

"In the village I returned from, the Nikanus received information. Lawrence bid Maillard to come to Halifax and help negotiate peace between himself and the People. Maillard was given free religious exercise in Halifax if he accepted."

"And?" Eagle Feather asked.

"He accepted."

"Do you agree, my father?"

"I am confident the British will do anything in their power to reign as masters of this land. The guerillas have decreased in strength and are too few to regain control. Any left wandering have long since dispersed, and we are vulnerable without them. We save the People who are left and prolong the agony no longer than we need to." White Cloud peered into Bear Cub's eyes. "You have doubts, my son?"

Bear Cub lifted his chin. "Are we not renouncing our rights too easily? How can we walk beside the ancestors with heads held high if we cede to the British?"

"We are a People whose children are walking in our footsteps. Maillard will negotiate the land, the hunting and fishing grounds, so our children can live in freedom. He will treat for the best possible peace for their survival…for our existence."

"Then you are confident he's the right person," Bear Cub said.

White Cloud grunted an affirmative. "He has lived among us for countless Winters."

"I don't have your courage," Bear Cub replied.

"This is the right time."

"It is dishonourable for us to solicit for our land, but there is no alternative," Eagle Feather remarked.

White Cloud finished his son's thought. "Other than continue the bloodshed until there is no one left."

"Do you think more settlers will come?" Bear Cub asked White Cloud.

"My son, it has only begun."

# Chapter Thirty-Two



*I*t was the first quarter moon, and the runner had travelled along the Tewapskik where newly arrived settlers had been spotted. He brought news of a peace treaty signed at the Spring Moon by the Nikanus of the LaHave Mi'kmaq, Paul Laurent. White Cloud had called for a community circle.

The runner listed the terms Laurent had agreed upon: He promised not to molest the King's subjects; any quarrels with the English could not be individually retaliated upon but could only be settled through applying for redress according to English laws; all held English prisoners must be released with the promise to have other villages do the same; any assistance given to the King's enemies was prohibited in any form, trade or otherwise; if ill designs were known against the King's subjects, they must be reported to the governor; any trade, barter, or exchanges must only be conducted at truck houses appointed by the governor; before the Animal-Calling Moon, a minimum of two prisoners of the LaHave Mi'kmaq must reside as hostages in Lunenburg or elsewhere appointed by the governor; and such hostages would be used as an exchange at the governor's request.

The spirit and intent was not what White Cloud considered to be a relationship treaty to benefit both parties. Reactions varied, particularly in regard to the omission of land and hunting terms. It was probable that some villages would not be signing. As far as White Cloud was concerned, he had the right to live and walk where he pleased. *How can we all share Mother Earth's resources and have enough left over for our children?* he wondered.

On this drizzly morning, the canoes moved toward the mouth of Oqomkikiaq. En route, Bear Cub glanced at the building by the riverbank, which had been abandoned after Bear Cub and Eagle Feather's capture. It was still empty, the door ajar, remnants of a once-bustling trading post. It dawned on Bear Cub that they had not encountered Hallett since the running of the tomcod, and when they had harvested birds' eggs on Penatkuk during Pnatmuiku's, they had encountered no other settlers.

At the weir, Bear Cub stood at the lowest point within its confines, up to his knees in the cold salt water among hundreds of spawning shad. A few mackerel were also scooped up in the mix. Baskets were quickly filling to the brim as water gushed from woven pores. Two sturgeon also lay trapped at low tide.

Eagle Feather scooped more shad by hand than with nets. Bear Cub was impressed. Even though his brother taught him to grab the fish behind the gills with his thumb, he just could not grasp it. "It won't work for me." Bear Cub laughed as a shad slithered from his hold.

"Keep practising, you will catch on," Eagle Feather said encouragingly. "Get a hard grip. That is good...Ah, now try again." He gave his brother a sidelong glance. "You still have a few Springs to sharpen your skill before you teach your son." He snickered.

"Daughter!"

"That remains to be seen. To save me from your needless prattle, I wish it to be soon!" Eagle Feather sharply sliced the water with his hand, giving Bear Cub a good dousing.

Bear Cub paid his brother back tenfold. Not getting a response, he asked, "What do you see?" Bear Cub looked in the direction of his brother's stare.

"I am sure I saw Hallett. He ducked into the woods there with four men."

White Cloud, who had been working nearby, stopped. "You are uneasy. Danger?"

"Moqwe," Eagle Feather said and explained what he had seen. "They are gone."

"We have enough," White Cloud called to everyone.

BEAR CUB'S STOMACH LURCHED WHEN he could not find Singing Sparrow as soon as all the canoes had returned. It was unusual for her not to greet him. *Something terrible has happened*, he thought. When he reached their wikuom, a tiny old woman shooed him away. "You cannot come in. I will come to you when it is over." Oddly, it never occurred to him that his wife was in labour until he heard a cry of pain. When the old woman lifted the door-blanket, he could see Singing Sparrow walking back and forth, aided by two women. "Ah-ah!" the woman curtly said, waving her forefinger like a pendulum. "This is forbidden to you." Then she grinned before closing the door to his prying eyes. From behind, a young girl touched his shoulder. "Lise is with us," she shyly stated, and ran away.

For the remainder of the day, there was no concentrating on anything. Bear Cub's ears picked up every sound. After almost cutting himself with a knife, he put aside the beech paddle he was carving, much to the relief of anyone who had noticed him in his pitiful frame of mind. Repairing his spear was equally futile; his brother removed the weapon from his hands in case he injured himself. Between the restless pacing and incomplete tasks, he was sure he was the entertainment of the day. It was the last straw when the women chased him away after he tried to help clean the fish.

Darkness fell without him receiving any word about Singing Sparrow. "I could give you words of wisdom, but you are not ready to hear them," White Cloud teased. "It pains me to watch this. Come with us—it will be good for you. You like duck hunting." He waited, then added, "This is not a request." He raised his eyebrows.

Bear Cub looked up from where he sat cross-legged in his misery. "My lack of awareness could cause me to drown."

"Highly unlikely, my son." White Cloud gave Bear Cub's foot a slight kick. "You can do nothing here."

HALF A DOZEN CANOES GLIDED along the river then separated into different coves. There was nary a breeze when Bear Cub, his brother, and White Cloud manoeuvred inside a sheltered inlet far away from the others. Eagle Feather pulled up the oars. They lay down out of sight and waited as the water currents carried them slowly among the sleeping ducks and geese. Bear Cub listened to the monotonous chirping of frogs bubbling up from the marsh.

White Cloud nudged Eagle Feather. After the torches were lit, they made a clatter of noise, which created a terrific flutter of wings and splashing about them. In confusion, the birds barked out harsh honks and quacks. As they rose and flew around the flames, the birds were clubbed one by one. Eagle Feather wrung their necks after he plucked the stunned ducks and geese from the water. As one flew passed Bear Cub's head, he was swift to take it down.

"There, the last one," Bear Cub said, staring at the limp bodies. He left no doubt in anyone's mind that he was anxious to return.

"You will not sleep, my brother. I will stay with you. I will get no rest either."

"Ach! You worry as well."

BY THE TIME THEY SETTLED, most of the camp was already sleeping and peacefulness descended. Bear Cub lay still, desperately hoping to hear even just a whimper of a baby's cry. Instead, his wife's groans made him flinch. Waiting was agony. Thoughts of Papa resurfaced. Bear Cub wondered if he himself would turn his back on his own child, given the same circumstances.

"I can hear you thinking, my brother," Eagle Feather said.

"Mmm," Bear Cub grunted. "I have no wish to face Papa again. Our differences are insurmountable, and he's too stubborn to concede."

"We all have our weaknesses, but he is not your entire family."

That cut to the quick. He missed his sisters, especially Hanna. He nodded but stated unequivocally, "I was foolish to return."

"We can never know what outcome lies ahead." Eagle Feather inhaled deeply. "I, myself, have lacked good judgment, making foolhardy decisions with no regard to the consequences. I know hatred well."

"You?" In the glimmer of the firelight, Bear Cub focused on his brother.

As Eagle Feather finally related what had happened after he left the village, Bear Cub could hear the difficulty his brother had in the telling. Eagle Feather told him they had raided in the dark, preying on families farthest from the town.

"There was to be no violence, no scalps taken. Fear of our presence could be enough, I told them. If it was not, we would take prisoners and turn them over to the French. But we found rum. I was drawn into my brothers' drinking, their resentments. The night hid many things. But the light revealed all. The darkness swallowed me whole at the sight of those bodies." His voice cracked as he whispered, "The worst…the worst is…I do not remember."

Bear Cub stared at his brother.

"There was a boy lying on his bed as if asleep." Eagle Feather cleared his throat. "The blood dried into the cracks of my skin. I still wake from my dreams to find myself scraping my nails into my palms to scrub the stains away."

"Was that the only time?"

He shook his head. "A farm. As my brothers drank more, it was easy to feign my own drunkenness after only a small bit. To save the young girl and her father, I held a knife to her throat and told my brothers to leave. After they disappeared into the house, I hid the girl and her father under straw."

Eagle Feather turned his head away. Bear Cub could hardly hear him when he said, "It was Hanna."

Something evil instantly took hold. Before Bear Cub even realized what he was doing, he had restrained his brother, grabbing the leather string around Eagle Feather's neck and tightening it. Bear Cub leered down at him. His own veins throbbed as he twisted the string tighter.

Eagle Feather's hand clawed at the string. "No-no harm came to her…or your father," he sputtered, gasping for air.

Bear Cub released his grip on his brother. He screamed out his anguish, pounding his fist onto the earth until he fell, panting. His heart thumped hard within his chest.

The camp awoke and a testy White Cloud appeared, demanding an explanation. When none was forthcoming, he said, "Then settle your differences before the sun rises."

When his father left, Eagle Feather said, "They are safe, Bear Cub."

He could not look Eagle Feather in the eye.

"Verdammt! She could have been..." Bear Cub could not bring himself to say it.

"You think I do not know that?" Eagle Feather shouted. "It never leaves me. Never!" He threw a stone into the fire. "But it did not happen. I would not allow it."

"*You* would not, but someone else would have." Bear Cub inclined his head. "It's all too clear how vulnerable they really are." He gave his head a shake. "They came so close." He forced himself to breathe slowly and deeply. "Ach! I am just sick of this damn war!"

Eagle Feather said nothing.

Moments passed before Bear Cub spoke again. He still couldn't look at Eagle Feather, but he had calmed down somewhat. "It took courage for you to tell me." He stood, brushing the dirt from his skin. "In times like these, I wish I was there for Hanna. Did she recognize you?"

"E'e."

A baby wailed and Bear Cub ran.

Not sure if he should barge in unannounced, Bear Cub anxiously paced outside and waited for permission. The old woman greeted him, smiling from ear to ear. "You have a daughter."

"I knew it!" He stepped inside the stuffy room. Singing Sparrow lay beneath a blanket with the tiniest baby Bear Cub had ever seen nursing at her breast. The women left them alone.

"My husband. I give you Ma'li."

He lay down beside her. His heart burst at the seams as he stared at the button nose and the wee fingers resting in the palm of his hand. "That is what you decided? Are you sure?"

"E'e. It is my gift to you—to remember your mother and my sister, Ma'li. Would you prefer she be called Maria?"

"Uh-uh. Ma'li is good. It is the same name as Maria. We will explain this to her."

They watched this small life suckle for the first time.

"Our daughter has been born into a far different world than the life the ancient ones were born into. Too many Elders have taken sick and died. She will not hear Calm Water's stories of our ancestors."

"His spirit is always here to guide us."

"It can never be the same. When he told the stories, he made them leap alive before us."

Singing Sparrow started to sing a song that had come down to her from the old times. Bear Cub remembered that Morning Dove had always sung it to her.

WHEN BEAR CUB WENT TO search for Eagle Feather, he found him alone, sitting cross-legged in front of a small fire. So as not to disturb, Bear Cub stood back in the shadows of the trees. He watched as his brother fanned whiffs of smoke to his eyes and ears. There were words he could not hear. He left him and walked back to camp where everyone in the village was gathering in celebration of his daughter.

Singing Sparrow was the giver of life. Drums were beating as the women danced in rhythm around her and the newborn. The children took Lise by the hand and joined the circle. When White Cloud commenced chanting, others followed in unison.

Ma'li was wrapped in soft moose skin edged with red and white quillwork. As Singing Sparrow held the sleeping infant, Bear Cub could see a sparrow and nuthatch she had painted on the moose skin during her pregnancy. He broke circle when his wife removed their daughter's coverlet. Gathering Ma'li, he lifted her upward to Kisu'lkw, then placed her on the ground, symbolizing her relationship to Mother Earth. Singing Sparrow sprinkled a dusting of earth over their daughter's bare skin. When he lifted her again, Eagle Feather was standing within the group.

Bear Cub placed the baby in his brother's arms, and the dancing and singing suddenly ceased. He had broken with tradition.

"Your niece," he said, and searched his brother's black eyes. "You and I have endured adversities, but our bond always remains unbroken. You have accepted me into the fold. You are my brother, more than any blood could ever be. I wish it to remain so." Eagle Feather nestled his niece in one arm, gripped Bear Cub's hand with his free one, and clutched his brother's hand tight to his breast.

"I truly know your pain," Bear Cub said.

It was Nipniku's, the Summer Moon, when life's cycle turned south, revitalizing the trees with bright green foliage. Singing Sparrow carried her daughter on her back, strapped onto the cradleboard, as she dug an ash stick deep into the sand to expose mouthwatering clams. Large clear jellyfish, abandoned by the receding tide, littered the beach by the hundreds. As more women joined his wife, Bear Cub rounded the cliff along the beach with Eagle Feather, heading to their canoe. They were on their way back to meet up with White Cloud.

As they paddled down a tributary to Oqomkikiaq and passed through the waters toward the estuary, Bear Cub's back dripped with perspiration. When they reached the spot where the river narrowed around the curvature of land, he lifted his paddle.

Eagle Feather turned his head. "Keep up. Why did you stop?"

"Shh. Listen. Do you hear that?"

His brother let the paddle drag in the water. "Moqwe. What is it?"

They waited a few moments. "Nothing, I guess. Thought I heard cows mooing."

His brother made a face. "Put some sweat into it! Move! I see my father's canoe."

Half of the weir was exposed from the receding tide. White Cloud waded toward them.

"Why is everyone here and not down the inlet?" Eagle Feather asked.

"There are many fishing schooners closer into these waters." The answer came not from White Cloud but from Ambroise, who was walking toward them. Bear Cub was taken aback. "Kwe'," Ambroise said. "There are a dozen anchored just as the river widens."

"Kwe'." Eagle Feather returned the greeting. "This is not unusual."

"The European fishers are not strangers here," Bear Cub noted. "They come and go."

"This is different," White Cloud said. "We will take you there."

It was not Bear Cub's mind playing tricks. Very vocal livestock were off-loading from several three-masted vessels. Women with simple straw hats tied under their chins and dressed in brown homespun dresses with soiled aprons carried yokes of water buckets. Older children were scrubbing clothes, and toddlers were running about makeshift houses that stood among countless tents and partly constructed timber-framed buildings. Trees were toppling.

They stayed concealed to observe from across the river. The longer they watched, the more people came into view, going about their daily lives completely unaware of who had detected them.

"This is not temporary by any means," Bear Cub said. "There must be at least two hundred people."

"We will greet them. First, we bring food," White Cloud exclaimed.

They returned well before the sun set. Smoke rose from firepits where the women were stirring heavy iron pots that hung from tripods. A state of alarm arose when their canoes beached. Women hurriedly pulled the children away and hid in the protection of their tents. A dozen men pointed guns at the intruders, but White Cloud straightened up and threw his musket onto the white sand. The remaining foursome followed suit. But no one waivered. Bear Cub remained motionless as he looked from one face to the next. Then Hallett strolled to the forefront, ordering the settlers to drop their weapons. Bear Cub's shoulders relaxed. Ambroise stepped forward and laid two baskets overflowing with clams at Hallett's feet. Bear Cub and Eagle Feather carried cod, mackerel, and lobster to the newcomers, while White Cloud gave them smoked eel and gull eggs. Even though the settlers were apprehensive, many did greet them openly. As Hallett extended his hand to White Cloud, Bear Cub found himself facing Philip Knaut, who had just approached him.

"Guten tag." Philip was nonchalant. "You are in a state of shock, Christian, nein?"

"To say the least."

"I sailed here with Captain Cobb, who's responsible for the transportation of these good people. This is quite a gesture," he said as he surveyed the foodstuffs. "I'm hoping this is not a trade. If it is, you are in violation."

Bear Cub quickly shook his head. "Why are you here?"

"Truck house. There is the possibility Herr Gerrish is resurrecting the old one here."

"Gerrish?"

"He is the newly appointed Indian commissary. The government has assumed all risks for the project and guaranteed him a percentage of proceeds from all sales to Indians."

"A monopoly like this can easily become mismanaged. I would keep a close eye on this Gerrish fellow."

"Hmm," Philip uttered.

"Are you still in close contact with my family?"

"Of course. It's been three years, nein? Hanna has grown to be quite an astute young lady. Sixteen years in September, I believe. Another baby is forthcoming for Elisabeth and Georg, and in my absence, she may very well have given birth."

Bear Cub's next question gnawed at his insides like a beaver on a log. "And Papa?"

"I am surprised you ask. You left on rather alarming terms, I hear. Ah, forgive my manners." Philip raised his hand in protest. "I should not be so bold. He's doing well."

"You need not berate yourself. I'm afraid what little affection Papa and I had between us was long gone before we left the Faterland. Believe me, I've accepted what fate has dealt me."

Their stay was short. As Ambroise and White Cloud pushed the canoes back into the river, Bear Cub felt bereft. He was reluctantly being pulled back to his German family.


Singing Sparrow was at a loss to speak the right words of comfort to her husband. She knew he was torn to leave her, but it was the one thing Bear Cub needed to do, and she would never stand in his way. "It is not forever," she said.

"It's Hanna who pulls me. Philip said she has grown up; she is no longer my baby sister. I miss her greatly."

"One day, I wish to meet her."

"And that you shall. You will adore her."

"As I do you, my beloved husband." She laid her head on his lap and relished in the closeness as Bear Cub stroked her hair.

# Chapter Thirty-Three

JUNE 1760

*D*id you see Barbara's face when the reverend announced that an English minister will be sent to us instead? Heaven saints alive!" Frau Born said. "We ask for a German pastor, and we get an English one. An English schoolmaster is asked for, and Gottlob Neuman is put on our doorstep with no understanding of the language. Do you see the irony in this?" Frau Born shook her head.

"Elisabeth and I know a few words of English. It's difficult to learn, but we can now follow the entire service," Georg told her.

She ignored the comment. "Where's your good wife? Ach, I see her now," she exclaimed, and waved. "Elisabeth!" she called. When Elisabeth joined them, Frau Born said, "Look at this little one, two weeks old. My, oh my. Markus is his name, right?" She gave a heavy sigh. "The good Lord has not blessed us yet with another." Frau Born had miscarried another baby midterm. "I must go now. I see my Martin patiently waiting. He says there's work to be done at the tannery, and on a Sunday! Tsk, tsk. There truly is no rest for the wicked."

Elisabeth kissed her farewell on both cheeks. "See you tomorrow with the children."

"Gut. I look forward to it." With this, Frau Born left.

"Who had your attention all this time?" Georg asked.

"Barbara. She's certainly not in favour of Herr Neuman. All I can do is listen, as I don't trust myself to give an opinion. Ach, my head is spinning."

Georg laughed. "You're safe now, my love." He reprimanded Petie, saying, "Don't tug at my breeches so. We will go now. Nein, no ships today. We're going home."

"Congratulations, Philip!" Then Michael said, "Ah, maybe I should withdraw my sentiment. By your face, are you sure you want the job?"

"It's not my being truck master that worries me. It's Herr Gerrish, the commissary. Many of the goods he trades are from his own store. I fear he's not giving the Indians a fair price. On the other hand, Herr Francklin assures me that the Mi'kmaq are shrewd and know a good trade." Philip paused a moment to clear his throat. "Herr Gerrish is a very prominent merchant in Halifax with an even greater influence on council. You know, this entire body is truly a merchant oligarchy." He sneered. "Do you think it's biased?" His sarcasm was unveiled.

"I gather things did not go well this term?"

Philip shook his head. "This session was no better than the first one. It was fraught with biases and clashes within council. Bills were rejected. And any talk of crop bounties was either fought over or dismissed. Enough of that, my friend. Have you thought more on the sawmill?"

"I am interested." Michael grinned.

"Gut. Come to our house with Hanna tomorrow. I know Anna wants to spend more time with her." He was about to walk away, then said, "By the by, I was lucky enough to run into Christian while in Liverpool. He asked of you." Philip tugged at his earlobe. "Forgive my boldness, but it's doubtful you'll see him again, Michael. He sees no hope for the two of you."

Michael crossed his arms over his chest, frowning. "That's not my fault."

"Oh? From where I sit, you have trouble hearing Christian." Before he departed, he added, "You will regret this, my friend."

HANNA COULD HEAR HOLLERING, THE orders barely audible over the noisy clamour of timber. Seabirds congregated and screeched over the shoreline while she walked with Anna down the hill from King Street onto Montague. On this Monday afternoon, the waterfront was energized as cordwood and lumber were loaded onto schooners. Pieces of partially eaten fish littered the wharf where gulls had dropped their unfinished meals. Hanna wrinkled her nose at the odious stench.

They made their way along the street still wet and thick with mud from this morning's rain. To avoid the mess, they kept to a small path covered with irregular flat stones. They passed the stocks where a man sat asleep on a bench with his ankles locked in the pillory. Only four licences were allowed in town for the sale of liquor, and he reportedly was caught selling rum with a forged licence. Two small boys mercilessly removed his shoes and tickled the soles of his feet, resulting in horrid profanities from the young man.

Anna pulled her skirt away as a wagon loaded with grain rumbled by. Hanna slipped and almost took a tumble before Anna pulled her from harm's way.

"I regret now bringing you here. Look at me, I must look a sight!" Anna brushed the mud spatters from her linen petticoat. "I must learn to not wear my best. Are you alright, my liebling?"

Hanna nodded. "Do not scold yourself. To be away from

my wearisome routine is a joy no matter what calamities we encounter. And I know you had no wish to be tripping over the feet of those workers building your new parlour."

"Nein! We're here now." Anna straightened her straw hat, then took in a deep breath to compose herself.

The cooperage building was made of clapboard painted light grey. The large blue door was rolled to one side, leaving the inside open to any ocean breeze that might alleviate the heat from the chimney corner. Hermann and his apprentice were surrounded by staves, metal hoops, and partially finished barrels. When the two women entered, the owner laid down his drawknife and rose from his shaving horse. The floor was strewn with wood chips, and the slightest of movements caused sawdust to dance in the sunlight. Hanna barely listened to the conversation. Instead, she moved to the open side-window. The oppressive air made it difficult to breathe.

"What are you looking for, Frau Knaut? Slack barrels or tight?"

"Slack. Three pails and a butter churn."

Hanna, drawn to the cooler outdoors, left the two to their business. Two armed soldiers marched by. Three natives, tethered at the neck and with hands restricted behind their backs, walked between them. The middle one with head down had much lighter hair, which was tied back beneath his cap.

"Christian!" Hanna ran after them, but when she reached the party and extended her hand to him, the light-haired man stopped and stared at her bewildered. She was immediately disheartened. The bruised face was not that of her brother.

"Stand back, ma'am!" the soldier yelled before moving on. When he shoved the prisoners forward, the Indian fell. His captor gave him a hard kick before pulling him up by the scruff of the neck, but he collapsed.

"Leave him be!" Hanna cried out and held him until he steadied again. "Where are you taking them?" The captive still had a hold of her hand.

"That's none of your business," the soldier said and grabbed her arm. "Stand back before you get hurt."

"Unhand her, sir, or I will report you to your superior!" It was Anna running toward them.

"My apologies," he said abruptly and started to explain the circumstances.

Anna interjected. "Stop. There's no need to explain. I have witnessed enough. If I'm correct, these men are willing hostages?" When he replied with a curt nod, she continued, "Then I'm correct when I say this treatment does nothing; it is horribly needless. As per their peace treaty, they are here on their own accord for possible exchanges."

"Ma'am, you know nothing of this situation. I'll treat them as I see fit. You may report me, but I'm sure the colonel will support my reasons."

Hanna could see the fire in her friend's eyes.

"Then you are unaware of my influence, my dear man. A report of your conduct will indeed go higher, as my husband is a member of the legislature."

"That same document states that there shall be no molesting of the King's subjects." He stared at Hanna, who dropped her hand from the Indian's hold.

Anna lowered her voice and spoke menacingly. "You are an impertinent cur. You underestimate me, sir."

The soldier did not so much as flinch. "You're attracting a few nosy onlookers, I see." With that, he moved his prisoners toward the palisade gate.

The bystanders walked away, and so did Anna and Hanna.

Her face red and her hand clenched, Anna suppressed her frustration.

Her friend was always the epitome of etiquette, and Hanna had never seen such a display. "I would have hit him," she said, and inclined her head.

Anna eventually cracked a smile. Hanna could not help but laugh.

Anna frowned. "Ach! We're being approached. I hope she didn't notice us earlier, as I'm in no mood to—Guten tag, Frau Rudolf," Anna declared brightly.

"Do call me Dorothy. We have known each other long enough, Anna, to dispense with the formalities." Her attention turned to Hanna. "I don't believe we have met."

"Not formally. I am Hanna Heber. Pleased to meet you." She gave a quick curtsy.

Dorothy looked down at her with chin held high. "My! It's good to see a courteous young lady in town. Our circumstance here tends to make us forget our manners." She relaxed. "You too may call me Dorothy." She gave a second glance at Hanna before giving all her attention to Anna. "We were extremely distressed to hear of David's death. We very much wished to be there for you and Philip."

"It's kind of you to say so. We're doing very well. Danke."

Since returning, Anna had had difficulty speaking about her son. Hanna steered the conversation to what everyone had been talking about. "You must be pleased with your husband's appointment as judge."

Dorothy nodded. "It's good to finally have an Inferior Court here. It made no sense at all to send our malefactors to Halifax just for common pleas. Leave the capital to handle the more serious crimes." She looked at Hanna again more pensively. "Are you Michael's daughter?" When Hanna replied yes, Dorothy said, "Your brother lives with the Indians, does he not? To have such disgrace brought upon your family must be quite disconcerting."

Hanna's temper flared. "Not at all. Why would you think such a thing?"

Dorothy was clearly flabbergasted at Hanna's tone.

Anna spoke up. "You are well acquainted and on friendly terms with Herr Francklin, are you not?"

"Why, yes, of course. His integrity and courage speak volumes among our friends."

"Then you agree he does not bring you and Leonard dishonour or shame."

"I should say not. What are you getting at, my dear?"

"There is great respect on both sides. When it came to trading, Herr Francklin earned the trust of the Mi'kmaq."

Dorothy was speechless at first, then waved it away. "You can't compare. He was captured. Hanna's brother—"

"Guten tag, Frau Rudolf!" Anna linked her arm with Hanna's, leaving the other woman stuttering.

"I do not like her!" Hanna said vehemently, and Anna politely urged her to lower her voice.

WORKING IN THE KITCHEN NEXT to her sister, Hanna jiggled the cross so that it dangled away from her clammy skin. Any outside chores had to be done first in the morning; it was impossible for Hanna to continue working in the rising heat as the day progressed. She usually tended to the livestock, and Papa was steadily scything hay. With the addition of cattle from Philip, Hanna was feeling the strain. But with Papa's starting wage at the mill of five shillings a week, she wanted it to work for him. They assisted one another no matter what the task entailed.

In the daytime, work kept her mind busy and away from her worrisome thoughts. It was in the nighttime when dark descended in the quiet hours that the reflections came back with a vengeance, resulting in wakeful nights. Was the petition sitting at the bottom of the legislative pile of items considered to be of lesser importance? After hearing about the discord with the council, things did not look promising. Then her mind would slip to the frightened Mi'kmaw woman. Her bloodied lip was a vision Hanna could not erase. She wondered if the man was still alive. She had agonized over Christian, until Philip had returned with news of him. She hung onto every word of his conversation with Christian so she could play it over again in her mind. *He was alive!*

That morning, Elisabeth had brought the children over. Petie was teaching Marta to gather eggs, while Markus slept. Elisabeth was nothing less than infuriating when she would make light of Hanna's attempts to help the Mi'kmaq. Hanna's venom was biting: "Do not patronize me, dear sister." She disliked herself for having said it.

Elisabeth had stopped the plunger in the churn. "You do mean well," she said. "But deep down you must realize the government won't help them. Anyhow, the London Board can no longer justify the victual continuation for us."

"There are still some who are needy enough and grateful for it."

Elisabeth resumed churning. "And I would venture to say even those small few will be self-supporting soon. Any monies the governor requested, the British Parliament has declined. Apparently, this province's parliamentary grant has been reduced."

"So where does this leave the Mi'—?"

"Don't say it. Isn't it enough to get this farm thriving?"

Hanna's accelerated whisking of the flour and milk mixture left wet droplets on the dusty table. "How can you just sit there, Elisabeth, and overlook anyone in despair?"

"That's unfair. Need I remind you—"

Hanna interrupted. "Nein, you need not." Her irritation knocked the wooden spoon out of the bowl, spilling raw egg onto the floor. Exasperated, she bent down to wipe up the drippy mess. "You must be quite comfortable now that our population is growing." Without intention, her words still came across as belittling. "I heard Lawrence was given permission to dam and flood four acres of land. This, to have water for a sawmill and a gristmill."

"I don't see what you are driving at."

"Do I really need to spell it out for you?"

Elisabeth turned away. "There still are plenty of other places for the Indians. In any case, those few acres are a small price to pay."

"Ja, we move in and they move out. Quite convenient, I must say." That was as derisive as Hanna dared. "From what Christian told me, it's not that simple."

"I refuse to listen when you're like this. If you will, go talk to the governor. He arrived yesterday. Evidently, we're his first stop before going on to Liverpool then sailing for Minas and Pisiguit."

"Indeed. I intend to."

"I'm sure you will, Johanna!"

Hanna stared at her disdainfully. Rarely did Elisabeth use her full Christian name, and when she did, it was in a spiteful way. Hanna opened her mouth to retaliate then thought better of it. "Elisabeth, one day Christian will come back again."

"Nothing you say will convince me of that. He may have

children of his own by now." Elisabeth shook her head. "Nein! He has no reason to return."

Hanna was unshakeable. "When he does, will you accept him?"

Elisabeth became extremely uneasy, tripping over her words. She stopped churning again and stood to smooth out her apron. "There, it sounds like we should drain the buttermilk off." She lifted the churn lid.

"You are avoiding my question!"

Elisabeth diverted her eyes from Hanna to the open door. "Petie and Marta are coming now." She turned to go.

Hanna's patience dwindled to a mere trickle. "Hear this, my sister. Because you are imprisoned by your silly fears, you are blind to the possible."

Elisabeth had stopped in the doorway, and Hanna thought, just maybe, her words had penetrated her obstinate sister. But Elisabeth left without turning back.


As CHANCE WOULD HAVE IT, Philip had spoken with the governor before his ship sailed again to the new township, but the meeting was not as favourable as Hanna had hoped.

"Unfortunately, he was not as receptive—a complete turn-around from when we last spoke of it," he said.

"Maybe, from the onset, he was only pacifying you," Anna suggested.

"Without a doubt—words are cheap. Have the Indians been back?"

"I've not stopped looking for them, but thus far, nothing," Hanna replied. "There was only one sighting that I know of. Up along the LaHave, Herr Feder came across a family to whom he gave food."

"Perhaps now there are fewer in need," Anna said. "Notwithstanding, there are not as many that are willing to sign this new petition."

"Philip, you have always stated that the Board is constantly pushing the governor to develop goodwill with the Indians. Helping them goes much further to a resolution of peace." Hanna was sure her simplistic views would appear naive in Philip's eyes.

"Be that as it may, the Board's priority is increased settlements to make this province viable and for it to remain British in the interim. In their eyes, peace must come in other ways, on Britain's terms, with the least possible strain on their coffers. The idea is to placate the natives in order to get what they want. You know, the Board expected us to be self-reliant long before this, but in my opinion, it was unrealistic."

"I haven't changed my mind or turned my back," Hanna stated. "If it's required, I *will* disobey Papa."

LATER IN THE DAY, HANNA sought out Anna and found her carding wool beneath the oak. "I see Philip walking in from the field, so I imagine you'll be leaving soon. Where's Catherine?"

"Oh, she trotted off to find him. In her mind, he surely must be working on something much more engaging than what I'm doing."

"The apple does not fall far from the stem," Hanna jested. Setting herself down, she stilled Anna's hand. "I can't thank you enough for your help. You are a godsend. And Papa's very grateful for Philip's kindness."

"Ach, it's the least we can do. Michael is learning quickly. Philip says he now has the confidence to leave the sawmill in his hands. And the apprentice has changed his mind on the position in Mahone Bay. He is staying on as well." Anna laid the paddles on her lap. "The petition…" she started. "I so wish the situation had resolved itself as fast as we had hoped. Philip's doing the best he can."

"I realize that." Hanna placed a wad of wool on the carder and began combing it. *This precious time together is calming*, she mused as she listened to the grasshoppers sing. "Were you aware Reverend Moreau speaks the Mi'kmaw language?"

"Nein."

Hanna looked down at the wool in her lap, and she sensed Anna's eyes upon her.

"Are you thinking about Christian?" her friend asked. "Until Philip came home, you had barely spoken of him."

"Do not misconstrue my silence for indifference. He's never far from me."

Anna slipped her hand into Hanna's. "I know, my dear."

"Maybe Elisabeth is right though. She thinks I should not poke my nose into affairs that don't concern me."

"How do *you* feel?"

"Ja, I am content here on the farm, but I can't wear blinders either."

"It's good to see you're speaking from your instinct. Pay Elisabeth no mind, nor anyone else for that matter. Don't change, Hanna, for the sake of compliancy. If you resign yourself to the fetters of narrowmindedness, you're only betraying yourself."

"Elisabeth refuses to face anything concerning our brother. But at least she doesn't fly into a rage like Papa has done."

"Can you not yet speak of Christian in his presence?"

"It's definitely not smooth sailing."

"Your sister just needs more time to accept the circumstances. She'll eventually come around," Anna soothed.

A few leaves fluttered to the ground, catching Hanna's

attention. She picked one up and twirled it by the stem. "These trees have witnessed countless generations of Mi'kmaq. They would have seen their joys, their sorrows, their children. Do the trees know the Mi'kmaq have not returned? I would like to think they sense their absence." She paused for a moment and let the leaf drop from her fingers. "The Reverend spoke to me about what it was like here before we came. From this harbour the French shipped lumber to France along with cargos of fur and fish."

Anna nodded.

"The Mi'kmaq lived and fished beside the French. In time, they adopted St. Anne as their patron saint. Each summer, the Mi'kmaq would assemble in this very area for the Feast of St. Anne, and here they would receive instructions from the French missionaries. I can just imagine what it was like as they congregated together. For all those years, this was *their* place." She gazed over the field. "Humph," she uttered.

"What is it?"

Hanna turned to her friend. "Our lives here just seem to go on, no matter. When I hear of the laws put in place to run this province, the taxes...then the new counties and their borders, new towns. All regulated and named under British specifications. All this has happened as if the Mi'kmaq don't exist." She sighed.

It was Anna's turn to sigh. "Has the Mi'kmaw woman come back?"

Hanna shook her head. "The truck house will help when it opens."

"You can ask Philip about it. Here he comes now."

"Look at you two!" Philip mopped his brow. "Keeping cool while your husband sweats."

"I see Catherine found you," Anna said as her daughter leaned into her lap. "Did you help Papa?"

"As much as a seven-year-old can muster," Philip answered for her. "Run to the barrel and get your papa some water." To Hanna, he said, "The last acre of hay has been cut." He moved the rag to the back of his neck.

"Papa will be pleased."

"He won't be at the mill until there is enough rain. The river is too low to generate the saw. Tell him I'll be back here tomorrow."

"I will. Danke."

"Hanna was wondering if the truck house is open now at the fort," Anna said.

"It is. Herr Wiederholt is managing it for me today. Why?"

"You know my concern."

"I must stop there on the way back. I will ask if a Mi'kmaw woman has shown up with a child."

"Are the prices fair?" Hanna asked.

"The council settled the prices with the Mi'kmaq in February. For a pound of spring beaver, they can buy thirty pounds of flour or fourteen pounds of pork."

"Are you still sailing to Liverpool next week, my dear?" Anna asked her husband.

"Indeed I am. Looks like the post will open. Herr Cobb and I will be discussing guidelines for that area. Ah, thank you," he said, as his daughter handed him a cup of water.

Hanna caught movement through the trees of a nearby wooded area and did not hear Philip's next words.

"Hanna?"

"Hmm? My apologies. You were saying?"

"We must depart now." He followed her gaze. "Is there something wrong?"

"Nein. 'Twas just an animal, I believe. It's nothing."

The conversation turned to a lighter nature as they prepared to bid farewell. Hanna studied the edge of the woods once again, but it was still. Nonetheless, she would go. There was ample time to be back before Papa returned. Once her friends had departed, she filled the basket and crossed the field. When she set the provisions down in the same area as before, a twig cracked. Hanna turned to see a woman dart among the foliage. In pursuit, Hanna called after her, which only caused the woman to run deeper into the woods. Hanna lifted her skirt to run through the bushy undergrowth. She slowed her pace and stood quietly. She called again. A pheasant startled her when it crossed her path, wings rapidly thrumming.

From behind, someone called, "Fraulein!"

Hanna spun around to face Detleff Jessen. Her mouth gaped open.

"Sorry if I frightened you." He smiled.

"Just surprised. I didn't hear you approach." Hanna swallowed hard to slow her breathing.

"Were you running from something?"

"I just lost my bearings. I'm fine now. Why are you here?"

"I might query you as well."

"I'm not required to explain myself, Herr Jessen. This is Papa's land."

He was unperturbed by her terseness. "I was following a recent report of an Indian sighting near here. For your safety, you should return home."

"Of course they would be seen. The truck house has just opened. You make it sound as if their presence is untoward."

"One report has suggested as much. For your own well-being, I would be happy to escort you back."

"That won't be necessary." Then, over his shoulder, she saw the Mi'kmaw woman staring at her from behind a tree. "On second thought, perhaps you're right. I'm grateful for the offer."

As soon as Detleff left their farm heading for town, Hanna returned to where she had left the food. The basket was empty.

Caught up into a vortex, brittle leaves rattled the death knell of Summer as Autumn briskly took hold. Thus far, none of Singing Sparrow's promptings had encouraged Bear Cub to depart earlier. Nervous of what might greet him, he prolonged making a firm decision. Now it was October, the time when the women dismantled the wikuoml, carefully rolling the sheets of birchbark for the journey inland. It was time to follow the migration for the fatted moose and caribou. Bear Cub could delay no longer.

Days passed on the numerous tributaries and portages. Now, as he sat by a small lake roasting eel, he doubted his decision. *If it weren't for Hanna, I wouldn't be here.* As much as he had wanted Eagle Feather to join him, Bear Cub needed to do this alone. He pulled the animal pelt tighter around his shoulders and leaned against the overturned canoe. A light dusting of snow fell as he chomped into the fish.

He would finish the trek on foot. Even though it was a different route than before, he knew the general direction of the farm. He walked around a large swamp, then heard cattle in the distance.

"Bitte, come back!" A female voice was barely audible. Bear Cub stopped in his tracks to listen. It drifted closer. Picking up his pace, he ducked behind a large boulder at the sound of someone quickly approaching. When the running ceased, he heard weeping. He raised his head and saw a girl walking away from him. She must have detected his movement because she turned her head back, then screamed and bolted. "Hanna!" he called. Running after his sister, he quickly overtook her and grabbed her arm. She struggled before awareness set in.

Resistance gave way to an embrace from which Hanna could not withdraw.

Sitting at the kitchen table with the hearth ablaze felt alien to Christian. His long-ago dreams of owning a farm were just misty memories. To live again in an enclosed wooden building, he would feel trapped. For now, he savoured his sister's presence, Hanna keeping a tight grip on his hand. Papa would not be home for another couple of hours.

Christian kissed the palm of her hand. "Look at you! You're a beautiful young lady, with manners, no doubt." He smirked. Then, suddenly serious, he said, "Forgive me. I didn't mean to frighten you."

"How could I recognize my brother with such a growth?" She snickered, touching his beard. "Though it does become you. You know I don't scare so easily, but of late the soldiers search these woods as soon as they hear the smallest hint of harassment, imagined or not. There are those who are against the truck house, and they make no bones about it. Because of it, I have been feeling ill at ease." Hanna paused. "No more of that talk, Christian. You have another nephew. Elisabeth gave birth to Markus in June."

"Ah, that's wonderful. Elisabeth is doing well?"

"Ja. And you?"

Christian saw the sparkle in his sister's eyes and inclined his head, grinning. "We named our daughter after Mama. In Mi'kmaw, we call her Ma'li."

Hanna wrapped her arms around him. "I'm so pleased for you. Things have changed so much, have they not?"

They sat fixated on one another to relish each moment.

"Why were you crying earlier?"

Hanna explained about the woman and her family. "When I try to approach, she runs. My only wish is to know her. At first,

I thought she feared for her daughter's safety, but she doesn't bring her."

"And her husband?"

She shook her head. "I fear the worst."

"She is distressed, I'm sure, especially after the run-in with Papa. What you are doing for her, leaving her food, is enough for now. Eventually, she'll warm to you, which is what everyone does when they meet you, nein?"

Hanna half-smiled at him. "Do you think the war is over now that Montreal has surrendered?"

Christian gasped. "I didn't know!"

"Last month. Philip doesn't think so, as the war is more far-reaching than what we see here. Besides Europe, there are other countries involved that I've never heard of."

Christian shrugged. "Maybe for us, the war has ended. Let's hope so. Our missionary, Maillard, has been persuading different bands to sign peace treaties in Halifax."

"I've heard his name. He was here. But that's all I know. Most of the people are faint-hearted and cower at the least mention of an Indian. Elisabeth is one." Hanna went on to explain their sister's encounter.

Christian relayed a tragedy near Annapolis when British soldiers ambushed a Mi'kmaw settlement—killed them in their sleep. "They had been in a festive celebration the night before," he said. He looked away, and Hanna reached for his hand.

Christian faced her again. "Eagle Feather told me how he hid you and Papa away from danger. Hanna, my brother had no concept of whose farm it was, until he saw you."

She laced her fingers through his. "I know."

"Although I understood what was behind his desire for punitive actions, I didn't agree with his plan when he left. However, if any of you had been struck down in cold blood, I could easily justify avenging your death."

Hanna nodded.

"Once this war is over, maybe we can paddle down the rivers unrestricted. On the LaHave, I avoided the lower part where there are many ships at least ten miles upriver and even larger vessels five miles in. The Mi'kmaq call it the Pijinuiskaq. The British don't realize what they are doing to us."

"They do know, but they don't care," Hanna said.

"The king doesn't replace our government, and we wish it to remain so. The Mi'kmaq have offered their friendship and tolerance to limited settlements if there are no interruptions to their way of living." Christian turned his gaze away. "We're aware of the new colonists south of here."

"Philip told me about your chance meeting."

"More prime food sources taken from our mouths. When we are relocated, we must learn new paths taken by moose, where the geese will land, major fish spawning grounds, safe routes across the winter ice, the best traplines." Taking hold of Hanna's hands, he said, "I must leave before Papa returns."

"Will you be back?"

"I need to return before winter sets in." Christian lifted her chin. "I promise to come back in the spring when the trees start to bud. I wish so much for you to meet my family. Would you?"

"Ach, I would love that!" Hanna exclaimed. "But how? When?"

"I'll come alone in April at the same place we met today. Watch for me. You will know if you see this medicine pouch placed on that rock. Wait for me there."

"What about Papa? And Elisabeth?"

"We can all meet the next day at Paul Labrador's place. Easier access down the rivers that connect to the lake there.

Hanna, don't set your heart on Papa and Elisabeth's approvals. I very much doubt—"

Hanna pressed her finger to his lips. "I'll try."

NOVEMBER BROUGHT MOSTLY FOG AND rain. Papa had turned in early. Hanna moved the candle closer to shed more light upon the letter she had received from Anna last week. By rereading it, she could imagine her friend sitting beside her.

*October 23, 1760*

*My dearest Hanna,*

*The last warship to Europe is departing tomorrow with a planned stop in Lunenburg. What better time to send news to my friend. Upon receipt, you will notice a few blank sheets of paper so you may feel free to write to me in return. Of late, writing paper has been hard to come by, especially in Lunenburg, I expect, and I must say, very dear these days.*

*I'm writing this four days after Governor Lawrence died. Two weeks ago Philip and I attended a ball at which he was his usual affable self. Soon after he took a chill and resigned himself to his bed. It was a shock to learn of his passing. He was such a strong, energetic man, it rather seems to go against his very nature to die from such an insignificant malady. If you knew him, you would agree.*

*The funeral procession was as stately as his coffin, which was most suitably dressed in the manner you would expect for an exalted Brigadier-General. However, the funeral sermon preached by Reverend Mr. Breynton was so piteous the good Reverend required comforting himself.*

*At present, Chief Justice Belcher has been appointed as the Administrator for Nova Scotia. Needless to say, because of Lawrence's untimely death, no reports were completed for the*

*London Board. Unfortunately, this means more delays for our*
*relief petition.*

*I must sign off now as Philip is patiently waiting to deliver*
*this to the captain.*

*Do please write back before the weather determines if a ship*
*departs again from Lunenburg to Halifax.*

*Yours affectionately, Anna Knaut*


Hanna smoothed out the edges of a blank sheet of paper and began.


*My dear Anna,*

*It is late when I write this. Papa's sound asleep, which I*
*envy as I've been restless and lying awake many nights. It's*
*almost December and I have yet to tell anyone but you of my*
*short time with Christian, nor have I approached Papa with*
*what my brother proposes for April.*

*Over the mantel are the evergreen boughs Papa so carefully*
*hung last week. This, to denote life and gaiety to get us through*
*the dark winter! But alas, I feel absolutely no joy in my heart*
*knowing what I must face.*

*I cannot find enough courage…*


She stared blankly at a droplet of wax slowly moving down the side of the candle. Hanna could only imagine the backlash from asking Papa to bring Christian back into the fold. As the house grew chilly, she clutched her shawl around her neck. She dipped for ink.


*With the increase of lumber produced at the mill, Papa*
*speaks of nothing but profit and the good fortune that has now*
*come upon us, especially with the vast increase of livestock*

*here and the copious amounts of hay and oats harvested this year. The root crops were indeed enough to aid not only the few needy, but also to send a surplus to the Halifax market. And, he says, the continued influx of settlers to these new townships can only mean good things. I think not, but I do well to only give my opinion here. That is, I say not for everyone.*

Hanna laid aside the quill to rub her weary eyes and briefly laid her head down on the table.

She awoke suddenly to a soothing brush upon her head. "You'll catch yourself a terrible chill," Papa whispered. "Go to bed." Hanna shivered as she rose from the table.

In the dim light, he gave a half-smile, all the while fixated upon her. Hanna tilted her head as she stood before him. "Papa?"

He cupped her chin, and she could feel the rough calluses on his hand. "Memories tease me of your mama when I see you. So, so very long ago…" His eyes glistened. "You and Elisabeth are all I have left of her." It seemed more of a plea than a statement.

Hanna pressed her hand to his, then kissed his palm. She felt it was safe to assert, "And Christian."

He rapidly pulled his hand away—a pained expression dulled his features.

"Papa, how long can we go on like this?" she pleaded. "Take a good look at what you're doing to me. In your presence, I am distraught to speak of my brother, dreading your reaction. When I spoke to you of Eagle Feather, I thought things would be different, but you have proven it's not to be. Should I not be able to express my worries about Christian? My love for him? He cannot be simply erased from our lives as you so demand." Passion took hold. Hanna lowered her eyes. "Only by the grace of God, he came here to find me."

The colour drained from Michael's face. "When?"

"It doesn't matter. You were at the mill." Hanna folded her arms in front of her.

"And you didn't ask him to wait, I suppose."

"In all truthfulness, would it have made any difference?" For the first time, Hanna thought he was breaking, so she pressed on. "He's returning with his family in April, before he leaves for good. Let it be known, Christian holds no hope of you ever changing your mind toward him. But I'm begging, will you come with me?"

Papa's scornful expression was all too clear. As he turned his back, Hanna screamed, "Do not include me in your apathy for your son! I can no longer endure how this is pulling us apart."

Papa simply walked away. "You're not going. That is final."

Hanna banged her fist against the table and squeezed her eyes tight to keep the tears from flowing.

# Chapter Thirty-Four



*Y*ou're putting yourself in extreme peril!"

Again, Hanna only had half an ear to what Elisabeth declared—the same irrational argument over and over, one Hanna had no intention of heeding. On this warm spring day, as through the course of the winter, her sister stood firmly with Papa. They both agreed that Hanna lacked judgment, that the plan to meet Christian was incautious. In the end, she had only the astute Georg to argue her side.

"Honestly! Christian is bringing his family. What part of this do you see as perilous?" Georg waved his hands in aggravation.

Papa had left some time ago for the calm of the outdoors. Hanna could see him, hands shoved deep into his pockets, pacing near the barn.

"No amount of convincing could ever result in me bringing our children." Elisabeth raised her chin in defiance. "And don't purse your lips at me so, husband. They could kill us and take the children for their own."

Hanna drew in a sharp intake of air. Her patience was wearing thinner than a skim of ice on a pond. "Pray tell, my sister, on what feeble reasoning do you base this?" When Elisabeth drew back, she continued, "Just as I thought, you have no grounds for it." She silently pleaded to Georg, who had already shown signs of defeat. "Do you really think Christian would put his own children and wife in harm's way?"

"It's a ploy. When all is said and done, it wouldn't surprise me if only our brother showed, and with others."

"Christian? You test my endurance to no end." Hanna breathed deeply to calm herself.

Georg sat Elisabeth down at the table and held her hand. "My dear sweet and sensible Elisabeth." His voice was quiet. "You're allowing your own experience to cloud any logical judgment. I have every intention of being there with Hanna and our children. Nothing is going to happen other than a union of two families. Christian's gesture is nothing but sincere, and he could never put any of us in harm's way. I beg you to rethink this."

"I cannot believe this! The two of you sit there as if what happened to me was trivial." Elisabeth stood up. "You expect too much of me."

Hanna's temper flared. "Do you think you're the only victim? This war doesn't play favourites. Our sister-in-law suffered as much." When Elisabeth gave a puzzled look, she continued. "Do you think cruelty is one-sided? British soldiers accosted her, and not just once. Her life was in danger!" Hanna took a deep breath, then exhaled. "Singing Sparrow's mother was murdered. So you see, there are victims on both sides."

As was typical, Elisabeth's response was to occupy herself with a distraction. She added more wood to the fire. "The children will be back soon. They'll be hungry."

"Hanna, I'll speak to your papa," Georg said.

She forced herself to smile.

THOUGH PAPA WOULD NOT BE there, he knew Hanna would not be alone. She was at the mill, waiting for him to walk home. Standing outside a fenced landing, she leaned over to watch the water splash over the large rotating, wooden wheel. She could smell the fresh spring rush as it roared below her. It barely drowned out the repetitive scraping of the blade inside sawing at a hundred and fifty strokes a minute.

The production of lumber was at its peak, which meant ten-hour days for Papa. Hanna could hear the wood rattling along the shaft as she watched him pull the rope on the tension gear. He appeared to be a seasoned operator with years behind him.

The assistant who had just delivered lumber returned with the news that King George had died suddenly—a week after the governor. "We still have a King George though," he jested. "His grandson, the third. The Assembly has dissolved now until further notice."

Hanna's face brightened. "Anna and Philip will be home soon."

"Next month, most likely," he answered, then disappeared briefly to close the gate. The wheel stopped and the blade ceased working, resulting in a silence that was almost deafening. Hanna followed the stout man inside the mill.

The assistant spoke to Michael. "There's one bit of news I overheard. No change in the rates, but hemp and flax bounties are extended another three years, and oats for two. Any hay cut from the upland will have the same rate for one more year before it drops to one shilling a hundredweight for three years."

"Gut! Better for us to supply Halifax with our hay than New England," Michael commented.

"As long as they can catch the swindlers. I can name a dozen who are still getting certificates for the grasses cut, not from their own land."

"Who's vouching for these farmers?" Michael asked rhetorically.

"I do know if Sutherland doesn't appoint a fit person to inspect these lands, the corruption will continue. We could lose the bounties altogether."

"Bring it forward to the Inferior Court. Sutherland is the JP."

"Ach, does he have time? His promotion to Major of the 77th Foot has him in Halifax often."

Hanna was anxious to depart now, as she wished to check one more time today to see whether Christian had arrived. The talk was moving in the direction of war, of which she was weary. "Papa, excuse my interruption, but we should return. The sun will be down before we know it."

"We'll go now."

ANOTHER WEEK PASSED BEFORE HANNA found the medicine pouch draped over the rock. She and her brother arranged for everyone to meet the day after tomorrow; she would hear Christian playing his flute as he and his family paddled toward them. He was surprised to learn that she had not hidden the flute in his sack, and Hanna wondered if Papa was responsible. Knowing about the flute gave her the backbone to try once more. The next morning, she found Papa in the barn.

"Tomorrow is the day."

"For what?" He stuck his pitchfork deep into the hay.

"Don't pretend, Papa." Her voice was low. Hanna was treading ever so lightly so as not to inflame him.

Papa's eyes narrowed. "Ach. So he's been here already." He resumed hurling the straw into the stall. "You know my answer."

"I also know you placed his flute into the sack I prepared."

He hesitated. "So?"

"Papa! This is your last chance to make things right again. You must feel something, otherwise you wouldn't have returned his flute to him. It meant a lot to Christian when he found out you put it there."

"Hanna, it's not to be." His expression hardened. "Much too late," he said as he walked away.

She took his hesitation at the door for a change of heart, but his words were cold. "Don't expect me home early. It will be busy at the mill today."


THE FOLLOWING MORNING, GEORG CAME by early to accompany her to the lake.

"Are you ready for this?" she said when he greeted her.

"Of course," Georg jested, and waved to Michael, who was walking from the barn.

"Can you give me a few minutes?"

Georg nodded and Hanna ran to Papa. "I thought you had left for the mill." She didn't know what else to say. "I'm in good hands."

He gave a half-grin. "I keep telling myself that."

Hanna reached her arms around him. She pressed her cheek against his face—his beard nuzzled into her chin. "I love you."

He squeezed her tight and would not let go. He sighed. "There was a time the top of your head used to fit under your papa's chin. But that now, like many things, has changed."

He released her. "Wait," he said, and disappeared briefly inside the barn. He reappeared carrying a small bag, neatly tied with a drawstring. He laid the cloth sack into the palm of her hand. "Can you give this to him?"

Hanna was elated. "Of course! What is it?"

"Seeds. Christian will know what it means. Tell him—" He struggled for the words. "Tell him, I should have been listening."

"Bitte, come with us." For a moment, she was sure he would have a change of heart.

He bowed his head and fidgeted with a strand of straw between his fingers. "Nein."

Hanna was not sad, not in the least. She beamed. "It's a start, Papa."

THE FOUR SHORT YEARS SINCE Hanna had spent time with Paul and Magdeleine seemed a lifetime ago. Now only a simple framework of birch poles, a ghostly refuge, still stood, marking two lives. Even undressed, the empty door enticed anyone to take their place inside.

Elisabeth stood back with Markus as Petie and Marta ran to the lakeshore. Hanna had been taken by surprise when she learned her sister had changed her mind, but she was certain it was more to protect the children under her own keen eyes than to admit to a desire to see her brother. Knowing her temperament well, Hanna was wound up tight, nervous about how Elisabeth might react.

Hanna laid a carefully folded blanket on the rock beside her. She had woven it over the winter just for this very day. She caught a glimpse of a canoe moving toward them just before the rich notes of a flute floated up. Georg held her hand as Christian, sitting at the stern, steered into shore. Singing Sparrow was paddling at the bow and did not seem the least bit hampered by the baby strapped onto her back. Their older child sat quietly on the centre bench, a small dog next to her. Hanna wished others were here to witness this picture of a family like themselves, which was so contrary to the disparaging remarks spreading throughout the colony.

Hanna noticed her brother searching beyond her. She caught his eye and gave her head a small shake. Christian hid his disappointment as he warmly greeted everyone and introduced his family. He was dressed in his Mi'kmaw attire of vest and leggings, his sealskin-covered feet firmly planted onto the sand. A necklace of beads hung against his bare chest, and a small part of Hanna knew the Christian who stood before her was not the same brother at all. A second canoe soon moved in. Hanna recognized Eagle Feather at the stern but not the older man, who had such a formidable presence. Elisabeth stayed rooted where she was as the two new arrivals waded from the boat onto the beach pebbles. The older man was introduced as White Cloud—Christian's protector, his father in all but blood. White Cloud was very amicable; Hanna and Georg warmed to him immediately. When Eagle Feather stepped onto the beach, he placed a basketful of herring down then directed his gaze at Hanna. Bear Cub said, "And of course, you know my brother."

Hanna could not explain why, but butterflies twitched within her belly as Eagle Feather stood before her.

She attempted to welcome him in Mi'kmaw as Christian had taught her. "Pjila'si." It sounded so weak, she was not sure if he heard it, but he grinned at her.

Suddenly, Singing Sparrow took her by the hand and led her to the canoe. "For my sister," she said in Mi'kmaw and placed a bracelet onto Hanna's wrist. It was made of colourful quills. Christian translated.

"I will treasure this," Hanna said, hugging her tight and kissing her on both cheeks. "Come with me." She led her to the rock and draped the soft blanket over Singing Sparrow's arms. "Pjila'si."

"Wela'lin. It's beautiful." Singing Sparrow beamed, stroking the fleecy coverlet. But her expression quickly changed when she saw Elisabeth wringing her hands. When Singing Sparrow approached her, Elisabeth fell back.

"Do not be afraid," Singing Sparrow said to her. "Bear Cub has explained. I truly understand." As Christian translated, Georg stood by his wife's side with his arm around her waist. Singing Sparrow untied her red- and yellow-beaded headband and slowly raised it, indicating that she wished to place it on Elisabeth's forehead. Elisabeth hesitated, then stepped closer and nodded. Singing Sparrow moved behind her, set the headband in place, and tied it at the back of her head. Tiny white shells hung from the loose ends and tinkled at the movement. Elisabeth turned and touched Singing Sparrow's hand.

"Christian, tell our sister-in-law, I know she has endured agony, and I have no words to express how very sorry I am."

Little Lise took hold of Marta's hand to lead her away. Elisabeth pressed her fingers into her daughter's shoulder to keep her from going.

Singing Sparrow inclined her head. "This is good." When her brother translated, Elisabeth gave her sister-in-law a half-smile and let her daughter run off with her new friend. Petie sat with Markus and Ma'li, etching animals into the sand while Alawei barked at any ducks that floated on the water.

White Cloud invited all to sit in a circle. He carefully unwrapped a red cloth revealing a pipe. He held the bowl of the pipe in his left hand and the long stem in his right. Christian translated through Eagle Feather's narrative. The bowl represented the woman and the stem, the man, he said. Joining the pipe together represented a union and balance between the male and female facets of the world. Elisabeth had remained standing, and Hanna watched her sister move about, still unnerved. She caught Elisabeth's eye and breathed a sigh of relief when her sister renounced her discomfort to sit beside her.

The same red cloth held a small container with bits of dried leaves. Christian explained that it was sweetgrass, which White

Cloud lit, directing the smoke toward himself. He then moved the pipe through the scented vapours.

"The smoke cleanses any negativity," Christian said.

White Cloud pressed a small amount of tobacco into the pipe bowl and offered a pinch of leaves to Kisu'lkw above. He raised his eyes skyward. "We recognize you, our Giver of Life. All things come from you. Your leaves and flowers are our medicines. We walk beside your animals and swim with your fish, who give up their lives to feed us. Your plants nourish Mother Earth and the People." White Cloud spoke to Grandfather Sun, Grandmother Moon, then to Mother Earth. "We are all one People, and we share all things you have given us."

White Cloud gave tobacco to the spirits of the East so they would help. "As Grandfather Sun rises, so the cycle of life begins. Mother Earth is awakening from her Winter slumber. We see the trees bursting with buds and the flowers unfurling from beneath." White Cloud continued until he had prayed to all the spiritual directions. With each of the directions, he turned the pipe four times.

He held an inflamed twig over the pipe bowl and drew deeply on the stem, coaxing the tobacco to catch. Hanna was transfixed. She listened to his deep nasal intakes of air as his face became flushed with effort. Veins bulged on his forehead and around his temples. Finally, small clouds of smoke drifted upward from the corner of his mouth. With his cupped hand, he directed the smoke up his body and over his eyes and head. He gathered more smoke and covered his ears. Each time he puffed to fill his mouth, he methodically blew it in each direction and prayed. In his hands, he rotated the pipe stem in a circle. After the last turn, he passed the pipe to Eagle Feather who inhaled and exhaled, cupping the smoke over his body. Turning the pipe, he handed it to Hanna who was careful to accept the stem in her right hand and bowl in her left. As per Christian's instruction, she was not required to inhale it. Instead, she said a prayer as she held it, touched the stem to her shoulders, turned it, and passed it to Elisabeth.

When the pipe had made its complete circle, White Cloud said, "We walk together as one People on this new path. O Great Spirit, we ask for wisdom to open our ears and hearts." He smoked the pipe until the tobacco was consumed. After he separated the pipe, he cleaned and rewrapped it.

The small group did not break. White Cloud relayed a story about Eagle, and the children took to him immediately. Then more stories were shared into the late afternoon.

When White Cloud rose to place the pipe ashes at the water's edge, everyone scattered. Hanna found herself alone with Christian.

She handed him Papa's gift. When her brother opened it, his hands shook. "He said you would know."

Christian nodded.

Hanna touched his hand. "He regrets not hearing you."

Christian stared down at the grain.

"Say something!" Hanna cocked her head to one side. "Is it too late?"

"I dare not speak for fear I might humiliate myself." Her brother's lips formed a partial smile.

"It may not be as you had hoped. I tried my best to persuade him to come. But he is reaching out."

"Really, Hanna, don't look at me with those big eyes of yours." He grinned. "I'm truly happy."

"You told me once the tether between us never breaks. But maybe it can never bounce back as it once was."

"True. Otherwise we don't grow. A love must be secure enough to allow the freedom to change."

"That's the hardest thing for a person to do."

"Just remember, Hanna, the tether can never separate in life nor in death. White Cloud and my brother have both taught me this. We cannot sever that which we are all born with—spirit. Everybody and everything are as one."

"We leave soon." It was Eagle Feather who startled them. "Our father is tiring." His eyes lingered on Hanna's.

Staring up at him, Hanna was captivated. She remembered those penetrating eyes, those high cheekbones. She had not seen a man show such unrestrained emotions as he had when he hid her and Papa in the haystack. She had been somewhat nonplussed to witness a man baring himself so openly.

After Eagle Feather left, Christian raised his eyebrows at her.

Hanna gave her head a shake. "What?"

"He is intrigued by you."

"He has told you this?"

"Not in so many words."

Hanna cleared her throat. She refused to look at her brother for fear he could read her thoughts. She distracted herself by ruffling Alawei's fur. "Well, I've never met anyone like him."

"Oh?"

"Do not grin at me like that! It's too difficult to put it into words. I can't help but be drawn to him."

"I would say you just expounded quite well. You did encounter one another under rather unexpected circumstances."

"It's time to end this conversation." Hanna stood up and left in a huff.


Hanna's tears flowed unchecked. Singing Sparrow embraced her, whispering, "Our hearts are one now." Christian translated and Hanna could not release her brother from her hold, not knowing if she would ever see him again.

"What did I say?" He held her at arm's length. "Remember what we talked about."

Hanna nodded.

Christian tossed Papa's gift into the air and snapped it up with one hand.

"What do you have there, my husband?" Singing Sparrow asked.

"A lifeline," he replied.

As Christian pushed the canoe onto the lake and climbed aboard, Hanna approached Eagle Feather. She wanted to speak with him before he left. "Wela'lin," she said. "You saved our lives."

She knew nothing of what he said in return. His hand briefly brushed over hers as he moved to push his canoe into the water. *Was it perchance?* No matter. His touch had awakened something inside that was oddly comforting. As he started to paddle away, she realized she wanted him to stay.

Hanna watched the canoes gradually become two dots upon the water, then turned to Elisabeth, who had come to stand beside her. "Your being here means very much to me, as well as our brother." Hanna leaned in to rest her head on Elisabeth's shoulder.

"I saw what Papa has done. I couldn't push Christian further away than he already is."

Hanna squeezed her sister's hand. "I'm glad you have resigned yourself to it."

"I still have to come to terms with it."

"It's time, ladies! It will be dark soon," Georg called. "Come, children."

# Chapter Thirty-Five



This moon was now fading to give way to another phase. It was the time when seal pups are born and moose cows are close to bearing their young.

They had left when the ground was saturated with snow melts and fresh, soaking Spring rains; forest growth inched higher toward the sun's warmth. They were to meet an encampment along the Niktuitk, southwest of Kejimkuji'jk. They hoisted the canoes over their heads and travelled between waterways, where hosts of returning migratory birds seemed to have mapped out the course for them. Both the People and the birds moved southwest to safer grounds.

Before the horizon was barely lit, they reached Oqomkikiaq upstream from where the New Englanders had landed. It had become evident to Eagle Feather and Bear Cub that their father was growing increasingly feeble. Singing Sparrow's motherly attention to their father was not in any way readily received. Her only recourse was to step back from her instinct to help.

On this day, White Cloud rallied to the point of being his tireless self once more. His sixty Winters of life were no deterrent to his now revived vigour and stamina. White Cloud was always the pinnacle of strength, and Eagle Feather relied on him for guidance. His father's counsel was a quiet influence. After Eagle Feather's absence three Winters ago, he had wished his father was not so discreet.

White Cloud lifted the bow of the canoe to dislodge it from the sand. "Give me a hand!"

Eagle Feather did not respond.

"My son, you seem troubled." White Cloud wiped the dirt from his arm.

"During the Winter after my mother died, you never asked about my absence. Before I had left, you laid down your argument, but you did not stop me from leaving. Why?"

White Cloud straightened. "Would it have made a difference?"

Eagle Feather did not answer. He knew it would not have. He also was deeply aware of his own need to push his remorse elsewhere.

"The door swings both ways. You could have come to see me," his father said.

"I could not face you."

"Are you doubting your decision to leave?"

"You must know what happened."

"If in your telling your burden is lifted, I will sit," White Cloud said, setting himself down on a flat rock.

"I cannot," Eagle Feather said, rubbing his hands together. As he paced, he revealed the entire ordeal, at least, all he could remember. And just as Eagle Feather expected, his father did not criticize, though a small part of Eagle Feather wished for some sort of reproach.

Instead, White Cloud said, "A close friend told me once, 'When in doubt, do nothing.' It is only when you are free of uncertainties that it is time to lead with courage."

"I allowed my brother's family to be put in danger."

"You cannot dwell on what could have been. My son, you are a better man now because of your decisions. It is not in vain." White Cloud smiled faintly, crossing his arms. "Our journey in this life is about learning. Then, still more learning."

"When I close my eyes, I see that dead boy and wonder…"

"If you learned the truth, would you find solace?"

The question churned inside Eagle Feather. It was unreasonable to search for a thread of comfort in the tragedy by wondering whether or not he was the cause. The fact is that the child died because of his intent to cause anguish. How it happened was of no consequence—he was still to blame.

"You need to come to terms with it and move on."

"And if it is impossible?"

"You must. What has happened is finished. What matters are your actions now." White Cloud stood up, holding his head high. "I am giving this back to you." He laid the bear claws in his son's hands. "I am not long in this world. This is your walk." He lowered his voice and whispered, "Listen to your doubts, my son, they are telling you something."

WITH THE CHILDREN BEDDED DOWN beside Singing Sparrow, Bear Cub sat across from Eagle Feather. The small fire danced between them as White Cloud slept soundly at the back of the wikuom. Bear Cub quieted his voice. "You haven't said two words since the hunt." The reddish glow of the fire illuminated his brother's face. "Is it your father that troubles you?"

"He talks of his death."

"You are reading too much into it. He was in good health today."

"He is keenly aware, Bear Cub. My grandfather knew." Eagle Feather crawled over to the side. "I will sleep now," he said, pulling the caribou skin over his body.

Bear Cub looked down at his brother, his face strained. "Your concerns are for naught. Seeing him today, you would never know he was unwell."

"You are wrong," Eagle Feather said and closed his eyes.

Eagle Feather's sleep was deep but restless with disturbing dreams. At the open door, his father, now youthful and fully clothed in animal skins, gazed back at him, an arm raised to support a small boy upon his shoulders. The vision was faded, almost colourless. Eagle Feather dug the palms of his hands against his eyes to rub away the mist. When he removed them, his young father stood there still, and the realization that Eagle Feather was the toddler on his shoulder sent a chill down his spine. Eagle Feather rose from his bed and glanced over at White Cloud who was still sleeping soundly. He followed the ghostly apparitions outside.

"Courage," the spectre spoke, beckoning. Eagle Feather tried to go after them but was stopped by a sudden gust of wind. He clutched at his necklace just as it dislodged from his neck, falling to the earth. Then, as quickly as it had come, the wind died to a sinister tranquility.

"Do not go!" His father blurred, wavering before him, his arms dropping to the ground. The figure of his father diminished until a black bear formed in his place. His father was no longer human, and the toddler was now a baby. As the bear lumbered away, a dove flew in circles around him. When Eagle Feather cried out for his animal spirit-helper, the wolf emerged from the woods anxiously pacing, pitying eyes fixed on him.

"Courage in your convictions," a distinct voice uttered into his left ear. He was no longer deaf! As everything disappeared before him, he stood in silent acquiescence.

Eagle Feather awoke, shivering, with rain pelting down. His

hair was drenched, clumped strands adhered to the back of his neck. Somehow, he was standing outside the wikuom, the bear claw necklace around his neck again. To the east, mounds of clouds parted to reveal brighter skies. His first thought: *My father is dead.*

A commotion confirmed that fact. He could hear the frenzied voice of his niece. "Wake up! Wake, my grandfather!" He could hear his brother soothing Lise. His sister's mournful wail sliced through him like a knife.

WHITE CLOUD WAS WRAPPED IN a birchbark shroud and tied up with a beaver robe. They carried him downriver to the ancestral burial ground. Each spoke in turn, revealing the times of laughter, their sadness, and their gratitude for his life path so intricately webbed within theirs. It was Bear Cub's most intense loss since his mama's death. White Cloud was the father who had protected and directed him. Bear Cub knew that White Cloud's presence would walk within his own shadow for as long as he lived.

Several nights passed before they decided to follow Ambroise to Niktuitk. It niggled Bear Cub; he wondered if moving from the safety net of truck houses was really in their best interest. If they stayed, trading would ensure their survival. They needed new guns and ammunition. Sure, Eagle Feather had said, they would barter for them but not to the extent to threaten their brothers' and sisters' existence.

"Already the beavers have left here," Eagle Feather said. "We do not need truck house food to live."

Bear Cub shrugged.

"White man's insatiable appetite knows no bounds. They get high prices for fish back where they came from. The greed never stops." Eagle Feather pointed downriver. "The People are my concern. We will go where Ambroise told us, where the new people do not know the hidden lakes and rivers. There, the beaver and cod know us intimately."

Bear Cub gathered the speared eels, laying them in the canoe. "We need to return. Singing Sparrow will be on edge."

His brother pushed the canoe out and climbed in, but he sat very still. "Do you hear?" He narrowed his eyes.

Bear Cub picked up the sound of hammering, then the monotonous hum of a saw drifting upriver toward them. He could just barely see the top of a building tucked away within a stand of trees.

"A sawmill," he said and started to paddle away. "What are you doing back there?"

"I want to see this." Eagle Feather steered them down a side river. "This is wrong." He examined the water beneath them. "It is the time of fast-running waters."

"What do you mean?"

"Not a ripple. I have never seen it this calm. Take the canoe in there."

Just before the river curved, they alighted onto an embankment. Eagle Feather waded to the weir. "It is empty. At this time, there should be hundreds of salmon here."

They ducked into the woods and travelled about three hundred paces before catching sight of a dam that cut across the river. Floating near the mill were hundreds of cut logs. When they walked closer, the sound of the rushing water intensified. The massive wheel turned with a force such as Eagle Feather had never seen. Any noise that might alert the settlers to their presence was drowned out by the rush of excess water pouring onto the rocks below. Holding the river back were logs stacked on top of each other. If Bear Cub were to stand on his brother's shoulders, the structure would be even taller.

Eagle Feather crouched down to scoop up the water. As it drained through his fingers, a residue of fine brown bits clung to his palms. "What is this?"

"Sawdust, from the mill."

A shot splintered the air, hitting the tree above and barely missing Bear Cub. Profanities followed them as they raced back through the forest to the canoe. By the time they heard a third musket fired, they had disappeared back upstream.

AFTER SEVEN NIGHTS, THEY REACHED the Niktuitk below the falls. The river meandered through a forested corridor that widened onto magnificent lakes. At Bear Cub's feet, Alawei dutifully sat with front paws perched on the edge of the canoe, Lise beside her. Singing Sparrow was nursing Ma'li, and her humming lulled Bear Cub into contentment.

When they neared the estuary, Eagle Feather slowed the canoe—British ships drifted on the ocean. They watched as four started upriver toward them. The vessels were at such a distance, their canoes would not be detected.

"I don't believe this!" Bear Cub said.

"You should not be surprised, my husband. We were forewarned."

"But not this far to the south," Eagle Feather said. "Turn around. We go partway back."

They retraced the route but turned from the main river down inlets and around small islands. Bear Cub spotted Ambroise and raised his arm to signal him. Ambroise greeted them as they manoeuvred beside him. "Pjila'si. Where is White Cloud?" His face quickly paled. "I gained so much by knowing your father. He was a good friend to me." He roughly brushed his hand across his eyes. Ambroise turned his canoe around. "We are on this side of the island."

"How far have you been down the main river?" Eagle Feather asked.

"If you are asking me about the ships, I have seen them," Ambroise said.

"It doesn't appear they know this area we're now in." Bear Cub was optimistic. "Maybe they'll not find it."

Ambroise raised his eyebrows. "For now."

It was a matter-of-fact answer, but to Bear Cub, it sounded like the beginning of the end.

Hanna sat in the afternoon sun to warm herself from the cool May breeze. She broke the seal and opened Anna's most recent letter. She liked to read them alone, so she waited until Papa had left for the mill.

*Saturday, April 25, 1761*
*My dearest Hanna,*

*Philip had a few loose ends to tie before departing Halifax. We will be back the first week of June. I am quite miffed over this delay but do understand.*

*The Act to prevent any private trade with the Indians was rejected by the London Board. Corruption by a few truck house merchants has reared its ugly head. When Herr Gerrish was managing the whole affair of these truck houses, he profited immensely while the government coffers remained empty. Once he's proven guilty, he, in all probability, will be removed. Philip is most disgruntled over this wretched situation.*

*Chief Justice Belcher will continue to conduct the government here, which has left a bad taste in the mouths of the Assembly. Thus far, he hasn't proven to be the best choice to run this province. For one, he does not sit well with the Halifax merchants.*

Hanna crumpled the letter into a tight ball. It was a grim
prospect her friend had painted. What did the future hold for
Christian and his family? She was more determined than ever
that hopelessness not be their lot. To be knocked down before
she had a chance to make another stand fuelled her drive. Tears
were useless.

Hanna turned at the sound of loud bleating to see two
wolves running alongside the fenced paddock. A black one
broke from his companion. His yellow eyes peered at her before
he scampered into the woods. Then he turned to watch her,
more intently, before he became one with the forest.

Christian had said to her once, "The wolf rids us of our
weaknesses in order to strengthen our spirit, so that we might
humbly ask for guidance."

An eagle feather lay near Hanna's feet, a message
from Kisu'lkw.

BEFORE THE EAGLE PUSHED OFF the rocky ledge, he directed
his gaze toward the young woman who now held the feather.
He silently flew above the cries of the sheep and grazing cattle,
then gained altitude. He circled around and upward, above the
colonists bent over their plows. He soared above the shrieking
sound of the sawmill that arose from the river, then glided
over the town. Wooden cargo barrels noisily rumbled down

the gangplanks. The incessant chatter escalated as newcomers milled about the town square, bartering their wares. Higher still, the eagle's powerful wings carried him farther down the coast, passing newly arrived ships, swaths of cleared forests, and wooden dwellings. Mile after mile, he strayed farther from the cacophony of strange sounds and away from a people who allowed fear to rule, avarice to prosper, and biased assumptions to sprout. The newcomers were ignorant of a grounded belief—all that live within Mother Earth come from the Great Spirit and do not exist to be fought over or divided. The greed and intolerance of the newcomers squeezed out acceptance.

The eagle drew nearer to the familiar, to the birchbark wikuoml and the Mi'kmaw chants. To the steady pulse of the drum, the ceremonies, and the Knowledge Keepers. To L'nu'k. The eagle regarded the People below who did not deserve the destiny that had been dealt them.

# Author's Note

At the Burying of the Hatchet Ceremony on June 25, 1761, at Governor Jonathan Belcher's farm in Halifax, the treaties of peace and friendship were signed by the governor, as president of His Majesty's Council and commander-in-chief of the province, and the Chiefs from the Mi'kmaq Nations called Merimichi, Jediack, Pogmouch, and Cape Breton, on behalf of themselves and their people. Daniel Paul, in *We Were Not The Savages*, writes, "Father Maillard, known by all as the 'Apostle to the Micmac,' died in Halifax on August 12, 1762. The Mi'kmaq Nation owes him a great debt. Without his efforts, all of our ancestors may well have perished."

The Seven Years War, the global war that had spanned five continents (and encompassed the French and Indian War), officially ended with the signing of the Treaty of Paris on February 10, 1763, which forever closed the door on a French claim over Nova Scotia and Canada. On October 7, 1763, a Royal Proclamation was issued by King George III that established the basis for governing the North American territories surrendered to Britain.

The Proclamation recognized the sovereignty of the First Nations People in North America and stated that the Indigenous People had the right to govern themselves within their own territories. It also stated that all land would be considered Aboriginal land until ceded to or purchased by settlers with the full consent of the Indigenous People. It forbade settlers from claiming the land unless it was first bought by the Crown and then sold to the settlers. Also, any land not ceded to or purchased by the settlers was reserved for hunting grounds; therefore, the settlers must remove themselves from such settlements.

In 1764, Sir William Johnson invited First Nations leaders to Fort Niagara to discuss the Proclamation. Over two thousand gathered, including representation of the Mi'kmaq. The Proclamation was read and explained to them in their own languages. The terms would become the foundation of a relationship between the First Nations People and the British Crown, and this Peace and Friendship Treaty was recorded through the issuance of wampum belts.

But even though the Proclamation gave recognition of Aboriginal rights, it also took away the right of Indigenous People to make their own determination about who they dealt with. In the end, the Proclamation did not protect First Nations People. Instead, it was used by British government to interfere with territorial rights of Indigenous People. The Crown used their authority to buy and sell lands that belonged to the People.

In subsequent years, there was minimal education of the Royal Proclamation, leaving an almost complete ignorance of it. The situation of the Mi'kmaq grew steadily worse through control and attempted assimilation. Their identities were denied. An "Indian" was considered a non-person with no rights, which through time brought them consistent injustices in court as they were undermined at every level. Indigenous People had to hide their ceremonies, which were prohibited. They had no voting rights, they could not sue the government, and they could not hire lawyers.

Instead of the Royal Proclamation protecting First Nations

People, it disappeared into obscurity, at most only mentioned in passing by colonial educators.

*Tethered Spirits* is a work of imagination based on my own distant German grandfather, Michael Hirtle, who emigrated with his family to Nova Scotia in 1751. For the purpose of the novel, I changed the surname to Heber but kept the Christian names unaltered. The main storyline of the Heber and Mi'kmaw families is pure conjecture, even though long and intimate friendships between the Mi'kmaq and settlers were common.

I deliberated a great deal on whether to tell a story that included the Mi'kmaq—they are the Traditional Knowledge Keepers of their history; however, the settler/Mi'kmaw narrative is intricately entwined, and to relate one without the other would result in an incomplete story. While it is not possible to fully comprehend the emotional complexities of our ancestors, an attempt to do so is crucial to the telling of our shared history. It is one thing to collect historical data, but it is our own human experience that adds to an appreciation of the past; it is here that we discover our shared humanity through the passages of time.

Through honourable research of other cultures, stories can be respectfully told to bridge the gap as we walk together to a deeper understanding. My hope is this novel is read in the context of its intention—to share what I have learned about the Mi'kmaq, revealing the egalitarian, consensus-based, and just society of a hospitable People who, at times, were pushed to take drastic actions.

During my research, I found numerous references to Merligueche, the Mi'kmaw name for Lunenburg, meaning "the place of barrels." This name continued to be used by the French in the seventeenth and eighteenth centuries. The Mi'kmaq also called it E'se'katik, meaning "at the place of clams," but I chose to use Merligueche.

The Maliseet of the Wabanaki (People of the Dawn-land) Confederacy were known by this name for centuries. Their Maliseet territory consists of the Saint John River watershed, extending from the St. Lawrence River to the Bay of Fundy. Today, they go by their traditional name of Wolastoqiyik (People of the beautiful river).

Paul Labrador lived on a seven-acre farm that straddled a brook running into the head of Lunenburg Harbour. His land was located west of the town of Lunenburg, south of what was then the west common. I found only one source that mentions Paul Labrador in the time after he and his family left Lunenburg, though it's unclear whether it is the same Paul Labrador. When the early English settlers arrived in what is now Chester in 1759, a Reverend John Seccombe kept a journal. In it, he wrote on September 16, 1759, "Paul Labrador, an Indian, brought five partridges to Mr. Bridge's, and lately killed four moose and two bears; brought also dried moose and tallow."

Colonel Patrick Sutherland left Lunenburg in the summer of 1762, after seeing the settlers through the town's most difficult years. The governor and council granted him the seven acres of land "formerly in possession of Paul Labradore." Major Sutherland died circa 1766.

Dettlieb (Detleff) Christopher Jessen became Justice of the Peace in the early 1760s; he became a member of the House of Assembly and represented Lunenburg County between 1785 and 1793. During my research, I learned that Detleff was known for his compassion and generosity throughout his public activities. I decided to portray him as a product of his environment, someone whose actions during war, fulfilling commands as an officer, were in conflict with his true character. Jessen died on August 12, 1814, and was buried in the crypt of St. John's Anglican Church in Lunenburg.

Philip Augustus Knaut continued as a member of the House of the Assembly until his death on December 28, 1781. He and Anna had five children. The only indication of Anna's death was Philip's second marriage to Jane Brimner in 1781.

The storm I describe in chapter 29 was a hurricane of epic proportions that struck the night of Saturday, November 4, and Sunday morning, November 5, 1759. It caused severe damage along the coasts of the Atlantic provinces.

The place where Province House sits now was the original site of the first governor's residence in Halifax. The elected Legislative Assembly, the first of its kind in colonial Canada, initially met at the courthouse at the corner of Argyle Street and what once was Buckingham Street. Of course, the true beginnings of participatory governance in this land now known as Canada lie in the Indigenous traditions of sophisticated leadership levels and consensus decision-making.

The teacher George Bailly died in Lunenburg circa 1807. Gottlob Neuman was eventually hired as the schoolmaster but abandoned the teaching of English. He continued to teach for the next twenty years. To quote Winthrop P. Bell in *The Foreign Protestants and the Settlement of Nova Scotia*, "Illiteracy apparently prevailed until well into the nineteenth century. The majority of children in every settlement in the county had been unable to read, either in that language (English) or German, the tongue then most generally used." German was spoken in Lunenburg well into the 1800s.

Reverend Jean-Baptiste Moreau died on February 15, 1770. By 1771, the German Lutherans had built their own church, with the first service held in the fall of that year. The building was the result of voluntary labour from numerous individuals. There is a record of "the cost of the 11½ gallons of rum and 20 gallons of spruce beer provided for the raising of the frame."

On November 1, 1772, the first Lutheran German minister, Reverend Friedrich Schultz, was inducted.

The new deputy surveyor, Benjamin Bridge, surveyed the three-hundred-acre lots and was paid twenty-five shillings for every one laid out with a ten-pound monthly advance until the work was completed, by September 1763. Starting October 3 of that year, the settlers began the first of three drawings of the lots with the last drawn on April 15, 1766.

The situation of the Mi'kmaq severely declined through history to the present day. From 1759 to 1768, approximately eight thousand New England Planters emigrated to Nova Scotia and New Brunswick, with thirty-five thousand Loyalists arriving after the American Revolution in 1783. The Mi'kmaq were always perceived as a threat. To control them, the British created laws that deprived them of their independence and customary food security, and their lands dwindled. As white settlements flourished, the Mi'kmaw communities, given no assistance nor taught to survive in their new world, languished. The introduction of reserves away from their traditional hunting and fishing grounds forced many to live on lands that were swampy and rocky, devoid of fertile soil and abundant fish and game. Their dependency on a non-traditional food supply gradually led to malnutrition and starvation.

Over the next century, many petitions, similar to the ones written in this novel, were submitted to the government. They were ignored. This left small pockets of white settlers to provide some form of relief where they could. At various stages of the nineteenth century, famine, the devastating effects of excessive alcohol consumption, and begging put the Mi'kmaq in closer contact with white settlements. With their compromised immunity, they succumbed to disease. By 1838, there were only 1,425 Mi'kmaq left in Nova Scotia.

From the 1830s onward, residential schools across Canada stole children from the security of their families; the last one closed in 1996. The schools treated their charges as prisoners instead of students, pulled families apart, decimated language and culture, and instilled shame of their birthright into the children. Children were forcibly assimilated into European society under dehumanizing conditions; they were subjected to unspeakable crimes if they spoke Mi'kmaw. Many of the children never returned home. The devastating impact of the residential schools manifested intergenerationally when the survivors had families.

The Mi'kmaw language is a sacred tongue, given to the People by Kisu'lkw. Expressive and intricate, it is key to how they view their relationships with the dynamic world around them. Their world gives prominence to interdependence and alliances with the living landscapes and all things, both animate and inanimate. Their language is so much more than a way to communicate. It lives within their spirit. To lose it, as was the result of residential schools, was to disassemble the individual and their whole heritage.

Even more important than owning our past is how we treat each other in the present. Symbolic apologies are only a small beginning; the healing truly begins when accountability repairs and stops the injustices of today.

On April 7, 2022, legislation recognized Mi'kmaw as Nova Scotia's first language and will support efforts to preserve and promote it for future generations. On October 27, 2022, Canada's House of Commons unanimously recognized the Indian residential school system as genocide.

Responding to the demands of Indigenous groups, the Vatican, on March 30, 2023, repudiated the Doctrine of Discovery, which allowed the seizure of Indigenous lands.

I can't help wondering, what if the Document of Discovery did not give credence to conquer and convert, but simply to explore? What if the newcomers had chosen the path of discernment, humility, and respect? How vastly different the story could have been.

Because of a narrow-minded belief that people should meet certain standards determined to be "civilized," the Indigenous were not recognized by settlers as a free and independent People with their own government. Sadly, the historical injustice and political control portrayed in this novel is still present today.

To be truly inclusive, we cannot hide or suppress one culture in favour of another. In the acceptance of all races and cultures, our differences are honoured, not demeaned.

Seek to know the person behind the eyes. The Mi'kmaw voices have always been here. Listen for them, hear them, embrace them.

# Acknowledgements

*Tethered Spirits* would not have been possible without the help of specific people from the Mi'kmaw community, listed below. All have given me their individual gifts of knowledge, wisdom, and encouragement. During the writing of this novel, I took the utmost care to maintain the integrity of the storytelling. Any error found is my responsibility, and mine alone.

My deepest gratitude to Dr. Bernie Francis, linguist from Membertou First Nation, an accomplished musician, storyteller, and translator. Your guidance was instrumental in making this book happen. You were more than giving of your time, making me feel at ease through our correspondence. I could never have navigated through the correct spellings, meanings, and pronunciation of the Mi'kmaw language without you. You truly are a gem.

To Mi'kmaw Saqmawiey (Eldering) Daniel N. Paul, CM, ONS, I am sincerely grateful to have had the opportunity to collaborate with you before you passed from this life. In addition to your generosity throughout my research, you also took on the momentous task to act as my sensitivity reader, incorporating your expertise and vision of historical events and the Treaties. Your encouragement came at a time when I had doubts about continuing to write.

A heartfelt appreciation for Dr. Roger J. Lewis, MA, Keptin, former Curator of Mi'kmaq Cultural Heritage, Research, and

Collections at the Nova Scotia Museum. Your kindness, Dr. Lewis, knew no boundaries through all my questions about everything from Chief Jean Baptiste Kopit to Mi'kmaw terminology to smudging and from beavers to fish weirs.

A special thank you to Rose Meuse of L'sitkuk (Bear River First Nation), who extended to me a gracious invitation to attend the Fall Harvest Gathering at Bear River First Nation, which allowed me to experience the Mi'kmaw culture. Rose said, "Do not give up." These simple words kept me going in my darker days of uncertainties.

To Carolyn Landry, member of Annapolis Valley First Nation, alumna of Acadia University (MA, Sociology), entrepreneur, and artist, a huge thank you for reading the manuscript and giving me invaluable advice.

Huge thanks to Matthew Connolly, Speaking Wolf of the Qalipu Band in Corner Brook, NL, Aboriginal veteran, who graciously accepted my invitation to create the front cover illustration and to review the manuscript. I am truly honoured.

Theresa Meuse's book *L'Nu'k: The People* was my constant companion throughout my writing. Theresa once said to me, "When good intentions and the heart are in the right place, you cannot go wrong."

Finally, I am indebted to my caring editor, Marianne Ward, whose expertise and commitment smoothed out the jagged edges of the raw draft, turning it into a polished, readable story. I am grateful for your keen eye, dedication, and guidance throughout the process, which only deepened my respect for the world of editing. It was indeed a pleasure to work with you.

I am grateful for having been given the privilege to include the story of Muin and the Seven Hunters as it was written in the book *The Language of This Land, Mi'kma'ki* by Trudy Sable and Bernie Francis.

For all I have learned, to say just thank you seems inadequate. Jane Meader, Mi'kmaw Elder, drummer, traditional singer, artist, and craftsperson, states that "wela'lin" and "wela'lioq" mean so much more than simply "thank you." They mean, more aptly, "you have blessed me with your kindness." To the Mi'kmaw community and all who have met me on my path, wela'lioq. You have enriched me more than you will ever know.

# Glossary

## MI'KMAW LANGUAGE

<u>Mi'kmaw Moons of the Year</u>

**Apiknajit** (ah-boo-ga-nah-cheet): Snow Blinder, February 3–March 5

**Kisaqewiku's** (gee-sa-ha-we-gooz): Harvest Moon, August 7–September 7

**Keptewiku's** (geb-day-we-gooz): Ice-Forming Moon, November 7–December 3

**Nipniku's** (niba-nee-gooz): Summer or Leafy Moon, June 5–July 6

**Pnatmuiku's** (binada-moo-ee-gooz): Egg-Laying Moon, April 4–May 5

**Punamuiku's** (boona-moo-ee-gooz): Frost Fish or Tomcod Moon, January 5–February 3

**Si'ko'ku's** (see-go-gooz): Spring Moon, March 5–April 4

**Sqoljuiku's** (skwoi-joo-ee-gooz): Frog-Croaking Moon, May 5–June 5

**Wikewiku's** (we-gay-we-gooz): Animal-Fattening Moon, October 8–November 7

**Wikumkewiku's** (weegum-gay-we-gooz): Animal-Calling Moon, September 7–October 8

**Amaqapskekek** (umma-hup-skay-gek): rushing over rocks; Gold River, Lunenburg County

**E'se'katik** (ay-say-gah-deek): at the place of clams; Lunenburg

**Kejimkuji'jk** (geji-ma-goo-jeek): the place of the fairies; a large lake and the surrounding area in southwestern Nova Scotia (Note: While "the place of the fairies" is the common translation, the nineteenth-century missionary, ethnographer, and linguist Silas Rand recorded an entirely different definition, told to him by the Mi'kmaq. For his account, see *The Old Man Told Us: Excerpts from Mi'kmaw History, 1500–1950* by Ruth Holmes Whitehead.)

**Kespukwitk** (ges-boo-gwit-k): end of flow; one of the eight Mi'kmaw districts, west of the LaHave River to Yarmouth / Cape Sable in south-southwestern Nova Scotia

**Kjipuktuk** (jeh-book-dook): great harbour; Halifax

**L'sitkuk** (el-set-kook): flowing along by high rocks; Annapolis and Digby Counties

**Merligueche** (mare-lee-guech), presently called Malikewe'j (mally-gay-wedge): the place of barrels; Lunenburg

**Mi'kma'ki** (mee-ga-mah-gey): territory of the Mi'kmaq, which includes the island of Newfoundland, all of Nova Scotia and Prince Edward Island, much of New Brunswick and the Gaspé Peninsula, and part of northeastern Maine

**Niktuitk** (nig-du-it-k): the water flow divides; Tusket River, Yarmouth County (Thank you to Melanie Robinson-Purdy of Wasoqopa'q First Nation, Yarmouth, NS, for her research to find the correct Mi'kmaw word for Tusket River and to

Bernie Francis for his slight variation to the spelling in order to right a wrong of a previously published English misinterpretation of a Mi'kmaw word.)

**Oqomkikiaq** (oh-home-giggy-ahh): a dry sandy place; Mersey River

**Penatkuk** (benott-kook): bird nesting place; an island in Shelburne River

**Pijinuiskaq** (bee-gee-noo-wiska): at the long reach; LaHave River

**Pisiguit** (piz-ee-geet): the Acadian name for what the Mi'kmaq called Pesegitk (bezzy-geet-k), meaning junction of the waters; Windsor, Hants County

**Siknikt (see-gan-ik-t):** drainage area; one of the eight Mi'kmaw districts, which includes the Miramichi River and the Acadian Coast and Bay of Fundy Region

**Sipekne'katik** (sah-bay-gin-nay'gah-deek): area of wild potato/turnip; Shubenacadie District and the Minas Basin coast (one of the eight Mi'kmaw districts)

**Tewapskik** (de-wab-sgik): at the outflow; Annapolis River

<u>Words and Phrases</u>

**e'e** (eh-hey): yes

**Elen** (ay-lan): Helen

**ji'kmaqn** (jigga-mah-hon): chanting stick; a split-ash rattle played by hitting it against one's hand or knee

**ka't** (gaad): eel

**Kisu'lkw** (gee-zoo-lk): "the one who created us; he, she, it who (or that/which) created us"; this definition comes from *The Language of This Land, Mi'kma'ki*, by Trudy Sable and Bernie Francis (Cape Breton University Press, 2012), who explain, "There was never one word for Creator in the Mi'kmaw language, but rather a number of different verbs, mostly transitive verbs, that articulated different processes of creation." Here are the definitions they give for the other terms used in the novel:

> **Ankweyulkw** (un-gway-oolk): he, she, or it who (or that/which) looks after us
>
> **Jikeyulkw** (gee-gay-oolk): he, she, or it who (or that/which) watches after or over us
>
> **Tekweyulkw** (deg-gway-oolk): he, she, or it who (or that/which) is with us

**kitpu** (git-boo): eagle

**kjika'qaquj** (ook-chee-gah-hah-hootch): raven

**Kluskap** (gloos-cap): a cultural hero who travelled the earth, shaped the landscape around Mi'kma'ki, and taught the Mi'kmaq valuable lessons

**kwe'** (gway): hello

**L'nu'k** (ul-noog): the People

**Mi'kmaq** (mee-gum-ach): the tribal name and the plural form of the noun

**Mi'kmaw** (meeg-um-ow): singular form of Mi'kmaq, also used as an adjective and as the name of the language spoken by the Mi'kmaq

**moqwe** (mohk-waa): no

**Msit No'kmaq** (mm-sit noh-goh-mach): all my relations

**Na'ku'set** (naa-guu-zet): sun

**Netukulimk** (na-doo-goo-limk): "a traditional way of life based on interconnective relationships that the Mi'kmaq have with natural resources and the earth around them, including past, current, and future generations. When actions are guided by Netukulimk, all of these relationships are respected." (definition provided by Nadine Lefort, Communications & Outreach Manager, Unama'ki Institute of Natural Resources)

**Nikanus** (nee-ga-nooz): head spokesperson of a village / community (Note: The word *Chief* has a specific connotation in English that Mi'kmaw does not have.)

**pjila'si** (ub-jee-lah-see): welcome

**plamu'k** (ba-la-moo-g): salmon

**puoin** (boo-o-win): shaman, one who communicates with the spirit world

**Saqmawit** (sah-ha-ma-wit): district leader

**Sulia'n** (soo-lee-un): William

**Tma** (da-mah): Thomas

**waisisl** (why-ee-zeesil): animal spirit helper

**wela'lin** (weh-lah-lyn): thank you, to one person

**wela'lioq** (weh-lah-lee-oh): thank you, to a group of people

**weliaq** (weh-lee-yah): you are welcome

**Wiaqtaqne'wasultijik na Kjijaqmijinaq** (we-ahh-donnay-wasaut-dee-jeek ook-chi-jahmee jin-ah): Tethered Spirits

**wiklatmu'jk** (wig-ah-lah-dah-mooch): little people or fairies

**wikuom** (wi-gwom): dwelling; wigwam

**wikuoml** (wi-gwom-uhl): dwellings; wigwams

## GERMAN LANGUAGE

**bitte**: please

**danke**: thank you

**frau**: used to address married women

**fraulein**: used to address unmarried women

**guten abend**: good evening

**guten morgen**: good morning

**guten tag**: good day

**herr**: used to address a man

**hier**: here

**ja**: yes

**liebling**: darling, favourite

**mein Gott**: my God

**nein**: no

**onkel**: uncle

**schnell**: quickly

**tante**: aunt

**verdammt**: damn it

# About the Author

After twenty-five years of adventures in Toronto and Calgary and a forty-year career in the travel industry, Corinne felt the pull to return to Nova Scotia, where she grew up. Her first novel, *Call of a Distant Shore*, based on her own history as a direct descendant of one of the first German settlers of Lunenburg, won the Silver Medal for Canada East, Best Fiction 2009, from the Independent Publisher Book Awards.

Corinne loves the mysterious, mystical, and diverse world we live in and believes that just because we cannot see it does not mean it does not exist. Her life encompasses lively games with her bridge friends, gardening, practising Tai Chi, and hiking with her husband through hemlock forests and unspoiled nature trails in out-of-the-way places.

A member of the Writers' Federation of Nova Scotia, Corinne lives in the Annapolis Valley with her Dutch husband and a British Blue cat named Toby. Corinne and her husband have four grandchildren.

Visit Corinne's website at corinnehoebers.mywriting. network.